Praise for Jen Frederick and her novels

"This story is written with breathless intensity, and Frederick portrays the seriousness of anxiety and phobias without reducing her characters to walking collections of diagnoses. The secondary characters add enjoyment, giving readers updates on past starring couples and anticipation for stories to come." —*Publishers Weekly*

"A cute and sweet read." —Under the Covers

"Kudos to Jen Frederick for writing another winner." —Book Binge

"Rife with passion and wonderfully paced romance, *Revealed to Him* asks how much a person is willing to overcome for a once-in-a-lifetime love." —*BookPage*

"Such a sweet, emotional read! I adore childhood romance stories and this is one of the best ones I have ever read! Jen Frederick is an amazing writer and she really has a knack for pulling your heartstrings in the best kind of way." —Amorette's Reviews

"A fun, sexy romance that will delight romance readers who enjoy watching the redemption of a seemingly unrepentant hero." —Smexy Books

"[*Unspoken*] has everything from heart-wrenching moments to lighthearted intelligent banter and intense, sexy love scenes that will leave you breathless." —Harlequin Junkie

TITLES BY JEN FREDERICK

Heart and Seoul

THE HITMAN NOVELS

Last Hope

Last Kiss

Last Hit: Reloaded

Last Breath

Last Gift

Last Hit

Jen Frederick

JOVE
NEW YORK

A JOVE BOOK
Published by Berkley
An imprint of Penguin Random House LLC
penguinrandomhouse.com

Library of Congress Cataloging-in-Publication Data

Names: Frederick, Jen, author.
Title: Heart and Seoul / Jen Frederick.
Description: First Edition. | New York: Jove, 2021.
Identifiers: LCCN 2020057943 (print) | LCCN 2020057944 (ebook) |
ISBN 9780593100141 (trade paperback) | ISBN 9780593100158 (ebook)
Classification: LCC PS3606.R4297 H43 2021 (print) |
LCC PS3606.R4297 (ebook) | DDC 813/.6—dc23
LC record available at https://lccn.loc.gov/2020057943
LC ebook record available at https://lccn.loc.gov/2020057944

First Edition: May 2021

Printed in the United States of America
1st Printing

Book design by Kristin del Rosario

To my brother, Andrew,
who looked like me in a world when no one else did

HEART AND SEOUL

CHAPTER ONE

WHEN I WAS TEN, MY DAD, PAT WILSON, JOKED THAT I should've had my tear ducts removed with my tonsils. I understood where he was coming from. I used to cry all the time. I cried when my crayons broke. I cried when I lost the red bow that was tied around my favorite stuffed bear. I cried when I broke the back door to the garage. Dad seemed like he was going to cry over that one, too. *Hara, you're eight. How in the hell did you pull the door off its hinges?*

I can't remember how I broke the door, but the reason I was crying when I was ten is still vivid in my memory. Why that's the memory of my childhood that has stuck with me I can't explain, but humiliation is like superglue. My elementary school days are a mosaic of failing the spelling bee, tucking my skirt into the back of my tights, not realizing I had peanut butter smeared across my sweater for a whole day, seeing my crush confess his feelings to another girl on the same day I was going to declare my fourth-grade heart, and then this one. I'd like to say that these past hurts stung and I moved on, but I can recall the day with perfect clarity. It was sunny and the school term was nearing its end. We were all anticipating summer break and perhaps that was why we were testy with one another. During recess, a couple of stupid kids asked if my face was flat because I'd fallen off the monkey bars and landed facedown. One, I had never fallen off the monkey bars. I was strong as hell even at age ten and I could fly across those damn things. Second, my face is not flat. If anything my face is too round. My chin is curved and my cheeks are plump. I don't have a prominent forehead or deep-set eyes, but that's not a bad thing. It's an *Asian* thing.

Even though I knew this, I felt ashamed of my face and so I cried because that's what ten-year-olds do when their feelings are hurt. The tears bothered my dad.

Hara, are you seriously crying because some kid said you had a flat face? What's the big deal? Hara, tears aren't going to make other kids stop making fun of you. Ellen, tell her to stop crying.

He wasn't wrong. Crying didn't change anything, and a year later, my tear ducts closed up and haven't worked since—not even at times when they should, such as when the hero or heroine dies in a book after you were promised a happy ending or when Allie remembered it was Noah reading the stories to her in *The Notebook* or when I'm sitting in the funeral parlor with my dad's body in a casket next door.

Even if I could produce tears on command, there isn't much to cry about today. Dad and I hadn't had much of a relationship since I was eleven and he'd decided that the fatherhood experiment wasn't working out for him. He'd been busy finding himself, which entailed him taking boys' trips to places he couldn't afford, shacking up with women half his age, and generally making Mom miserable. I was glad he'd kept his distance, because any interaction between them ended up sending Mom spiraling. We once joked she cried enough for two people, but it wasn't just a joke. She wished I would cry more and I wished she would cry less. I'd turned into my dad at some point, I guess. How depressing.

"Drink this. You look thirsty." Mom shoves a mug into my hand.

"I'm good." The thought of putting anything in my mouth makes my stomach roil. Not only is the body of my father lying in a box in the next room, but all the prep work for the deceased is done in this very building. I'd rather eat my own toes than digest this funeral food.

"You haven't eaten or drunk anything all day. I understand if your stomach is upset, but at least put some liquids in you."

I pretend to sip because getting into an argument over a cup of hot water at a funeral doesn't seem like the best course of action. It's easier to give in.

"Your eyeliner is smudged."

That's from earlier when I thought if I poked myself in the eye, it might produce tears. It didn't, even though it hurt. Mom licks her finger and drags it underneath my eye as if I were a little girl again and had dirt smeared on my face. Her action leaves an uncomfortable wet spot above my cheek that I itch to wipe off, but because I don't want her to feel rejected, I let my face air-dry. She's already on edge.

"Your dad is probably livid at this." She waves a hand toward the table someone set up with a poster board filled with photos. "It's so low-rent. And the lack of people . . ." She clicks her tongue against the top of her mouth. "He'd be devastated. I can't believe Geoff Kaplan didn't come. Those two had a business together, for crying out loud."

A failed one, if I recall, but Mom is absolutely correct. Dad would not be happy with this event. If this were Geoff's funeral, Dad would be in the corner with a golfing buddy declaring that this joint was both dull and tacky. The reception table has a grocery store cake, an assortment of cheese slices on a tray with the UPC label still visible on the black plastic, white disposable cups, liters of off-brand soda for the punch, and two tall stainless steel hot liquid dispensers filled with coffee and tea.

Dad would take this all in with his social smile—the salesman grin that seemed permanently etched into his face like the Joker's scars—but inwardly he'd be fuming. The attendance at the wake is sparse and no one sounds like they miss him. Even the second Mrs. Wilson is occupied with trying to keep her toddler from drooling all over the punch bowl instead of sitting still in her black dress weeping delicately into a handkerchief.

The last straw would be the fact that the sun is shining and there's a whole row of yellow and pink tulips sprouting in the funeral home's flower beds that line the walkway. Pat would want wailing and rain and a scene full of black umbrellas. He liked drama and attention, which is how he ended up with Nina Mathews. My mom has purses older than Nina.

The second Mrs. Wilson was a waitress at a bar that Dad liked to frequent. One thing led to another and she got pregnant. I was informed via text: Hey sport. Brush up on your baby facts. You're going to be a big sister soon.

The second-fatherhood thing must've terrified him so much that his heart gave out. That and the fact that his arteries were as hard as a cinder block.

"This whole thing looks so . . . *cheap*," Mom declares with a sniff. "But what do you expect from someone like her. Trash only knows trash."

I wince. Mom hasn't always been this antagonistic toward Dad's new wife. Up until yesterday, Mom's primary emotion toward the current Mrs. Wilson was one of pity. *That poor girl better start hiding the grocery money* or *She's wasting her youth on that man.* But last night, the new Mrs. Wilson revealed that Dad left a mortgage bigger than the value of the small two-bedroom that they lived in and a car loan that was three months late. Oh, and an insurance policy of twenty grand. Mom had demanded I get half. Dad had died without a will, and per the law, I guess I was entitled to some share. Mrs. Wilson countered that it was all that young Ryder would have to put toward his college education. *You've already been to college and gotten a degree*, Nina had said, her small face looking more pinched than normal. *Don't be selfish.*

Mom disagreed, loudly, and maintained that as Patrick Wilson's daughter, I deserved an equal portion. Nina then made the mistake of saying Ryder deserved it more because he was the *real* child. I'd had to drag Mom out of the house before she committed a homicide. She was that angry. *How dare that tramp say that about you? Of course you're his real child!*

What Nina meant, what everyone means when they say that I'm not Pat Wilson's real kid, is that I'm adopted. I don't look anything like my parents and this has been the cause of a great deal of confusion to strangers who would sometimes stupidly ask Mom where my actual parents were. Mom always responded tersely that she was my real mother. *Real because I'm the one who raised you. It doesn't matter who gave birth to you. I chose you. I supported you. I raised you.*

And she did. She wiped my tears, made my lunches, took me to my appointments, paid for my college, bought me a car, and even helped me with the down payment on a condo, which makes me the envy of all my millennial coworkers. I'm actually doing fine because of her and don't need half of the insurance policy, although I know my friends would tell me to take it and go on some wild vacation. I glance toward my purse, where a folded email rests. I've been thinking about traveling lately . . . but, no, if I take that trip I'll use my own funds.

The insurance proceeds are necessary for Nina because saving money wasn't Dad's forte—using all available cash on reckless get-rich schemes, such as opening a taco franchise when there were already two in the same zip code or buying up a bunch of biotech stock based on a tip he overheard at lunch, was what he was good at.

So while Mom might be mad at Nina forever, I'm fine with not getting anything. I'd also be fine with not being Pat Wilson's real daughter at the moment if that meant I could leave.

The slight chemical smell of the funeral home, the hushed whispers, and the casket sitting in the other room were all making that space between my shoulder blades—the one I can't reach from either above or below—begin to itch.

"Ellen, my goodness. I wondered if you would come. How are you holding up?" A big woman with a beak of a nose dressed in a black floral dress leans down to envelop Mom. I breathe in a wave of lavender and eucalyptus, which makes my empty stomach turn over. "I can't believe Patrick is gone and so young, too. I heard it was a heart attack?"

"Yes, while he was mowing the grass, can you believe it? His arteries were a mess. I always told him he needed to lower his cholesterol."

"How could he when he was married to you, though? You always made the most delicious desserts. Potlucks haven't been the same since you and Pat got the divorce. Do you still make that chocolate mousse? You told me your secret once and I forgot."

"Ice," Mom explains, happy to be distracted. "Everything needs to be cold. I even freeze the whisk that I use to whip the egg whites. That's the key to a perfect piecrust, too. Cold butter. So many people forget that. I have this book I adore even though I know paper books are outdated these days."

"I love paper cookbooks, too!" declares the other woman.

The two fall into a discussion about the merits of print versus internet recipes. The new ones can't compare. Since Mom is occupied and the overwhelming perfume is threatening to make me sick, I decide to move. Over the woman's head, I point to my barely touched tea and mouth that I'm getting a replacement. Mom gives me an encouraging smile and motions me off.

I drop my cup into a nearby trash can and wander over to the memory table. Set up near the poster board full of pictures is a television monitor. It plays a loop of photos and videos of Dad's life. Nina put it together so I'm not surprised that large chunks of Dad's life are unrepresented in the movie, but I find myself engaged anyway. There are baby pictures. A montage of old school photos with Dad holding a baseball bat and then a football and then at a track-and-field event. There's an image of him leaning against a bright blue sedan and then another at prom followed by a young Patrick throwing his graduation cap in the air.

"It's such a pity about Patrick, isn't it?" a woman says behind me. "He couldn't do much of anything right and now he's left behind a young widow and a baby."

"He finally got a kid after years of trying. At least he was successful at one thing before he died," answers a man.

I wonder if criticizing a dead man is normal discourse for a funeral. It feels like it's in bad taste, even if it is accurate. After the text, Dad invited me to dinner. Over pasta, he'd admitted to being a bad, absentee father. The specific words were: *I had shit for brains when you were a kid, Hara. I didn't do good by you so I think I should make it right by being there for my son.*

I nodded and told him it was fine. Even if it wasn't fine, I would've said it was because Dad is—I mean, was—a salesman and if he suspected that I didn't agree with him, he'd try to "sell" me on his ideas. I saved myself from that exhausting experience.

"Didn't he have a child from a previous marriage?"

"I think so, but not a real one. Apparently his first wife couldn't have kids. Or maybe she had kids before they were married because she has a daughter. Anyway, this is his first real child—and a son, thank goodness."

I should move. There's no point in listening to this conversation anymore. I look down at my feet and order them into motion but they remain planted.

"I knew it was something because when I first heard he was having a baby, I offered my condolences. Who wants to parent a toddler at the age of fifty? But Pat was thrilled to death. He said that he hadn't ever got to experience the whole bottle-feeding, diaper-changing bit and that he couldn't wait."

"Crazy. I'd lock myself in the bathroom for the next five years if my wife told me she was pregnant."

"Same, but Pat was beside himself with excitement." The woman tsks. "Too bad. It's all so tragic."

That's enough funeraling for today, I decide. It's not just the conversation that's unsettling; it's that save for my mom, Nina, and Ryder, everyone else is a stranger to me. I don't know how any of these people are connected to my father. Were they coworkers? Golf partners? Part of a swingers' club? I have zero idea and the more I think about it, the greater my head aches. If I stay much longer in this oppressive room with its tinny classical music soundtrack and the spiteful extras, I might climb onto a table and ask to be embalmed. I turn to make my way back to Mom when a wave of my coworkers streams through the door, blocking my escape.

"Hara, my goodness, how are you?" My supervisor, Lisa, envelops me in a big hug before I can sidestep it. "Why didn't you tell us when your father's funeral was? If Kelly hadn't come across the obituary, we would not have known!"

Behind Lisa, Kelly winces and mouths, "Sorry," as she's aware I deliberately kept my mouth shut. I don't like the spotlight in any way. Sometimes people ask me if I have any writing aspirations, but I don't. I'm happy as a copy editor, where I pay attention to detail, rather than as the author of a work, who has their name in the byline. There's something safe and secure about laboring behind the scenes.

"I can't believe you came to work yesterday. You should have told me your father had passed. I would've authorized another two days of leave for you." Lisa clucks. "Here, we brought flowers. Jeffrey, where are you?"

"Here they are. We ran into your sister outside, too." He shoves a bouquet of lilies into my arms.

"Sister?" I don't have a sister.

"It's me." Boyoung Kim steps out from behind the bevy of co-workers to give a small wave.

"You aren't sisters?" Jeff asks. "Aren't you both Chin—"

"Korean," Kelly interrupts. Her eyes plead with me not to say anything because we all know Jeffrey falls into the ignorant rather than hateful category. "They don't look anything alike. Hey, Boyoung. Nice to see you again."

"I'm sorry for your loss, Hara." Boyoung dips her head and offers a white envelope, extending one hand while using her other to hold up her elbow. It's a polite Korean gesture that I've seen Boyoung make to many people, including clerks at stores when she hands over her credit card.

"So you two are like cousins? From Korea?"

"They're not related," Kelly snaps. "Come on. Let's go inside." She grabs Jeff's arm and drags him into the reception room.

As they're leaving, Jeff can be heard saying, "They look alike and they're both from Korea. What are the odds?"

I exchange a wry smile with Boyoung. It's not the first time we've been called sisters, because, unfortunately, all of us Asians look the same to a lot of people around here, but side by side, Boyoung and I are as different as stripes and polka dots. Boyoung is small, coming up to my nose. She has big, wide eyes that always tend to make her appear slightly surprised. Once she told me that she wished she had had the double-eyelid surgery because everyone mistakes her for being far younger than her actual age of twenty-six. Her hair is cut in a chin-length bob and she has a Bratz-doll lower lip and a thin upper one that tends to disappear if she doesn't wear lip gloss.

At five-six, I'm tall for a Korean. My hair is long and layered and, if I'm feeling energetic, sometimes I curl it into big beach waves. I have *a lot* of hair. My eyelids do have a crease, which Boyoung envies. The shape of my eyes is not almond—I don't know any Asian whose eyes are actually almond-shaped and I'm not certain how that became a thing—but rather they curve inward near the bridge of my nose. Boyoung says that they look like a dragon's eyes. She always has the nicest descriptions of my features.

"The lecture went overlong and I was not able to come earlier," my friend explains, still holding out the envelope.

I reluctantly accept the money. Boyoung is small and speaks softly, but there are certain things that are immovable for her, and the giving of gifts is one of them. It's a custom in Korea to bring a gift everywhere.

"Thanks for coming at all." I walk inside to deliver the gift and bouquet to the memory table. "You didn't need to do this."

"I wanted to. Are you doing well?" Boyoung tilts her head to the side, her glossy black hair shifting like a dark curtain.

"Do I have something on my face? It's my eyeliner, isn't it?" Had more of it migrated after Mom tried to wipe it off? I have never gotten the hang of applying eye makeup. I'm decent at other things. I make a killer apple pie. I'm pretty good at my copyediting job. I've figured out that my long torso and short legs look good with high-waisted things. I know exactly what shade of red lipstick complements my skin tone. That last one took five years and several hundred dollars, but I've figured it out. Eye makeup still remains a mystery. One of these days, I'll get Boyoung to help me. She does a killer wing.

"No. No. It is a . . ." She rubs her finger under her eye.

"A smudge?" I offer with a slight smile. I know she loves learning new words.

"Yes, smudge," she exclaims. Her voice is a little loud and a few heads turn our way. Boyoung winces, but I don't mind. I'm glad she's here. There's something comforting about not being the only Asian in the room. I don't feel so alone at this, my father's funeral.

CHAPTER TWO

"YOU SHOULD TAKE A TRIP SOMEWHERE," KELLY SAYS, SUCKING on her vape. "Like to Bermuda. Bereavement leave should include one week where you can go anywhere in the world."

"I'd go to Vail," Jeff says.

"It's May, Jeff," Kelly reminds him.

"What? People don't die in the winter?" He reaches down and takes the Juul from her. They argue so much, sometimes I forget the two are dating.

Kelly rolls her eyes and addresses the rest of us. "I'm sorry for the hundredth time for Jeff's rudeness."

I'm used to it and if Boyoung is bothered, she doesn't show it. She's busy messaging someone. The four of us found our way to Denny's after the funeral, collectively agreeing that eating anything at the funeral home would be worse than starvation. The remnants of a pancakes-and-skillet breakfast that we shared for dinner are shoved to the center.

"Where would you go, Boyoung?"

"For a vacation?" She glances up from her phone. "Maybe Hawaii?" she answers tentatively. If the Korean girl thinks it's weird that we are discussing post-funeral getaways, she doesn't show it. I wonder how funerals are handled in Korea. Is there a wake? Is there a burial? Do they have pallbearers? In high school, one of my Jewish friends had an aunt who died and the official process of mourning took place over an entire week.

"So two for sun—"

"One for fun," Jeff cuts in with a bad attempt at a rhyme.

Kelly rolls her eyes before turning to me. "Where would you go?"

"Korea." It pops out before I give it much thought.

"Korea?" The three people at the table say it as one.

Their surprise takes me aback. I peer around the table. "What? Why can't I go to Korea?"

"You've never mentioned wanting to go to Korea, like, ever," Kelly says, retrieving the Juul from Jeff.

"I know. It's an idea." One that I can't seem to push aside.

"Why there?" Jeff frowns.

"It's where she's from, dummy." Kelly flicks Jeff's ear.

"But you don't know shit about Korea, right, Hara? Ow, Kells, that hurt." Jeff rubs his biceps—the one Kelly punched after attacking his ear. "Remember when I asked her the date the Korean War ended and you guys all got up in my face about it, saying it was racist and that I can't use her as a reference dictionary and that just because she's Korean doesn't mean she has to know anything about Korea?"

"Two plus two doesn't equal fish," I reply a bit tartly, and maybe it's because I'm tired of Jeff or maybe I'm feeling defensive because he's right. I don't know shit about Korea. I opened my browser the other day to look something up and realized I couldn't even type in a phrase because I didn't have the Korean keyboard layout down-loaded onto my computer. My knowledge of my birth country is so shallow it would barely fill a thimble.

"Just because Hara looks Korean doesn't mean she is a real Ko-rean. Not like Boyoung," Kelly replies. "Hara's American."

Ouch. The *real* thing again. But do I have any right to be mad at Kelly when I've tried to separate myself from my Asianness as much as possible? I've been asked more than once where I'm from and I always answer, *Here*, which is never enough because the people who ask that question don't want *here* to be the answer. The question has context, which is *you look different from me so you must be from some-where else*, definitely not *here*. I know this is what they're asking but I hate the question so I always repeat my answer. I'm from *here*. From Iowa. From America. Just like you. Plus, I don't feel Korean—whatever that feels like—but I know that next to Boyoung, the dif-ferences are stark.

It's not the language difference either. There's something about Boyoung that is innately different, from the way that she dresses (al-ways up) to the expertly applied makeup (I've tried to copy Boy-oung's eyeliner technique, resulting in comedic black-eye results) to the mannerisms (never show your teeth while laughing, eating, or smiling). I actually hadn't realized how *not* Korean I was until Boy-oung came along.

"I didn't know you wanted to go to Korea," Boyoung says softly.

"Like I said, it was just a thought." A thought brought on by a sur-prise email, my father's unexpected death, and this uncertainty that has surrounded me for too long. Lately, wherever I walked, whatever I did, didn't feel right. It is as if my life is this once-favorite jacket that I'd washed in water that was too hot and now it is tight around the arms and the zipper works only half the time. It doesn't mean that the jacket will fit right if I go to Korea, but maybe it's time to try.

"What would you do there?" Jeff asks. He's confused. "I saw this video once of them eating live squid."

"It wasn't alive." I'd seen the same video going around social media. Soy sauce was poured onto a dead squid and the thing rose up and danced in the bowl because of some chemical reaction between the salt in the condiment making contact with the cephalopod, but from the reaction to the video, you'd think a fish massacre was taking place on the table.

"It was Japanese," Boyoung murmurs.

"What?"

"She said it was a Japanese video," Kelly says with exasperation. "There isn't one Asian country, but Jeff is sort of right. You don't speak Korean, do you?"

Next to me, Boyoung stiffens. "Do you?"

"No."

And my friend visibly relaxes. I pat her shoulder. "Don't worry. I've never understood a word you said to anyone on the phone." Not that I've heard her talk all that often, but sometimes she's spoken to someone in Korean. I don't know if they all speak as quickly as she does, but I couldn't even begin to tell where the sentences began or ended.

"How would you get around? How would you order something to eat or find a bathroom?" Kelly asks.

"All good questions," I say.

"And?" my friend prompts.

"The subway has signs in English," Boyoung pipes up in my defense. "And in tourist spots there are helpers who speak English and Chinese. Many restaurants have English menus, and in Itaewon, there are many, what do you say, expats?"

Jeff claps his hands. "Maybe we should all go."

"To where?" Kelly wonders.

"Korea," Jeff says. It's his turn to be irritated. "We can all go and then you guys can't call me ignorant anymore."

"I don't have the money for that," Kelly laments, sliding halfway down the booth seat until only her shoulders are above the table. "Isn't it expensive, Boyoung?"

"No. Food is cheap or expensive depending on where you go. It is the same with places to live. There are poor places in Seoul and rich places, too."

"What's it like there?" Jeff wonders. We all lean forward.

Boyoung is quiet for a long time before she says, "Beautiful."

And some free-floating piece of my heart slides into place with an audible click.

IT WAS A month after I'd gotten the Hey sport text that I signed up for the DNA matching service. Kelly had come to work and announced that she was one-sixteenth Inuit based on her DNA test results and that she might have second cousins who lived in Canada. She was excited about this and told me I should sign up and find out what I was made of, at least for health reasons. I once told her that filling out doctor's forms at a clinic took no time because I didn't have to answer any of the family history questions. When I was a kid, Mom had suggested I undergo genetic testing but Dad balked because it was too expensive. After the divorce, Mom had other things on her mind and never followed up.

But at twenty-four, I was curious so I swabbed my cheek and sent off the kit. A few weeks later, the envelope of results returned noting that I was 98.2 percent Korean and 1.8 percent Japanese. There were no genetic warnings and no pings to anyone else's results. I was slightly disappointed. I didn't want to admit it, but I think I was hoping there would be some long-lost relative. I'd once read that two adopted siblings found each other—one in America and one in France. Having a French sister would be awesome. I've always wanted to visit. However, that was not the case for me so I buried my expectations in the box of "things better forgotten" along with my dad's dream that I'd be some kind of super athlete and my mom's fantasy that I could be the next Gillian Flynn.

The real-life truth is that I'm clumsy, spend my days fact-checking and editing, and have a greater chance of winning the lottery than finding information about my biological family. And it's not that I care to know about the people who abandoned me on a street corner in Seoul twenty-five years ago. I'm just . . . curious about whether I have siblings. Maybe aunts and uncles. I grew up as an only child of an only child. Mom's mother passed away fourteen years ago and it's been the two of us against the world ever since Mom kicked Dad out.

Knowing I had extended family would be cool—or, at least, that's how I justified it in my mind. And when nothing came of it, when there were no notices in my inbox, when the weeks of silence turned into months and then a year, I'd essentially forgotten about it.

Until that one morning, three months ago, when an email had popped up between the half dozen newsletters I didn't remember subscribing to and the spam that somehow finds its way to my inbox despite the so-called filter. It took a moment for me to register that the subject line was in *Hangul* instead of some odd mass of characters designed to get around the spam block.

I'd copied and pasted the characters into the translation website but the English text made little sense. After some research, I'd discovered that the Western machine translation was inaccurate and misleading. In sum, I wasn't to rely on it.

But I didn't know any human translator. I lived in Des Moines, Iowa, a place so homogenous that my adoption likely increased the Asian population in the city by an entire percentage point.

This was before I ran into Boyoung at the coffee shop near my office. After I did get to know her, it didn't seem right to whip out the email upon our first meeting or even our sixth one. *Hey, new girl from across the ocean, we barely know each other but can I use you to translate this email?* It seemed rude so I never asked, never felt like asking . . . until now.

CHAPTER THREE

IT TAKES ANOTHER WEEK BEFORE I ARRANGE TO MEET BOY-
oung for lunch. I tell myself that it's not because I'm afraid of what
the email says but rather I'm engaging in safe bereavement behavior
and not making hasty decisions so soon after my dad's death. This
isn't lying to oneself; it's self-care.

I end up arriving at the mall thirty minutes early because I'm a
ball of anxiety. I don't know if I'm making the right decision. I keep
wavering between two sayings: "Ignorance is bliss" and "Knowledge
is power." The knowledge one is winning out mostly because I already know something. My ignorance was pierced when I received
the email. Or maybe it was when I ran the email through the machine translation. What I think I know is eating away at me. The
saying should be "Full knowledge is power" because half knowledge
is something that drives you to the brink of disaster.

I try to kill the extra time by wandering in and out of the stores
close to the restaurant. The makeup-store display lures me in.

"Want a cut-crease tutorial?" an eager staff person offers. "It's free."

Who can turn down free? Not me. "Sure. Why not?"

Eye makeup, particularly eyeliner, has always been a struggle for me—as evidenced by everyone from my mother to Boyoung trying to fix my eyes at the funeral last week.

"Do you have a look you want to try? Like an evening out or a work face?" the clerk asks as she leads me over to a vanity station.

"I'm pretty helpless when it comes to eyeshadow. I don't think I even know what a cut crease is." I climb onto the stool in front of a brightly lit makeup mirror. When I see my reflection, I realize it's too well lit. I can count every pore in my nose.

"Oh, a cut crease is perfect for you because your fold isn't that pronounced so you can create extra definition in your eyes by using color." The staff person gathers a few supplies, applies a primer, and then starts to dab color onto my lids with small brushes. "Are you meeting up with a guy? Or is it work? Close your eyes."

"A friend. A female friend," I answer as I lower my lids.

"Cool. She'll be so jealous. This color of brown is going to look gorgeous on you. Okay, open your eyes."

I start to obey when the woman orders, "No. Sorry. Close again."

This process goes on for a few more minutes. The clerk mutters to herself and then I feel a damp cotton round swipe across my eyelid.

"I think the brown was the wrong color. I'm going to try something different," the clerk says.

I don't even have to see my reflection to know this is not going well, but I do anyway. The color, which I'm sure looks great on everyone else, makes me look like I got punched in the face.

The clerk meets my gaze in the mirror. "I'm sorry." She grimaces. "Let me try again. This color normally works well with every skin tone. If you—"

I wave her off. "Nah. It's fine. I have the same problem. I've got to run anyway."

And it's true. Time has gotten away from me, and Boyoung is probably waiting at the restaurant. She's always punctual. The hostess at Tofu greets me with a Korean hello—*annyeonghaseyo*. I try to echo it back but based on the funny expression on the hostess's face, I can tell I've butchered the pronunciation again. There are a handful of Asian people in this town and I sense that I've embarrassed myself in front of half of them.

Boyoung is at the table near the window overlooking the parking lot. A slight smile dances around the corners of her mouth.

"Did you hear?" I slide into my side of the booth.

Boyoung nods. "Your pronunciation is getting better," she lies.

"It's terrible, but thanks for not laughing at me. One of these days, I'm going to say it perfectly. It might be the sole Korean word in my vocabulary, but I'm going to sound like a native when I say it."

"That's not true. You sound like a Korean when you say *ottoke* and *ppalli ppalli.*"

"'What to do' and 'hurry up' and 'hello.' I feel like I could navigate the whole of Seoul," I joke.

Boyoung giggles, bringing her hand up to cover her mouth.

"How's class?" I ask as we wait for our pizza to arrive. Pizza is Boyoung's favorite American food, yet she only likes it from this Korean restaurant that serves the most amazing fried chicken around as well as super-cheesy oven-baked pizza. They don't make it in Korea like they do here, she's said repeatedly. In the months that I've known Boyoung, the girl has eaten pizza here every week and it's always the same—cheese with pineapple and ham.

"Great. I am almost done with my fellowship paper." Boyoung is part of a cultural educational exchange at the local college. It was a new graduate school program that started this spring and my Korean friend was one of the first participants.

I feel like some proud mother whenever Boyoung talks about her project. She picked a college here! In the Midwest! All the way from Korea! Boyoung fascinates me. I don't know many Koreans. There is the couple that run one of the three Asian groceries in town. I'm a little abashed to go in there because I don't know what half of the items on the shelves are for. I've used the internet to decipher what I could about the things that Mom made at home when I was younger like the vermicelli noodle dish with the dried mushrooms and the *kimchi jjigae*, with a broth made out of dried anchovies and seaweed, which sounds terrible but is one of my favorite dishes ever. I took Boyoung there and she explained a bunch of things to me and even bought a few ingredients for me to try. A certain type of ramen was the best and had I tried cheese in it? No, never, and it was shockingly good. Microwave rice beats instant rice by the length of a marathon or three. Curry vegetables out of the refrigerated section weren't half bad.

She's also introduced me to Korean dramas. I mainlined the shows *Kingdom* and *Signal* like they were Grade A drugs. I guess they were in their own way. With each minute I spent with Boyoung, I regretted how I acted when I was younger, immature, and, well, stupid.

When I was little, Mom took me to Korean cultural programs in Minneapolis—"dragged" is a more accurate word. I hated attending them and for the entire five hours or so that it took to get there, I pretended that counting the cows was more interesting than any of my mom's attempts at conversation. I was a real brat. The music they played sounded odd and foreign. The smell of the food seemed to cling to my clothes for days after. If a schoolmate asked me where I spent the weekend, I'd lie and say I was home sick.

The sad thing was that those visits were the only time I was surrounded by people who looked like me. I should've been more comfortable, but it served to remind me how different I was from my friends. Eventually, Mom stopped forcing me to go.

I'd intentionally closed my eyes and ears and now I was paying for it. If I'd continued to attend those programs, perhaps I'd have learned a little Korean and I wouldn't be forced to ask Boyoung for help today.

But that wasn't my story, so I reach inside my pocket and pull out the printout that I made today. It's a new one. The copy I've been carrying around has been creased so much that some of the *Hangul* is indecipherable. It doesn't matter to me because I have it memorized, but Boyoung needs to see all the characters correctly. It's important that the translation be perfect. "I have a favor to ask."

"Of course." She smiles and gestures for me to continue.

I take a big breath and lay the sheet in front of her. I don't know why I'm nervous but I'm glad I haven't had any of the pizza yet. It'd be in my throat right now. "It's a translation request. I looked it up online but you've said I can't trust machine translations, so . . . would you mind?"

"Yes, yes." She takes the paper and scans the contents.

The email is short—a few sentences. I recite the machine translation to myself as Boyoung reads it to herself. I can tell she's finished because her jaw drops and her dark brown eyes grow wide.

Strangely, I find this shock reassuring. It means my own translation wasn't that far off. "It's from my father—my biological one, isn't it?"

My friend nods slowly and her words stumble out. "How did you— Where did you— When?"

She sounds as confused and as surprised as I felt the first time I read the email.

"A while back," I begin vaguely, not wanting to admit that my father's announcement that he was having a biological child sent me into a panic at my big age, "I signed up for a DNA matching service on the internet. You send your blood in along with whatever details you have about your adoption, and then, if both parties consent, you are contacted if there's a match. I didn't get a response, so I figured either there was no match or my birth parents didn't consent." I tug the paper out from under Boyoung's hand and trace a finger over the *Hangul* at the end. Lee Jonghyung. That was my father's name—my *biological* father. My mind keeps inserting that adjective, as if I'm going to forget. "The sperm donor" would be Mom's term for him. "I figured there was no match because, you know, I was left on the street."

Boyoung nods again. I'd shared my backstory not long after Boyoung had met Mom. The questions filled her eyes but she was too polite, too well-mannered to ask even a single question, unlike Jeff, who shouted across the break room one day to ask what baby mart Ellen had bought me from. He got written up for that but I told HR it was no big deal. It wasn't, either. His wasn't the first dumb question I'd ever fielded on the matter of my relationship to Ellen. It didn't bother me. Not really. Or, at least, not much.

But while I wouldn't ever tell Jeff the circumstances of my adoption, the story spilled out to Boyoung without much thought. After dinner at my house, we'd gone out for ice cream, and over a giant banana split that was nearly bigger than my head, I'd told her that at a few weeks old, I'd been left on the street near a police station in Mapo-gu, a busy and central neighborhood in the capital city of Seoul. A policeman found me and took me to an orphanage, where I was fostered out. I stayed with a foster family until I was adopted at the age of one by the Wilsons.

"Your *abeoji*—I mean, your father consented to this information being shared?" Boyoung's girlish voice is pitched one octave higher in disbelief. She clears her throat and tries again. "You should be careful. I love my country, but there are bad people everywhere. This person probably wants to take advantage of you. Many in Korea believe that all of you Westerners are rich, especially Americans."

"He didn't consent. He didn't reach out to me at all, in fact. There was a data breach and the system sent me his name and contact information." Lee Jonghyung. That would make me a Lee. Hara Lee sounds pretty Asian. To be more precise, it would be Lee Hara.

Boyoung taught me that the last name—the name of a person's clan—always comes first because that's the Confucian ideal. Family first. But, obviously, not always, because I was left on a street corner and then sent to America, so sometimes it was every man—and child—for himself. Not that I'm resentful. I don't have any right to be. I have a great mom. I have a job, a condo, a ten-year-old car, good health insurance, and no debt. That's a lot for a millennial. No, I'm not resentful, and if I keep telling myself that, the sour feeling in my stomach will eventually settle. "I waited. I deleted the message." I smile wryly at my own mind games. "But I fished it out from the trash and sent him a message. This is his reply."

> I am Lee Jonghyung. When I was twenty, I was told by my sweetheart that I had gotten her pregnant. I did not believe the baby was mine and sent her away. But now I wonder if it was you. My heart is heavy and I am afraid that if I do not reconcile this issue, my ancestors will reject me upon my death. I would like to meet you.

"Hara, what if it was not your father? You said it was a data breach. This could be any random person. Why did you not ask for my help?" Boyoung is distressed. Really distressed.

Her concern spikes my blood pressure. "I . . . I thought I could do it myself."

And I wasn't ready to share this. I'm not ready now, but I was so uncertain of my own translation and I didn't trust the internet, so I came to you.

Boyoung presses her lips together in a disapproving line before holding out her hand. "Let me have the email and I will do some research for you. Once I find out who this man is, I'll help you write a response. I don't want someone to take advantage of you."

I curl fingers protectively around the printout, as if the email isn't starred in my inbox and couldn't be reprinted a thousand times. "It's okay. I'm not going to do anything rash. I was curious."

I mean, yes, I've looked up tickets to Korea, but I haven't bought any. I might have applied for a passport, but that hasn't arrived in the mail. I haven't done anything concrete. It's all dreams and imaginings. I fold the paper up into a tiny square and tuck it back into my pocket.

"Do not reply without talking to me first," Boyoung urges. "Promise?"

Our pizza arrives to save me from lying to my friend.

CHAPTER FOUR

"AND AFTER SEEING KAREN AT THE WAKE, WE THOUGHT IT would be good to get together again. Apparently, Pat's coworkers aren't fond of that woman either. Everyone thinks your dad was a fool to remarry and have a kid at his age. Karen kept asking what was Pat thinking, but that's the problem. He wasn't. At least not with his big head." Mom presses the plastic wrap into the top of the honey lemon curd cake she's making.

I wince at the vague reference to my dead father's penis and decide it's not a good segue to the confession I have to make. It's not the trip that will freak Mom out, but the reason. I did contemplate lying like a coward and saying I'm going on a vacation out east, but that would require keeping up an elaborate story, which I'd mess up within the first twenty-four hours. Besides, can you ever lie to your mom? They have some inborn sixth sense about their kids. I've never been able to get away with a thing, and if Mom wasn't preoccupied with Dad's death and the other Mrs. Wilson, she'd catch on to the fact that I'm jumpy as a piece of corn in a hot skillet.

I bend my head over the wax paper in front of me and pipe out the squat bodies for the chocolate ganache bees with which Mom plans to decorate the cake.

"Karen was shocked that our names weren't listed first in the obituary. It should've been me and then you and then her and that child. How many people did I say were coming?" Mom's sudden change of topic doesn't confuse me. I'm used to it. I acquired my nervousness from her—not biologically but through the process of living with her for eighteen years. You take on the traits of those people you're around. I'm firmly in the nuture-over-nature camp.

"Thirteen, and his name is Ryder."

"Oh my Lord. Don't even get me started on that name. Who names their child that?" She taps my wrist. "Make the ganache bees fat. Everyone likes a good amount of chocolate with their lemon."

It's better than *Hara*, I think as I pipe extra-large bees onto the wax paper and then stick the slivered almond wings onto the bodies. The start of every school year was always a joy, as I had to listen to each new teacher massacre my name. It's *ha-rah*, not *hair-a*. I should've made a sign and pasted it onto my chest. Unfortunately, that minor trial didn't prepare me for the embarrassment I'd experience in college when I learned from one of the Asian exchange students that my name was the same as some famous Korean porn actress's. Each time I passed one of the few Asian students, I swear I'd always hear a slight twittering of laughter, so I never hung out with them—not that I was asked. International students are a tight bunch. They all spoke at least two languages, if not more, and when they said something to me in Korean, my only response was a dumb, blank stare.

I didn't belong with the Asian international student clique, and it wasn't simply that I lacked the ability to communicate with them. I didn't understand the language puns they made. I didn't know the foods they referenced or the cultural landmarks. Lotte Tower? My-eongdong? Gwanghwamun Square? Every cultural reference escaped me. I was *other* with them as well. The single commonality we had was that our features were similar.

Boyoung is the first Asian friend I've ever had.

"He'll be spelling that name for every teacher from preschool through graduate school—not that she'll be able to pay for that even with that measly insurance policy. It's a good thing you have a job; otherwise, that would be one more area where *he* let you down."

I keep my mouth shut. Mom doesn't want my input.

As expected, she barrels on. "I'm making three different kinds of sandwiches, but I'm not sure how many to make. Perhaps two per person? So that would be . . . How many people did I say were coming?" She abandons the cakes and rushes to the refrigerator, pulling out cucumbers and cream cheese and salmon spread.

"Thirteen." I grab the bag of white chocolate and lay down the stripes on the backs of the bees.

"Thirteen. Right. That's not a good number. I should've invited one more person. Although do I even have enough chairs for thirteen? Maybe that's too many. What about something to drink? I've tea, of course, but should we have a dessert wine? Do they serve dessert wines with high tea?" She leaves the vegetables and spreads on the counter to grab her phone.

I slide the sheet of finished cake decorations into the freezer and stash the pies in the refrigerator. With the dessert completed, I tackle the finger sandwiches. At least Mom is serving something that I can make. At the last party she hosted, Mom had wanted to serve four different types of homemade pasta composed of things like spinach and pumpkin. Together, we mangled ravioli pouches and fettucine noodles for hours before I gave up and ran to Whole Foods for packaged pasta.

"Oh, champagne. Of course. We'll serve mimosas, then. Do I have orange juice? Hara, you'll need to stop and pick up champagne tomorrow after work. I have that cheap bottle from New Year's and I can't serve that to your dad's old work colleagues."

I decide to make these twenty-eight sandwiches and then confess. No, not confess, because that feels like I've done something wrong. It can't be wrong to want to know more about my past—that yearning is normal. Even Boyoung, who has been arguing with me for the past week about being careful about strangers on the internet, isn't against me connecting with my birth parent. She is concerned about me being ripped off. Understandable. A couple of days ago, she texted me a mass of *Hangul* with stern instructions to paste it into the reply section of the email. I didn't, though. The machine translation made it sound like an angry rebuke along with a command to never contact me again.

Mom won't think it's a con artist, but she'll be hurt. She'll take this as a direct assault on her parenting, even though this isn't a binary thing where if I go to Seoul to meet Lee Jonghyung then I'll denounce Ellen Wilson.

"Mom, listen."

"How many bottles of champagne do you think I should buy? Three? Or maybe two because Karen will bring a bottle of wine, don't you think? She's the type to bring wine everywhere. Macy might, too. She said she wanted to help out—"

"Mom—"

"Three is a good number. I'm bound to have guests over again, so if we don't drink the three bottles I'll be set for next time."

Talking isn't getting me anywhere. I abandon the sandwich assembly line and pluck the phone out of Mom's hands.

She jerks to attention. "What is it?"

Of course, now that I have her attention, my courage falls somewhere around my knees. "I'm ... I am ..." I pause to clear my throat.

Mom's forehead creases. "You're not ill, are you?" Her hand comes up to rest against my cheek.

"No. It's not that. It's, well, I got this email, you see." I reach around her and drag my purse across the counter. The folded email falls out.

Ellen looks at the paper and then at me. "What is this?" She doesn't want to touch it, somehow sensing she's not going to like the contents. I unfold it and hand it over.

She takes it reluctantly. The paper shakes a little as she brings it close enough to read. "Is this a time-share?" She tries to laugh. "You know those things are rip-offs."

"No. It's not a time-share," I say softly. "It's an email from my dad."

"Pat?"

"No. My—" I almost say "real" but stop myself at the last second. "My bio dad."

"The sperm donor?" Mom blurts out in shock. Her eyes quickly scan the document, stopping at the blue inked translation that I'd penned after my pizza dinner with Boyoung. Mom starts shaking her head. "No. No. This— You can't."

I press on. "I signed up for one of those adoption DNA matching services and I received this in return."

Her lips thin. "Is this because your father died?" She lets the paper flutter back onto the counter and shoves by me. At the cutting board, she begins to slice the cucumbers into ragged, uneven bits. "You should get some counseling. You didn't cry at the funeral. I know you don't like crying, but it's good to do sometimes. It gives you a"—Mom fists her hand in front of her chest—"a release. I've been thinking of going to therapy myself. We could go together."

"It's not because Dad died." It was that he'd tried to make a new life without me; it was because of the email that I'd received; it was because I've never truly felt that I fit in here among everyone with their blond hair and their prominent brows and their high nose bridges, but I didn't fit with the Asian crowd either. My shoes are either too tight or too loose, but I feel like there are answers somewhere in that small peninsula on the other side of the ocean. "I wonder things," I finally say.

"What things? Why he abandoned you? There's nothing to be curious about. You already have a father." Mom stomps over to the counter and haphazardly throws the cucumbers down onto the bread I laid out earlier. "You don't need to get in touch with this stranger. Besides, you know what happened to Nicki's family. That was horrible. She went through so much trauma, and unnecessary trauma at that."

Nicki was an adoptee from Minneapolis whom I'd met a few times during annual cultural festivals. Through the adoption grapevine that Mom had once been hooked into, Nicki's unhappy reunion story spread like a spark falling on dry hay. She'd gone to Korea on a trip hosted by her adoption agency and met with her bio father and two older siblings. They were poor, which was why they'd given young Nicki up for adoption. They were still poor when Nicki, now a med student, returned. They'd demanded money from her, stating that it was her filial duty. She'd grown up in a posh home with wealthy doctor parents, wanting for nothing, while her biological family had scraped by. She'd given them money, but the requests were nonstop to the extent that Nicki had to cut off contact. She regretted ever meeting her bio family and never wanted to return.

"He didn't say he wanted money." The few responses I'd received from Lee Jonghyung were brief. *Come and visit me. I would like to meet you.*

"Why else would he contact you?"

Mom doesn't mean to hurt me, but the offhand way that the sentence is phrased, as if there couldn't possibly be any reason other than money, leaves a shallow mark across my chest. I pretend that I'm unaffected. "Perhaps he's curious, too."

Mom sniffs. "He could be one of those fisher people, trying to take your identity. A lot of people over there do that."

"Over where?" I don't like where she's going with this and before she can say something we're both going to regret, I move on. "It's phishing, not fisher, and I'm not going to give him any information. In fact, he wants me to come to Seoul. He's not asking me to pay his way here. Mom, I know it sounds ridiculous and that it's a dead end, but I'd always regret it if I didn't do anything."

She mashes bread on top of the carelessly strewn cucumbers. "Aren't I enough? Yes, Pat was a bad dad, but he did love you in his own way and I love you so much. From the moment that I saw your picture, I have loved you. There's nothing for you in that country. They literally threw you out like trash and abandoned you."

I suck in a breath and hold it, surprised at how much simple words can hurt. She's mad, I tell myself, and hurt. "There's lots of reasons. Medical, for instance. Whenever I have to fill out medical forms, I can't answer any of the family history questions."

"Are you sick? Is there something you're not telling me? You should've said something before I planned this party!" Mom's voice is getting high and thin.

"No, Mom, I'm not sick. I'm just . . . I'm curious." I rub my throat, wondering if the tightness there is from a summer illness or the fact that this conversation is going exactly as badly as I expected.

"You can be curious here. There are lots of resources. The internet exists for a reason." She smacks her hand on the counter. "What if you do meet up with him? What answer can he possibly give you that would make you feel better? I already told you that your mother gave you up because she wanted a better life for you."

That's the story Ellen has told me all my life, particularly at night, when there was a tiny bit of moonlight seeping in around the edges of the shade that's cut shy of the opening. Because at night is when the doubts would creep in, when I would lie awake and stare at the popcorn-pebbled ceiling and wonder why my mother gave me up. Why she, as Ellen so plainly put, threw me out like so much trash. The painful, hurtful thoughts would run around in my head like a hamster on a wheel until I worked myself up so much that I felt like I was actually the hamster—small, insignificant, unworthy. These were the source of the tears that Dad had hated so much. *Stop crying. What's the use of crying? Not going to change things.*

"I want to see him. I want to touch his hand. I want to . . ." It's inexplicable. I don't have a full explanation because I don't fully understand the yearning myself. I only know that it exists and it's pulling me, like a rope around my heart tugging me east.

"There's nothing for you there. Your life is here. Your job is here. Your friends are here."

"Mom. They said I didn't look like Dad. At the funeral."

"Who cares what they said!" She throws her hands in the air. "You don't look like me either. Does that mean I'm not your mother? Does that mean that I haven't been there for you every time you fell? Every time you had a success? Every time you were sick or you were happy? It was me that was there for you. I'm your *mother*!" The last word is said more like a plea than a declaration. Her outburst isn't followed by a torrent of tears, but a thin-lipped, tight-faced expression, and somehow that's even worse.

"I love you." I don't know how to explain myself. How can I put words to something that's a feeling in my chest? "I love you, Mom. I'm not leaving you." Not like Pat did. "I'm just . . . I want to go."

CHAPTER FIVE

"I'M SORRY," BOYOUNG REPEATS FOR WHAT SEEMS LIKE THE tenth time since I landed. After I unfolded my body from the cramped airplane seat and turned on my cell phone, a host of messages from Boyoung greeted me. She couldn't meet me at Seoul Station as we originally planned, she was very sorry, and she would make it right.

"It's okay." What was the Korean term? I remember hearing it in a song that Boyoung liked to play in her apartment. *Gwenchan-ah? Gwenchan-ahyo?* I try it out, my tongue tripping over the unfamiliar syllables. *"Gwen-chan-ah-yo?"*

Boyoung tries to suppress a laugh but a small sound escapes. "More hard *k* sound than the *gw* one, but it's the right term. Thank you for understanding. My brother is sick and I'm afraid to leave him."

"It's no problem at all." There's a train that runs directly from the airport in Incheon, a small island city northwest of the capital, and deposits me at Seoul Station. From there, I need to take one more train and then a bus to get to my rented room. Boyoung thought that it might be too complicated. While the subway had English signs, the buses did not. Plus, I needed a transit card and she couldn't remember where the English kiosks were at the subway station, which made sense because she would never have had the occasion to use them. In the back of my head, I can hear my mom chastising me for coming to a foreign country when I barely know three words. Of course, I will not be admitting my unease to Boyoung. She's clearly distressed.

"It is not good, but what can we do?" She sighs. "After customs, go downstairs and through the doors. Straight ahead will be a telecom desk. You can pick up an internet modem there. The clerks will all speak English so there will be no problem. Do not take the train. I have hired a driver."

I grimace. That sounds expensive, and with Mom against this trip, I'm on my own financially, so I need to be careful. "I'll be fine with the subway. You said all the signs are in English at Seoul Station."

"You have luggage. No. The car is the right thing. The train cars have this small space for bags and you have to transfer at Seoul Station, which is very busy. I'll show you tomorrow, okay? Make sure you go to the man wearing a blue suit and a red tie. He will wait for you near the rental station for the internet modem. Also do not worry because he speaks English, too. He has your mobile number and will text you if you can't find him. I told him where to go, but show him your address and he will take you directly there. Please, Hara, or I will worry too much about you."

There's genuine grief in my friend's voice, and since I don't want to add to her burden, I capitulate. "All right, but I'm paying for the car when we see each other tomorrow." Boyoung makes some noises of protest but I ignore them. "One of the security guards is glaring at me. Let me call you back after I get through customs and find the driver, okay?"

"Yes, good."

We say our goodbyes and I allow myself a brief moment of panic as I tuck my phone away. I give a tight smile to the uniformed officer, whose facial muscles do not move, and proceed through the customs line.

I'm an adult. I've traveled outside of Iowa before, so while the Incheon airport looks more like a small, futuristic city than a travel gateway, I feel confident I can find my way to the Airbnb, especially if I have someone dropping me off at the front door. It's a splurge but worth it. Plus, Boyoung sent me a handy cheat sheet of words—not that I can pronounce any of them, but she assured me if I showed my phone to any traveler, someone would help me.

"People are nice in Seoul," Boyoung had said when she finally realized that I was making this trip no matter how many times people told me it was a mistake.

It was strange how the more people told me not to go, the more I wanted to leave. No one could change my mind, not even my supervisor, who said that while my two-week vacation could be approved, I wouldn't be able to take one more day off for the entire year, not even around the holidays. I didn't care. I went home and started packing.

Once Boyoung realized I was coming regardless of any argument that anyone could offer, she said—actually demanded—that I allow her to be my tour guide. Like I would say no to that. Because her classes had ended for summer break, Boyoung returned to Korea first while I waited for my passport to arrive in the mail.

The sixteen-hour flight was long and tedious. The seats were cramped and despite the on-board entertainment, I couldn't focus on anything. I tried to sleep, but an odd sense of excitement buzzed through my veins.

It's cool to be here, all alone, in the country where I was born. If Boyoung had traveled with me, I might have felt the need to appear unaffected. Instead, I am free to gawk and not feel stupid. Everywhere I look, there's a sea of blue-black hair. Of oval-shaped eyes. Of round cheeks, smooth foreheads, small noses. These are faces with features that are similar to the ones I see in the mirror, the face that sometimes I forget I sport until I catch my reflection in a shop window. *Oh, I'm Korean*, my brain will stupidly supply.

Here, I don't have to pretend I belong. I look like I belong. There are other travelers who stand out—a redhead with curly locks, a tall Caucasian businessman with blond hair, a family of five with varying hues of brown mops. Others look at them, but not at me.

No one would ask me where I came from. No one would question if I spoke the right language. No one—

"Passport, please." The customs agent's voice interrupts my little fantasy.

With a sigh, I hand the blue book over. Okay, so maybe there are people who will ask me questions, but they won't be dumb ones like if I can see when I smile or whether my sex is slanted like my eyes or how I look like Constance Wu even though she's a whole Chinese person and I'm Korean. There wouldn't be any of those dumb questions that I still remember even though most were asked so many years ago that I should forget but can't. I guess you remember the things that make you feel foreign in your own backyard.

"What is the purpose of your visit? Business? Travel?" The agent peers through the plexiglass at me. "Family?"

The options filter through my mind and I discard them one by one before settling on, "Yes, family."

The customs agent stamps my passport and hands it back to me with a small nod. See? No dumb questions.

A silly smile spreads across my face. I've not even left the airport and I already feel at home. When I stroll through the automatic doors from baggage claim, I immediately spy my driver—tall, dressed in a perfectly tailored blue suit with his dark head bent over his phone. I keep my eye on him while I lease a Wi-Fi travel modem.

I've noticed that the men here are particularly fine—not that I'm here for some vacation romance, but every man I've seen has been well-groomed, well-dressed, and generally very easy on the eyes. Boyoung has been keeping things from me. How rude of her.

The clerk at the rental kiosk does speak English as Boyoung promised. The transaction is painless and in minutes I'm hurrying over to the man in blue.

"Hello!" I call out. "I'm Hara. Hara Wilson."

I nearly fall on my face when he looks up from his phone. I'm not a chatty person, but I've never been at a loss for words. I've always got something to say, but not this time. It's as if my tongue is glued to the roof of my mouth.

He is beautiful.

It is not a term I'd generally use for a man but there's no better adjective. He's magazine beautiful. Photoshop beautiful. Beautiful in the way that if I uploaded a picture of him on Instagram, the post would go viral. It's possible I've conjured him much like a thirsty woman in the desert imagines an oasis, but in reality she's licking a sand dune.

I've been up for nearly twenty-four hours. It's hard to sleep on a plane when you have two inches of leg room and are scrunched between a businessman wearing a bottle's worth of cologne and a woman who takes selfies every five minutes before passing out on your shoulder. I probably have a film over my eyes that's acting like a real-life blur filter. I blink twice, but when I refocus, he's still there, except now he's staring at me like I'm the odd thing.

"I'm H-Hara," I stammer out, but there's not even a flicker of recognition. Then I remember that he probably knows of Boyoung since she arranged for him to be here. "Boyoung Kim. I mean, Kim

Boyoung," I correct myself, remembering that last names go first. "Kim Boyoung arranged for you to drive me to my rental."

The man looks from my face to my hand and back again. That feeling of home is leaking away and a familiar sensation of otherness creeps over me, turning my cheeks red. Suddenly, I realize that when Boyoung was telling me that everyone dressed up here in Seoul, it wasn't a commentary on Seoulites, but a gentle piece of advice that my preference for sweatpants was going to make me stick out like a red crayon in a box of neutrals. I didn't get the message and now I'm regretting my choice of joggers, an old Puma T-shirt, and sneakers. The heat spreads to my ears.

I'm about to turn away when he reaches out and clasps my hand. He has long, piano-playing fingers and a firm, dry grip. The contact snakes a line of electricity from his palm to the back of my neck and other places farther south.

"Choi Yujun," he says in perfect, hardly accented English. "You're American." It's not a question.

What was left of my "I'm a local" bubble deflates, as does the surge of energy from his handshake. I pull away and wrap my fingers around my purse strap. "How did you know?"

"The accent or, rather, the lack of one." The left corner of his mouth quirks up slightly.

"You don't have much of an accent either," I point out. This driver speaks English like my coworker Jeff but for a faint hint of an accent that I can't place.

Boyoung has one and she doesn't like it, which I understand. There's always some dumbass back home ready to mock you for your *Engrish*. If I had a dollar for every time I heard *I love you long time* at a bar, my bank account would rival Bill Gates's.

"I studied in the States," he admits.

"Oh, really?" I'm about to ask where when it strikes me that the conversation we're having is an odd one for a driver and a passenger. He probably doesn't want to field personal questions about his educational history from some random American he's ferrying to a rental. I drag my attention away from his perfect face and his delicious body to the task at hand. "So Kim Boyoung arranged for you to take me to my rental. Do you have the address?"

He shakes his head. "I do not, but if you provide it, I will be glad to assist."

This surprises me, because Boyoung's the type of person who calls ahead to see if the pizza place is serving fresh and not canned pineapple, but maybe this is the way it's done here in Korea. I don't want to look stupid so I pull up the address on my notes app.

The man angles his head toward mine and I get a whiff of something warm and citrusy. If I sniff his neck, will he call a customs agent to deport me back to America? I better not risk it.

"Do you know how to get there?"

"I'm familiar with the general area," he concedes.

"Great. Great." I'm so very awkward. "Um, this is all I have." I point to the large red case at my side along with my wheeled carry-on.

The handle of the big case is in his grasp and he's moving before I process what's happening. "Wait." I trot to catch up with him. Does he not realize his legs are twice as long as mine? "I can push my own luggage."

"Yes, I'm sure you can," he replies but doesn't return the case. "My car is this way."

Unless I want to wrestle him, I don't think he's going to let me handle my own luggage.

"I lived in America for a few years when I was young," he says when I catch up. "California, to be precise. What part are you from?"

"The Midwest. Iowa." I'm not surprised at his blank face. My state's not called a flyover state for nothing. "Near Chicago."

That he knows. "I visited once. The water is lovely." This time the smile is deeper and I make a devastating discovery. He has dimples. I can tell by the way the shadow hits that should he really smile, the divot would be caverns deep.

"Yes, lovely," I echo. *Oh no.* There's a song that Boyoung shared with me about dimples, and one of the lyrics was about whether the crease was an angel's kiss. This is a sign that God plays favorites. No man has the right to be beautiful and have a dimpled smile.

"Your family is okay with you staying at a rental?" he asks, gesturing his elegant hand in the direction of my phone.

"I, ah, don't have family here. At least, not that I know of. I'm adopted," I blurt out. Then I bite my tongue in regret. Why did I tell him that? What a dumb thing—

"That's interesting," he muses. "My mother—"

"Sir. *Sir!*"

Mr. Dimple stops walking and we both swing around to see a man, also wearing a dark blue suit, running toward us. He says something in Korean and the man beside me replies, sliding me a swift glance. These two know each other.

"Ah, just a minute." He strides over to meet the new arrival. The second man, shorter and stockier, shoves his sleeve back and taps his watch. Mr. Dimple replies with a shake of his head and turns back toward me. The second man follows, still speaking.

A tickle of apprehension itches at the back of my neck. What car service has two drivers? Is this a scam where they pick up unsuspecting travelers and then steal their luggage? That would explain why he doesn't know Boyoung and why my destination was a mystery. It also explains why he's so attractive. He's a lure. Who wouldn't choose to ride in a car with him, even knowing you were going to be kidnapped and fleeced of all your belongings? He's *that* attractive.

What a disappointment. I guess that's how it works in life. You don't get to be super-good-looking and have a decent personality. It's not fair to the rest of the world. The existence of a dimple that deep, that cute, requires some kind of sacrifice.

"Actually, I'll get my own ride." I reach over and tug at my suitcase, but he doesn't release it.

"Please. A moment." He holds up a hand as if to stop me from moving and, surprise, it does. I'm curious, against my better judgment.

The other man speaks again and my mother's admonition repeats itself. Coming to a country where I don't speak the language is looking dumber by the minute.

"Yes, I know the car is at the entrance," the would-be body snatcher says, and this time I understand because he is speaking English. "But Hara-nim needs a ride."

"The meeting for dinner is in an hour and the traffic is not good," replies the second man, also in English, but with a very heavy accent.

"My new friend needs a ride," Mr. Dimple repeats, and this time his voice carries with it a certain firmness that signals that's the end of the discussion.

Maybe for him and the second man it is, but not for me, because while he might play a very large role in my pre-bedtime fantasy, I am not going to be a statistic. "I'm going to catch the train."

"With that?"

Both of them gaze dubiously at the large piece of luggage and my smaller carry-on. It does seem unwieldy, but I'm sure I can manage. I reach for the case again but Mr. Dimple rolls it out of the way and starts walking.

"Hey, wait. Give that back."

"I'm your driver, remember?"

"No. No, you're a complete stranger."

He stops abruptly and I nearly run into his back. "I introduced myself, didn't I? We're at least acquaintances now."

Oh, that was nicely done. He's criminally attractive and charming. *Get a grip, Hara, before someone stuffs you in the trunk and sells you for parts.* "You could be an organ seller for all I know."

"Choi Yujun is no criminal," the second man bursts out with so much indignation that I almost start to feel bad.

A dimple on the other side of Choi Yujun's face appears as his hand returns to his pocket. There's a gasp behind me and then the sound of something crashing into something else. I don't need to look to see what happened. Obviously, another traveler caught a glimpse of this man's smile and lost her mind—completely relatable because here I am contemplating getting into his car.

"I'm not," he says. "But to be honest, I'm also not a driver as you assumed. I'm an ordinary citizen who got off his flight from Hong Kong and was waiting for my car to arrive."

My brows crash together. "Then why didn't you correct my assumption?"

His dimples deepen. "Because you're adorable and you apparently needed a ride."

Adorable. He called me adorable! He's lethal. I take a step back.

"But what about the car Boyoung ordered for me?" I look back toward the terminal and look around for another blue-suited man and find not one, but several dotted all over. Many of them are holding signs. In fact... I squint. I think I see my name on someone's iPad. "Oh no." My purse slides to the ground as my stupidity finally sinks in.

"It's okay. Anyone would've made the same mistake."

It's a lie, but a nice one. With burning cheeks, I bend over to grab my purse and to hide that I'm completely humiliated. I give myself an internal slap. It's time to stop being a foreign fool and start acting like a person with manners and sense.

Straightening, I gather my composure. "I'm sorry. I'm tired and obviously mistook you for the driver my friend had arranged, but he's over there." I laid eyes on Choi Yujun and decided, irrationally, that he was my ride, and I didn't even bother to look for someone holding a sign with my name because in my lust-induced myopia, it couldn't be anyone else.

"It's a long trip from the States," he sympathizes. "I'm not a very good traveler myself, and in a foreign country it is easy to get confused. I find America very challenging. Please allow me to help you." He folds my hand between his two large ones. He's so sincere and he's so warm and there's not one hint of mockery in his voice or expression. "As a proud citizen of the Republic of Korea, it is my duty to make sure that your adventure here starts off right. Allow me to take you to your home as I promised so that I can face my mother and tell her she raised me right."

"Of course," I find myself saying, and I think it's because he's holding my hand and it's so nice that I'd probably agree to about anything at this point. Besides, I can't allow his mother to think poorly of her amazing son.

"Excellent." He flashes two dimples at me and my knees weaken. "Let's go deal with your driver." With those words, he walks us quickly to the driver holding my name on his iPad. He speaks in rapid Korean and, before I can say anything, takes out his wallet and gives the driver some bills. The driver smiles and bows to him, obviously thanking him profusely. With a quick grin at me, Choi Yujun turns back toward the exit doors. "Now, we'll make plans in the car."

It all happens so fast that I almost miss the last part. "What do you mean 'plans'?"

CHAPTER SIX

I'M A MEME NOW. SPECIFICALLY THAT *RECORD SCRATCH* *freeze frame* one where I look at the camera and say you're probably wondering how I got myself in this situation. The situation being me in the back of an expensive black car with a delectable stranger in a foreign city. The problem is I can't precisely recreate my decision-making process. It's a blur. One minute I was trying to catch up to long-legged Yujun, and the next moment, my luggage was disappearing inside the trunk of a black sedan so glossy I could see my reflection in its finish. I recall hesitating, but both men waiting beside the open car door and a stream of curious onlookers drove me into the back seat. Yujun flashed his dimples, and we were off.

It takes more than an hour to drive from the airport, which is situated on an island connected to mainland Seoul by two long bridges. I don't even get a moment to text Boyoung because Choi Yujun, who insists I call him Yujun, has all sorts of questions: What do I do in Iowa? Copy editor for a home-and-garden magazine and web portal. Is this my first trip to Korea? Yes. Do I have any definitive plans? Yes, but none that I'm sharing. Those I keep to myself. I've already panic blurted out too many details.

In between the questions, he reveals that he was on his way to a dinner, but it was with his mother and she will understand why he's late. Based on the irritated looks the driver keeps sending my way in the rearview mirror, I have some doubts.

Yujun either ignores his driver, Park Minho, as he stiffly introduced himself, or doesn't notice the other man's irritation. Yujun is busy pointing out landmarks—the tall needle-pointed building to the south is Lotte Tower, the tallest building in South Korea. To the north is Namsan, one of the five mountains—or guardians, he calls them. He tells me both are can't-miss tourist destinations and I file that information away. I do want to see things while I'm here—museums, historical sites, the markets. Maybe I'll do some of that with my dad. *Lee Jonghyung.* I wonder where he lives. South by the Lotte Tower or north by the mountains? Does he live in one of the thousands of mid-rise concrete-block apartment buildings or in one of the houses with the clay-tiled roofs? Will he cry when he sees me? Will *I* cry?

The freeway gives way to city streets, which narrow into a residential neighborhood with roads that aren't made for two cars. I find myself holding my breath as Park maneuvers between oncoming cars, pedestrians on the street, and outdoor displays in front of a succession of small stores. Finally, the long vehicle stops at the base of a set of very, very, *very* steep stairs.

My mouth drops open in dismay. Had I known that it was a literal mountain climb to reach the rental, I'd have packed lighter. I'd have put everything in one backpack, but instead, I stuffed in about a month's worth of clothing changes because I couldn't decide what to wear to meet my father. Were jeans okay? Maybe I should wear a dress? Or perhaps even a suit?

I packed it all and now I regret everything.

The Airbnb instructions were deceptive. *At the #3786 bus stop, go straight until the first light and then take a right*, the email had said. *Continue for three blocks until you reach Ahjussi's Chicken. From there, it is a short walk up a hill to a house with the number.*

Short walk my ass.

"What number did you say your house was?"

I look at my phone. "Fifteen, I think."

"Hmm." He peers over my shoulder and his warm lemony scent drifts into my lungs. I try not to sniff like a dog but it's hard.

"That's about halfway up. Not so bad. Let's go." He climbs out. Park Minho has the bags waiting, and before I can grab one, Yujun has his hands wrapped firmly around the handles.

"I'm not getting that away from you, am I?" I sigh, even more regretful that I packed so unwisely because when I was stuffing the hundredth item into the suitcase, I was thinking of how easy it would be to roll into my apartment, but now that someone else is shouldering the burden, guilt creeps up my neck.

"No." He smiles, and a shallow right dimple and a shadow of a dot on the left appear, but they have the same deadly effect.

I wrinkle my nose and force myself to turn away. Briefly, I entertain the image of me wrestling the bags out of his clasp and carrying the unwieldy things up the mountain like a trophy over my head. In reality, I'd fall down and cut myself on the asphalt, and then he'd take me to the hospital, all the while politely declaring it was his fault. To save myself that humiliation I avoid the wrestling match. "Can I at least carry the small bag?"

"No." He starts walking.

Beside me the driver, Park Minho, makes a disgusted sound. I don't know if he's madder at Yujun or me. Probably me.

"It's not my fault," I say quietly, but I'm not sure Park understands me.

"Coming?" Yujun calls back.

"Yep, saying goodbye to your friend."

That generates a grunt. I give the driver a little wave and scurry up the stairs after Yujun.

"I'm going to owe you some giant steak dinner," I say as we make it to the second level of stairs. I'm out of breath and he hasn't broken a sweat. He doesn't look very muscular under the suit—he has sort of a swimmer's build, lean and trim—but apparently there's more to him than meets the eye. Unlike the information about the landmarks, this isn't data that I need in my memory bank. He probably has abs and defined arm muscles. I could climb him like a tree and he'd not sway even an iota. Does he have calluses on his hands from lifting weights? I rub my lips together and try to remember. His grip had been firm and warm and—

"I accept."

"What?" My mind was distracted by the endless possibilities of what his body actually looked like without clothes and I'd missed what he said.

"I accept your offer of a giant steak dinner."

"Oh, okay."

This is definitely one of those polite things people say so as not to make their companion uncomfortable, but my silly mind immediately starts creating the fantasy date, which is a good thing because it takes my mind off the long climb and I don't even realize how my thighs are burning until we stop in front of a gate. Under the dim light attached to a post, his brow glistens. Of course it makes him more attractive. I need to get away from him or I'll spend my two weeks in Seoul chasing this boy around instead of reconnecting with my father.

"Hand me your phone," Yujun orders.

"Why?" But I do as he asks because my mind doesn't seem to have any control right now.

He takes a photo of his own phone screen and hands mine back. "There. Now you have my number. You can save it as Yujun from Seoul."

"You're the only Yujun I know."

"You are the only Hara I know."

We stare at each other for far too long under that amber light. It's okay to be charmed, I tell myself. It's okay that your heart is beating a bit faster than normal. That your feet feel light and that there're butterflies in your stomach. You're not falling for a dimple, a show of strength, and a few compliments. It's the entirety of the circumstances. You're here in Seoul, your birthplace. You're about to meet your birth father. This—him—it means nothing.

"Call me when you're settled so that we can have the steak you owe me."

He squeezes my hand and then starts the descent. His hands are in his pockets. His dress shoes make small tapping noises against the asphalt. I hear a faint tuneless whistling. Nothing. It means nothing.

Resolutely, I turn to the gate and press the buzzer. "It's Hara Wilson," I say into the intercom. "I'm here about the rented room."

CHAPTER SEVEN

"WOW," SAYS THE PETITE BLONDE WHO COMES DOWN TO OPEN the gate. "Is that your boyfriend? And, not to be rude, but why are you staying with us? He should be putting you up. I'm Anna, by the way. Did I already introduce myself? Let me take that. Wait, are you Korean? *Annyeonghaseyo, jeoneun Anna-ibnida.*"

I catch the "hello" and "Anna" bits, but I'm not sure of the rest of it. "I don't speak Korean and I'll handle these cases. The big one weighs as much as you. I packed way too much."

"I'll get the small one, then." Anna darts behind me before I can protest. "I'm the one that is subleasing this place, although we're not supposed to but since we have an empty bed, why not? You aren't going to throw any wild parties with your *chaebol* boyfriend, are you?"

"Who has a *chaebol* boyfriend?" asks a new voice from inside.

"Our new girl." Anna jerks a thumb toward me as I lug my suitcase up over the threshold. A half dozen shoes—mostly sneakers with their backs folded down—are scattered along the small entrance.

"A *chaebol*?" The taller girl leans her frame up against the wall and watches as I slip my shoes off. "Which one? I'm Jules, by the way."

"Don't know. Which one?" Anna asks as she turns to me.

Since I have no idea what Anna is talking about—*chaebol* is not on the list of things Boyoung has taught me—I shrug. "He gave me a ride here as a favor." It's a little shading of the truth, but to admit I climbed into a car with a total stranger in a foreign country would create an image I'm not enthusiastic about. The farther Yujun is from me, the more foolish my actions appear. "I don't even know what a *chaebol* is."

"Oh, you speak English."

"She does," Anna says. "American, right? She's American," Anna confirms without me saying a word. I guess I look it. Or smell it. Surreptitiously, I sniff my shoulder.

"Did you two meet when he was overseas for college? All the rich kids go to America for college, where they smoke weed and have orgies."

"Sometimes England, too," interjects Jules.

"Yes. Oxford, Cambridge, Imperial College London. Anything that sounds Western is impressive."

I feel like I'm getting a crash course in some sort of cultural context, but it's zipping over my head.

"Technically, a *chaebol* is a company, not a person, but it's shorthand for anyone who doesn't have to suffer the ills of *helljoseon*," says Jules. I nod even though I don't know what *helljoseon* is, though I can guess after climbing the hill.

"You're scaring her," Anna chides. "Seoul is like any big city. There are good parts and bad parts. You see fewer of the bad parts if you're rich."

"The good parts have elevators instead of stairs." Jules points upward.

Chaebol or no, Yujun did me a huge favor lugging my suitcase up the hill. I lift the fifty-pound behemoth past the shoes and over the small threshold onto the main floor. Hopefully, I only have to go up one flight of stairs. I may not make it if there's more than that.

"Don't mind Jules. She had one bad experience with a guy and now she hates all of them." Anna sets the smaller case on the wooden floor and swipes her blond hair away from her eyes.

"I do not." Jules lifts the carry-on and sets it at the base of the stairs. "But the first thing you should know about Korean guys is that while they remember shit like the first date and celebrate little things like your hundred-day anniversary and bring you pretty gifts, they're as terrible as American men. It's a universal truth. Jane Austen wrote about it."

"I thought she said the universal truth was that a single man with money wanted a wife," I reply.

"Exactly. They want a wife, not love. Besides, it doesn't matter because the good ones aren't going to marry a foreigner anyway, although it might be different for you because you're Korean." Jules's eyes narrow as she inspects me.

"It was a ride," I protest.

"Stop grilling her." Anna shakes her head. "She just got here."

"I'm trying to prepare her."

"Do it later." Anna starts up the stairs with the small case, waving her hand for me to follow. "Come on. I'll show you to your room. It's up on the third floor, so you might want to unpack down here and carry your stuff up in smaller batches."

Filled with the foolish confidence of someone who is eager to escape an uncomfortable situation, I tighten my hand on my suitcase. "Nah, I'm good." By the second floor, my arm feels like a noodle and

I'm beginning to regret so many things, such as why I didn't listen to Anna, who lives here and has trekked up these stairs multiple times. I should learn to be less hardheaded.

"You okay?" Anna asks halfway up the second flight of stairs.

"Yeah. I've got it. I know I may sound like I'm a dying cow, but I can make it." I lift the suitcase two inches off the ground.

Anna suppresses a small smile but bounds up ahead. "Sorry about Jules. She doesn't hate all men and definitely not all Korean men. She dated a teacher for a while but it didn't go anywhere. Her feelings are bruised."

"I understand." My dating history hasn't been wonderful either. It's not that I've sworn off men entirely but that there doesn't seem to be a need for one, which is why my instant reaction to Yujun is odd. Maybe it's because I've been without for so long that I wanted to jump him at the first flash of his dimples. Or maybe it's because I've never been in such close proximity to male perfection. Or maybe it's because I'm apprehensive in this new country, and his was the first kind face I've seen. I guess it doesn't matter because nothing will come of it. Years from now, it's a story I'll tell on drunken nights back in Iowa with Kelly and Jeff.

"Here's your room." Anna pushes the door open to reveal a small bedroom with a twin bed, a dresser, a chair, and a nightstand. The pictures made the room look bigger, but it has everything I need. "Our one bathroom is the door at the top of the first flight of stairs. Do you have shower shoes?"

"I do." The instruction sheet, which I'm guessing Anna wrote up, said to bring my own towels and a pair of rubber shower shoes that I needed to wear inside the bathroom at all times.

"Great. Don't forget to wear them." She scrunches her nose. "Jules is a stickler for it. The Wi-Fi password is 'Seou!tast1c,' but put an exclamation for the *l* and a one for the *i*."

I drop my suitcase and pull out my phone. While I tap the password into the device, Anna lingers at the doorway. "Hey, I know we just met, but we are going to be roomies for two weeks, so my advice might be totally unnecessary, but some of those rich Korean boys think foreign women are kind of . . . easy. I hope you don't think I'm overstepping my bounds."

Heat flares in my cheeks. "No. I hear you."

"Good." She pats me on the shoulder. "We're having barbecue tonight. If you want in, it's ten thousand won. We'll be on the back deck. Come and find us when you're ready."

Anna clambers down the stairs, leaving me to eye the bed with longing. I could take a quick nap, something like fifteen minutes long, and catch my second wind. My stomach grumbles in protest.

"All right. We'll eat first and then sleep." I'd scheduled my flight purposely this way. A Korean beauty guru had written an online article saying that the best way to combat jet lag was to fly in at six at night, go out for Korean fried chicken, and drink soju. After the meal and the booze, she'd pass out and awaken totally refreshed.

I resist the urge to sit down because I suspect if I do, the chicken-and-beer plan will be tossed out the window. I drag the suitcase to the end of the narrow twin bed and unzip it. Tucked into the corner are my towel and the new rubber slippers that are still connected by one of those plastic loops that will cut off your circulation if you try to rip them apart. I fish around for my manicure set and use the fingernail scissors to clip the plastic tie. In my stocking feet, I head down to the bathroom. The entry has a high ledge and inside the door on a rubber mat are three pairs of rubber slides. Anna wasn't kidding. Everyone has their own shower shoes. I drop mine onto the mat and then step over the threshold. Awkwardly, I toe the shower shoes on and nearly fall on my face. This is going to take practice.

The shared bathroom is a little messy. There's a towel on the floor

near the door and a pair of washcloths draped over the side of the
sink. If I was less tired or if I'd paid more for my room, I might've
cared more about the condition, but the water is clear and hot and
after a few splashes across my face, I feel more like a human and less
like a crumpled piece of paper.

As I'm leaving, I nearly forget to remove the slides. Practice, I remind myself. I'll get it in time. Back in the bedroom, I trade my
sweatpants for a pair of jeans and a pale pink knit shirt that I bought
at H&M. It's a little chilly out so I find my favorite oversize cardigan
sweater and shrug it on. Finally, I pull out my phone again. Flopping
backward onto the mattress, I text Mom.

> **ME:** I'm at the rental. It's nice. Looks like the pictures.

Because I know she's going to want a proof of life, I take a selfie
and then a few snaps of the room. Mom's reply comes so swiftly that
I feel guilty for not sending her a message earlier.

> **MOM:** Thank goodness. How is the neighborhood? Is it safe?

> **ME:** There are a thousand steps to get to the apartment. If I
> was a criminal, I'd choose an easier victim.

> **MOM:** ?? Are you saying it looks dangerous? Should I book a
> hotel?

> **ME:** Kidding. Bad joke. Lots of stairs. No criminals spotted.

> **MOM:** Don't joke about your safety. You're thousands of miles
> away. I worry about you!

> **ME:** I know. Sorry.

If I tell the car story back home, Mom cannot ever hear of it. She'd lock me in my childhood bedroom and throw away the key.

MOM: Is everyone nice?

My mind immediately flits to Yujun.

ME: Very

MOM: I'm happy then. You must be exhausted. Get something to eat and then go to bed. Call me in the morning! I love you.

ME: I love you too

I allow myself one last minute of lying on the bed before pushing to my feet. Let me get some food inside my body and then I'll rest. I make my way to a small outdoor patio off the kitchen, where Anna, Jules, and one other girl are seated around a small table a foot off the ground. In the middle of the table rests a grill. The redolent smell of caramelized meat travels at lightning speed into my nose and down to my stomach. It rumbles loudly as introduction.

"Climb on up," Anna instructs, patting a yellow cushion beside her. "You're in time for some *samgyeopsal*."

"I have no idea what that is but it smells amazing." I cross my legs and scoot close to the table.

"It's pork belly. You'll love it. Our chef tonight is Mel. Mel, this is Hara Wilson from—"

"Iowa," I supply.

Anna snaps her fingers. "I knew it was one of those vowel states. She's renting Sara's room for the next two weeks."

Mel waves her tongs in the air. "Hey. Here for work or fun?"

"Fun," I say because I don't want to launch into a long explanation of why I'm here. "I have friends here," I add. It's not a complete tale. Boyoung is a friend. Yujun from Seoul was very friendly and so he counts, too—at least for this argument.

"Awesome." Mel reaches across the table and places a piece of meat on my plate.

"Mel and I teach at a *hagwon*, which is basically a private English tutoring school," Anna explains. Mel is a small brunette with hair down to her butt and skin so pale she sort of glows in the moonlight. "You met Jules—she works for Hallywu Air."

"It's private air travel, so if you've got an extra three million won lying around, I can hook you up with a sweet jet."

"I'll keep that in mind. Thanks."

Anna pours me a drink. "Cheers to our new roommate."

I down the clear liquid. It's tasteless at first, but there's a kick at the end. My glass is refilled almost before I set it down. Mel finishes cutting up the meat with a pair of scissors and then parcels out the food in equal portions on everyone's plate. Jules dabs a little red sauce in the middle of a lettuce leaf, adds the cooked meat, and folds it into her mouth. I do the same and nearly moan out loud as the pork almost melts in my mouth. As Anna promised, I do love it. I assemble another wrap as the small blonde goes on to explain the rest of the house rules.

"We change the Wi-Fi password once a week. The password is on the chalkboard in the kitchen. For food, everyone buys their own stuff. Write your name on whatever you don't want anyone else to touch. You can either get it delivered or go to the market. Don't cook anything smelly inside the house, so no beef or fish."

"Or fried chicken," Mel pipes up. She pours me another glass and motions for me to drink up.

"Right. Or fried chicken. Don't leave the *gimbap* in the fridge longer than a couple days or the fish will stink up the fridge. Korea is super strict about recycling, so if you find a bag of trash in the freezer, don't be alarmed. All the food waste is put in that bag. There's a dry-erase board on the door for bathroom shower use. Sign up the night before. What else?" She scans the other members.

"We clean on Sundays," Jules adds.

"Oh right." Anna snaps her fingers. "Every Sunday we clean. Since you just got here, no one expects you to do much, but starting next week, you'll need to chip in."

"No problem." I've stuffed two lettuce wraps into my mouth and I'm starting to feel sleepy. I make another one, though, and decide that food should always be wrapped in a lettuce leaf with a tiny bit of hot red paste. It's literally the perfect food.

The girls' conversation swings to where they plan to go over the next school break. Jules suggests Hong Kong because there's a near-empty flight scheduled and she'll smuggle them aboard dressed as staff.

After the fourth piece of wrapped meat and more booze refills than I can count, my vision starts to blur. I would like to go up to my bedroom and pass out, but I don't want to be targeted as a bad room-mate before the first night is out. "Are there dishes to wash? I could do those now?"

"You look like you're ready to fall asleep. Go to bed. We'll take care of things tonight." Anna makes shooing motions with her hands.

The other girls nod in agreement. I'm too tired to argue. I bid everyone good night, pick up my plate, and disappear inside. I have enough energy to wash my dishes and set them on the drying rack next to the sink. The trek up the two flights of stairs seems endless, and by the time I reach the top, my eyes are half-closed. My phone pings to let me know I have a message, but I can't bring myself to answer it. Tomorrow will be soon enough.

I'm asleep before my body hits the mattress.

CHAPTER EIGHT

I WAKE UP TO A POUNDING IN MY TEMPLES. I DON'T REMEMBER drinking *that* much soju last night, but from the way a drumline has taken up residence in my head, I must be suffering a massive hangover.

I close my eyes tight and will myself back to sleep. Sleep cures everything. I hold myself still, inhale through my nose, count backward, but all I hear is the incessant thumping. Food, then. Hangovers can be cured by food. I toss my pillow on the ground and sit up.

"Hara? Hara? Her name's Hara, right? Or Haru?"

"It's Hara," I mumble, finally realizing that the knocking is Jules's fist on my door and not from inside my head.

"Just a minute," I yell. I jump out of bed and promptly fall on my face. "Crap," I say into the floorboards. I'd forgotten I moved my suitcase from the end of the bed to the side.

"Hara?"

"Give me a minute." I climb to my feet and hop to the door, rubbing my bruised toes along the back of my calf.

When I swing the door open, I find a sober Boyoung standing on the other side along with Jules.

"Ah, finally. Someone here to see you," Jules states the obvious.

I'm not prepared for a visitor. My bones ache as if someone ran over me with a truck. My eyes itch, there's a gross film coating my teeth, and my tongue feels swollen.

"Hey, Boyoung," I say from behind my hand. I know my breath must reek.

My friend gives a worried look and then, with uncharacteristic rudeness, pushes past Jules into my small room. Boyoung sets a shopping bag on the floor that I hadn't even noticed the girl was carrying.

"I tried to text you last night and this morning." Her tone is slightly chastising.

I release an apologetic sigh. "I passed out before I could answer."

I hobble over to my purse and pull out my phone. It's dead. I forgot to plug it in last night. "Ugh. Sorry. It needs to be charged." I grab a charge cord and look for an outlet.

Boyoung comes over and shoves a battery pack into my hands. "Here. Use this. You should text your mom and then . . ."

The odd tone in Boyoung's voice draws my attention. I stop hunting for an outlet. "What is it?"

She holds out the bag. "I need to take you somewhere and I brought you this because I didn't know if you had packed something like it."

I set aside the phone and peek inside the shopping bag. There's a dress—a black one. I don't want to jump to conclusions, but the last time I wore a black dress . . . I leave the thought unfinished as the soft, silky fabric snakes through my fingers. Boyoung says nothing either and so I have to ask, even though I don't want to.

"This dress is"—the words come out raspy and harsh—"this dress looks like it's for a funeral." I raise my eyes to see the denial, but when Boyoung still can't meet my gaze, that's when I know. I've lost two dads.

I stumble, the backs of my knees hitting the bed. The black dress spills out of the bag and spreads across the floor like a dark stain between Boyoung and me.

"I'm sorry, Hara. I'm so sorry," Boyoung says, as if this is somehow her fault.

My first instinct is to say that it's no big deal or that it's okay, but I don't feel okay. My chest feels heavy, as if there's a thousand-pound weight pressing down on a very fragile organ. I swallow once and try to speak, but no sound comes out.

"I will wait downstairs," Boyoung says, likely thinking I need privacy to change, but when the door closes and I'm left alone with the black dress lying at my feet, I can't move.

Pat was big into all sports. He didn't measure time by months or seasons, but by sports. Football was in the fall. Basketball took over in the winter and ended in June. Baseball was in full swing by then. He tried to get me interested, but I was afraid of small balls and would duck whenever Pat threw one at me. My legs weren't very long, so track was out. In a desperate attempt to prove to my father that we had similar interests, I professed a deep interest in hunting. In truth, I was as scared of guns as I was of balls, and the idea of killing anything as cute as Bambi made me want to barf, but my love for my father and my need for his approval outweighed all of that.

I went through a six-week training class to learn about gun safety. After getting my certificate, I went to the range and fired the shotgun three weekends in a row despite the kickback causing so much bruising on my right shoulder that I had to carry my backpack to school with my hand. Despite all of that, I looked forward to winter for once. We were going on a big weekend trip together. When the first snow fell, Pat got me up at four in the morning and we drove to a field. Dressed in an orange hunter's jacket that was two sizes too big for me, I walked along the tree line behind my dad, clutching the shotgun in my hands. It was so quiet that I could hear the freshly frozen blades of grass crunch beneath my boots.

Pat found a valley and put me at the top of it. "Don't shoot anything without a rack because I'm not hauling a doe out of the valley."

I nodded and tried to ignore the sick feeling in the pit of my stomach. Pat chucked me on the chin and said, "Good girl. I'll see you at lunch."

He wasn't joking. I didn't hear or see him for the next six hours. At some point, I'd dozed off despite the cold seeping through my several layers of clothes. A loud, booming, echoing sound woke me up. Something brown and fast bolted, tearing through the clearing and up the hill. I clutched the shotgun to my chest, the smell of gun oil and powder tickling my nose. Another shot rang out, followed by a thud.

I didn't even see the deer. I only heard the fall of the body onto the forest floor. By the time Pat arrived, the carcass had been hauled away, leaving behind streaks of rust and brown in the snow. I started crying and couldn't stop. I'd made such a racket that the hunter who had killed the deer complained that I was scaring the animals away. I was eleven. Pat had been furious—both at losing the deer and at having to cut the hunting trip short. Crying over a dead deer was dumb, he'd fumed. Killing a deer was the whole point of hunting. That night I dreamed Pat was chasing me through the woods, telling me to stop crying. It was the last time I'd gone on a trip with him. The last time I'd cried, too.

I rub my fingers under my eyes. They come away dry. Why should I cry over a man I don't know? It would be more unusual if I did cry. I know nothing of Lee Jonghyung other than his name. I don't know what he looks like and I have doubts I would be able to pick him out of a lineup. My eyes catch my reflection in the mirror over the dresser. Would he have my eyes or my chin? Or rather, would I have his eyes or his chin? The tiny drum starts thudding again, but this time it's at the back of my skull. My throat feels scratchy and my face feels heavy—as if the day's news is physically dragging the corners of my mouth to the floor.

I dig the knuckles of my thumbs into my eyes and command myself to move. There's no point in wallowing in self-pity. No amount of feeling sorry for myself will change my circumstances.

I pick up my towel and toiletry kit and make my way down to the bathroom. Thankfully, there's no one signed up for a shower time slot right now. I strip and brush my teeth. A hollow-eyed shell stares back at me.

"There's no reason to be upset about this," I order my reflection. "You never knew the man. He abandoned you, for crying out loud. Your mother had to give you up because this penis wouldn't step up to the plate and parent you." I slap myself lightly. "You're tired. You're emotional because you're tired and attending more than one funeral a year at the age of twenty-five is an affront against youth."

After a fast, hot shower I feel marginally better. I know Boyoung is waiting so I hurry back to my room and drop the dress over my head. It falls perfectly around my shoulders and settles at my waist as if it was made for me. The neck is a simple crew but there are pleats down the front and small polished black buttons for details. The skirt is a perfectly cut A-line that swishes around my legs as I walk. I briefly wonder where Boyoung got this dress. It's too big for the smaller Korean and it seems too early for stores to be open. The garment also feels expensive—more than I would've spent on a dress I'd wear once.

What does it matter, though?

I close my eyes and inhale and exhale until my breath steadies. I guess now I'll find out what a Korean funeral is like. It's ironic in that sort of horrible what-if-you-met-your-soul-mate-only-to-discover-he-was-in-love-with-someone-else way.

CHAPTER NINE

"HERE. I GOT THIS FOR YOU." BOYOUNG HANDS ME A SMALL plastic card as we clamber down the steep hill. "It's a T-money card. You can use it on the bus and subway. You can even buy some stuff with it at convenience stores."

"Okay." I tuck it into the black purse that I found in the bottom of the shopping bag. Boyoung had thought of it all—black dress, black purse, black hose, black flats.

"Was the ride okay? From the airport," Boyoung clarifies when I don't answer right away.

"Yeah." I don't explain the airport mix-up because all of that feels as if it happened in another life, maybe to another person—one who didn't have two fathers die within the space of weeks. "How did you find out about this?"

"When I returned to Seoul, I went to your father's address. He wasn't home but I gave my phone number to his landlady. She called me when he died."

"I see." I don't really, though. I suppose Boyoung went to check out if my dad was a grifter, and that sends a minor ping of irritation down my spine. She should've told me or asked me if that was okay, but at this point, complaining would be silly. If she hadn't gone to visit, I wouldn't have known he'd died.

She grabs my hand and pulls me down into the subway station. After a twenty-minute ride, we transfer onto a crowded bus. No one speaks. I want to ask where we're going, but the bus is eerily quiet. No one is talking. Thinking back, I realize the subway car was similarly silent except for the sound of the train moving on the tracks. Everyone's head is buried in their phones except for Boyoung's. She's looking worried and distracted.

I'd say the scenery was interesting, but unlike yesterday, when I couldn't tear my eyes away from the window because I was drinking in the sights, today I don't see anything but a blur of one building after another. Nothing is registering. I see things, but they're only shapes, not things. My brain has stopped working.

The bus is half-empty when Boyoung reaches up and presses a button to signal the driver to stop. There's something comforting about the universality of buses and subways. Swipe the card upon boarding. Press a button to get off. At least I'll be able to navigate my way around the city.

We walk down a paved street with tall buildings on either side. The sidewalks are narrow with barely room for two people to walk next to each other. Several times, I have to step off the sidewalk to make way for oncoming traffic. People do not move for us. Boyoung mutters something under her breath and I assume she's irritated. I don't really care. It's not as if I'm in a hurry to reach my destination. No matter how slow I walk, though, I end up at a gated entrance. Beyond the iron fence is a plain midsize glass-and-concrete structure and behind that looms a much larger building that sports a green plus symbol next to a few *Hangul* characters in black. The symbol tickles my memory bank but I can't quite make the connection. My efforts to decipher the meaning are interrupted when a camera crew nearly knocks the two of us over. There's a flurry of bowing and apologies before the crew rushes off into a van idling down the street that I hadn't noticed before.

"What's that about?" I ask.

"I don't know. Perhaps there must be a celebrity who is having a funeral. This is a funeral hall"—Boyoung gestures with her hand toward the shorter building—"and behind it is the hospital. Many people hold their funerals here, in separate rooms. There isn't one room, not like in America."

Boyoung buys two white flowers from a vendor situated just to the left of the entrance. She hands one flower to me along with a thin rectangular white envelope. It's exactly the same as the one she'd given me at my father's funeral—my other father's funeral. It's a money envelope.

I fish out cash and tuck several Korean won inside. When I'm done, Boyoung leads me inside. The hallway is thick with black-clad people. Boyoung wasn't kidding when she said many people were having funerals here. Some have armbands around their suit sleeves. Others are carrying flowers similar to the ones Boyoung bought outside. A profusion of wreaths with long silk banners dangling to the ground lines the hallways.

"Oh, it's them," Boyoung says, stopping before one of the rooms. The camera crew that almost ran into us is setting up.

"Who?" I ask.

Boyoung drags me away before she explains quietly, "There was an article trending today. There was a couple from the same clan who fell in love. It's not against the law, but their families must've been very traditional. Most Koreans won't marry someone within their same clan. It's . . . inappropriate. These two jumped off the Mapo Bridge into the Han River together. They were twenty-two."

I can't hold in my gasp. "They were so young."

"*Ne.*" Boyoung grabs my hand. She doesn't realize she's spoken in Korean, but it's that kind of moment.

Boyoung once told me that *ne* in Korean doesn't merely mean "yes," but that it is a word of acknowledgment with its meaning changing with how one emphasizes it, what kind of emotion one puts behind it. And, today, I understand. *Yes*, the couple was young. *Yes*, it was tragic. *Yes*, this is terrible. *Yes*, I know you are full of grief and hearing about this is very hard. *Yes*, I'm here with you.

It's a good word. *Ne.*

I clutch her hand tightly as we walk down the long hallway, the scent of flowers making my stomach clench. The pretty decorations seem more macabre than comforting. At the end of the hall, the decorations grow sparser; the mourners are fewer. It begins to feel more like a hospital and less like a graduation ceremony.

A woman dressed in a knee-length black sheath, wearing a wide-brimmed black hat, sweeps by. Boyoung stops so abruptly I almost trip over her. My friend's eyes linger on the elegant figure for a long, strange moment. There doesn't appear to be anything remarkable about the departing woman other than she seems like she should be visiting the rooms at the front of the hallway, not down here in the antiseptic, spare part. Her clothes fit her well. I admire the hat. It's a nice accessory.

"Do you know her?" I ask.

Boyoung doesn't respond, but my voice appears to jolt the shorter girl from her trance. She gives herself a brief shake and then dips her head toward a small room at the end of the hall. "Your father is over here."

"Over here" is a tiny rectangle of a room, with a plain table at one end. On the table is a picture of a man with a ribbon wrapped around the top corners. In front of the picture is one small bowl of fruit, a wreath of white flowers, and a pot containing three incense sticks. The smoke curls off the ends, dancing in the still air. It's the only movement in the room, as the two women kneeling to the side with their heads bent don't stir.

Boyoung motions for me to slip off my shoes and then urges me inside. I balk. My feet want to turn and flee, run after the lady in black and use the big black hat as a shield all the way to the airport.

This was a mistake—coming to the funeral, coming to Korea, believing I was going to find something from a stranger. There are no answers here, and the sense of belonging that infused me when I was at the airport has curdled into a rock in the pit of my stomach. I should go back home where I understand what everyone is saying and the losses in my life are still at one. I'm twenty-five. I should be mourning a romantic breakup, not the death of my second father—or my first one. I don't know anymore.

I'm pivoting away from the door when one of the kneeling women rises, her black traditional Korean dress belling out like the bloom of a dark flower. The older woman shuffles toward us, confusion writ large across her face. I don't need to know the language to guess that she wonders who the hell we are. Boyoung begins to speak, and with each Korean word that comes out of her mouth, my window of opportunity closes.

Boyoung softly translates. "You can bow if you'd like and then greet the family."

"Family?" Why hadn't I made that connection? This was my birth father. Of course the mourners would be my relatives. The rock in my stomach feels lighter, and something like excitement begins to bubble. I lean close to the older woman and inspect her face, looking for signs of familiarity. My mom, Ellen, looks a lot like her mother. They shared the same eyes, nose, and mouth. I don't see any of myself in this round-cheeked woman with the downturned eyes. The skin around her cheeks has fallen. There are long, deep lines, and her eyes look tired. My eyes shift toward the younger woman, who is watching us curiously. Is this—my breath catches in my throat—my mother?

"Ah, no, I'm sorry. Not family. They are . . . the older lady is Yung Hyejin. She is—I mean, was your father's landlady."

My heart drops.

"And the other?"

"Your father's . . . friend. Kwang Miok." There's a note of disapproval in Boyoung's voice although I'm not sure if it's because the friend came to the funeral or because my father had a girlfriend at his age. Then it strikes me that I don't even know how old he was. I guess around forty-five based on his email where he said he was twenty when he learned of my bio mom's pregnancy.

"You can light a stick of incense and lay your flower down next to the fruit on the table." She clucks her tongue. "There should be plates, but there are not. Bow twice to the family," Boyoung instructs. I do as she tells me, walking toward the small table that serves as the altar. I sink down in front of it and my fingers shake a little as I strike the match and light the incense stick. The smoke rises, snaking its way up toward the ceiling to join the other plumes like a tiny death cloud. Someone's tears should fall from that, but everyone here is dry-eyed. Maybe crying isn't appropriate at Korean funerals.

My gaze falls upon Lee Jonghyung's portrait. The photo isn't large—slightly bigger than the size of one of my school portraits Mom has hanging on the hallway wall. She bought the eight-by-ten-inch version each year and had them framed. The hallway served as a storyboard of sorts showing my progress through the years. At age five, I had three missing teeth and wore my hair in two pigtails. I wore dresses picked out by my mom. As I grew older, I smiled less, my hair was straighter, and my clothes were more casual. From ages eight through ten, I had a sports uniform. That was before Pat gave up on me. In my teen years, smiling during photos was for losers and straights. I wore too much blush and my eyeliner skills were tragic. The senior photos were taken at a park, because unlike other kids, I had hobbies that didn't photograph well. There were only so many poses one could do with books.

Lee Jonghyung isn't smiling in his photo either. By itself, the photo doesn't tell much of a story. The background is plain. He's wearing a collared shirt with the top button undone. It's not quite DMV quality but it's not much better. There's a grainy texture to the portrait, as if someone took a smaller picture and enlarged it. Maybe that's why I don't recognize him. He has a thin face and even thinner lips. I touch my own fat lower lip. *I wonder where you got that. Not from your father.* His eyebrows need grooming. They're dark and unruly. It gives him a slightly sinister expression.

His hair is dark, his eyes brown. That's as much as I see of myself in him. Is our DNA match really 98.2 percent? Shouldn't I see something of myself in this picture? Shouldn't it be like an actual damn mirror? I want to pick it up and run to the bathroom so I can do a side-by-side comparison. I want to turn to the people in the room and ask them to point out the similarities.

I stare at the image for a long time, cataloging a mole on the right side of his neck and a scar near the left earlobe. I press my hands against my cheekbones, pulling the skin tight, and then drag a hand down my chin, trying to feel a connection, but there's nothing. No flare of recognition. No immediate sense of belonging. I rub my eyes and look again. Still nothing.

Disappointment leaves a lump in my throat. I get to my feet, bow twice, and then straighten. I don't know what to do now. I thread my fingers together and bow again. I might've kept bowing had Boyoung not come over to take my hand and escort me from the room. She leads me into a large common area where small wooden tables about knee-high are surrounded by black-clad mourners. Boyoung finds an empty table in the corner and folds herself onto a mat. Silently, I follow suit.

A server comes by and leaves a small collection of dishes—soup, some sides, rice. Boyoung makes a request and the *hanbok*-wearing waitress returns with a green bottle. "Soju," Boyoung explains. "It's how you get through one of these." She twists off the cap and pours the clear liquid into a small glass in front of me.

"I'm sorry," I say. Of all the things I imagined experiencing here in Korea, attending the funeral of my father wasn't one of them.

Boyoung tips her head. "For what?"

"This can't be any fun for you."

"Fun? No. Not fun, but not fun for you, either."

"No. Definitely not."

"Drink. It will make you feel better." Boyoung pours herself a glass.

"What is this place?" I ask.

"Our funerals are all held in these places except if you're very, very wealthy, and then you don't go to this *jang-rae-shik-jang*, but somewhere private. For everyone else"—she shrugs—"this is it. Your father's landlady and his friend have already cared for the body. Tomorrow, they have prepared for your father to go to the crematorium, unless you want to make other arrangements."

"No. That's fine." With the glass halfway to my mouth, I pause. "Who is paying for all of this?" I don't know how much funerals cost, but it doesn't seem right that a landlady and my father's current girlfriend pay. On the other hand, is it right for me to do so? Pay for the funeral of the man who abandoned me? Mom wouldn't approve of that.

"It's been taken care of. Don't worry." Boyoung holds up the soju bottle. "Drink and I'll refill your glass."

And that's how it goes for the next hour. Boyoung gives me a lesson in funeral etiquette in between shots of soju. After a bit, my butt and head both feel numb. Perhaps copious amounts of soju are the only way to get through these things.

"Did he look like me?" I blurt out after the two of us empty three bottles.

"Your father?"

I nod vigorously, almost too hard. I have to catch myself on the edge of the table so I don't tip over. "I didn't see it. Are you sure we're at the right place? That you have the right guy? Didn't you say that there are only a few last names in Korea? That it's common for people to have the same name?"

"It's not uncommon, but"—Boyoung bites her lip—"this is the right man."

"No. We don't know that for a fact. He doesn't look like me at all," I insist. I'm warming to the idea that this is all a mistake. In a city this big, with this many people, Boyoung could've gotten this man mixed up with my father. Relief pours through me, warming me in a way that none of the soju has been able to. "Yes. It's not him."

Boyoung gives me a pitying look. "He is the man from the email, Hara. I verified it. I would not lie to you about this."

"Oh." I deflate like a popped balloon.

"You do look like him. You have his eyes. They're shaped like dragon eyes, long and dark, sloped like a fishhook. Very pretty. You have very pretty eyes. Mine are too small." Boyoung covers one of her own pretty and, in my opinion, large eyes shyly. "Plus, because your eyes are long, you have a nice eye smile."

"An-n eye smile?" I don't know what that is. When I was little, kids would make fun of my eyes, calling them "rice eyes" because they were the shape of a grain of rice, or sometimes "almond eyes." I'd once held both a grain of rice and an almond to my eye. Neither had the same shape.

Boyoung closes both her eyes and smiles. Her black lashes form two small curves on her face. "Eye smile," she repeats and then her lids pop up. She gives me a moment for this to sink in, as if she can sense that I'm having an epiphany.

Holy shit. An eye smile. There's a name for it and it's considered attractive. I feel like my worldview is shifting on its axis. I test out the eye smile. Behind my closed lids, in the darkness, I envision myself and it feels . . . nice.

"Should we go?" Boyoung asks.

My eyes fly open. How long has Boyoung been sitting there while I squeezed my eyes shut? I nod. "Yes, let's go," I say, before I start making random faces and asking if there are names for those, too.

Boyoung starts to lead me away, but as we pass by the funeral room, I spot the old lady and my dad's friend still kneeling in the room—alone.

"How long will they stay there?"

"Until tomorrow."

"Tomorrow?" I'm shocked. "Are there places to sleep here?" I look around but see only floral wreaths, black-clad visitors, and darkened doorways.

"They will take turns, but, yes, we observe a funeral for three days. On the third day, the body is prepared for, um, its final rest."

Cremation, Boyoung had said earlier.

I glance down the hall toward the exit and then back at the two small figures, the bare altar, and the incense that's almost burned away. Maybe it's the soju. Maybe it's something else, but I don't want to leave now. "I'm going to stay."

"But you don't speak Korean," Boyoung protests.

"I know." I don't care. There's something wrong about walking out on my blood when two strangers are sitting there observing the rituals. "I'm staying anyway."

I leave Boyoung in the hallway and return to the room. The two women look up in surprise but say nothing as I step inside and take up a position next to the younger woman. She smells of rice wine and incense—and I think I'll always associate this with sorrow. I lower my chin to my chest and send a few prayers into the universe. I didn't know this man. He abandoned me, but he died alone. The least I can do is stay here.

STAYING LITERALLY MEANS sleeping sitting up in the room, I discover later. As I take my turn in the bathroom, I wonder if I made my decision too hastily. It's not like anyone is around to judge me and my fitness as a daughter. I'm earning no brownie points unless I'm making a deposit in the karma bank. But if I'm dead, will I care if there are people who come and kneel in the room where my body lies?

I peer into the mirror again and try to see if I like the eye smile. Not really, I decide. It makes my face look too round. It looks better on Boyoung. I slap myself lightly, splash water across my face, and then, after a moment's hesitation, I cup my hands under the stream of water and drink. I don't know what the tap-water situation is in Seoul, but I figure I'm not going to die from ingesting a tiny bit from the sink. It's better than dry mouth. That done, I run my dampened hands over the skirt of my dress. There isn't any dirt on it. The one advantage of taking off one's shoes before entering any building is that the floors are pretty clean. It's wrinkled, though. Silk isn't made for hours of kneeling.

The ladies with the big voluminous skirts of the *hanboks* have the right idea. You could hide a lot under that fabric—a basket of fruit, a Thanksgiving turkey, a few Oompa Loompas from Willie Wonka's chocolate factory. A giggle bubbles in my throat. I choke it down. It's one of those hysterical laughs that want to burst out at the most inappropriate times. Like now. At a funeral—I search for the right word—hotel with a bunch of strangers who speak an entirely different language and have different customs. *Now is not the time to lose control, Hara*, I order.

I grab the edge of the stone countertop and remind myself to breathe—that it's one inhale and one exhale—and I concentrate on those, counting each one individually until the sudden hysteria passes. Once I've regained my composure, I return to the room and settle into place beside the landlady, who reaches out and pats my hand. I try to return the gesture but end with our fingers entangled, and that's how I spend the rest of the night, with my hand clasped around that of a strange woman. The only thing we share is the man that we're mourning.

At some point the next morning, two men dressed in black suits with white armbands around their biceps arrive to remove the body. The ladies rise from their kneeling position, pulling me with them. I hobble out into the hall, feeling about as nimble as the landlady. My knees ache and my back feels like it might crack in two if I move wrong. The silk of the dress is crushed. I hope that this wasn't some favorite outfit that Boyoung sacrificed for this event because I don't think a cleaning will fix it. Some of the creases seem permanent.

The two women either have experience in doing this or are far more limber than me. Maybe it's both. The sunlight feels odd on my face, and as I shield my eyes with my hand, I think of the black-hatted lady. She was onto something. The older woman at my side says something that, of course, I don't understand, but my companions know this by now. They figured it out last night and we've been able to have limited exchanges through hand gestures. It's rudimentary but has worked so far. The landlady grabs my hand again. I don't protest. I belong with these women now. They lead me to a bus stop and through hand motions ask if I have a pass. I show them the card that Boyoung gave me yesterday and they nod with approval.

Verbal communication is overrated, although I admit I'm curious as to what the two talk about. They've spoken to each other in Korean, and for all I know, they're spilling all kinds of secrets about Lee Jonghyung. I want to know about him. The longer I knelt in that room, the more I wondered about the man in the picture. I wondered about small things like how tall was he or what was his favorite food. I wondered about big things like where was his own family and then really big things like who is my mother.

I guess that's why I'm following these two like I'm their new duckling. They have answers. Sadly, they are all in Korean.

We ride three buses to get to a neighborhood where small buildings with hard concrete and cinder block walls are stacked on top of one another. The asphalt is cracked and loose gravel has me looking down more than ahead. The only real vegetation is unruly dried vines that spill over the sides of the walls and climb into and out of the spidering splits in the concrete.

The two women walk steadily ahead, ignoring the man on the side of the street who's busy relieving himself. This is not the same Seoul I saw in any of my internet searches.

In the middle of the alley, the two women stop in front of a three-story building. Unlike the others, it's free of the growing vines and the exterior is relatively clean. When they step inside, the older woman points to the stairs on the left and then disappears inside the first door. The younger woman begins a descent. At the bottom of the stairs, she pushes open a dark apartment door. There's a thin line of light from a window that's too high to open or close. There isn't much inside the apartment and it's not very large. I can make it across the space in less than ten strides. A few thick blankets are rolled up and stacked in the corner. Near the door is a sink set into a row of cabinets and a very short refrigerator. My dorm-room refrigerator might have been larger. Resting on a squat table is a single burner. There isn't even a bathroom attached to this room. He must've shared a communal one.

The entire place is tidy and clean, but it's so spare and small. This is not the home of a man who was capable of raising a family. A tiny arrow pierces the bag of resentment that I hadn't realized I'd formed. The sound of the door opening catches my attention. When I turn around, the younger woman is there holding a blue-flowered fabric-covered package. She presses it into my hands and then nods toward the door. It's time for me to go, she is saying.

The questions I have will go unanswered. My guess is that they don't know the answers and there isn't anything left for me here. Not in this near-empty room. Maybe not in this country.

CHAPTER TEN

THANKS TO THE BATTERY PACK BOYOUNG GAVE ME, I HAVE ENOUGH juice on my phone left to reply to a text from her asking me if I need help.

ME: I'm okay.

She sends me the instructions on what buses to take and where to transfer, but my brain is dead and I'm afraid I'll screw it up so I walk until I find a taxi. There's some confusion when I slide into the back seat since I don't speak Korean and the driver doesn't speak English, but showing him a screenshot of my address seems to do the trick. When he drops me off at the base of the stairs leading up to the house, I barely register the cost. The money I allotted for this trip has already been eaten away by the unexpected funeral. What's another thirty dollars? As I trek up the hill, the black dress that Boyoung lent me sticks to my sweaty back. The package Kwang Miok had given me weighs my right arm down. In the taxi, I'd discovered that the package was three different plastic containers of food. Not wanting to spill anything on the back seat of the cab, I'd retied the cloth and stuck it between my feet. Halfway up the hill, I consider abandoning it, but afraid I'll get arrested for littering, I transfer the food to my left hand and power forward.

The dry dust on the asphalt mixes with the stale air of the funeral room and fills my lungs with an acrid, bitter taste. My feet feel as though they are weighed down by concrete blocks instead of shod with delicate black flats. The shoes, like the dress, are ruined. At the top of the hill, I pluck at the sweat-soaked bodice of my dress. I'm ready for a shower and a nap. Inside, Anna sits at the kitchen table painting her nails.

"Is there a place I should put this?" I ask, wearily holding up the cloth-wrapped containers.

"Is it food?"

"Yes. I think it's kimchi and some other stuff." I'd peeked in the taxi.

"The kimchi goes in the middle section. God, homemade kimchi. I can't wait." Anna caps the polish and hurries over to take the container from me. She carries it to the table, and with one tug on the knot, the wrapping falls apart. "Everything in Korea is always presented so nice. I swear even if it was dog poo, they'd put it in a special dish and wrap it with a cloth. How was the funeral?"

"How'd you know I went to a funeral?"

"Your friend showed up in a hurry with a shopping bag full of black stuff and then you disappeared for two days. What else could it be?" Anna lifts the lid of the fermented cabbage and takes a long whiff. "This stuff smells good." She flashes me a smile. "There's nothing wrong with the market kimchi, but it doesn't have the same flavor as the stuff the aunties make. What else do we have here? Marinated bean sprouts? Fish cakes? Nice. So who was it? The funeral."

"Oh, my father's."

She nearly drops the plastic container. "Your dad? Oh my God. I'm so sorry. I've been rattling on like it's—"

"I didn't know him," I interrupt before she can pile on the condolences. The only thing I'm feeling sad about at this moment is that I rented a room at the top of the steepest hill in Seoul. "I'm going to shower."

Maybe under the hot water, some kind of revelation will come to me about whether I should stay or go. I know what Mom would say. *Come home immediately. The death is a sign.* Boyoung would likely vote for me to leave, too. My roommates won't care as long as I pay my leasing fee.

"Okay. Hey, wait. Are these yours?"

Hand on the railing, I turn a tired eye in Anna's direction and squint. The smaller girl is holding up a photo. Wait. No. Not a single photo. There are five in total. I nearly fall down the steps in my rush back to Anna's side. In each one, my father has an arm slung around a pretty young woman. Sometimes the arm is around her shoulders; sometimes it's snug around the waist. The women have a sameness about them, as if my dad had a type—sloped eyes, small nose, and round chin. My hand rises to touch my own curved chin, which I've never liked because Ellen's chin is so strong and square.

"There's something on the back," the girl points out.

I flip the first photo over. On the back a collection of characters is written in small, neat handwriting. My heart beats a little faster. The characters are grouped in three-syllable sets, and from my limited knowledge of Korean, that's how names are written. Names. Photos. Faces. This is the real gift the two women have given me— not the food that Anna was excited over, but the five photos.

"Who are they?" Anna fans the photos out.

"My mother."

"For real? Like, all of them? Your dad was in a commune or something?"

"Is that a thing here?" I ask in surprise. I hadn't considered this a possibility.

She shrugs. "Hey, it's possible. I mean, probably not here in Korea, but it's possible other places. It looks like there are names on the back, see?"

I'd guessed correctly. "What do they say?"

Anna gives me a side-eye. "Do you not know how to read *hangukeo*?"

"*Hanguk*— Do you mean *Hangul*?"

"No. *Hangul* is the alphabet. *Hangukeo* or just *gukeo* is the language itself."

I grimace. I don't know what I don't know. "Obviously, I'm pretty ignorant."

"I guess you'll pick it up as you go. How long did you say you were staying?"

I stare at the photos. Five minutes ago, I was considering taking the first flight home. Now my plans seem to be changing. "I don't know."

"Not to be an ass, but there's a no-cancellation clause. If you leave, we're not going to be able to give you a refund."

"Yeah, it's no problem." I'd already paid the housing fee so I'm not going to worry about money already spent. "These names . . . can I google them?" How hard would it be to find these five women?

"I mean, you could, but you wouldn't get anywhere. No one uses that here. We all use Naver, but it's not going to be of any use for you until you read *Hangul*." Anna pulls out her phone and types one of the names in. My heart is racing. I hadn't even considered I could find my mother now that Lee Jonghyung is dead, but the photos and the names are filling me with hope. It leaps into my throat and makes it hard to breathe. A bunch of results show up on the screen. "Lots of people have the same name, and"—she squints at the tiny photos—"none of them look like their old photos. Are you going to hire a private investigator?"

I gnaw on the corner of my mouth. "I don't have the money for that."

Anna grimaces. "This might be impossible, then. South Korea is small, but millions of people live here."

I inspect the internet search results but it's as if I'm looking at a code without the key. *Hangukeo* is supposed to be the easiest language to learn—at least that's what it said online—but I haven't managed to even memorize the simple alphabet. The results are a collection of undecipherable characters. I squeeze my throat and tell myself that this is a hurdle, but not an insurmountable one. I have Boyoung. She'll help me.

"I'll ask my friend. She can help." I pluck the photos from Anna's hands and hurry to my room. I need to plug in my dead phone.

"Mind if I eat some of your food?"

"Feel free." She can eat all of it. The only important thing is the photos.

In the room, I charge the phone, strip off the dress, and dart down the stairs into the bathroom. After taking the quickest shower possible, I run back to my phone. By the time I get back, the phone has a 10 percent charge and a number of messages have downloaded, including one from my mom.

The excitement over the pictures fades a little at the sight of Ellen's name on my phone. I shouldn't feel *this* excited over the possibility of finding my birth mother. I rub the space between my eyebrows and wonder how much Mom needs to know. Definitely that my father is dead, but the mother news seems unnecessary. The photos are leads. That's all. There's no actual confirmation that one of these photos is of my birth mother or that I can even find this woman. Seoul is home to nearly ten million people. Plus, these photos might not even have been taken in Seoul. Lee Jonghyung could be from the other side of the country for all I know and have recently moved to Seoul. There are so many ifs and contingencies that it makes no sense to wind my mother up. If I find my birth mother, then I'll have something to share with Ellen; otherwise, she will be emotionally distraught over nothing.

I unlock my phone and start reading.

MOM: Miss you. Hope everything is going well. I read about the spy cams. You should do something about that.

MOM: Are you okay? Is your phone working? Do you need anything?

MOM: Honey. I haven't heard from you in nearly a day. Do I need to start calling hospitals?

Oh no. I check my voicemails. There are four—all from Ellen. I double-check the time zones. The clock says that it's ten in the morning, which means it's eight in the evening at home. It's early enough to call, but I don't want to. It's easier to duck Mom's questions if we're communicating via text.

ME: Phone died. I was with Boyoung. Sorry. Am fine. Safe.

The response is immediate, as if Ellen has been waiting by the phone.

> MOM: I was so worried. Where is your extra battery charger? Is your passport safe? Are there spy cams in your room?
>
> ME: I don't think so. There are a bunch of women who live here.
>
> MOM: You can't assume!!!!
>
> ME: I'll double-check. I promise.
>
> MOM: Go and check and then give me an update.
>
> ME: I will.

I have no idea how to do that so I pass the time by checking my emails and downloading the Naver app that Anna mentioned. I pull up the website that promises to teach me the entire alphabet in fifteen minutes and study the *Hangul* characters. It's not easy. Fifteen minutes pass and I'm still not fluent, but I have wasted enough time that my mother will believe I've done all the things she wants me to do.

> ME: All clear.
>
> MOM: Thank goodness. Bring your charger with you wherever you go. I love you.
>
> ME: I love you, too.

It's not until I hit send that I realize I didn't mention Lee Jonghyung's funeral, but also, Mom didn't ask. It's possible that she doesn't want to know that information. Perhaps she's pretending

I'm on some cultural exchange visit that has nothing to do with searching for my biological parents. I flop onto my back and stare at the ceiling. If that's how Mom is dealing with this trip, then I'm definitely right to keep the information regarding the five women to myself. It's not as if Ellen, all the way back in Iowa, can help me here in Seoul.

There's one person who can, though. I call Boyoung.

"Pictures?" my friend screeches.

"Five of them," I confirm. "It's him—my dad—and five women."

"Five?"

The stunned silence on Boyoung's end erodes some of my excitement and forces me to acknowledge that Lee Jonghyung was kind of a jerk. He'd hooked up with five women all around the same time and they could all potentially be the woman who gave birth to me. It's like I won the bad-dad lottery twice.

"I know. It's a lot."

"No. I didn't mean it like that," my friend apologizes, which is silly.

"I want to find all of them, but I will need your help."

"Of course," she responds immediately. "Should we meet?"

"Yes." I sit up in excitement and look around for my clothes. With Boyoung's help, this won't be the impossible task that Anna suggested it would be.

"I can't today, but tomorrow. Let's meet for lunch. I'll come to you and we can grab a bite to eat nearby."

"Sounds perfect," I lie. I'd forgotten Boyoung has a family here in Korea. She's not at my beck and call. "In the meantime, I'll make friends with my new flatmates."

"Oh, Hara, wait," Boyoung calls out as I'm about to disconnect.

"What is it?"

"I wouldn't say anything about those pictures to anyone. Or why you're here. People might view you differently if they know you are adopted. There's nothing wrong with it, obviously, but some people are old-fashioned," she tries to explain.

"Right. I remember." We actually had this conversation back home. Boyoung has said that people in Korea are working to make it more acceptable, but the cultural focus on bloodlines puts adoptees somewhere on the social scale above drug dealers and sex addicts, but only by a little. Okay, maybe that's an exaggeration.

But the assumption is that there is something wrong with the abandoned kids, else why would they be abandoned? And even if the child isn't flawed, the parents must be, because true, decent human beings wouldn't give up their child, regardless of their circumstances. It's not so different back home. I overheard one of Ellen's friends say that Ellen was so brave to adopt because you just didn't know what you'd get. I even read stories about adopted children being given away like animals that the adoptive parents had tired of. It was called re-homing, a hideous, awful practice that should be illegal but apparently isn't. So was South Korea any different? It will change, Boyoung claimed, and there are even important, powerful people who are trying to make that happen. Laws had been enacted, but the government can't change the hearts and minds of people.

Objectively, I understand this, but there's still a pinprick of hurt. Just a pinprick, though. The friend who was loud about her opinions on adoption held no weight with my mother. The friend became an acquaintance and then a stranger in my mom's life. Likewise, I wouldn't be here long enough for anyone's opinion of my adoptive state to matter. I'm going to find my biological mother and then go home. "I won't," I promise, omitting that I'd blurted out the details to Anna just a few moments ago.

Boyoung hangs up and the exhaustion of the past couple of days causes my knees to give out. I flop back on the bed and stare at the photos. I want to meet Boyoung now. I want to find out the identity of all five women now. I want to meet the one who is my mother now. I wonder if she knows that Lee Jonghyung has died. Maybe she's the woman with the big black hat. Did she and the new girlfriend get into a fight and that's why my mother didn't stay? Is she—

I sit up. I need to move. I need to get out of my room and away from these photos so I don't start spinning ridiculous fantasies about my birth mother like I did when I was a child. I need a distraction. Unfortunately, Anna is gone when I get downstairs. The food from my dad's female friend is tucked into the refrigerator and there are freshly washed dishes sitting on the counter, but Anna is nowhere to be found.

The small home is suddenly both stifling and too large at the same time. I decide to explore the neighborhood instead of twiddling my thumbs. I'll find the perfect place for lunch with Boyoung tomorrow and practice my Korean.

Armed with my phone and a small notebook where I've written out the *Hangul* characters for reference, I set out. I go up this time, which is only two flights of stairs, instead of down, because I can't stomach walking up that hill today. At the top are more apartments, but it takes longer to find shops and restaurants. At least the terrain is flat. My calf muscles send up a silent thank-you.

My expedition is one part successful, two parts failure. The successful part is that I find dozens of places to eat. There's a fried chicken place and coffee shop on every corner. Halfway down a small street, I discover a bakery that specializes in apple desserts. It takes me nearly a minute to type the characters into the Papago app, but I complete the task and repeat the word *sagwa* under my breath until I feel it slide into my regular vocabulary. I also learn that the word is the same for "apologize" and that Koreans will often give an apple along with their apology, which is *adorable*.

The failure part is the weariness that sets in as the sun bakes into my black hair. There are also other small stores selling electronics and shoes and beauty supplies. Everyone in the advertisements plastered on the sides of buses that zip by and in store windows sports poreless glass skin. I rub the side of my thumb against my less-than-perfect cheek. I look like I'm Korean and yet I'm not. None of this feels familiar. It isn't merely that the signs above the stores and the advertisements in the windows are all full of *Hangul* characters and not English letters, but it's the buildings wedged together, the noise of the traffic, the smell of something tangy and dry. All of it is foreign. I stop in front of a convenience store with fruit sitting in a display outside. The man tending to the fruit stand says something to me that I don't understand. When I try to tell him that, he gives me a suspicious look like I'm mocking him. I'm not but I don't have even enough Korean to tell him I don't speak his language and I don't think saying *sagwa* in this circumstance is useful.

It's time to go back to the apartment.

When I arrive, it's still empty. I drag myself up the stairs and lie down. My body is tired and even as my feet ache and my head hurts, I still can't sleep.

The hamster in my head is running again. One of these women is my mother, which means there's someone in this city, in this country, who gave birth to me. *Or she could be dead*, my brain unhelpfully supplies.

Yes, or she could be alive. Ellen always theorized that my bio mom had been poor, and that's the conclusion that I had come to as well. It's the story that made the abandonment hurt the least. She was poor and couldn't afford to raise a family. Abortions aren't legal—not then or now. It fits with the state of my father's place—small and bare. An ache blooms in my chest, and when I press the heel of my hand against my heart, it doesn't go away. I don't know if it's an ache of sadness or hope. Sometimes they feel the same way inside your soul.

I finally drift off into some stage of restless sleep until a buzzing of soft laughter, excited chatter, pulls me out of my semiconscious state. I creep downstairs to find my flatmates in various stages of dress. The smells of hair spray, curling irons, and perfume tell the story. They're going out for the night.

Anna stops on her way to the bedroom, a mélange of hair products clutched against her sizable chest, and looks up at me on the stairs. "You woke up at the perfect time. We're going to Club Dance. It's this swanky club over in Incheon, and normally I wouldn't go all the way to the airport but rappers from a famous group are supposed to be there and they never perform alone like this. I know you just had the thing"—she waves her hand as if to brush aside the unpleasant thought of my dad dying—"but if you need a distraction, this would be it. I don't want your time in Korea to be a bummer."

Stay home and mope or go out and distract myself? It takes me a split second to decide. "What should I wear?"

Anna beams. "Something sexy, of course!"

"Not too sexy," Jules chides unseen from another room.

Some Korean men think Westerners are easy, I remember her saying. I trot back to my room and dig through my suitcase. Despite overpacking, I don't find any club clothes. They didn't seem appropriate attire for a meeting with my biological father. I have leggings, sweatpants, skinny jeans, and a denim skirt that stops somewhere in the vicinity of my knees. Also a frock. With its thin white stripes against the black background, the elastic waist, and small bow ties at the side, it is a dress you wear to Sunday brunch or a meeting with your dad, but not one you'd wear to grind out on the dance floor.

I opt for jeans and a black silky T-shirt that has a scoop neck.

Around my neck, I tie a velvet ribbon for decoration. The shoes that Boyoung provided with the funeral gear will be perfect with this outfit even if the soles are worn out. I have to pay her back for all of this. I keep forgetting and she isn't saying a word. I'll settle up with her tomorrow. It seems fitting to wear my funeral shoes to a nightclub. It's a sort of weird clash of experiences that have summed up my three days in Korea. Even if I don't know why I'm here, at least the experience is memorable.

CHAPTER ELEVEN

CLUB DANCE IS FOUR STORIES OF LED SCREENS STITCHED TO-
gether to project enormous illusions. The exterior of the club is so
fancy, so technological, so full of lights and screens and moving images, that I half wonder if I'm inside a gaming console. I wouldn't be
surprised if a flying car speeds across the sky just below the planes
taking off and landing. The airport is within spitting distance.

The line to get in is long, which is expected given that even I,
whose knowledge of Korean culture is shallower than a puddle, recognize the performers. I don't mind, though, because there's so
much to look at and I don't mean the architecture. It's the first time
since the airport that I've paid much attention to the people around
me. There's the occasional wildly dyed head, but for the most part
everyone has jet-black hair. I reach up and run a hand over my own
straight locks. In this line, I don't stand out. The people in front of
me are staring, but not at me—at my flatmates. I fit in. I fit in so
much that at the door, the bouncer frowns when I present my passport as my ID. He stares at the document a long time before inspect-

ing my face with his flashlight. This time I don't blurt out that I'm adopted, but I won't lie, it's on the tip of my tongue. *Sorry I'm confusing you. I'm adopted. Not from here. Or, I was originally from here, but then I got sent to America, where I grew up next to the corn and cows. And insurance. Iowa is big on insurance. It's the second-largest insurance capital—*

He grunts and passes me through. Access to the club is via a winding staircase lined with vertical brass bars that leads into an enormous two-story space with more strobe lights than at a stadium concert. The line to the bar seems longer than the one to get inside, and when we reach the counter, the bartender barks out something in Korean. And, of course, I have no idea what he's saying. Beer should be a universal word. Everywhere you go, you should be able to say, "Beer me," and everyone would know exactly what you want. That and "bathroom." "Where's the toilet" and "Beer me" will be the first language edicts I make when I'm in charge of the world.

Anna pushes me lightly to the side and gives our order. I don't miss the slightly puzzled look the bartender throws in my direction, and I suffer a slightly traumatizing flashback to that Korean club meeting at college. Since I won't ever be Supreme Leader of the Universe, I should've studied Korean instead of Spanish. *Hola* isn't going to work here. I hope this guy doesn't think I'm a porn star. Everyone here will be sorely disappointed. The one very Asian thing about me is my tiny chest.

The beers get delivered to our table and I get a quick lesson in drinking etiquette. Age matters. No one pours their own glass, and the younger ones should turn to the side and cover their drink. Everyone skipped over this before. "We didn't want to overwhelm you," explains Anna.

Thinking back, I do remember seeing people at the funeral home turn to their side and lift a hand before downing their booze, but the action hasn't registered until tonight. I'm younger than everyone but Jules so they put me in charge of the pouring, which is good because I have something to do.

The two-story club is massive. There are strobe lights flashing red and blue and white in sync with the heavy bass of a very familiar Western song. At least four disco balls twirl in the ceiling, splashing a kaleidoscope of colored dots everywhere. In this dark circus, I can't tell the color of anyone's hair or even make out many features. I could be in a club in any large city.

"Are you having fun yet?" Anna screams over the noise.

I nod because this should be more fun than lying on my bed trying to work the translation app and winnow down a hundred thousand search results in a foreign language to locate five women, but the drumming in my head is back. Not even one beer down and I'm already thinking fond thoughts of my sublet room and its quiet solitude. Pushing the corners of my lips up into what I hope is an agreeable smile, I turn to the side and down my drink. It glides down my throat with ease, but when it hits my stomach, there's turmoil. I don't remember eating anything today and I still have all the funeral soju in my system. At this point, I might be 80 percent fermented rice water.

I take a steadying breath through my nose, and when that doesn't work, I decide that I better move.

"I'm going to get some air," I shout. I think Anna heard me but I'm not sure about the others. I escape anyway. There is a steady stream of partiers arriving but they're all too intent on getting inside to take much notice of the single female taking the stairs a little fast. The fresh night air hits my face, and despite the heat it feels good. I lift my face and walk over to a steel tubular railing that's set up to prevent drunks from falling into the hedges below.

I lean against the metal and take a deep calming breath. My

emotions are all over the place. One minute, I'm excited to dance the night away. The next, I can't breathe. I don't know what's wrong with me. I clear my throat, run a hand through my hair, and tug on the waistband of my jeans. I wish I had a glass of water instead of the soju.

I haven't felt this disoriented since my freshman year during the Drake Relays when I drank for four days straight and woke up on the fifth thinking I was blind but really my eyes were just glued shut from all the alcohol I'd imbibed. It was the first and last real bender I'd ever gone on. As I rest my hand against the railing, I remind myself I'm no longer eighteen and away from my mother for the first time, but an actual adult so I don't need to down liquor like I'm never getting another chance at the bottle. I close my eyes and count my breaths. Inhale one. Exhale two. Inhale one. Exhale two. The faint roar of the airplanes taking off fills the night air, but it's still quieter. My chest no longer feels like it's about to cave in.

Incheon looks like a scene out of a Marvel movie. The buildings are sleek and rounded. Tall, statement buildings. Dozens of cranes, heavy machinery, and scaffolding fill the skyline. It's a manufactured place and none of it seems entirely real. Maybe if I stretched out a hand, it'd pierce the computer-generated image and I'd stumble forward to find myself in my apartment back home.

"There you are." A voice slices through the silence like a whip.

Electricity arcs up my spine. I know that voice. It might be the only familiar one in all of Korea other than Boyoung's, and so I shouldn't be surprised when I spin around and find Choi Yujun standing on the first landing of the wide stairs that lead up to the entrance of the club. I am, though, and my return greeting sticks in my throat.

"We met at the airport," he says, as if I could ever forget. His long legs cover the stairs two at a time and he's in front of me, within dimple-poking distance, even before I can blink. He's dressed in black slacks and a silky shirt whose top two buttons are undone. A hint of his clavicle peeks out. I scrape my teeth along my lower lip and wonder when collarbones became sexy.

"I remember," I reply, a little too breathlessly. *You're not eighteen, remember, Hara?* "Choi Yujun. You gave me a ride home."

"You're supposed to call me Yujun, remember?" He grins and the left dimple winks into existence. I'm glad I'm still holding on to the railing. "And take me out for a giant steak dinner."

I'd forgotten that. The news of my father's death followed by the funeral and then the discovery of the five photos had shoved everything else out of my brain. I'd forgotten my mother, Boyoung, and this man. Thinking back, though, I never would have called him because Yujun from Seoul was as much a mirage as the images that flash along the exterior of Club Dance—a dream. Perfect but not real.

But he is real and he's standing in front of me looking so delicious that my hands start sweating and my skin starts to pebble with goose bumps despite the hot, still air. A light, bubbling sensation replaces the rock in my stomach and the corners of my lips are curving upward of their own volition.

"I was unpacking," I blurt out, realizing belatedly that it's my turn to speak. I don't know what it is about this man that renders me so dumb. It's his looks, I guess? And his charm, which he wears like a garment that was made just for him. And the smile and the height and the way his eyes dance when he looks at me, as if *I'm* interesting and delightful. "I brought too much stuff," I finish weakly. This is not a good excuse. I'll think of one tonight, hours later when I replay this humiliating exchange in my head a thousand times.

He's an angel because he doesn't call me on the bullshit but instead asks, "Are you enjoying the show?"

"The show?" I repeat because my brain cells have their tongues on the ground and things are slow upstairs. *All right, Hara, get your act together. Stop acting like you can't understand his perfect English and reply in full, cogent sentences.* "Right. The show. It's good." What a lie. I can't remember a single song that was played.

He cocks his head. "You sound uncertain."

"No. No. It was good. Really good." Everyone inside is jamming out. It isn't that the music isn't good. My head isn't in the right place.

"If you're leaving, my chauffeur services are available. I'm driving myself today. Taxis at night can be unpredictable."

"I'm not leaving," I say in a hurry. "I was catching a breath of fresh air. This place is incredible."

Yujun doesn't let this half-truth slide. One side of his mouth quirks up. "Is it the cranes or the airplanes that you like the best?"

"Cranes," I quip. "I've got a thing for construction and heavy machinery."

We share a smile at my silliness. Hints of Yujun's dimples appear like tiny crescent shadows, and I lean a little closer, feeling the weight of the past three days ease a bit. Silence stretches between us and it should be uncomfortable but instead makes it easier for me to be standing here in this place I thought would feel like home but isn't in any way familiar. The expression on his face is fond and admiring and seems to be saying that he understands me. Or, at the very least, sharing this space, this moment, pleases him. We aren't the only two people here in Incheon or at this complex, but I don't notice anything but him. My entire vision is of his long legs and broad shoulders, his glossy black hair with the side part, his dark eyebrows, straight nose, and full lips. My lungs are full of something warm and pleasant. My hand rises and I'm on the verge of doing something stupid like poking my index finger into the divot on the side of his cheek when a newcomer pops up and saves me.

"Hey, I'm ready to go inside," a man announces, coming up to drape an arm around Yujun's shoulders. The blond peers intently at me. "Who is this?"

I peer right back, surprised at how good the wheat-gold hair looks on this Korean man. It suits him better than it does some Scandinavians back home. It helps that this particular man is so good-looking that he could be a webtoon character come to life. The most sophisticated computer programs in the world couldn't have crafted a better combination of that sharp jaw, high cheekbones, bold brows, and high nose bridge.

The two of them are perfectly awful together and I think it's unfair how good-looking people congregate like this. There should be a law against it. Only one attractive person per two square meters for the good of the general public—a social-distancing rule to prevent pandemics of fatal attraction.

Yujun's smile widens until shadows form deep indentations. I have a feeling that this is Yujun's normal state—happy and smiling. That, more than his good looks, is what draws my eyes, what makes me want to bask next to him as he exudes sunshine and warmth. "This is Hara. Hara, this is—"

"I'm Ahn Sangki." The man breaks away and briefly takes my hand in his. "Where did you two meet?"

"At Incheon," Yujun explains. "Hara's airport transportation vanished." I quirk my eyebrow at the shameless lie but keep my lips sealed. No way am I going to correct him with the embarrassing truth.

Sangki shakes his head, his bangs falling forward to nearly cover his eyes. "An outrage. We're a very safe country, you know, as a result of all the cameras." He points a finger upward. "They're always watching. I know you Americans aren't fans of that, but we're used to it."

I tip my head back and see a camera mounted at the top of a light post. I hadn't noticed it before. "How did you know I'm American?"

"The accent. Or lack of accent. I heard you as I was approaching."

"You two are pretty good English speakers," I point out.

"No," Sangki denies. "You have that perfect, second-generation, born-in-America speech."

Yujun nudges his friend and gives him a tiny but firm shake of his head, telling Sangki wordlessly that perhaps these observations should be kept to himself. To me, Yujun says apologetically, "What is the saying? You can't take him out."

"You can't take him anywhere," I correct. I'm amused rather than offended.

"Exactly. I can't take you anywhere," Yujun says. I can tell by the way he allows the other man's arm to rest along his shoulders and the easy way the two interact that they've been friends for a long time.

"Do you have family here in Seoul?" Sangki asks.

Boyoung's warning to keep my adoptee status to myself pops into my head. I've told Yujun, but from how he protected me earlier by saying my transportation got screwed up instead of how I mistook him for a hired driver, it's likely he's not sharing any information with Sangki. But is it that big a deal? And even if it is, what do I care if these very pretty men think differently of me? Being adopted is part of my story as much as having black hair and brown eyes. It's baked into my bones because all of my life I've had to explain why I don't look the same as my mother—or nearly anyone else around me. And I'm not ashamed of it. After all, I wasn't the one who did the abandoning. I jut out my chin. "I'm adopted. I thought it was time to visit the place where I was born."

The admission elicits no reaction from Sangki. My confession isn't the Hester-Prynne-wearing-a-scarlet-letter-around-town-on-her-dress Boyoung made it out to be.

"We should go inside. The main act is about ready to perform," Sangki suggests.

"Or we can stay out here. I haven't finished counting all the cranes yet," Yujun says, a silent offer to remain with me, but I'm done getting fresh air.

"No," I say with a shake of my head, "I want to hear them."

Sangki bounces on the balls of his feet like an excited boy. His anticipation is infectious and I'm tempted to give him a pat on the head, but I settle for exchanging grins with Yujun like we're old friends. This feels comfortable. In this other country, Yujun and now Sangki are this comfortable island. I'd like to attach myself to them—Yujun specifically, and hide in his pocket or maybe put him in mine and take him out whenever I'm feeling nervous or need reassurance. Sangki bounds up the stairs, a bundle of energy. He bypasses the front entrance and instead approaches the side of the giant cube. One set of the LED screens opens as if someone has been waiting for him. I guess Sangki isn't an ordinary person.

"I don't want to be a bother," he explains. "If I go through the front, I'll be creating more work for everyone."

"Sangki is famous here," Yujun adds, confirming my suspicion. I feel bad for not recognizing him.

"Famous everywhere." Sangki laughs as he ducks underneath a rather tall security man's outstretched arm.

"Famous in his head," Yujun replies drolly.

I'm too embarrassed to admit that I've never heard of Ahn Sangki, so I keep my mouth shut and smile and nod as if I'm in on the joke. First chance I get, though, I'm googling him. Or maybe it's navering in Korea? Wait. I don't know how to spell his name, either in English or in *Hangul*. I guess I'll remain ignorant until I get home or I see Boyoung. *Along with finding my mother, can you explain who Ahn Sangki is and how to spell that?*

"You came with someone, right?" Sangki asks as we walk down a dark hall.

"Yeah. I should get back to them." Maybe Anna and company can supply the answers.

"Invite them here! I won't take no for an answer." "Here" is a private room overlooking the dance floor. Two uniformed waitstaff stand at strict attention as we enter the room. One of them is dispatched to find Anna and the others. Sangki explains, in an apologetic and serious tone, that going down to the floor could cause a problem.

"He is actually very famous," Yujun admits. "He doesn't want to take away anything from his friends."

The friends being the other very famous people onstage. I'm starting to realize that Sangki is famous here in the way that someone like Bieber is back home. He must be some sort of a musician—a rap star? A pop star? An actor? One of those. My guess is partially confirmed when my flatmates are ushered into the private space and gasps of shock and screams of glee fill the space.

"He puts on a brave face, but he's shy," Yujun murmurs next to me. "Watch his ears. They will grow red like the trees on Mount Chiak."

In the face of this very loud, very obvious adulation, Sangki gives a small bow and smiles, but Yujun is correct because the very tips of Sangki's ears turn a charming, endearing pink. Sangki turns and gestures for Yujun to step forward and there are introductions all around. While Yujun talks to the staff about drinks, Jules takes up the empty spot next to me.

"Why didn't you tell us you knew DJ Song?" she hisses into my ear.

"Who is DJ Song?" I ask. "Oh, you mean Sangki?"

My flatmate's brows crash together and she jerks a thumb over her shoulder. "You call him Sangki?" she asks in shock.

"That's what he said his name is."

My flatmate sighs. "You don't know anything about this country, do you? There's a strict age thing here and you have to use honorifics with people or you're going to offend someone. It'd be different if you looked foreign, but you look like you're Korean, so people like the waitress are going to speak to you in the language. You should learn some *Hangul*, too, because not everyplace has stuff in English. Plus, you'll be treated better."

You look like you're Korean. Jules doesn't mean anything by it, but the words bite anyway, mostly because Jules is right. I don't know much of anything about Korea and haven't put the time or effort into learning. Korea wasn't even on my top five places to visit despite what I'd blurted out at Denny's after the funeral. I'd come here on a whim and that foolishness is starting to pay dividends I don't like.

"What should I call him?" I ask, trying to learn.

"You said you're twenty-five, right?"

"Yes. Is this like the booze thing where I have to pour the drinks and turn to the side?"

Jules nods. "Yeah, in Korea, it's all age based, so if you're the same age as DJ Song-nim then you could get away with calling him something like Ahn Sangki-nim or DJ-nim. Don't use *oppa*. It's cringey, particularly from a foreigner."

I don't even know what *oppa* means, but I file it away.

"The full name?" That's a mouthful.

"The full name unless you are same-age friends and you decide together that you don't need that formality; then you can call him Sangki-ah and he'd call you Hara-ya."

"That sounds awkward."

"Well, your name isn't super Korean so that's why."

With that last twist of the knife, Jules turns away. I rub my chest lightly. It's all in one piece but it feels like I should be bleeding somewhere.

"Is it too loud in here for you?"

I turn to see Yujun—no, Choi Yujun-nim—in the place Jules had occupied.

"No, it's great." The music is good and I'm not going to let a few truth bombs drive me away. I'm glad Jules educated me. Sure, it might've been a little harsh, but better that I know than I continue to embarrass myself or, worse, offend someone.

Choi Yujun studies me for a moment and then puts a hand over his stomach. "I feel a sudden onset of a stomach pain. Oh no."

I see what he's doing. A reluctant smile tugs on the corners of my lips. "Stop."

"It's very painful." He bends over.

Ahn Sangki appears out of nowhere. "What's going on?"

Still bent over, Choi Yujun peeks at me, waiting for a sign. If I want to leave, he's given me an out. I shake my head slightly. *I'm good*, I tell him.

He straightens and flashes a warm smile at his friend. "A cramp."

Ahn Sangki-nim shoots the two of us a narrowed suspicious gaze before raising a green bottle and three shot glasses. "I have soju," he says, like he's brought out the Christmas turkey. "What would you drink in America?"

"Watered-down beer," I tell them, watching the soju bottle like a hawk so I can snatch it up. I'm not going to mess up the beer-pouring protocol. If there's one thing a twentysomething should know, it's bar etiquette. Along with how to do your taxes and laundry, knowing how to act in a bar should be in the first two chapters of those little handbooks they sell at the bookstore by the checkout counter.

"This is the opposite of watered-down beer." He turns to Choi Yujun. "What did you drink when you were in college?"

"Beer. Vodka. Wine out of a box."

"Out of a box?" Ahn Sangki looks half-horrified, half-intrigued.

"It is not good."

I wonder where Choi Yujun went to college.

"But cheap and American," he tacks on as if that explains everything, although it sort of does. We are a to-go society and I have yet to see anyone on the street in Seoul drinking or eating, whereas back home, you couldn't go one block without seeing someone with a Starbucks coffee cup in their hand.

"American is good. Cheap is good," Ahn Sangki declares and pours the soju into the small cups before I can grab the bottle. He hands them out and clinks his glass against mine and then Choi Yujun's. *"Gun bae!"*

"Gun bae!" Choi Yujun echoes.

I repeat it in my head and down the shot of rice wine, frowning slightly at not getting the chance to do the pouring and then kicking myself when I belatedly remember to turn my head to my side. Everyone else but the two men turn away. If there is a test on social skills, I'm failing.

Jules asks Ahn Sangki a question in Korean and by the way she touches her hair, I'm guessing it's about his very good dye job. The washed-wheat-gold color looks better on him than on natural blonds. It's kind of amazing and I begin to wonder what I would look like blond. I run a hand down my own plain black hair and think of all the times I wanted to be a blonde growing up. I could've been but I didn't have the vision. Damn.

Next to me, Choi Yujun leans back against the cushions and eyes me from beneath the fringe of his eyelashes. Both names are a handful in my head. I want to shorten it, make it more familiar. He specifically told me to call him Yujun, not Choi Yujun or Yujun-nim or even—what was it that Jules said was cringey? *Oppa?*

"You have questions in your eyes."

"It's the strobe lights."

His own eyes twinkle as the corners of his mouth quirk up. He rolls his empty shot glass between his fingers a couple of times before saying, "I'm very good at listening. My *eomma* says it's my best quality."

"What? Not your dimples?" I jest.

He grins and I pretend I'm unaffected.

"Those are a very close second," he says, putting his thumb and forefinger millimeters apart. "But I scored high on my listening skills in aptitude tests. Try me out. See if what I'm saying is true."

He did ask, I suppose. "Age is important here."

He nods.

"So I'm going to ask even though it feels unnatural. How old are you?"

"Ah. We actually ask what year you were born. I was born in ninety-two and so was Sangki-ah, so he is my same-age friend. A *chingu*. And you?"

"Twenty-five."

"That would make you a ninety-five-liner, which would make me your *oppa* since I'm older." He says the word a little cheekily, as if he's inviting me to call him something that's slightly inappropriate.

I eye him suspiciously. "Do I want to know what *oppa* means?"

"Older brother," he supplies readily.

I can see how calling a man who is not related an older brother is cringey. I'm glad that Jules warned me. Of course, this means that all his warmth that I took for flirtation is actually a gesture of friendship, which is disappointing, but I'll live. I mean, maybe I'll cry into my pillow tonight and erase all the mental scribbling where I put our names inside a heart, but I will live. "My flatmate told me I shouldn't use it but you're telling me I should call everyone *oppa*?"

"No." He shakes his head firmly. "Only me."

The twinkle is back and I don't think it is the strobe lights causing it. It's been a while since I've interacted meaningfully with the opposite sex, but now it seems like he's flirting again. Maybe "older brother" has some other connotation here in Korea. And while Yujun is up for explaining a lot of things, I sense he's not about to give this one away. I'll have to ask Jules—or maybe Anna since she's a mite less prickly—later.

"And what about Sangki—I mean, Ahn Sangki. What should I call him?"

Yujun glances over at the other man, bracketed by two of my flatmates. They're all enjoying the show below.

"You won't need to call him. You have my number, remember? Yujun from Seoul." He taps the back of my phone. And there it is again, that hint of flirting.

"What would you call me," I ask, "if I was Korean?"

His eyes widen. "But you are Korean."

"No. I look Korean," I correct him. I want to tell him I feel foreign and strange here even though everyone around me is some version of myself, but this is a club and you don't do that kind of thing at a club. Clubs are for the *F*s: flirting, fun, frolicking . . . fucking. My eyes sweep downward to Yujun's lap before I realize what I'm doing and jerk my gaze toward a twirling disco ball suspended over his left shoulder. On the list of things that I should not be doing, speculating about Yujun's package is up near the top—somewhere under getting arrested but above pissing Jules off. That said, thinking about Yujun's body is better than bemoaning my ignorance.

When I stepped off the plane and saw a sea of black hair and faces that were shaped like mine with eyes like mine and skin color like mine, I thought this was home. But now I'm not so sure, and it's not because I don't know the language or the customs. I can't tell what the gold characters pinned to the wall mean, although I assume it's "exit" or "bathroom," or maybe it means "secret hideaway." Who knows. It could say "organ transplant" for all I know. I came here without doing any homework and I know nothing.

Yujun doesn't agree. He shakes his head emphatically. "You're Korean. You don't know all about your background yet. That's an easy remedy. There just happens to be a very charming English-speaking Korean who is available for tours and language lessons."

A slow warmth spreads through my bones. "Maybe I can't afford this tour guide."

"He is in great demand," Yujun allows, "but perhaps he can be convinced to lower his prices."

"What would it take?"

"I think meals. Definitely several meals together. Lunch and dinner."

I'm slow, but not that slow. A heady rush of endorphins sweeps through my system and it's hard to hold back a smile. "You're very good at this—making it seem like I'm doing you the favor."

"I'm very good because it's fate. We never want to fight fate. As for what I would call you? I suppose you would be my charming *dongsaeng*, which means my young friend who I promise to look out for."

His answer is vague and evasive, but in the most charming way possible. I cock my head. "*Oppa* doesn't mean older brother, does it?"

"Oh, but it does." His dimple winks into view. "But your friend is right. You mustn't use it for anyone else."

CHAPTER TWELVE

I SLEEP BADLY. HALFWAY THROUGH THE NIGHT, I HAVE THIS
lovely dream with Yujun. We are walking down a tree-lined street,
holding hands. He is teaching me Korean, pointing out the words
for "tree" and "street" and "flower." Then we stop walking and I look
up to see the funeral home in front of me. Boyoung is waving me
inside. Yujun keeps up his instruction. The funeral is called a *san-
grye*. The money given in the white envelopes is *bujo*. I put my hands
on my ears and tell him to stop, except I call him *oppa*. Boyoung
morphs into Jules, who shakes her finger in my face and reminds me
that I'm not supposed to use that word. Since I've violated a rule, the
landlady and my father's girlfriend drag me away—one on each
arm—until we arrive in the mourning room. They all push me onto
the floor, dress me in white clothes, and start lighting incense sticks
around my body. I tell them I'm not dead, but no one seems to hear
me. Sleep paralysis seizes me and I can't move. The covers get heavier
and heavier. I try to kick my legs. I try to cry for help. Nothing works.

I moan and moan and struggle, and when finally I wake, I am sweating and panting.

Is this what it means to have a guilty conscience? I've buried two dads in the space of three months, but at the first opportunity, I'm making googly eyes at a stranger and trying to gauge the size of his dick. I guess it's been so long since I've been the focus of any hot guy's attention that I've let it get to me. That and it's far more pleasant thinking about Yujun than about two dead dads.

I've never been good at connecting with people. In high school and even the early years of college, I was too overeager, latching on to the first person who showed any sign of interest. If a girl complimented my lipstick choice, I presumed that we were going to be exchanging those interlocking BFFs heart necklaces and then I'd be crushed when I got skipped over for that girl's trip to the nail salon or the post-prom party at the Embassy Suites down by the river. In college, it was much the same way. I'd take the most innocent of overtures and blow it up into a lifelong friendship before we'd even had a meal together. I'd end up hurt, but wouldn't admit it. By the end of my sophomore year, I learned to stop making the effort.

The last real relationship I had, if you could call it that, was with Travis Bloom. He was a jock insomuch as a nonscholarship college athlete could be called one. He was fit, looked good in a pair of jeans, rocked intramural sports, said that he rushed but didn't want to conform. Later, someone told me that he never even received an invite to join a fraternity. It sounded about right. He often made small boasts that could never be verified—*was the best player on my high school football team but am not going to brag about it*—but I thought he was cool in the way stupid virgins who didn't have boyfriends in high school think men in college are cool.

He was bad in bed, although I was no better so I didn't complain. Our two-semester romance didn't make it past the summer between my sophomore and junior years. He went home to St. Louis and hooked up with his high school girlfriend, a former cheerleader if I remember correctly, and I learned how to make a chocolate raspberry mousse with my mom at a new kitchen store that had opened up in the East Village.

After that, I had a few random hookups but nothing serious. I slept with a lab partner for a semester mostly because we were both bored and it was easy. I hooked up with a minor league baseball player whom I met at a bar the summer I graduated from college. These experiences were pretty soulless and unsatisfying, so when I started working, I decided that my time was better spent as a single female. Men were too much effort, and friends? Well, I had my coworkers if I needed someone to hang out with, and there were other things in life that fulfilled me. Books. Binge-watching sitcoms made ten years ago. I took up knitting once with Mom. We tried to make a blanket together. It turned into a very large, very ugly scarf. I wonder where the monstrosity is right now. In the three years since I've been out of college, I've sort of retreated—to my apartment, to my hobbies, to my television.

Mom always pressed me to go out more, to be more social, but that wasn't my thing. Last night was an anomaly. All my interaction with Choi Yujun has been out of the ordinary. The point of this is to say that I'm likely misreading Yujun's actions and my dream of being smothered alive is symbolic of how embarrassed I will feel mistaking his friendliness for something more. In the light of day, when sleep and time have burned off the soju, it's clear he was being kind and not trying to get into my mom jeans.

I vow to be cool and less dorky the next time I see him—if I see him at all again, which is unlikely. Besides, I have more important things to do, none of which I can accomplish until lunchtime, when

I meet with Boyoung. I drag my stiff body out of bed and wander downstairs. Everyone is gone again. My flatmates are hard workers.

I decide to go for another walk. This time I don't need my notebook to recognize the chicken sign: 치킨 . If I'm ever lost and hungry, I'll at least be able to figure out where to eat. From the lettering on the windows, I'm able to figure out a few more words. Over the top of a laundromat I see a word that reminds me of *ppalli ppalli*—the first word I learned in Korean. When I check the translation app on my phone and find out that I'm very close—*ppallaebang*—I want to slap a gold star on my chest. Fluency, here I come. I almost text Yujun from Seoul but manage to talk myself down from that silly impulse. The instinct to share something with Yujun only happens three more times before lunch.

I manage to keep myself together until it's time to meet Boyoung at the *ttalgi* café she suggested. Two doors down from the café, a few older people stand in front of a four-story building that looks to be in the process of renovation. They are all holding signs with red-and-black lettering. My limited Korean gives me no insight and I add it to the mental scroll of all the things I need Boyoung to explain, but first are my photos.

The inside of the *ttalgi* café is adorable. Literally everything on the menu is related to that one particular fruit—strawberry milk, strawberry bread, strawberry muffins, strawberry ice cream. The seats are even covered with a red berry pattern. I love it and want to take it home with me.

Boyoung is next to the far wall with her head bent over her phone. She's always fifteen minutes early. I hurry over to where she is standing by the wall and we go together to the counter. I allow her to order for me but shove her lightly out of the way so I can pay.

Boyoung helps me navigate the checkout process. When the transaction is complete, Boyoung takes a small electronic disk from the clerk, which I assume lets us know when our order is done. We find a small table near the windows and from my seat I can see the protestors. "What's going on outside?"

My friend leans back to get a better view of the older people. "They are protesting the building. The owner wants to tear it down and build something bigger. The current tenants don't want that because it will mean a disruption in their business and higher rent. Protesting is a Korean hobby. We will protest anything from our favorite yogurt drink being discontinued to ousting a corrupt president." She shrugs lightly. "It works and so we keep doing it."

"That's not a bad thing." It's kind of cool, if you think about it. Actual voice-of-the-people stuff.

"It is not a bad thing," she agrees.

I want to whip out the photos and ask her to start the search now, but that seems rude. Back home, there were always things to talk about. I was eager to learn more about Korea and Boyoung never lacked for enthusiasm on the subject. She loved and hated it here. She hated the classism, where everyone was judged by where you went to school. She loved the culture and the food. She hated the misogyny, where sex crimes against women were practically ignored and women were paid a fraction of the dollar men received—even less than in the States. She loved her family and said that the company she worked for was the best ever. But now that we are here, in Korea, she seems distant and uncomfortable. Maybe it's because the social formalities that I never knew about matter to her now that we're in Seoul.

"What year were you born?" I ask.

"Ninety-four." She sets a small electronic disc on top of a painted strawberry. "But it doesn't matter. You're not Korean."

I try not to wince. *But you are Korean*, Yujun had said. I think Boyoung is right, though. To be Korean, wouldn't I have to speak the language, know the customs, actually have lived here? "Right, but I'm in Korea now and while I don't speak the language, I can at least observe the customs. So you're my *unnie*?" I struggle to remember the correct word for older girl.

Boyoung nods, looking half-impressed. "Where did you learn that?"

"I went to Club Dance last night in Incheon with my flatmates. I picked up a few things there."

Boyoung's eyes widen. "Club Dance?"

"I was tired of being a sad sack."

"A sad sack?"

Boyoung's English doesn't always extend to the weird idioms in my vocabulary. "I didn't want to bring down the mood of those around me. Plus, I needed something to distract me."

"Ah, the photos. Did you bring them?"

Yes! I don't pump my fist in the air, but I'm cheering inside my heart. I pull the pictures from my purse and fan them out on the table. "There are names on the back. I looked them up on the internet, but nothing appears." Actually, that's incorrect. There are a lot of results but none that mean anything to me. "Or, at least, nothing that I can decipher."

"You should use Naver," Boyoung says absently as she picks up the first photo. "Also Facebook. Lots of Koreans have Facebook even if most of them don't use it anymore."

She flips through the photos, hesitating when she gets to the third one.

Excitement spikes. I lean forward. "Do you recognize her?"

She shakes her head. "This will be very hard. Do you have any papers? Anything?"

"My mom had stuff from the adoption agency. Like how good of an eater I was. That I could use a spoon. That I smiled when I was around other people. I played well." The documentation from the orphanage wasn't extensive. Mom said it was because it was a private adoption and they weren't required to keep many records, so my file was thin—a half dozen papers and a few pictures. One of them made me look like a prison inmate—if babies were in prison.

Boyoung grimaces slightly. "You were so young."

I shrug. "It's fine. I mean . . . it is what it is. I don't think it matters if you're given up when you're two months or two years. It's all the same." I'd come to terms with it long ago. I was abandoned by one woman but chosen by another. You can dwell on the shitty parts of life or the good parts. I opt for the latter, although . . . does poring over these photos really mean I'm looking forward and not back? No. This is more like a genealogical study than anything else. A data-mining operation. A fact-finding mission. Cold, impersonal facts.

The disc on the table buzzes. Boyoung hops up. "I'll get the drinks."

While Boyoung is off at the counter, I look through the photos again, wishing that they were taken closer so I could better make out their features. Why don't I recognize even one of them? I hold up the third one, the one that Boyoung stopped at, and wait for something to stir inside me. Is that my nose on the woman? Is that my forehead? How about the neck or the fingers? We have a similar figure, fairly straight and not much on top, although the woman in the picture is more slender.

"How will you find these women?"

I jolt in surprise, the photos falling out of my hands onto the table. I hadn't realized Boyoung had returned.

"Do internet searches, I suppose." I take my iced Americano and gulp down a good dose of cold caffeine. "I emailed the DNA company yesterday and told them I deserved to know if there were any other matches—brothers, sisters, cousins."

"What about those other people? What if their families don't know that you were given away?"

This gives me pause. I hadn't given thought to the other people—only me—and it hits me how selfish that is. "I want to know," I say slowly. "I don't want to interrupt their lives or take anything from them. It's just . . . if they're out there, I want to know. Wouldn't you? Wouldn't you want to know the story? Wouldn't you want to know if you have sisters and brothers out there? Or cousins or aunts and uncles?"

"Family isn't all good. My uncle is a drunk who beats his wife," Boyoung says bluntly. "It broke my mom's heart to see her sister like that. It was the one good thing about her dying. She didn't have to face that anymore." My friend tilts her head to study me. "What will change if you know?"

I don't know how to respond to this. I tip a cube of ice into my mouth and chew—on the ice, on Boyoung's words, on the concept of "knowing." From the very beginning, Boyoung has wondered what I'm looking for, but what does it matter? Do I have to have an answer now? Don't you conduct a search to result in a find?

"I don't know. I don't think I'll know until we meet. It could be Oprah good or Maury bad."

Boyoung doesn't get those cultural references so I explain that both are talk shows that make people cry except Oprah brings people together and Maury brings people to fight.

"I didn't see those shows in the US." Boyoung sounds disappointed. "But we do have *Hello Counselor*. Famous people go on it and give advice to regular citizens."

"Famous people . . . like singers?" I think back to Ahn Sangki, who hadn't wanted to go down to the first floor for fear of causing a riot.

"Yes. Like singers. Idols, soloists, rappers, actors, MCs. Those types of people."

"Has DJ Song been on any shows?"

Boyoung's eyes widen. "DJ Song? You know him? I didn't realize he was internationally famous. I mean, you don't know anything about Korea—"

She cuts herself off in embarrassment.

I shrug it off. "No. You're right. I met him last night at the club."

"DJ Song was there?" Boyoung says his name as if I'm uttering the name of a minor deity.

"He was there at the club to support his friends who were performing."

"And you met DJ Song?" She keeps repeating his name. "I'm surprised he wasn't getting mobbed."

"I was outside getting some air and, wow, so this is a convoluted story, but when I was at the airport I mistook someone for the driver you sent, and well, a very nice guy drove me to the rental. I know it was stupid to get into a car with a stranger," I hurriedly add as Boyoung's face turns from awed surprise to horror. "But he was a stand-up guy—rich, I guess, based on the car. It was nice inside. Anyway, when I was at the club, I was outside getting some air because the funeral kind of"—I wave a hand beside my head—"messed me up and I wasn't exactly in the mood for a rave. Outside was this guy, Choi Yujun, and apparently he was waiting for Ahn Sangki. They're friends."

"Ahn Sangki and Choi Yujun . . ." Boyoung trails off, her voice growing faint, her pale skin going from pearl to porcelain.

Boyoung raises her arm, and while the scene unfolds as if time is being stretched like an elastic band, I can't react quickly enough to stop the disaster I see unfolding. Boyoung's arm rises. Her elbow pushes out. It strikes the glass of iced Americano that has been sitting long enough that much of the ice has melted and a sweat circle has formed on the tabletop. The glass, which is still half-full, tips over. I reach for it at the same time that Boyoung notices. Our hands collide and the glass totters. We both gasp and watch in horror as it falls over, spilling onto the pictures.

The minute the liquid strikes the table, I jerk into motion, sweeping the photos up. Boyoung throws napkins on the pool of cold coffee. A café worker runs over with a cloth, but it's too late. The photos are drenched. I shake them out, spraying tiny droplets of coffee-flavored water into our faces while Boyoung apologizes profusely, her English slipping into Korean.

Anxiety is building and my stomach begins to roil. I bite my lip. *It will be fine*, I tell myself. *These photos will dry and nothing will be ruined*. The spill is mopped up, the glasses taken away, and Boyoung collapses in her seat, a pained expression on her face. Is it a reflection of mine? I feel frozen and full of dread. Do I even want to look at the photos? We sit back down and spread the pictures onto the now-dry table. "It will turn out okay," I say.

"I'm sorry, Hara. I'm *jinjja, jinjja* sorry." Her hands shake as they hover over the photos. I want to push them away, push her away, but it was an accident.

"It's fine. It's going to be fine." I'm reassuring both of us at this point.

Her phone rings and then rings again. She has to go. "Let me take these with me. I will find a shop that restores photos."

"No." The denial comes out too sharp. I try again, this time with a forced smile and a nicer tone. "No, thank you. Once they dry out, it'll be fine." I fold a protective hand around the images.

"Text me if you need anything," Boyoung begs as she leaves. "I'll help you whatever way I can."

I can't bring myself to view the damage, not here in the *ttalgi* café surrounded by all the cute decorations. I wait until the images dry, stuff them into my purse, and run home, barely noticing the steep climb up the hill. Burning calves are no match for my panicked heart.

Once home in the empty flat, I dump out the contents of my purse onto the bed. As I'm laying out the photos one by one, I repeat my mantra that it will all be fine. No matter how many times I say the words, though, the outcome is unchanged. The photos are ruined. On two of them the colors of the photograph have bled together and the women's faces are no longer distinguishable. The names are smudged as well. The remaining three have curled corners, but the faces aren't damaged and I think I can make out some of the characters on the back. Maybe Anna remembers them.

I'm angry and upset and I sort of want to call Boyoung and yell at her, but it's not Boyoung's fault. It was an accident. There are still three photos that are in good condition, so I start with them. I take out my phone and photograph the front and back—something I should've done before I left the apartment. Then I carefully transcribe the names:

Kim Eunshil
Kwon Hyeun
Kim Jihye
Lee Mi—
Na Y—

The last two on the list are likely wrong because the ink smeared, but it's the best that I can make out. The final *Hangul* character appears to be a vowel, but it could also be *ya* or *yae* or *ae* or *eo* or *yeo*. Hell, I don't know. I find the Naver app and type in the names. I can't read the *Hangul*, but I scroll through the pictures, hoping one of them sparks recognition.

Boyoung said there was some of Lee Jonghyung in me, but I couldn't see it at the funeral and I don't see it now. While I don't like admitting this, part of me thought that if I saw one of my biological parents, I'd immediately know them. Some part of me would acknowledge some part of them. As I scan the results, all I see are words I don't understand and people I don't recognize.

Frustration and self-loathing creep through me. Why am I so dumb about everything? Why didn't I scan these photos into my phone before taking them out? Why didn't I learn Korean at some point in my life? Why do I even care so much about what anyone thinks, especially my dead dad—either of them? Who cares? Who cares? Who *cares*? I drop the phone and squeeze my nose bridge.

My heart is racing and a damp sweat breaks out along my hairline. The usual bindings I have wrapped around my emotions are fraying. I close my eyes and take a breath . . . and then another.

Get a grip, Hara, I order. *You have a translation app. There are people who will help you. Stop dramatizing things.*

I inhale again and pick up the phone. The first thing is to triangulate the age of the women I'm looking for. My birth mother was likely young and unwed, so I need to be searching for people within the ages of forty-three and, maybe, forty-seven? That narrows it down. And I have names. Granted I can't fully make out two of them, but three names and an identifiable year of birth are a lot. I pull out a notebook and make five columns. This is going to be challenging but not impossible.

As I'm creating my matrix, a text message pops up.

YUJUN: It's me. By my count, it's been fourteen hours since we last saw each other and that's too long.

The next text is an address.

YUJUN: You need to have korean beef. Best in the world. My treat. What time?

It's more of a demand than an invitation. The way it's worded . . . well, I can hardly say no. It's as if Yujun pulled the brake on my hamster wheel just as it was about to hit five hundred miles per hour and break away from the stand to go clattering off the counter and into a traffic pattern of doom. I can almost feel his long fingers curl around my shoulder and squeeze. At a time like this, when all of my life seems so uncertain, having Yujun is a comfort. So, yes, I do need Korean beef, especially if it's the best in the world, along with every other morsel of joy that being with Yujun brings.

CHAPTER THIRTEEN

BEFORE I MEET YUJUN, I DO AN INTERNET SEARCH FOR THE BIG-gest mistakes someone can make in Korea—something I should have done before I came here. Age is a big thing. I should offer to pay for the second round of any drinks. Most places do not require you to take off your shoes, but wearing socks just in case does not hurt. Don't talk on the subway or the bus—I'd already figured that one out from my ride with Boyoung to the funeral home—and don't point. Don't stick your chopsticks in your rice, as that's what they do at funerals. I didn't see that at my father's but he didn't have much of a ceremony either. Koreans are big into gift giving. I'll have to re-member that. I also find some simple Korean sentences for "hello," "how much," and "where's the bathroom." I try them out but know I'm getting the pronunciation all wrong. I bookmark the link and get ready, reciting the words as I wash my face, brush my teeth and dress. *Annyeonghaseyo, eolmayeyo, hwajangshireun eodiseyo?* "Hello, how much, where's the bathroom?" *Annyeonghaseyo, eolmayeyo, hwa-jangshireun eodiseyo?*

My options for date clothes are thin. I'd been focused on the proper attire for a family reunion, not trying to look sexy for a man. To be quite honest, though, my past attempts at sexiness have never been super successful. I don't have the body for it. I'm small on top and straight down below. It might not be an exaggeration to say a board has more curves than me. Since I wore skinny jeans to the club, I search for something different. I wish I had more skirts. There are so many girls and women here in pretty dresses—even on the subway I noticed it.

The nicest thing in my suitcase at the moment is the black silk funeral dress I need to return to Boyoung, but I want to clean it first. I put that on my list of things to do tomorrow. The other dress I have is more Sunday school than Saturday night, so I end up wearing a pair of regular jeans, a white camisole, and a slightly oversize pink and yellow plaid shirt, unbuttoned and knotted at the waist. It looks decent with a pair of pale pink flats and gold hoops. I'm not going to stop traffic but I look *okay*? I hope.

None of my roommates make it home before I leave, but I download an app a travel site recommends and input the address that Yujun texted. The app tells me how to get to the subway, where to transfer, and how long it will take—all in English. When I arrive at the restaurant, I feel competent enough to conquer a small country, or at least demolish some delicious Korean beef.

The eatery is small, with a half dozen empty booths lining the walls. Lattice-like partitions provide privacy for each table. There's no one at the front—just an empty register. I freeze, unsure of what to do, until the tall, lean figure of Choi Yujun appears from beyond one of the screens. He waves me forward in that Korean way with his fingers pointed toward the ground. A smile of delight threatens to bust across my face and make me look decidedly uncool. I rub my lips together so as not to blind Yujun with my eagerness as I hurry to his side.

"You look pretty," he says and pulls out a chair.

Whether he's lying or he means it, I don't care! It feels good to hear this gorgeous man say it. "Thanks." I beam, no longer able to keep the happiness off my face. I start to sit when my eyes fall to a pretty packaged gift on the side of the table. My smile slides off immediately. A gift. I'd forgotten to bring a gift. It was in the list of customs and practices that I'd reviewed earlier, but in my haste to get ready and arrive at the restaurant, I'd forgotten. Could I possibly run out and buy something real quick under the pretense of having to use the bathroom? Of course that would only work if I could recall the phrase for "where is the bathroom?" *Annyeonghaseyo* I remember, but what was the bathroom one? *Hwagon edeyeo? Hwagahaseyo?*

"Is something wrong with the chair?" Yujun asks.

I realize I'm hovering stupidly over my chair while Yujun looks on in confusion. "Nope." I drop inelegantly into my seat and try smiling again, but it feels awkward. Where was all the confidence I gained from navigating the subway on my own? Somewhere in my shoes, I guess.

Yujun returns to the other side of the table and presses a button. "Is it okay if I order for us? I know that can seem . . ." He pauses, not quite sure what word to use.

"It's fine. Great, actually. I'm going to leave myself in your hands." Your perfect, large, nicely veined hands.

"Wonderful."

A staff person arrives and Yujun gives the order. I listen closely and try to make out certain words. I think I hear "bulgogi" and *kalbi*, which I remember are marinated beef and short ribs, but *ddeokbokki* I'm not certain of, nor am I familiar with *soondubu jjigae*.

When I ask Yujun, he explains, "*Ddeokbokki* is a spicy rice cake, and *soondubu jjigae* is a soft tofu stew. Spicy and very good."

He reaches out to pour the water but I nearly leap onto the table to grab it. "I'm supposed to pour," I remind him.

He looks like he's going to fight me for a moment but eventually sits back and motions for me to go ahead. "So you are. Have you been researching?"

"A little bit," I admit, "but I forget more than I remember." I eye his gift again, which he's made no move to give to me. Maybe I'm overreacting and it's for his mom.

"Did you have a difficult time finding the place? I could have picked you up. I'm always available to do so."

"Your instructions were perfect and I enjoy riding the subway, I guess. I feel like I've accomplished something when I go places by myself. Like I'm a local."

"Have you been to many places since you've been here?"

It's on the tip of my tongue to tell him that no, I've spent two of my days in a funeral home. Part of me wants to tell him the whole story—how I got here only to find that my bio dad had passed away, how my inheritance was photos of five different women, how my friend Boyoung spilled my drink on the photos and I don't have the first idea how I'm going to find these women—but as I look at him across the table, his brown eyes bright with interest and a small smile playing across his lips, I decide not to. I don't want to taint this time I have with Yujun. He's like this light in the middle of a dark night. I want this memory of my trip here to be good, and I know this brief flirtation, these dinners together, the charming smile, will linger long in my memory so that no matter what else happens, I can pull these occasions out of my memory bank. That's what I want to take home with me, not the smell of incense and the single portrait of my father on a bare altar, missed opportunities, what-could-have-beens.

I don't want this, my homeland, to be a place that I associate with sorrow.

"I went to a strawberry café. It was adorable. Everything was strawberry themed, even the food."

"Oh? I like strawberries," he says, his right dimple flashing at me. "Did you like it?"

"I don't know if it's any good. I ended up spilling my drink and left after I cleaned it up."

"Then we'll have to try it out together." He beams.

I almost swallow my tongue. "Absolutely." Any time that I can spend basking in the sunlight sounds good to me.

"Any other places you visited other than the *ttalgi* café?"

I love how Korean sounds when he talks, more so than English. I wish I could understand more so that I could hear his native language with the soft *l*'s and the long vowels.

"I've walked around the neighborhood where I'm staying. There are five chicken restaurants, the strawberry café, a laundromat"—I tick the shops off on my fingers—"and some other stores. I'm not sure what they all are. I couldn't figure out from the lettering and I didn't want to stare through the window for fear the owners would think I was casing the joint."

"Casing the joint?" Yujun's eyebrow goes up.

"It means to survey an establishment to see if you want to rob it."

"Ah, interesting. Casing the joint," he repeats, folding the words over on his tongue so he can use the expression later. He stores English phrases while I file away Korean ones. We're the same in our different ways.

"I read that *Hangul* was designed to learn in one day, but I've tried and either I'm dumb or the people in King Sejong's era were mad smart."

He laughs, his hand coming up to cover a flash of perfect teeth.

"I don't think you're dumb, but it's possible people in King Sejong's time were brilliant. Have you visited his statue yet?"

"No. I haven't made it to that part of Seoul yet."

"Then I will put King Sejong's statue on your tour list. Any other requests?"

"I'm going to leave it in your capable hands." In between searching for the identities of the five women in my photos, I am going to spend as much time as possible with Yujun from Seoul.

He seems to like that. "Namsan, then, and the Seoul City Wall because those two have the best views of the city. Seoul Forest because it's quiet and shady and full of trees."

The right dimple, the deep one, makes a brief appearance before the waiter comes over and turns on the grill. Soon after, small bowls of what Yujun calls *banchan* are delivered.

"Cabbage kimchi, marinated soybeans, fish cakes, sweet potatoes, and scallion salad. The fish cakes are salty and don't taste like fish," he explains. "Every restaurant has their own *banchan*, a little like every restaurant in Italy serves their own *limoncello*."

"I didn't know that about *banchan* or *limoncello*," I admit.

Yujun shrugs lightly. "Another thing for your to-do list. Seems like I'll have to keep you around for a while."

It's a joke. I'm in Korea for only two weeks, but there's nothing wrong with the fiction that Yujun is spinning as long as I don't get caught up in the fantasy of this dinner being a regular occurrence.

He captures a piece of cabbage kimchi between his chopsticks and with one hand tucked under his elbow, he reaches across the table and places the food on the small plate in front of me. I wonder if I should do the same in return. Boyoung never covered dating rituals. I'm saved from asking these awkward questions when the waiter arrives with a huge platter of sliced meat. The waiter says something in Korean and Yujun replies, this time also in Korean.

"The waiter doesn't speak English or I would have replied in English. I told him we would cook our meat ourselves." He picks up a pair of tongs and starts laying strips of meat across the heated grill. My mouth waters as the *kalbi* and bulgogi start to sizzle.

"I used to live in America," he volunteers as he finishes placing the first round of meat on the grill. "My mother died when I was four and my father thought I needed a mother's influence, so he sent me to Aunt Sue. Her full name is Choi Soomin but she adopted the name Sue in America. It was easier, she explained, than having to say her name ten times before anyone caught on. She had this beautiful cottage close to Malibu Beach. I got brown as an acorn, running around on the shore, and I picked up the language quick. Kids do that," he says, trying to explain away his own natural brilliance.

"Sounds like you had fun."

"About as much fun as an Asian boy can have in a community that's mostly Caucasian. There are pockets of Los Angeles that are thick with Asians, but not Malibu."

Ah. We share a look of understanding. He knows what it's like to be Asian in America. How it's fine but also not fine. You aren't followed around in the store. No one thinks you're going to cause trouble, but for Yujun, it would mean that he wasn't manly enough, and for me it meant that I was pretty for an Asian. A few years ago during parents' weekend at college, a father of another student spent a good ten minutes trying to convince me to test out his hotel mattress. I reminded him that he was, well, old, and wearing a wedding ring. He'd replied that when you went to buy a new car at his age, you wanted an exotic, foreign model. At twenty-one I hadn't had the ovaries to slap him. If I could do it again, I'd at least throw a beer in his face. But Asian girls were presumed to be subservient and exotic. I think guys believed I would pull out some wild sexual maneuver when all I really knew how to do was swivel my hips.

"So a carnival of fun," I reply.

"I developed a bad stutter," he admits.

"No." I don't want to believe it because it would've taken a lot of awful comments to make a child stutter, and that sounds like an actual crime.

"It's true," he says cheerfully, clearly over that childhood trauma. He flips the meat over. Grease makes a spitting noise and smoke is sucked up the vent flume resting a bare foot above the grill. "My *appa* came over for a visit and I stuttered so badly that we could barely have a conversation. That was the end of my stay in America. He brought me back to Korea and I've been here since. Well, I did go to college in the States, which helped develop my English-language skills."

"They're better than mine," I tell him. "Was it better the second time around?"

"Much. I didn't stutter anymore and I even thought about staying and working there, but my *appa*"—he pauses and there's something that he decides against sharing—"and my *eomma* needed help. *Eomma* is 'mother' in Korean. She's technically my stepmother but we're very close. She helped me get over my stutter." He smiles fondly. "And when she took over our company, she made changes, some of which were very unpopular, but it helped so many people, particularly disadvantaged people." He speaks of his stepmother with a great deal of pride and affection. "Ah, enough of that. Have you been to LA?" He changes the subject.

"No. I went to DC on a class trip when I was in seventh grade and my mom took me to Chicago a couple of times. It's fairly close, relatively speaking."

"You mean in America terms."

"We do have a different standard of measurement when it comes to geography," I agree. Korea is roughly the size of Indiana but has eight times the people, so six hours can take you across the country here, whereas back in America, it takes you to the state's border. "Anyway, I'm uncultured. I admit it."

It's not a great feeling, either. I don't know why I haven't traveled more. There was the opportunity to travel to Spain with my Spanish class my sophomore year of high school, but I ended up staying home after getting into a fight with my then best friend, Sophie. One day at lunch she told everyone at our table that my refrigerator smelled like dirty socks. My mom had tried to make some kimchi but it didn't quite work out, and yeah, the house did smell bad, but it took me back to when I was in elementary school and kids made stupid—but surprisingly cruel—comments about stinky Asians. Sophie apologized and said it was a joke, but I hadn't wanted to spend ten days with her after that. I spent spring break baking apple pies and Mom stopped making Korean dishes.

"America has different standards of measurement for everything. Who measures things in feet?" Yujun serves me the cooked meat and I refill the grill. We get down a good system of cooking and serving. The meat is melt-in-your-mouth tender. *Hanwoo*, Yujun explains, is a special Korean beef that isn't allowed for export because the government wants to keep the best for its own citizens. "How long are you here for?"

"Two weeks. I guess a week and a half now." Four days have already passed. It feels longer. The time at the funeral seemed endless at moments.

"We'll have to stuff a whole fish while you're here."

I don't need an internet search to tell me what this Korean idiom means. We are going to try to do as much as we can in a short time.

"Yes, I'd like that."

The whole experience is lovely. The restaurant is another small one with what appears to be only one server, but he bustles about delivering *banchan* to newcomers followed by platters of meat and sometimes vegetables for roasting. I eat way too much but I don't want the dinner to end. A glow of warmth spreads as we talk and eat and drink. The whole dinner is like sitting in the sunshine with the rays warming me from my bones out. He's animated when he speaks—his eyes sparkle, his hands move, his right dimple pops in and out.

At times, I stop eating to lean my chin on my hand and enjoy the moment. I've never been good at that. It's always been a race to achieve one goal after another, whether it was the spelling bee or the science fair or premium marks on the SATs or graduating with honors.

"I'm talking too much," he says.

"No." That could never happen. Never in a million years could I imagine not wanting to hear him talk. Granted this is our first date, but sometimes you know things are true. Like when I look up and see that the sky is blue and down at my feet and see that the grass is green. Those immutable facts that don't change even when the grass sinks back to its seed to prepare for the first freeze and the skies turn stormy gray. "I want to know everything."

THE GIFT WAS a small box of chocolates. Yujun had said it was my dessert. I felt relieved it wasn't something more extravagant. When we saw each other again, I'd be prepared with my own chocolate. No, something that lasts. Not that I'd expect him to put a gift of mine on his desk, but something that lasts more than a day, more than a moment. I'll be gone, but I want there to be something that he comes across six months from now or two years from now that makes him smile with fondness—or something more. I'm not sure what.

The next day, I take the metro to a bookstore Jules recommended and buy a couple of books on learning Korean. I spend the rest of the afternoon practicing the *Hangul* characters, and by the time dinner rolls around, I feel like I have the hang of it. With help from the workbooks and YouTube tutorials, I can recognize the characters and make the basic sounds. It's putting them together to form actual words that's the problem.

But I have the tools now. I downloaded the Korean keyboard on my phone and laptop. I have apps, the textbook, access to videos. If I apply myself, I can learn. Of course, I should've done this before I came, but I'm doing it now and that's the important thing.

I know enough to begin my search and I start from the top: Kim Eunshil. It's not an uncommon name. There are hundreds of search results and based on a couple of the pictures, one is a doctor or, perhaps, a scientist given the lab coat she's wearing. Another one is dressed in a suit, and there are a few in their school uniforms. The thing is that none of the pictures strikes any chord of recognition. I scroll through so many photos and pages that it becomes a blur, like a Mark Rothko painting with giant swatches of colors bleeding together.

My flatmates come home from work, one after the other, looking tired. When Jules arrives, she's carrying two white plastic bags with something heavenly in them.

"Korean fried chicken," she says, plunking them on the table.

"Ten thousand won?" That was the buy-in price the first night.

"Yup."

I dig out the appropriate bill and slide it toward Jules. Anna pockets it instead.

"I paid." She sits down next to me. "Whatcha doing?"

"Looking up these names." I point to my list.

"What names?" Jules calls from the kitchen.

"She's trying to find her birth mother," Anna answers for me. "Remember? I told you she had the funeral a couple of days ago."

"Wow. You just got here and had to go to a funeral? That's rough." Mel carries over a stack of plastic cups and a pitcher of water. Behind her, Jules trails with plates and napkins and clear plastic gloves to handle the chicken.

"So these are your mom?" Jules pulls a glove on one hand and picks up the photos with the other. "What happened to these two?"

"Coffee accident."

"Sucks. Looks like the names are gone from these two. What else have you found?"

"Not much."

"Give me one." Mel wiggles her fingers.

"Yeah, I can do one, too," Anna volunteers. She plunks a picture in front of Jules. "You, too."

Jules makes a face.

"It's fine," I say quickly, reaching for the picture. "I've got this."

Jules moves it out of my reach. "I'll do it, but you should eat the chicken with chopsticks or you're going to get grease on your photos."

We all do, forgoing the plastic gloves in order to keep the photos in good shape. It's a thoughtful gesture from Jules, who oftentimes comes off as cold.

"Thank you," I tell her.

She shrugs and stuffs a piece of chicken into her mouth. With the photos passed around, phones and laptops come out. In between bites of crispy chicken—no wonder there's one on every block, the stuff is delicious—my flatmates and I search up the names.

"God, who could believe there are so many Kim Eunshils. This one is twelve." Anna holds up her phone for everyone to see. "She won a presidential award for excellence in linguistics, which means she speaks English well."

"Japanese, too," Mel suggests. "Everyone here learns two languages. Sometimes three, depending on how much money you have. How many languages does your *chaebol* speak?"

"Yujun?" I don't bother to correct her assumption that he's mine. "He speaks English." He had come back from a business trip to Hong Kong. "Maybe Chinese?"

"Oh, probably. And Japanese, too." Mel nods to herself. "That's pretty common for high-level execs. The more languages you speak, the better."

"How about this Kim Jihye? She kind of looks like the picture?" Jules interjects.

Anna turns Jules's phone screen around and holds the photo of Kim Jihye next to it. In my photo, Jihye is wearing a light-colored skirt with a high waist and a red T-shirt. A long necklace dangles low. Her hair is cut short and she has small circle shades on. The image on Jules's screen is a mere headshot. The hair is slightly longer, a little like Mel's chin-length bob. Her red lips are a straight, unsmiling line.

"It's hard to say because of the sunglasses." Jules squints at the screen. "How old is your mom?"

"My mother is—my adoptive mother is fifty-five."

"I think your bio mom would be younger," muses Jules. "Most women who give up babies are young, right?"

I have never done any demographic research but it's what I've assumed, too. "I don't know exactly, but it sounds right."

"This Kim Jihye is forty-four, and that would make her nineteen when she had you."

"Eighteen, actually," Jules interjects, flipping her long hair over her shoulder. "You're born one year old in Korea and then you turn a year old at the New Year, so you're not actually twenty-five here. You'd be twenty-six. Maybe twenty-seven depending on the date you were born."

"If she's twenty-seven, you'd have to call me *unnie*," Anna teases. "That's what younger girls call older girls. Jules is twenty-six here. If you're older than her, you get to tell her what to do."

Jules scowls at this. "What year were you born again?"

"Ninety-five. Same as you." She must've forgotten our age discussion at the bar.

"Right! You're same-age friends. Ninety-five-liners," Anna crows. "*Chingu* is the word—"

"For friend," I finish, feeling like I'm fluent because I know one word.

Jules's frown makes a reappearance. For some reason, she doesn't like the idea of being same-age friends.

"Mel and I are your *unnies*, which is essentially 'older sister.' If you were a boy, you'd call us *noona*."

"But she's not a boy and we're not Korean, so don't call me *chingu*. I think this is her." Jules shoves her screen under my nose. "She's the right age and if you put sunglasses on her, the shape of the face is the same—oval with a small forehead. You have a small forehead." Jules lifts my hand and presses it against my head. "See. It's three fingers, maybe four if you squeeze them together. This woman has a small forehead too. You don't recognize her?"

I shake my head. "No, but I'll check her out."

"What if she doesn't speak English?" Anna asks. "Do you want one of us to go with you?"

"I can't," Jules declares, pushing away from the table. "I've got a flight to Shanghai tomorrow. I'll be gone until Friday."

"I've got a full schedule tomorrow, too," Mel says with regret. "You do, too, Anna. We've got finals coming up."

"It's fine. I can get Boyoung to go with me or I'll use the translation app."

"Let's write down some phrases for her," Anna suggests. Jules sits back down and together the three huddle over the phone.

My hands begin to tremble although I'm not sure whether it's due to nerves or excitement. Tomorrow I could be meeting my mother for the first time. It's overwhelming. A surge of energy brings me to my feet. I could run laps around the hill and not be tired.

"Is there an ice cream or dessert shop still open?" I ask. I need something to do.

"I think the *ttalgi* café is open until ten. Why?" Anna asks.

"Because you all deserve a treat for helping me so much, and if I'm going to interrogate this woman tomorrow, I should bring a gift, right?" It's an excuse but a valid one.

"Ohh, good idea. I'll have the milk cake. That's so good." Mel rubs her stomach.

"I'll take a milk cake, too," Jules says.

"I'll go with you," Anna volunteers. "Let me get my purse."

While my flatmate scurries off, I study the image of Kim Jihye and wait for something to stir inside me, but it could be a stock photo. I have a more visceral reaction to Twitter profile pictures of people I don't know than to Kim Jihye. However, since I was dead inside when I saw my own father, I refuse to take this as a negative sign. I was left on the street as an infant. I shouldn't be expected to recognize my biological parents. I place a hand on my forehead and then look down at the screen. Jules does appear to be correct. Kim Jihye's forehead is the same size as mine.

"I think it could be her," Anna says, appearing at the door. "Do you think it is?"

"I don't know. I don't want to get my hopes up." But I'm already sweating.

"You could email her. She had a work contact on her profile."

My whole body tenses at that. Send her an email and have that out there, drifting around in the internet space while I wait for a response? The anxiety would keep me up all night.

"No. I should ask in person." Maybe it's foolish, but I'm holding out hope that when I see Kim Jihye face-to-face it will be different. There's no response inside me when I look at the photos, but in person, I imagine that the part of me that came from her will activate, as if we are two magnets that snap together once we are close enough. In fact, that elemental pull might be the very reason I'm here in Seoul right now.

"I can see that. It sucks that the first thing you did when you got here was go to a funeral. I know we barely know each other, but if you want to talk, I have a sturdy shoulder."

At five foot six inches, I'm not a giant, but I have at least five inches on Anna.

"What? I'm small but mighty." She flexes an arm, and if there's a muscle there, it's not visible to the human eye.

"I'm good," I tell her.

"All right. So besides the funeral, are you enjoying yourself here in Seoul?"

My mind flashes to the dinner with Yujun last night. It was one of the nicest dinners I've ever had. "Yeah. I think tomorrow I'll do something touristy. I heard there's a statue of King Sejong somewhere."

"Oh yeah, he's downtown at the Gwanghwamun Plaza along with Admiral Yi Sunsin. It's an easy subway ride. There's a ton of stuff to do over there. There's a museum and a palace. The entry fees aren't too expensive either. It's a nice way to spend the day." Anna chatters on, adding details about all the things I can do including lunch at the top of city hall, a couple of museums, and *hanbok* rental shops. If I rent one I can get into the palace for a discount. The strawberry café is nearly empty and it takes no time to buy our desserts. Milk cake for Mel and Jules and a strawberry-cream-filled white cake for Anna. At Anna's suggestion, I buy sugared strawberry candies for Kim Jihye instead of something perishable because "carrying around a cake in the subway is no fun," Anna declares as she swipes her phone across the payment pad. The staff boxes everything up in an elegant white container decorated with a green ribbon and paper tag with a smiling strawberry. Seoul isn't all funeral homes and dead dads. It is also darling packages, kind staff people, and welcoming flatmates.

"How long have you lived here?" I ask.

"A little under two years. I'll be going home soon. Oregon," she provides before I have to ask. "I'd love to stay longer, but even though the pay is decent and the rent is covered by my school, it's not something I can do long-term because of benefits and stuff. Plus, I miss my family. I know I'm going to miss being here once I leave, though, so it's bad either way."

"What made you come here in the first place?"

The corner of her mouth lifts. "A boy, but not in the traditional sense. I had the biggest crush on this Korean exchange student at my high school, and so I started learning all about Korea so I could talk to him. The more I studied the language and the history and the people, the more I wanted to come here and see everything for myself."

"What happened with the boy?"

"He had a girlfriend back home, and to avoid turning girls down, he pretended he couldn't understand you."

"That's sort of hilarious."

"I know, right?" Anna laughs. "Anyway, I'm glad I came. Korea's beautiful. Amazing food, super clean, the people are as nice as can be. I mean, sure, there's a lot wrong with it, but isn't there a lot wrong everywhere in the world? It's too bad you can't stay longer. It's hard to get a feel for a place being here such a short while."

"I didn't plan this well," I admit with a half smile. "I hardly ever do things like this. I like itineraries and schedules. I work best with them. Here, I'm flying by the seat of my pants and it feels . . . weird."

"Weird good or weird bad?"

"Neither. Just weird."

"Do some fun stuff so your memories aren't full of disappointments. I want you to go home loving Seoul like me," Anna advises. "But—and I don't mean to be a total downer—hooking up with a Korean guy you met at an airport might not be the safest thing. Rich guys here are a lot like rich guys everywhere. They've had an easy life and expect a lot of things."

"He's not like that," I start to reply, but I give up because I can tell by the expression on my flatmate's face that she doesn't believe me. To be fair, I would be telling Boyoung the same story back in Iowa. Beware of the dogs that lure you in with sweet smiles because their teeth are as sharp as the teeth of the ones that growl.

CHAPTER FOURTEEN

THE TEXT FROM YUJUN COMES RIGHT BEFORE I'M ABOUT TO turn in. A few years ago, I would've characterized this as a booty text. Any message sent after, say, eight in the evening is seeking one thing, which would be consistent with all the warnings I've gotten from Boyoung and Jules and Anna. If I was smart, I wouldn't even unlock my phone to read the message, but I don't have that kind of willpower. Didn't Anna say to do some fun stuff so I'm not filled with bad memories? I flick my finger against the screen and read the message.

YUJUN: Dinner tomorrow night?

Of course he's not sending me a booty call. This is a guy who carried my suitcase up a thousand steps—or what seemed like a thousand steps. Besides, for someone like him, there are plenty of women willing to warm his bed. There were women at the airport who tripped over their luggage when he smiled. Why he has an interest in me is a mystery, but I'm not going to question it. Why do that to my self-esteem?

ME: Ye—

I stop before the last letter. What am I actually doing here? Just because Yujun is decent and gorgeous and kind and has dimples deep enough to get lost in doesn't actually mean I should dive in. The warnings of my friend and flatmates weren't issued because they want to stop me from being happy but rather because they don't want me to get hurt. Yujun is a distraction—a sweet, wonderful distraction—but the point of this trip is to find my biological family. That's what I came here to do. Not run around with a rich boy who thinks it's cute to play tour guide, no matter how wonderful he is. *Damn.* I press the back button angrily.

ME: I'm sorry but I have plans. Thank you. For everything.

YUJUN: If your plans fall through, the view of Seoul from Namsan Tower is amazing. Daebak, we Koreans would say.

I'd seen that needle-pointed tower on nearly every travel site I'd visited as I was buying my tickets and getting ready to come here. It was even in a K-drama I'd watched with Boyoung, so turning down a visit to the tower, which is top of my list to visit, is very sad.

ME: Thanks

It's sufficiently terse that I don't get a reply. Not even an attempted one where the three dots appear, causing you to hold your breath in anticipation. I plug in my phone, climb into bed, and try not to be upset that Yujun took my rejection to heart. The audacity of him to respect my wishes!

I get no sleep. I'm mad that I turned Yujun down. I'm mad I don't know more *Hangul*. I'm mad my dad died before I got here. I didn't even get an opportunity to curse him out for abandoning me. I didn't hear his excuses about being poor and unprepared for fatherhood. I didn't get to tell him how it didn't matter that he gave me away because I lived a good life—am currently living a good life. I was robbed of that and it pisses me off.

I roll out of bed at dawn with scratchy eyes and a sore throat. The bathroom mirror says I should go back to bed for at least five days, but I know if I lie down again, I will want to text Yujun, spam email Kim Jihye, and basically do all the things that aren't good for me. I have to get out of the house. I don my single Sunday dress and toss a cardigan around my shoulders. I'm halfway down the walk when I realize I've forgotten the strawberry candies. I dart back into the house and stuff the box into my purse.

I wander down one alley and then another, avoiding the main six-lane road and keeping to the small passages where it's easy to forget that I'm in a city of millions. Seoul in the early morning is quiet. There aren't many cars on the streets and the city feels like it's still sleeping. Metal gates are rolled down, covering store windows. The lights are off inside cafés and coffee shops. A few people stream in and out of the occasional twenty-four-hour convenience store carrying small plastic sacks of goods. Some are even sipping coffee from to-go cups. I'd like to go inside and get my own coffee but I don't think I'd know how to run a machine or communicate with a clerk, so I keep walking.

I haven't paid much attention to the city itself since I arrived. I've scouted the area around the place I'm staying and it's a mix of midrise buildings filled with restaurants, cosmetic stores, and other small businesses. There always seem to be a lot of people walking with purpose. In the underground subway tunnels, there's another city, with vendors selling hot foods, umbrellas, socks, and shoes. Music drifts out from the stores like a conveyor-belt radio station. Move down one storefront and you get a different song.

The other thing that strikes me about the city is how clean it is. There are no empty cups or napkins or cigarette butts lining the streets. The garbage cans aren't overflowing. For a big city, it doesn't feel as massive as it should. It reminds me of home in some ways. There aren't the towering high-rises of Chicago or New York. On this side of the river the building heights are limited. The skyscrapers are to the south, whereas here, the taller buildings can't be much more than twenty or thirty floors. I read in one of my searches that this is because the old palaces are here and city zoning laws limit how high the buildings can get. Everyone deserves to see the palaces. I want to visit one. You can't see what they look like from the outside, as tall walls surround the entire grounds, and it's partly because they're hidden that my curiosity is piqued. After I hunt down these five women, then I'll go.

I don't know how far I walk but my feet grow sore and my calves ache and there's a low pain in the middle of my back and all of that is good because I've been able to successfully distract myself for a few hours. The traffic is starting to pick up and the quietness of the streets is being erased by the sounds of cars, buses, and people. The sun is baking my dress to my back.

Near one of the city gates, I discover the remnants of an old fortress wall. The stone stairs leading up disappear into a cove of trees. I find a burst of energy and clamber up the wooden steps. A woven burlap mat covers the dirt trail, providing cushion and grip. My thighs and calves appreciate it. Under one dense collection of trees, a bench appears. I collapse on it. I'm not fit enough for all this walking. Back home, I drive everywhere.

Around five minutes later, an older man, in his seventies, dressed in a sports coat and loafers, strolls by with his hands clasped behind his back. He barely gives me a nod of acknowledgment. A little while later, two ladies dressed in exercise gear huff up the hill. The two eye me with a frown, likely wondering why I'm not at work.

I pull out my cell phone and duck my head, pretending to be preoccupied, which is a mistake because the last text I have is the one I sent to Yujun. I scan my messages and am shocked to see my mom so low. I haven't talked to her in a couple of days. I'm a little surprised she hasn't texted me, though. I tap her name and then stop. Maybe it's best that I don't contact her. She might ask questions that I don't feel comfortable answering, and I don't want to lie to her. Plus, if she hasn't contacted me, it means she's occupied, which is good. Better not to wake the sleeping dog.

As for Yujun—or even Kim Jihye—I don't know what to do about either of them. The one brings me anxiety and the other brings me joy, and it gets mixed up in my head and my heart until the dampness on my skin isn't from the sun but from something inside me.

I turn my phone off and get to my feet. Doing something is better than sitting here and turning into a roasted potato in the shade. I follow the meandering trail up the hill, focusing on the immense skyline of Seoul below. It's an intimidating sight. I laugh a little at thinking that Seoul was small. Up here, it feels like even the mountains are dwarfed by the massive number of buildings squished together. In this great big city with its ten million people, do I even have a chance of finding my family?

A lump develops in my throat—the small, wiry kind that scratches whenever I try to swallow. I rub a hand across my forehead. What exactly am I trying to prove here? Was I trying to find my mother or something else? I hate this uncertainty. I hate having all these emotions. It is messy and unsettling and I wish for a hot minute I was back in Iowa where there is nothing but flat land, cornfields, and serenity.

"Ha!" The bark of laughter escapes me. As if. If my Iowa self was so happy, why'd I come here?

That thought tumbles through my head as I walk, taking a turn here, branching off there. The sun beats down on my head, my legs grow tired, and my mind empties out as I navigate the trail. I walk by a driving range, through a large parking lot filled with more luxury cars than the country club back home, past giant rocks with etchings on them set in a garden of sand. The path leads me down, down, down until I emerge at an intersection eight lanes wide. My eyes skip from the asphalt roadway to the lights hanging over the center of the crosswalks to the large banner arching over the entrance to yet another steep incline.

Namsan Park.

I pluck the dress away from my chest, read the letters again, and shake my head.

> If your plans fall through, the view of Seoul from Namsan
> Tower is amazing.

If I believed in signs, this would be a big one.

I REMEMBER WATCHING *The Hunt for Red October* with my dad. Pat loved spy movies—the Bond movies, Jason Bourne, John le Carré adaptations. The plots of the movies all sort of run together for me. Men with guns chasing more men with guns. Sometimes there are airplanes involved. Most of the time there are explosions. I don't have any specific recollection of exactly what *The Hunt* was about, but I remember a bearded actor with a low-pitched voice

spending the whole movie looking for someone inside the subma-
rine. That's all these spy movies were about—the search for someone.

At this moment, as my legs grow numb and my eyes begin to
water from staring at the glass doors of the office building in front of
me, I feel a little like the ship captain looking endlessly for someone
and coming up empty-handed.

Paper crinkles in my grip. Okay, not literally empty-handed because in the three hours that I've stood in front of the building, I've
had about fifteen flyers shoved in my hand. People stream in and out
and it's hard to track everyone. All I have is a small screenshot of
Kim Jihye's face and I'm not sure I could pick out Ellen's face from
this big crowd.

Perhaps I should go inside. I could say I was delivering flowers or
that I was bringing over a business proposal from America. Of
course, that would require someone inside to speak English because
I have no idea how to say any of that in Korean. Those weren't options on the list the girls prepared for me. I should've brought Boyoung, but I had this wild idea this morning that I could do this on
my own. I found Namsan Tower on my own! I could make out the
Hangul letters! I was fluent! Not really, but a few hours ago I had
convinced myself of my own power. Now, not so much.

Straightening my shoulders, I decide to brave the building. It becomes immediately apparent that I'm not dressed appropriately. Everyone who has entered or exited the high-rise has looked polished
with their nice dress shoes, dark pants, and white shirts with the lan-
yards strung around their necks. I'm wearing a black cotton dress with
thin white stripes, a black cardigan, and a pair of sandals, which were
perfect for my day of sightseeing, but it doesn't say "smart businessper-
son," which is the attitude everyone but me is selling.

No one pays a dot of attention to me as I enter the building. I
aim straight for the lobby desk manned by two men wearing dark

suits. Neither smiles as I approach but one dips his head and says something in Korean that I don't understand, as per usual.

"I'm sorry. I don't speak Korean, but I'm looking for this woman." I hold up my phone. "Can you help me?"

The man's face shows a flicker of surprise and he exchanges a look with his coworker. They both peer at the photo.

"Fourth floor. Daehoon Group is on the fourth floor." He points upward.

I almost drop the phone. I didn't expect them to answer. "F-fourth?"

I'm not sure why I'm surprised. I'm standing here in the lobby of this office building because the internet told me that Kim Jihye works here. But suddenly my heart is beating faster and my stomach begins to somersault. I'm standing in the same building as my mother. We're breathing the same air. She's four floors away.

I press shaky hands against my face. The cell phone feels overly warm against one cheek. I bow and then move toward the elevators. One of the men speaks sharply to me. When I turn back, I see him pointing at my chest.

"ID," he says.

ID? I blank out for a moment and then fumble in my purse for my passport. "Here." I hurry back and show it to him.

He scrutinizes it and then picks up a phone. Oh. He's calling Kim Jihye. That's not good. The woman won't know who I am. She won't let me up. My mind empties out and I react in panic, grabbing my passport from security and motoring toward the elevator. Someone behind me shouts but I don't listen. I'm too close and I won't be stopped because of some office protocol that does not apply to me. I speed around the corner, ignoring surprised office workers who stop to watch me scurry to the elevator bank. Once there, I jab the up button repeatedly. I hear footsteps racing toward me.

"Come on. Come on," I mutter, watching the lights above the elevator doors count down to the lobby floor.

The doors slide open, but before I can climb on, a whole mass of people pours out of the cab. Irritated looks drive me backward and into the arms of a security guard. He glares at me and points to the exit.

No. Not today. I dart inside the elevator and smack into another person, who screeches and falls backward. I grab the woman's arm and pull myself upright.

"Jamsimanyo," the woman says. Wait a minute.

I open my mouth to respond, but nothing comes out because I'm staring at the face of Kim Jihye—the woman with the three-finger forehead and the oval face.

"It's you," I blurt out.

Kim Jihye blinks at me and then says something else. I can't respond, and for the umpteenth time I mentally slap myself for not learning my mother tongue.

"I'm sorry. I don't speak Korean. I'm from America. I'm . . . adopted." The word falls from my lips, half apology, half accusation.

Kim Jihye responds with a nod. "Ah, I do not speak English well. Sorry. Do you need help?"

Yes. A lot of it. I pull out my phone and try to pronounce one of the sentences that Anna and the girls wrote out for me, but after three stumbling attempts, I give up and go straight to my English. "I need to speak with you. Can I buy you a coffee?"

Kim Jihye cocks her head.

"Please," I beg. *"Ko-pi ga-ju-se-yo,"* I stammer out in broken, barely comprehensible Korean.

The woman makes no move toward the door. I consider grabbing the woman's hand and dragging her out, but I can feel the grim stares of the security guards.

"Hara! Hara!"

I spin around to see Boyoung racing toward the elevator bank, her jacket billowing behind her like a superhero's cape. I've never felt so happy to see anyone in my entire life. I almost collapse in relief.

"Boyoung!" I exclaim. "What are you doing here?"

"I called your home and your flatmate told me you would be here." Boyoung tucks a strand of her hair behind her ear and peers around me. "Is that one of them?"

Together we look in the direction of Kim Jihye, who is inching toward the exit door. I grab Boyoung's hand. "Please help me. I want to talk to her. To ask about—you know. Can you help me?"

Boyoung squeezes my hand. "Yes. Stay here."

She hurries over to the other woman's side. The two engage in a brief conversation. I'm not sure what Boyoung is saying, but it works—whatever it is. Boyoung gestures for me to come join them.

"She'll have a cup of coffee and hear you out."

I nearly collapse on the floor in relief. "Thank you. Wonderful." I turn to Kim Jihye, who is eyeing me warily, and bow. "Thank you. *Gamshamnida.*"

At the coffeehouse, Boyoung places the order and I pay.

"Do you have the photograph?" Boyoung asks when we settle at an empty table.

"Yes." I pull out the original, barely able to take my eyes off the older woman. She has a short bob that curls close to her chin, and she's wearing what seems to be the office worker uniform of dark slacks and a white button-down shirt. There's a small flower broach pinned above her left breast. It looks old—either Kim Jihye has a liking for vintage or it could've belonged to my grandmother. There's a whole slew of questions on the tip of my tongue. Is Kim Jihye married? Do I have siblings? Are my grandparents still alive? Can I go to

Kim Jihye's house and look at all the photos, see where she sleeps—okay, maybe not that, but the rest of it, yes, I want answers to all of it.

Boyoung says something to Kim Jihye, who then picks up the photo. She stares at it for a long moment, shakes her head, and then sets it down. I don't like the look on the woman's face. It's denial. I want her to pick it up again. I want the woman to explain how she met Lee Jonghyung. Was it at school? At a club? Were they neighbors? How long were they in contact? What happened to end the relationship? Why did Kim Jihye give me up?

"She says she doesn't remember Lee Jonghyung-nim," Boyoung says.

"No." That's not the way this meeting is supposed to go. "Ask her to look again."

Boyoung points to the picture, but Kim Jihye shakes her head again. She says something in Korean and this time I don't need to know the language to understand it.

I lean forward. "Please, try to remember," I plead.

Boyoung shoots me a sympathetic look. "She says she doesn't recall him and that she's never had any children. She's very sorry."

That can't be the end of it. I refuse to take this answer. "I know it's long ago." I pull out a printed copy of the email he sent me. "Maybe this will help."

"I am sorry," interjects Kim Jihye in heavily accented English. Her eyes meet mine directly, and as much as I want the outcome to be different, the sincerity in her gaze tells me that the answers I seek are not with her. Kim Jihye is not my mother. A rock in my throat, I fold the email into a tiny packet and tuck it back in my purse.

Kim Jihye says something to Boyoung, bows her head slightly, and stands. I want to grab her arm and force her back into the chair. I want to change this outcome and make her my mother so that I don't have to keep looking.

"Please," I whisper, but she doesn't hear me or maybe she doesn't want to. She gives us another nod and walks off. I clench my teeth together—hard.

"She wishes you the very best and hopes that you find what it is that you seek," Boyoung says as we watch the older woman leave.

A ragged stone of sadness and regret chokes me. "I bought candies."

"What?"

I turn toward Boyoung. "I bought her sugared strawberries from the *ttalgi* café as a gift and forgot to give them to her."

I squeeze the heels of my hands against my temples and wish for a redo. Maybe if I go back into that building and meet Jihye again, the outcome will be different.

"Let me see your list again." Boyoung stretches out her hand. I nudge my phone toward her with my elbow. "Technically, every Korean who is born is registered in a family registry. These records are kept by local governments. As long as your mother is in Seoul, a local ward should have that information."

I drop my hands as hope begins to stir. "Do some people not register?"

"Yes. It's possible, but to get government benefits like health care or a pension, you must. We should think positively." Boyoung smiles brightly. "The ward offices will open at ten and I'll start the first thing in the morning."

"I'll go with you."

Boyoung shakes my head. "It will be faster if I do this by myself. Trust me, okay? You should do something fun. Go to a *jjimjilbang*—a spa—or rent a bicycle and pedal along the Han River."

I spend the next five minutes arguing with my friend, but she's adamant that there will be nothing for me to do because she will need to search the ward books and they are all in Korean. Basically,

I'll slow her down. The language barrier is too great. There's no way I can go to a ward office and search a registry. I don't even know what a ward office is or where to find one, and even if I did, I'd not be able to read the entries. I can barely make out the *Hangul* characters, let alone search for a name.

I'd never be able to navigate this without Boyoung, and so if my friend wants to go alone, I will respect that.

"Thank you. I appreciate it."

Boyoung presses her lips together. "I also do not want you to be disappointed. I may find nothing."

Her words don't go down easily, but I know she's right. What I need is a distraction. The Namsan Tower sign flashes in front of my eyes. I know exactly how to take my mind off Boyoung's search.

"I know. And I'm okay with that, but I don't want to leave without trying." I can see Boyoung doesn't believe me. I don't know if I believe my statement either. It's aspirational. The sort of mindset that I want to reach so if I say it enough times, it'll become my truth. "I will be fine. In fact, since this was a bust I'm going to go and do something fun."

"Oh?" There's a tentative, wary note to the question. "The Choi boy?"

"Yeah. The Choi boy." If he's still available. For all I know, he's escorting someone else to the top of Namsan Tower. And now that I've made up my mind, I want to be at the mountain immediately. I squeeze Boyoung's hand and scoot out before she can deliver another concerned speech. It wouldn't be useful. I've made up my mind. I made it up hours ago. Who am I to disobey the universe's demands?

Outside, I send a hopeful text.

ME: I found Namsan but they wouldn't let me up without a native tour guide.

I don't have to wait long for a reply.

YUJUN: That's terrible. Where are you? I'll pick you up.

ME: I'll meet you there. Riding the subway makes me feel accomplished, remember?

YUJUN: Don't get lost.

ME: If I do, you can pick me up.

YUJUN: I changed my mind. Feel free to get lost.

I laugh and the weight on my chest that has lingered since yesterday seems to fly off.

ME: I'll do my best to meet you at Namsan. Don't be late or I'll find another native tour guide.

YUJUN: Impossible. I'm the only one in Seoul that knows about Namsan. It's a hidden gem.

ME: It's in all the tour guides.

YUJUN: Sounds like a lie to me. See you soon.

CHAPTER FIFTEEN

"YOU DID NOT GET LOST," YUJUN SAYS, HIS FACE FULL OF MOCK disappointment, as I climb the stairs out of the metro. I'm glad I'm wearing my sole frock when I spy him. He's dressed in a pair of sharply tailored dark slacks hemmed right at the ankle bone with a white shirt tucked into the waistband. It's likely normal office attire for him but comes off dressy and put together, and I'd look odd next to him wearing jeans or sweatpants.

"The Namsan Tower signs were hard to miss." I don't tell him I've been loitering in the subway for an hour, moving from one café to another.

"I'm glad you changed your mind." He gives me a warm smile, one that doesn't harbor an ounce of resentment that I first turned him down.

He's different and no one will change my mind on that. "Me, too." And because he's different, I decide to be honest—something I've not always been in the past with other guys I've dated. With other people, I've put on an act, pretended things were okay when they weren't. I don't feel the need here. Or maybe it's that he's always been so open with me that it feels right to give that same vulnerability in return. "I'm leaving in a week, you know. And, well, you are here and I will be in America."

The curve of his lips softens and understanding lights in his eyes. "Yes, I know. It's a long way between us." He swings his finger in the space between us and takes one step closer. He reaches out and brushes a wisp of my hair over my shoulder. A small sound catches in my throat. "But while you're here, we can enjoy each other's company?" It's softly stated, more of a declaration than a question.

His hand hovers over my shoulder, close enough that if I shift a tiny bit to the right, he could cup my cheek. I feel myself listing in his direction and catch myself at the last second before I fall into his hand.

"Yes. Yes, we can." I'd agree to anything at this point. Drink a cup of poison with me? It's delicious. *Sure, fill my cup to the brim.*

Yujun's hand drops to his side but I don't feel too sad about it, as the dimple makes a reappearance. "There are three ways up to the tower—cable car, bus, and your feet. Well, we could also take a taxi."

I stare up at the thin cable wire and then down at my flimsy sandals. "I'd rather walk." It can't be all bad. Yujun has dress shoes on.

"It can be steep in places," he warns.

"Walk. Definitely walk. I rode one of those cable cars at a fair and I spent the whole time with my sweaty palms curled around the safety bar, wondering if I'd survive if the line broke."

A smile dances around the corners of Yujun's lips. "And your conclusion?" he queries.

"In some places, yes, but with many broken bones. I don't think there's even one safe spot along this cable line." The wire carrying the cable cars from the top of the mountain down to someplace on the street is barely visible.

"There is quite a bit of open space between the cable car and the ground," Yujun concedes. "But it hasn't failed yet."

"Have you ridden it?"

"Oh yes, but not for years. I think I was fifteen?" He considers it for a moment. "Yes. Second grade—that's second year of high school here," he clarifies. "I came up here with *hyung* and a friend of ours. Our friend had moved here from Busan and he wanted to see what the city looked like."

"Hyung?"

"Ah, have you forgotten our lessons already?" he teases. "*Hyung* is what I would call a male friend who is older than me. If Sangki-ah wasn't my same-age friend, but older, I'd call him *hyung*."

The conversation we had the other night about proper titles is starting to come back to me. "But I wouldn't call him *hyung*, right? I would call him . . ." I'm not sure how to say Sangki's name anymore after the talk with Jules. What was the respectful way to say another person's name? "DJ Song?"

"Still against *oppa*?"

"I thought you said that I shouldn't call anyone else *oppa*."

Yujun's lips quirk up at the corners. "That's right."

"Are you going to tell me what that means? I have this feeling it has some hidden definition."

There's a light sigh, as if Yujun doesn't want to share, but he says, "All older males are called *oppa*. If Sangki-ah were your brother or you were very close with him, you'd call him *oppa*. But if you were to say it to someone you liked, you would use a different tone. We would know.

"I suppose you could call me *sunbae*. It means older, respected person usually in the same profession. If you were a lawyer, anyone who passed the bar before you would be called a *sunbae*, although if you weren't close you would have to add *nim*, so *sunbaenim*. I am older than you and very respectable, yes?"

I'm starting to get it. "Yeah."

Oppa. I try it out in my head, but the word doesn't feel right. "Is it too American of me to call you Yujun?"

"No. Call me what you like."

There's something vaguely unsatisfactory about this, but I can't pinpoint what it is. But I don't want to dwell on it because as I told Yujun, I only have eight more days left in this city and with him. I concentrate on the smooth pavement under my feet and the soft, warm breeze in the air as we make the climb up toward the tower. Tall trees on either side of the wide road make this path feel private despite the occasional bus that barrels its way up the hill. The city seems far away from this canopy of green.

"I can barely hear the highway," I say.

"It's nice here," Yujun admits. "I like the Seoul Forest, too. The nice thing about Seoul is that there's always a place to hide out if you need it. Here, the Bukhan Mountain. Spots along the Han River. There's an island called Seonyudo in the middle of the river. It used to be a water-purifying facility but it's been turned into a park. And . . ." He trails off, slightly bemused by his torrent of words. "Sorry," he says. In the darkening twilight it's hard to tell if he's blushing, but I think he's slightly abashed. He loves his city and I find that utterly endearing. "It might seem overwhelming, but it's not all concrete and glass and dust," he finishes and tucks his hands inside his trouser pockets.

"I love it," I tell him. "What little of it I've seen, I love. Even the concrete, glass, and dust." As well as the mass of people, the humid heat, and the language, because all of that is part of this place that felt like home the minute I stepped off the plane and saw the sea of black hair.

"That's good, then." The hint of self-consciousness has disappeared.

"Tell me about the mountain. The one we're on right now." I want to hear him talk.

"It's the south mountain. *San* means mountain. Add *nam* to it and you have south mountain. This is part of the old fortress road that follows the ridges of the four main mountains in Seoul. Back in the Joseon dynasty, we used a series of fire beacons, a *bongsu*, to spread messages. The one here's called Mokmyeoksan." He points to his left, where a flight of stone stairs appears. "It's up that way—a bit of a trek, so we'll have to do it another day."

I like that—the way he always talks as if his tomorrow includes me. "All right."

Yujun flashes his perfect toothpaste-commercial teeth. As we climb, he continues to add a few tidbits about the mountain, Seoul, the trail.

"How do you remember all of this?" I ask. If he worked in my office, he would be able to answer the question about when the Korean War ended.

He shrugs and my eyes catch on the roll of his shoulders and the muscles that move smoothly under the still-crisp cotton shirt. "I like history. I read books about it."

I have a dozen questions. What's on his nightstand? What did he major in during college? What color are his sheets? What was the name of his last girlfriend and why did they break up? Does it bother him that I'm adopted? I manage to ask the appropriate one. "Did you major in history?"

"No. I studied business. Maybe, in my next life, I'll be a professor, but my mother and father have a business and I want to be part of it."

"What is it?"

"It's a logistics company. We move things—cargo, freight, concert equipment, animals, even people. But it's not so much about what we do as who we do it with. You can have the best-paying job in the world, but if you don't like who you are working with, it's terrible."

"You sound like you speak from experience."

"When I first got out of college, I joined a company that was very big, very prestigious, but . . . it wasn't for me." He moves his shoulders again as if shrugging off the bad memory. "What about you, Hara? Did you study copyediting?"

"No. That's not really a thing. I was an English major. It's an okay job. I want to move into actual editing someday, but I feel like that's a long way off. My coworkers are decent."

"And your family?"

"My mother is a real estate agent. My father passed away."

Yujun stops. "I'm sorry to hear that. Was it recent?"

How could he tell? Did it show on my face? Was it something in my voice? "It happened a few months before I came here."

Things are clicking in his head and I'm not sure I like that. He's drawing conclusions about my dad's death, my unplanned vacation here. Those are areas I don't want to get into. Not with Yujun. I want to keep him in this separate compartment that's completely clean and drama free, so I change the subject, quickly. "I read that Namsan Tower is famous in a lot of Korean dramas. Which ones?" I gaze up at the needle-pointed observation tower. It looks like other observation towers—circular with antennas at the top reaching toward the sky.

"*Boys Over Flowers*? Geum Jandi and Gu Junpyo get stuck in the cable car and have to spend the night there. She has a cold. Or maybe it's him who has the cold." Yujun frowns. "I can't remember. I watched that drama back in high school."

"I've never seen it. I've watched two K-dramas and both were ones that Boyoung recommended. *Kingdom* and *Signal*."

"No romances? I'm disappointed in this Kim Boyoung-nim. We have the best dramas," he boasts. "Where did you meet?"

"She's taking a gender studies course for international graduate students at the college in my town. I ran into her at the coffee shop."

"And she's from Seoul?"

"Yup."

"We should share a meal. When we have dinner, you bring Kim Boyoung-nim and I will bring Sangki-ah." Yujun looks pleased at this development.

"A regular matchmaker, are you?"

"We're a romantic people." He proves it to me when we arrive at the tower. The sun has fully set but there are still quite a few people about, taking selfies in front of the skyline, getting on and off buses, throwing coins into a fountain. Yujun bypasses all of it and walks me down a bridge. "It's the locks of love," he says. "Couples buy padlocks, write their names down, and fasten them to the bridge."

There are quite a few hanging on the metal railings, but not as many as I expected with a city of this size. "It looks like only a few of you are romantics."

"Wait and see." His eyes twinkle. As he leads me down a short set of stairs, the locks grow in number. We turn a corner and I gasp. On either side of the walkway, the padlocks line a railing that's chin-high. They're full of color, like confetti on the top of a cake. I run my hands along the metal locks and listen to them clink quietly against one another. The lettering is tiny, with the three-syllable Korean names fitting easily but the longer Western names running off the sides.

"There are more above." Yujun points his finger upward in the direction where we just were.

"How many of these are yours?"

"None. You can't put a lock up here until you've met your soul mate." He says it simply, as if it's a universal truth.

"I don't know that I believe in soul mates." I fiddle with a lock that says *Christina + Namjun*. I'd put money on the fact that they aren't still together.

"It doesn't matter if you believe. Soul mates exist regardless."

I peek at him under my eyelashes, trying to gauge if he's joking or serious. "You are romantic."

"It's the red string of fate, Hara. The gods tie the strings together and you can't ever separate them. Come. Let's go to the top of the tower."

I leave the locks behind as well as Yujun's statements. I won't rain on his sweet parade with my cynical point of view—that'd be like telling a kid at Christmas who is ripping into his presents that Santa did not deliver them. A crowded elevator takes us to the top. We spill out onto the observation deck, which isn't as busy as I thought it would be given the crowd outside. Yujun is quiet as we approach an empty window. I can see the skyline and the giant black ribbon that is the Han River snaking through the city. Down on the street, it's easy to forget how massive Seoul is.

"I want you to see something," Yujun says quietly. He leads me away from the windows to a bank of LED screens where I see people standing on a viewing platform, much like the one I'm on.

"What am I looking at?"

"It's Busan's observatory. There's a camera there and it broadcasts the interior of that tower to ours here. They can see us in real time."

Yujun waves and then smiles, poking a finger into one of his dimples. My knees nearly buckle at the cuteness. He turns to me and makes a V with his fingers and places them over my chin.

A couple on the screen do the same thing. It's adorable. The girl says something to the boy. At first, he shakes his head, but ultimately, after some cajoling, he gives a wildly exaggerated hand kiss. The girl folds over in laughter, covering her mouth. I bring my own hand up to muffle a giggle. I turn to see if Yujun is laughing, too. He's not. Instead, his face holds the fondest expression. My breath catches and then shudders out.

"Busan is three hundred and twenty-five kilometers away from Seoul. Not as far as Seoul to Iowa, but still there's distance, and yet, in the right place, it's as if you're right next to each other."

It makes sense when Yujun says these things. There's no distance in this world that can exist. Not with phones and planes and the internet. That's what he's saying. That my short stay doesn't have to be a barrier. Not if I don't want it to be.

CHAPTER SIXTEEN

I THOUGHT IT'D TAKE FOREVER TO FALL ASLEEP AFTER YUJUN
drove me home from Namsan, but I was out the moment my head hit
the pillow. I didn't even dream, which, I suppose, is par for the course.
We relive our nightmares, but the special moments are fleeting. When
I wake, I replay our last moments together in an attempt to embed
them in my memory bank. He drove me home in his Audi SUV because he wasn't about to have my experience in Seoul ruined by some
drunk *ahjussi* on the subway. His hand rested on the gearshift for
most of the drive and I spent an inordinate amount of time staring at
his long fingers. If I'd been braver, I might have covered his hand with
mine; instead I just fantasized about interlocking our fingers.

He left the vehicle idling and hiked up the mini-mountain with
me. At the gate, we said our goodbyes. I didn't want to go in and I
don't think he wanted me to leave. His hand came up and tucked my
hair behind my ear. I waited for him to kiss me, but he didn't. I think
it's because he didn't want to be that guy—the one that everyone has
warned me about. The guy who thinks foreign women are easy, and

to be honest, if he had made a move, I would've proven all those ste-
reotypes true. I was a second away from grabbing him by the shirtfront and taking him down to the asphalt but managed to summon
an ounce of dignity and slip through the gate before I did something
irreparably humiliating.

The next morning, I wake up to my phone chirping in my ear.
My hand shoots out to grab it and I end up knocking the phone off
the bed onto the floor. Then I nearly hit my forehead on the edge of
the table. In the end, it's not even a text from Yujun but an update
from Boyoung.

> **BOYOUNG:** I have not found anything but I will keep looking.
> It is taking me some time and I may not have anything until
> tomorrow. Please don't wait by the phone. I don't want you
> to be disappointed.

I wrinkle my nose at the screen. Too late. There are five messages
from my mother, who texted while I was sleeping.

> **MOM:** You haven't gotten sick, have you?

> **MOM:** How's the food? What are you eating?

> **MOM:** I miss you. Send me pictures.

> **MOM:** I love you.

> **MOM:** Don't forget to reply.

I send some photos I took of the locks of love on Namsan and the
Seoul skyline. None of them include Yujun, even though I find my
camera roll filled with him. I don't remember taking so many photos
of him, and sometimes it's just parts of him—his long, slender fin-

gers holding a red heart-shaped padlock; his side profile as his tall-tree form bends over a telescope on the observatory platform; his palm curled around the back of his neck when he stretched getting out of the packed elevator. Then there are the full-on pictures of him poking his dimple, holding his fingers in a V against his face. In almost all the pictures, he's smiling.

I can't send any of these images to my mother. They would generate too many questions and admonitions that I've already heard from so many others. I know what I'm getting into. I do. He was the respectful one. I was the one who wanted to tear our clothes off and enjoy some cross-continental loving.

The weather app says that the day will be hot. I pull on a white cotton button-down with navy stripes and pair it with light-wash denim. It's too hot for jeans, but I've noticed there's a distinct lack of shorts on the street. Most of the women wear pants or cute dresses—lots and lots of cute dresses. I'm going to shop, and tonight, well, tonight I'm filling my camera roll with more photos because Yujun is taking me to his favorite spot—the river.

"GET OFF EARLY?" I ask, raising my voice slightly to be heard over the din of people in the metro station. Yujun had decided not to wait outside, but met me at the turnstiles. It was our compromise because, again, he wanted to pick me up and, again, I refused.

Yujun glances down at his jeans, ripped at the knee. "It's casual day."

"Is it Friday?" The days have run together like a watercolor painting in the rain and I've lost track.

"It is. Most Koreans don't have casual day, though. *Eomma* implemented it a few years ago. We have a lot of Western influences at our office." He gestures for me to get on the escalator in front of him. Tucked under one arm is a paper bag. I eye it curiously.

"Like what?"

"It's not hierarchical. Remember the *sunbae* lesson? That's how it is in most companies. Age and when you entered the company are strictly observed, but at IF Group, we treat everyone the same." I can tell he's very proud of this. "We have an anonymous suggestion box and everyone puts their ideas on how to improve the company in it. Every Friday we meet to discuss the suggestions."

"If it's anonymous, don't you get a lot of people leaving bad comments about their coworkers?"

Yujun's eyes flare in surprise. "No. Do you have a lot of bad coworkers?"

"Some. I mean, you can't get along with everyone."

"That's true," he acknowledges, "but even if you have complaints, those should be discussed because the workplace is one where you spend many hours. If there is something I am doing that creates conflict, I would want to know so that I can adjust my behavior."

I wonder if there's such a thing as being too good a human being. "We're a lot more selfish in the West."

"Independent," he clarifies. "You're more independent."

Of course he spins it into something positive. "Did you have any suggestions today?"

"Someone thought we should paint the walls a color other than white."

"Was that someone you?"

He bursts out laughing. "Me? Why me?"

"You don't seem like someone who likes white."

"I love white. My apartment is white."

"All white?" I don't believe him.

"There might be some yellow pillows, but that's because *Eomma* forced them on me," he proclaims.

"You're wearing yellow right now."

"It's more of an off-white," he says, plucking at the front of his pale lemon button-down with its rolled-up sleeves.

"Only if you're color-blind," I tease.

He stops in front of a row of bicycles and waves his wallet in front of a sensor. "Are you saying that yellow isn't my color?"

"I don't think there's a color in the Pantone catalog that would look bad on you," I reply as he rolls a bike out of the rack.

Slightly pink in the cheek, he holds it out for me. "Is that right?"

I smile at his mild embarrassment over my compliment. *Yes*, I decide, *Yujun is too good and too pure and I hope he's always like this forever because the world needs people like him.*

"Are you going to tell me about the river?" I say as we pedal along the wide boulevard. There are joggers on the path along with quite a few people walking their dogs, and then there are people strolling along. The sun is going down and the air is cooling. It's a beautiful night and not just because I'm with my new favorite person.

"What would you like to know?"

Everything because I know nothing. "Where's the island you talked about?"

"The opposite direction. The river is . . . eighty kilometers long? Something like that. Well, not the river but the bike path. Obviously the river is much longer. It goes all the way up to North Korea. From the city, it empties into the Yellow Sea. When Korea rebuilt after the war, Westerners called it the Miracle on the Hangang. They say Korea advances so quickly that the Seoul you see today is not the one you will see tomorrow."

"What was it like in the nineties?" What had my mother faced? Couldn't she have sought help from the government to keep her baby? What about family support? Was she an orphan? Did her father kick her out when he discovered she was pregnant? Did she run away? What about Lee Jonghyung? Did he really not know that his girlfriend was pregnant? Would he have married my mother if he learned he was going to have a kid? Or would he have abandoned her? These questions pour out like candies spilling endlessly out of a vending machine until there are so many at the base of my brain my head starts to ache. When Yujun doesn't answer right away, I feel foolish. Why am I asking him questions about a time period when he was barely old enough to read? "I mean, if you know."

He slows down near a small park and climbs off his bike before replying. "I don't know much of any detail, but there were difficult times in the nineties. We had to get a loan from the IMF. It seemed astronomical at the time and many countries did not think we were a good risk. But we paid it off early." He gestures for me to follow him to a bench.

"How so?"

"We had a yellow-ribbon campaign." He waits until I sit before continuing. "I know in the West that's a sign of remembrance, but for us in Korea, it was a symbol for gold and selflessness. Everyone in the country, no matter how rich or how poor you were, gave up gold to the government to be melted down and delivered to the IMF to repay our debt. It was a national campaign. Everyone participated. Well, I was too young, but I remember that my grandmother gave up jewelry that she'd had since before the war. They put together a whole chest of things. Plates, jewelry, gold bars. Lee Jong-beom, a baseball player, gave up five years of trophies and medals. We paid off the debt three years early because of it." He starts to unpack the bag.

"Wow." This cultural identity—my cultural identity, one that I hadn't ever known existed, one I hadn't cared to explore, is fascinating. If I'd kept going to those Korean exchanges in the city with my mom, would I have learned these things? Would I have been prouder of my heritage? I would've at least known of it, right? My eyes fall to my lap as I recall how irritated I was at my coworker for asking about

Korea and how proud I was to be ignorant. *I'm American, like you.*
Hadn't I said that with my whole chest?

"There's a collectivism here that works well in times of trouble
but can also cause problems. It's hard to create social change when
we're all stuck thinking one way or another. It's like steering the
whole *Titanic* away from the iceberg." He hands me a small paper
box. "Like with every society, there is good and bad. I think the
good outweighs the bad. You have been here a week. What do you
think of Seoul so far?"

"It's big, busy, beautiful." I think back to the locks of love. "And
romantic."

"You are missing the best parts. Summer is the worst."

"What's the best?"

"Hmm." He ponders for a moment. "The cherry blossoms bloom
in late April and all couples love the cherry blossoms."

"So I should come back in the spring?"

He separates a pair of wooden chopsticks and places them on top
of the box. "Not necessarily. Fall is beautiful. The leaves turn and the
skyline looks like it's on fire from the color of the changed leaves. They
line the paths up the mountains and through the forests like a patch-
work rug. But then there's winter, and it's said that if you confess your
feelings when the first snow falls, you'll stay together forever."

Two cans of beer appear between us. Yujun's paper bag is the
equivalent of Mary Poppins's carpetbag and I'm as enthralled as the
Banks kids. Yujun pops open my box to reveal a seaweed-wrapped
roll. Is this sushi? "What's the least romantic season in Korea?"

"This is *gimbap*. There's seasoned rice, bulgogi, spinach, egg, and
a little radish. As for the least romantic season, it would have to be
now. Summer. It's hot and sticky, and who wants to hold hands with
anyone during the humid season?" He pops a slice of *gimbap* into his

mouth and stretches out his long legs far enough that a thin line of skin appears below the hem of his jeans and above his sneakers.

Summer is the least romantic season? I think as I stare at the reveal and wonder when I developed an ankle fetish.

"I came in the most unromantic months of the year? I'm destined for spinsterhood."

"An *ahjumma*, then," he teases.

"What's that?" The word sounds vaguely familiar. Last night hadn't he said I shouldn't ride the subway at night so as to avoid the drunk *ahjussis*? The radish *banchan* is delicious, crunchy with a slight sourness to it, offset by a tiny bit of salt and sweetness.

"Hallyu skipped you by, didn't it?"

"Hay who?"

"It's the spread of Korean culture. Dramas, sheet masks, BTS?"

"Yes, I've heard of them and they're amazing, but . . ." I trail off. I hesitate. How do I explain to this beautiful Korean man who speaks so lovingly about his country that I spent my whole life trying not to be Korean? It's embarrassing.

"But Americans think Asians are funny people, with funny accents, weird-smelling food, and almond-shaped eyes?" he fills in.

"Yes." I'd forgotten that he'd lived in LA. "Iowa is very homogenous. I think my mom doubled the Asian American population in the state when she adopted me."

He chuckles. "There are more Asians in LA than anywhere in America, and it has the best Korean food in the country, but Malibu has a distinct flavor. My aunt changed her entire name to Sue, remember?"

"Right." I get his aunt. "It's odd when you grow up around people who don't look like you because you start to envision yourself differently. When all you see are blondes or brunettes with high bridges and deep-set eyes, you start thinking that's what you look like, too, and then it's a huge shock when you catch your reflection." I hated reflections—and pictures—because they constantly served as a reminder of how I didn't quite fit in. Although I guess the one good thing about being the only Asian in school was that it was never hard to find me in the group photos. "Anyway, it's dumb. I feel like I'm complaining about dumb stuff here. It's not like I was afraid I was going to be profiled. I was never followed around a store like one of my classmates."

"Sometimes small cuts cause a lot of pain." He gives me a half smile and another piece of *gimbap* disappears into his mouth. "We need to make you some seaweed soup. Usually we serve it for birthdays but I think your first visit to Korea is like a birthday."

I put my chopsticks down.

The ever-intuitive Yujun asks, "What's wrong?"

"My mom used to make that for me."

"Oh really? But not anymore?"

"No. I made her stop." I'm ashamed.

"What happened?" It's a gentle question.

"About fourth grade, I think, I had some friends over and one asked why it was so stinky in the house. I don't even think it was the soup that smelled but the kimchi Mom served with it. Someone else said that it was my hair since it looked like seaweed. After that, I wouldn't eat it."

"That's terrible."

"I feel like a fraud now." I wave my hand. "I hated all this stuff growing up. Mom would want to take me to things or she'd send me articles on Korea. She offered to take me to a Korean concert once. I refused. I wanted nothing to do with it."

"I understand."

"Do you?"

"Yes. Remember Aunt Sue? She lives in a French country home on the beach among all those ultramodern glass and concrete structures or the art deco ones. She wears Ralph Lauren constantly and smells like rose water. She never spoke Korean in the house and pretended she didn't know it. She didn't speak because she was embarrassed of her accent. We hardly talked at all when I first arrived. I couldn't speak much English and she refused to speak Korean. Ironically, that's why my English is so good. If she still eats kimchi, it would be outside or in the garage."

I don't know if he's making this up to make me feel better, but I appreciate it if he is. There's something really freeing about talking with someone who understands, who has had the same experiences. I don't have to explain what it felt like to be othered. He knows all about the sensation of standing in a group and appearing so obviously different, of being asked questions that your friends are never asked. Where did you come from? What language do you speak? Do you speak ching chong chang? I inhale and let go of some of the guilt that's wound itself around my lungs.

"What do you want to know about Korea? I'll tell you as much as me and my phone know."

I ask more questions about the time when my mother would've been pregnant. While I eat, he shares all sorts of details. There was no KTX train and the movie *Train to Busan* couldn't have existed. He doesn't know what the fashion was, but his father had worn the big tinted sunglasses in college that are popular in fashion magazines today. "It's all a big circle," Yujun declares. He puts down the box and moves the beer cans. "Let's take a picture. Slide over."

He raises the phone with one hand and waits. I don't move. I like taking photographs, but I don't like being in them.

He lowers his arm. "What is it?"

"I hate pictures."

"Why?"

"Because . . ." I don't want to admit it because it sounds like I'm both insecure and fishing for compliments, which, yes, I'm a bit insecure about what I look like but I'm not fishing for compliments. I've never enjoyed how my face looks in photos. It's too round, for one. My eyes are too small. My nose is but a bump in the middle of my face.

"We can't leave without a picture. It's against the law." He does the hand gesture again, his fingers pointing toward the ground, pulling me forward with the invisible strings he's tying around my heart.

"What if I don't like it?" I ask, sliding reluctantly over to his side.

"You'll like it," he says with the utter confidence that he has about everything.

"But if I don't?" We're like the North and South Poles—opposites in every way. I'd like an ounce of his surety.

"If you don't, you can delete it. Say cheeseus."

"Cheeseus," I repeat dutifully. He takes a picture. Several of them. And then he holds out his phone in front of him so we can both see.

"See. The picture is perfect." He stops at the second photo. The sun is setting and the red-orange globe dipping its toes into the Han River makes everything glow. "You have a beautiful eye smile."

He taps the screen where my eyes are nearly closed and all that can be seen is a small crescent of black where my lashes fall over the dark brown of my pupils.

"My eyes are closed."

He tilts his head, my flat tone catching him off guard. "Mine, too," he points out.

I'm startled and examine the photo again. I was so focused on my own face that I didn't realize that Yujun's eyes had the same downward curve. In fact, his is more pronounced because his smile is bigger, the divots bracketing either side ocean-deep.

"Eye smiles are considered a very attractive feature." He lets his lashes fall and his lips curve up. He pokes a finger into one of his dimples and says, "Isn't mine cute?"

My throat closes up. In the picture, his eyes are like mine. They aren't the exact same shape. His turn down slightly at the inner and outer corners, looking more like a slight paisley curve, while mine are crescents, like a true upside-down smile.

I glance away from the phone screen only to end up staring into a gaze that is so full of tender warmth, I would swear that the sun was rising instead of the moon. But it's not the sun; it's a man who is so sweet, so kind, so *endearing* that I do what any other person in my position would do. I kiss him.

His eyes widen in surprise but he doesn't back away. He sets his phone down, curls his hand around the back of my neck, and angles my head to deepen the contact. My heart soars and my fingertips tingle. I press myself closer, forgetting the food and beer sitting on the bench between us. He pushes it all to the ground and hauls me so close I'm practically in his lap.

The tingles intensify and my fingers itch to touch him. They skate over his shirt-clad sides; they trip up the buttons lined up in front; they find their way to his collar. I dip inside and feel his Adam's apple bob against my fingertips. Electricity bolts through my bloodstream. I clench my legs together and open my mouth wider, willing him inside.

I don't know how long we kiss. It might've gone on all night if an older couple hadn't walked by and said something in a sharp tone that made Yujun set me aside abruptly. He stands and gives a small bow while I nervously pat my hair into place and wipe the wetness off my lips. He says *mianadae*, which I know is "I'm sorry." I bow, too.

The older couple gives us a stern nod and says something else, which puts a little color on the tops of Yujun's cheeks. Once they're gone, he bends down to pick up our mess. I join him.

"No kissing in public?" I joke, feeling awkward. We sweep up the remnants of our *gimbap* roll onto the paper boxes.

"Maybe not that . . . enthusiastically," he replies with a small grin, small enough that the dimple appears to be a shadow.

Yujun produces a small trash bag and then produces a second container of *gimbap*. "I didn't know how hungry we would be," he says.

I resettle on the bench with the newly produced food. "How hungry are you?"

"Ravenous." But he looks at me as he says it, which makes me think he's not talking about food.

The tingling returns and doesn't go away the rest of the night.

CHAPTER SEVENTEEN

YUJUN TEXTS ME FIRST THING SATURDAY MORNING TO TELL ME that he will be busy all day with work and into the evening because they have new employees—or "friends," as he calls them—joining the family and the company is treating them after work.

> YUJUN: We are celebrating new friends joining our family by taking them out for hanwoo and much soju. Let's meet tomorrow. I have a forest to show you.

In contrast, it's utter silence from Boyoung, and by midday all the warm feelings from my outing with Yujun have been erased. I don't want to bother her but I'm so anxious for results that I can't sit still. I turn off my cell phone and bury it in the bottom of my suitcase so I don't use it again—at least for the next hour.

Downstairs, the front door opens. Someone's home. It's probably Jules, but I don't care because a cranky Jules is better than sinking into my own head. I run downstairs to greet her.

"What's up?" I ask.

Jules doesn't look up from the small carton she's digging into. "Eating ice cream. What does it look like I'm doing?"

I tap my fingertips together. Jules is in quite the mood today, but ice cream for lunch sounds perfect. "Any more in there?"

"One carton, but it's mine, and if you eat it, you need to pay for it."

I reach inside and grab the small carton with the odd heart-shaped face and blue body on the cover. Jules is always buying this brand, but at least it's good. I prop myself up against the fridge and use the small wooden spoon attached to the lid to feed myself the creamy strawberry goodness.

"How's the job going?"

"It sucks. Pay is terrible. Rich people are the worst. They ask for the most outrageous shit and treat you like dirt when you can't get it." Jules mimics one of her passengers. "'What do you mean you don't have Armand de Brignac Ace of Spades? Veuve Clicquot is for cheap hookers.'"

"I have no idea what any of that means."

Jules makes a face. "Champagne, and she wanted a mimosa, which, why are you mixing four-hundred-thousand-won booze with thousand-won juice? Makes zero sense." She gets up with a huff, her chair legs scraping against the tiled floor, and stomps to the recycling bins. "If I had money, I'd be everyone's favorite customer. I'd tip well. Say thank you. Wouldn't give a rat's ass if my mimosa was made with five-thousand-won Brut or five-hundred-thousand-won Louis Roederer, which, by the way, is a hundred times better than the other stuff."

An idea pops into my head. It's a bad one, but it's better than standing around here all day holding up the appliances. "How much money would it take for you to be my translator today?"

Jules's head swivels around. "What?"

"I need a translator. How much would it cost me to rent you out for the next"—I check the clock—"four hours?"

Jules's eyes narrow. "A hundred thousand won an hour."

"Too much. What about twenty thousand?"

"And we use cabs, not the metro."

"Done." I might be better off paying Jules the hundred dollars an hour she asked for, but it's ninety degrees out and walking between subway stops doesn't appeal to me either. It's money well spent. At least I'm doing something.

"Fine. Let me get an extra battery charger. My phone's almost dead." She speeds out of the kitchen.

"Aren't you going to ask me what you need to translate?" I shout after her.

"Who cares? You're paying me and I'm getting out of the house. It's a win. Besides"—her voice becomes somewhat muffled—"it's about the women, right? The ones in the pictures?"

Jules is smarter than I realized. She appears at the top of the stairs. "Are we going or what?"

I jump to attention. "We're going." I run and get my own phone.

Jules doesn't ask a single question during the cab ride to my father's last home, and I find that disinterest almost comforting. I don't have to explain myself to her. She's along for the ride and the money.

Her silence doesn't last for long. When the driver drops us off, she immediately says, "You were born here? That explains a lot."

"I wasn't. It's where my dad last lived. I figured I'd go back and ask questions from the people who came to his funeral. It's a place to start."

"Okay. I didn't mean to be rude. It seemed to fit. This isn't a great place in Seoul, and if you were adopted, it's because your mom couldn't afford to keep you, right? Or she came from a super-religious family where she would've, like, died or something."

Jules's observation gives me pause. I never thought my mother's life would be in danger if she got pregnant, but that could happen, couldn't it?

"My father lived here before he died. I don't know if my mother did. That's what we're here to find out." Jules is right. If this is where I was born, it does explain a lot.

We pick our way past the loose rock, up the path toward the small building that had once sheltered my father.

"Why do you want to know about your birth family so bad? What are you going to find? That your parents are superrich and you're going to live that crazy-rich Asian life? Or you're secretly royalty? They don't have that here in Korea. That's Japan. And Thailand. And maybe a few other Asian countries."

I swallow a sigh. So much for not explaining myself. "No. I never thought any of that."

"Then what?"

I rub the soft spot between my eyes and wonder if I shouldn't be the one earning the money for having to endure Jules. "I don't know, okay? I never gave my birth parents much thought because I was left on the street. I had a better chance of winning the lottery than finding them. But my coworkers were getting DNA testing done, and I thought, why not, and when I researched the tests, there was this one that had an adoption matching service and so I went with that one. I forgot about it. Then there was this data breach and I had Lee Jonghyun's contact information. Suddenly, I had expectations. I had to know."

I omit mention of my adoptive dad's remarriage, new son, and death. They weren't the impetus for this hunt. They weren't.

"But what is it that you have to know?" Jules presses.

I let out a long sigh. "When you look at yourself in the mirror, who do you see?"

"Me."

"Who do you take after? Your mom or your dad?"

"Mom," Jules answers immediately. "I have her eyes and face and basically everything. Also her limp hair." She pulls at a hank of her blond locks. "It's so fine, I might as be wearing corn silk on my head. It's irritating. What's the big deal about looking like your family anyway? It's not like my parents were supermodels."

"One of my first memories is being in the grocery store and someone who hadn't seen my mom in a while comes up to her and asks whose kid is she watching. My mom answers, 'Mine,' and the other woman laughs like Mom had made a joke. So many times, the first words out of her mouth to explain that I belonged to her were that I was adopted."

And then I come here and I still have to explain where I'm from, only this time for other reasons.

"And finding your dad or mom is going to make you what? Feel like you belong?"

"I don't know." I start walking again.

Jules hurries to catch up and peppers me with a few more questions, which I refuse to answer because I don't know. I just don't know. Finally, Jules runs out of steam and I send a thank-you to the universe because I was very close to throttling the blonde in the middle of a Seoul alleyway, and given the prevalence of CCTV cameras in this city, I would be caught and thrown in prison and then never, ever get the chance to find my mother or eat *gimbap* with Yujun again.

"That's an odd look on your face," Jules notes.

"I was thinking about whether I was strong enough to choke someone to death."

"Nah. You're pretty puny. You're better off with a knife. Or poison. I think poison is the easiest way to murder a person. You can buy herbal cures at any pharmacy, plus there's a lot of off-market, unregulated supplements made out of faux-Eastern medicine available."

"You've given this a lot of thought."

"Flying is boring."

"You have had the same three roommates since arriving in Seoul until I subleased the room, right?"

"Yeah, why?"

"Just checking." *Because you don't come off as someone easy to live with.* I knock on the door before Jules can expound on the myriad ways to kill someone. After a few moments, there's some shuffling inside and a familiar face pokes out.

I pull out the photos and shove them toward the landlady. "Ask her if she knows these women."

Jules asks the question in Korean and the landlady shakes her head. "She says—"

"I can read the body language," I interrupt. "Ask her if my father was from here. No. Ask her how long he lived here."

"She says he moved here two years ago. Before that he lived in another district."

"Do you know where that is?"

Jules sighs. "It's southwest of the city. Kind of far away."

"Good thing we're cabbing it."

I ask Jules to translate a few more questions such as if his landlady knew where Lee Jonghyung was born or whether he had any friends or coworkers.

"She doesn't know anything. We're better off going to the other district and showing his picture around there," Jules informs me. We start to leave but the landlady lets out a spew of Korean, which I can't follow. Jules replies and the two have a long conversation during which my anxiety starts ratcheting up. Finally, the conversation is over and the landlady retreats inside.

"What was that all about?"

"She says that there's a woman at the sauna down the street that knows, or knew, your dad and that we should talk to her."

"What else did she say?" Because the conversation had gone on for longer than that.

Jules sighs. "No offense, Hara, but your old man was kind of irresponsible. He didn't have a job but was able to pay rent here because he got money from women. She didn't like him much but a renter is a renter. Five women in the space of a few weeks? That seems like a lot."

"I know this." It hasn't escaped me that Lee Jonghyung was a dickhead, but I'm not going to dwell on it. That seems extra pointless.

"But what if this is the information you're going to find? That your dad is a lowlife and your mom was a druggie or something. Isn't it better to know nothing?"

"It's too late for that." The veil of ignorance has been pierced and I won't ever know peace until I chase down every last lead.

Jules finds the woman at the sauna, which is not a wooden room heated to 130 degrees but more like a giant yoga room with mats on the floor. People inside are all wearing the same T-shirt and shorts, and many have towels wrapped around their heads with Princess Leia–like towel doughnuts above their ears. I stare at one of them for far too long, wondering how they manage to contort a towel into that shape. Jules has to physically drag me away from my inspection to the front counter. After we exchange greetings, Jules shows the photos, which prompts the sauna woman to reach over the counter and grab my chin. The woman jerks my face from one side to the other. I stand like a mannequin and allow myself to be inspected. My heart races and the palms of my hands grow sweaty. Is this my grandmother? Because she's too old to be my mother . . . isn't she? Or did this woman get pregnant by a young man who wanted nothing to do with me afterward and so the woman gave me up for adoption out of shame?

It's another scenario I hadn't considered.

"What's she saying?"

"Kim Eunshil is her daughter," Jules replies in a hushed voice.

Kim Eunshil? That was the woman in the third picture wearing the faded yellow turtleneck tucked into a pair of straight-leg jeans. "Is she my grandmother?"

"She doesn't know. She says her daughter has never been pregnant. She's never married. She did know of some, well, not very nice men who dated her daughter, but as far as she knows the girl never had a baby."

"If she was away from home for even six months, it could have happened." I'm not letting this go. I have a real lead here. "Please ask her if I can see her daughter. Please." I'm ready to get on my knees.

"Yeah. Yeah. I'm asking." Jules engages the woman, who finally releases me. I rub my sore jaw. That woman's fingers were tight.

"Her daughter sells dishes at the market and won't be off until tonight."

"Let's go to the market." I don't want to wait.

"Okay."

I jerk around in surprise.

Jules spreads her arms and shrugs. "What? I'm yours for as long as you want to pay me."

"Let's go."

We wave to the Korean grandmother, who shouts something after us. Jules mumbles that we better hope Kim Eunshil isn't my mother because *her* mother won't let her live if it's true. I'll figure out how to prevent this murder later. Right now, my heart's pounding faster than Secretariat running at the derby. The market is a five-minute cab ride, but it feels like an eternity. I have the door open almost before the cabdriver pulls to a stop. Behind me Jules yells to slow up but I don't pay her any attention. The alleyway into the market is small and there are small carts set up on either side of the road. The sound of people and the clanging of pots and the chimes of bells ring through my ears as I dodge through the crowd.

Jules catches up with a huff. "Do you even know where you're going?"

I point to the sign on the large four-story structure in front of us. "You said she sold dishes? The sign on the second floor is in English. It says 'housewares.'"

Jules presses her lips together. "So it does."

Housewares is four floors up. I race up the stairs while Jules climbs more slowly, grumbling all the way. The market is a maze of shelves filled with ceramics, brass bowls, chopsticks of every enameled color, and more pots and pans in one place than I've ever seen before. It's as if someone took every kitchen item from all the Targets in one state and shelved them in one space. As I round what feels like the tenth aisle, I spot Kim Eunshil spooning *ramyeon* into her mouth. She looks very much like the photo taken twenty-five years ago. Her face is unlined and her hair is cut in the same bob that is in the picture. She's ageless. I touch my own face. Is it the same? Do we have the same eyes? The round eyes that make upside-down crescents when they smile?

Having arrived, I find my feet glued to the ground. Unmoving, like I've been stapled in place, I stare at Kim Eunshil. Jules brushes by me and takes out her phone. She bows and says something, shows the picture, and then points to me.

This time, the response isn't like any of the others. There's no kind word and sad smile or bright interest and piercing inspection.

Instead, it's anger. Kim Eunshil erupts with a volley of angry words. She picks up her spoon and waves it menacingly at Jules, who holds up her hands in front of her face and ducks. The angry woman turns to me and makes another threatening gesture. I'm too stunned to move. Jules speeds toward me, catching my sleeve, and drags me backward. Kim Eunshil throws the spoon at my head. When it falls harmlessly to the side, she grabs another. I start moving then.

"What's she saying?" I ask as we run toward the stairs.

"She denies everything," Jules half yells.

There are more angry words hurled toward us, along with two more spoons. Something wet and sticky strikes my head. I take the stairs two at a time, passing up Jules. We escape the market and burst out into the sunshine of the outdoor alley, panting.

Jules places her palms on her knees. "I think your dad wasn't a great guy."

"You don't say," I reply, pulling a noodle out of my hair, and sniff. Shrimp-flavored *ramyeon*? The worst. I toss the noodle aside in disgust.

"She said your dad was a pig and a lot of other curse words that I don't have a translation for but basically she hopes that the root of his tree withered from poison. I don't know if she meant you or his dick," Jules offers unhelpfully.

"Thanks." I pick out more noodles.

"Who else is left on your list?" Jules comes to my side.

"I have one other name that I can fully make out. Kwon Hyeun." I take out my phone and show Jules. "My friend Boyoung was going to a government office and looking in a registry but apparently she hasn't found anything." I shake my phone, wishing that a text would appear like a message in the window of a Magic 8-Ball before putting it away and going back to combing through my hair.

"Yeah, the family registry would be helpful. We could do that."

"We could?" I stop fussing with my damp strands. That I smell like watered-down fish starch doesn't matter much with this new information.

"Well, I can't promise anything, but a big university here has been collecting family registries and putting them in a computer database. We need to find your dad living in the same ward as one Kwon Hyeun."

"Wouldn't Boyoung be doing this?"

"Dunno. Maybe she doesn't know about it. I only know because the president of the university was on a flight that I worked a couple of months ago asking for money from one of the *chaebols* who owns a private jet."

"Let's go."

CHAPTER EIGHTEEN

THE UNIVERSITY DATABASE YIELDS TWO RESULTS. *THIS IS IT,* I think. *One of these addresses is where my mother lives.*

"Don't get your hopes up," Jules cautions as we make our way to the subway station.

"Of course not," I reply, but we both know that I'm lying. It has to be. If not, I'm left with two blurred photos with no legible names on the back. One of these addresses is for Kwon Hyeun and she's my mother. There's a pull inside me, as if the magnet has been activated.

"Since both places are across the river, we might as well take the subway. The bridges are always overcrowded. It'll take longer by cab," Jules suggests. I don't argue. I'm running low on money.

The first address is right off the subway. Jules runs into a co-worker in the terminal. The two talk for a short bit. Jules tells me that even though there are ten million people in Seoul and it seems big, the city is actually small. Everyone's connected. Jules's sudden talkativeness is slightly unnerving because if the usually cold girl is consoling me, my prospects for the mother hunt must be dim. I reject that line of thinking. This is the one. Kwon Hyeun is the one.

We walk out of the tunnel and then up a hill. Everything in Seoul is uphill. Even though there is a high concrete wall separating the neighborhood from the train, the rumbling of the machines on the tracks shakes my legs. The road is narrow, with enough space for one vehicle to travel at a time. Small homes are stacked on top of one another like uneven building blocks. Stone walls provide a barricade from the street to the entrance of the homes but the walls aren't high enough to block out the upper units. Clothes hang from the upper balconies like colorful flags. Whether I'm breathless from the uphill climb or from the prospect of meeting my mother, I don't know.

"You look like you're about to pass out," Jules comments, her hand on the gate. "Should I wait or knock?"

I inhale deeply, press a fist against my thundering chest. "Knock. Definitely, knock."

As Jules pounds her fist on the gate, my mindset suddenly changes and I steel myself for disappointment. The last two visits have been a bust. The leads on two of my photos are ruined. My dad was an asshole, spreading his seed from one end of Seoul to another. Any woman who was dumb enough—

The gate creaks open and a tiny woman peeks her head out. Her face shows a few lines, but there's age there. I peg the older woman to be in her sixties—far too old to be my mother. My heart sinks to somewhere near my knees. The magnet is not engaged.

Jules and the woman have a brief exchange.

"What's she saying?" I ask as if I don't already know. I can read the body language.

"That she doesn't know any Lee Jonghyung."

"Of course she doesn't." But I'm desperate so I pull out the last won in my purse and hold it toward the woman. The door creaks open a little wider. "Have her look at the photo again."

Jules points to the photo and then to my face. The older woman's eyes dart from the picture to my face to the money between my fingers.

The older woman steps away from the gate, grabs the money from my hand, and says something sharp and quick before ducking inside. The door shuts firmly behind her.

Jules shakes her head. "She said you are very pretty and that if she did have a daughter she'd like it to be you and that if you want, you are welcome to return and meet your filial duties as a daughter by bringing food and money every Sunday."

I can't even be mad at the loss of money. I brought this on myself.

"You want to quit?" Jules asks.

"Nah. If I'm going to be beaten down, let's do a good job of it."

IT'S PAST FIVE by the time we make our way into Yangcheon-gu, south of the river. We are both hot and tired. Jules took me back into the subway to find a hat and a hair tie to cover up the wet *ram-yeon* look. I also got a cash advance from an ATM. Mom will murder me if she finds out that I'm charging everything. Even though it's been hours since I was baptized at the market, I can still smell the faint odor of the shrimp. I briefly contemplate doing the third visit another day, but I'm worried I'll never convince Jules to leave the house with me again. It's also possible I may never leave the house. I've gone past disappointment into a cavern of numbness. You don't feel anything there but emptiness. If you rattled me, all you'd hear is the clacking of bones echoing from one end of my frame to the other.

"My feet hurt so bad," Jules complains.

"Mine, too." I feel like we've walked the entire length of the city.

"You should carry me."

I gives Jules's long frame a once-over. "I'm not carrying you."

"Fine, but you're buying me beef and I'm talking *hanwoo*. I want the Korean beef that gets cooked over charcoal briquettes and not on an electric grill. There's a place in Myeongdong that my ex took me to. Actually, no, I take that back. You should be renting out the private room at Born and Bred." She smacks her lips together. "I've always wanted to eat there."

"Fine." I'm already bleeding money. The stripe on my credit card is worn down and the balance on the ATM receipt made me wince.

"Really? It's three hundred dollars a person."

"What?" I stop and glare at Jules. "No. I'm not buying you three-hundred-dollar beef. Geez, what's it made out of? Gold?" Is that how much dinner was with Yujun at his favorite *hanwoo* barbecue restaurant? No wonder it was so good.

"No one eats gold." Jules rolls her eyes. "Why did you even say that?"

I bite my tongue so I won't yell at Jules. When I have my temper under control, I mutter, "It's a metaphor."

"A dumb one."

"Is there CCTV here?"

"Probably. Why?"

"I might murder you, but since I don't want to spend the rest of my life in a South Korean prison cell, I'll wait until there aren't any cameras around."

"No need to get—" Jules cuts herself off, stopping in front of a gate. "Wait. Is this the address? Hand me your phone," she demands.

I slap my device onto Jules's wiggling fingers. As she double-checks the address, I search the gate for something out of the ordinary. Does Jules see signs of a cult house? Is it a celebrity home? The gate is large and wooden with a simple iron design hung in the middle. There is a black box mounted on a cement pillar holding up one side of the gate.

"Oh. My. God." Jules grabs my arm. "What if this is your grandparents' house and your mom had to give you away so she wasn't banished?"

I peel Jules's fingers away. "Are you a flight attendant or a writer?"

"Maybe both? I told you that being a flight attendant is boring work. Sometimes I make up stories in my head, mostly about how I'd push a passenger out the window." She rises on her tiptoes as if she can stretch far enough to see over the gate. "This is what my ex's house looks like."

"I thought you never met his parents."

"I didn't. I found his address by looking through his phone and took a cab to it."

I stare at my flatmate for a long, silent moment.

"What's with the judgy stare? Curb stalking is normal."

"Normal?"

"Yeah, it's not like I went into his house. And we were dating *dating*," she adds with emphasis and wiggled eyebrows. Then her face falls as she remembers how they aren't together anymore. "Anyway, I went by his house and it made a little more sense. Rich families here in Korea marry their kids off to other rich families. It's not about love or romance or soul mates. It's about how to keep your money for the rest of eternity so you don't end up living in an apartment next to the subway or in the basement or at the top of the highest hill with no elevator access."

Jules's tone is matter-of-fact, but there's hurt and bitterness in her words. If we were friends, if it were Kelly from back home or even Boyoung, I'd squeeze her shoulder, but this is Jules and she's more likely to bite my hand than appreciate my comfort, so all I say is, "That sucks." I mean it, though.

"It is what it is. Anyway, let's see if this is the house of your fairy godmother." Jules shrugs, pretending like the rejection of her ex doesn't still sting, but I'm an expert at rejection and know all too well how it lingers like a toothache. Wasn't that why I flew all the way across the world to track down my sperm donor and bio mom? I wanted an answer, as if hearing the truth—whatever it is—from the mouth of the people who created me would somehow salve that wound that still exists. I've papered over that sore—the one that exists because I wasn't good enough to keep—but it's always there in the back of my mind. It's why I cling so quickly and then back away twice as fast, and it's why I'm here, even if I don't want to say it out loud.

Jules casts a worried look in my direction. "Don't get hurt feelings if these people deny your existence. A child showing up out of the blue is going to be a huge embarrassment for them, and these people are all about face—looking good to outsiders."

"I'll strive to not care what my biological grandparents think about me."

"They're only people," Jules says, trying in her own way to be as encouraging as possible.

"Yeah. Just people." I knock on the gate.

"Nah." Jules muscles me aside. "This is rich Korea. Everything here is high-tech." She presses a button and shoves her face close to the black electronic pad on the wall.

"It wasn't at the last place."

"We aren't in the last place," Jules retorts and then smooths her irritated expression into a pleasant one before pressing a button and saying, *"Annyeonghaseyo."*

"Yeoboseyo?" comes the immediate response.

Jules waves her hand. "Hello. I'm here to see Kwon Hyeun." Jules drags me over so that my face is now in front of the hidden security camera. "There's someone from America here to see her."

There's a pause with no response.

"Do they think we're Jehovah's Witnesses? Do they have Jehovah's Witnesses over here?" I wonder, shifting from one foot to the other.

"Yes, but—"

The speaker comes to life and then a voice says, *"Jamkkanman gidaryeo juseyo."*

"What'd she say? What'd she say?" Hope burbles at the bottom of the empty cavern that is my heart. I clutch Jules's arms.

"She's home. She asked us to wait," Jules says, a bit breathlessly. "I think she's coming out."

"She is?" I squeak. I didn't expect this. I thought this was another dead end. I'm completely unprepared. I look like I was dragged through a subway tunnel attached to the end of a train. My hair is a mess. I'm sweaty as hell. Do I have time to slather on some foundation? I tug Jules away from the intercom. "Jules, how do I look?"

"Like you walked five miles in the hot Seoul sun."

I run the back of my hand across my forehead. "That bad?"

Jules nods. "Pretty bad. Do you have some makeup? Some CC cream?"

"Tinted sunscreen." I dig in my purse and squeeze some product into my hand. I slap it on, rubbing dirt all over my sweaty face.

"Rub it in some more. You look like you're trying to audition for the role of Casper the Friendly Ghost."

"Ugh, this is awful." I dig the heels of my hands into my cheeks.

Jules hands me a tube of lipstick. "Put this on, too."

But the gate opens before I can apply any color. The woman steps out, shutting the gate behind her. She stares at me for a long, awful, and wonderful minute. It's the woman in the picture. The one wearing the denim skirt, wedge heels, and the white short-sleeve sweater

with the pretty necklace. A shout of excitement builds at the base of
my throat. In my imagination, I'm bellowing out the biggest roar of
exultation, as if I'm celebrating the last-minute buzzer beater at a
basketball game.

I step forward with my heart beating so loud that everyone can
hear it. There's a buzz in my ears and a pulsing sensation behind my
eyes and my throat feels sore even though I've barely spoken today.
"M-M-Mom?" Mom? Is that what came out of my mouth?

The woman tilts her head to the side. "May I see the picture,
please?"

"You speak English?" I scan the woman's face. Is this what I'll look
like when I'm twenty-some years older? The woman looks more like
my sister than a mother. Speaking of sisters, do I have any? Is this my
mother's house? Is this my grandmother's house? Who else lives here?

"I . . . A little." She turns away from me to speak to Jules. The two
carry on a conversation and I hang on every unrecognizable syllable
and sound. Jules pulls the picture out and hands it to Kwon Hyeun,
who studies it for a long, silent, agonizing moment. Then she shakes
her head and says something to Jules.

I want Kwon Hyeun to speak English again. I want in on this
conversation. I nudge Jules to the side. "Please, do you know this
man? Did you have a baby twenty-five years ago?"

"She doesn't know you and she says she doesn't know Lee Jonghyung," Jules interjects.

"It's her in the picture," I insist.

"I know, but she's saying it's not. That she never had a child."

The excitement that had been buzzing before begins to turn
sour. I fist my hands at my sides so I don't take the older woman and
shake her until acknowledgment comes out of her mouth. There was
recognition on Kwon Hyeun's face. The magnet was polarized. This

woman knows something. "How can I have a picture with her and my dad and her not know him?"

Jules gives me a tight smile. "Single motherhood is pretty stigmatized and giving up your kid would be even worse, I guess."

I take the picture and hold it up in front of Kwon Hyeun. "This is you."

She shakes her head in denial.

"Here. Take this." Jules scribbles something on a piece of paper and shoves it into the woman's hand.

"I know it's you," I insist. "Listen, I'm your kid. This is my dad. Or, not my dad, but the sperm donor. I know it is." I'm shaking now, the words coming out of my mouth so fast they're tripping over one another.

Kwon Hyeun continues to deny it. "I'm sorry," she says in her Korean-accented English. "I do not know this man." She slides behind the gate. "And I do not know you."

The gate is shut quietly, but it rings loud in my ears.

CHAPTER NINETEEN

I STARE AT THE CLOSED GATE, MY HANDS BALLED INTO FISTS AT my sides.

"You look like you're about to Hulk out on the door and knock it down."

"Do you think I could?" The woman behind the gate is in the picture, and the fact that Kwon Hyeun's denying it makes the whole thing suspicious. She stared at me like she knew me, like she'd been expecting me.

"No." Jules clamps a hand around my wrist and starts dragging me down the street. "Besides, she's going to call the police and then you'll be put in a Korean jail and will either get deported or you'll have to stay there forever."

"Are you serious?"

"I mean, I don't have personal knowledge or experience, but I've watched dramas, and unless you're a sports star or celebrity, it's the lockup for you."

"Noted." I uncurl my fingers one by one, forcing myself to calm down, and not because Jules is telling me I'm going to go to prison for breaking and entering but because I'm not getting behind that gate unless Kwon Hyeun lets me in. So I have to figure out a way to get inside. It's time to retreat and recalibrate. I need a plan.

"Let's eat. I'm hungry."

I jiggle my bag. "I've ten thousand won. What will that buy us?"

"Not much." Jules shrugs. "I've got some won."

"Some won" is enough for a bowl of instant ramen and a six-pack of beers at a small store at the edge of a park not too far from the walled-in house. I take everything up to the counter to pay while Jules fills our bowls with hot water from a convenient dispenser along the wall. The clerk says something to me and I can't make it out. We end up staring at each other until Jules arrives and pushes me out of the way. She pays with her phone and then motions for me to grab the beer and chopsticks. I follow her out to the small table situated on the curb outside the convenience store. Jules sets the two bowls down and places the paper-wrapped chopsticks across the top.

"You're too stiff with your Korean. You pronounce every syllable like you're a translation app. Koreans slur their words, swallow half the syllables. You don't say *annyeonghaseyo*, you say *haseyo*. The *annyeong* part is said in the back of your throat and you don't even move your lips. Try it." She reaches over and squeezes my lips together. I mumble it.

"Good. And then when you're leaving you say *gyeseyo*. Say it like this and you can impress the hell out of your boyfriend."

"He's not my boyfriend."

"Nah, he is. The one thing about guys in Korea is that they get romantic real quick. They lose interest real quick, too, but while it lasts, you'll be showered in gifts. You know they celebrate the first day they started dating. Day one, they call it."

This isn't about me, I realize. This is about Jules's hurt and longing. The breakup is still fresh for her.

"You miss him, don't you?" I pop open a beer and slide it across the table.

Jules winces. "I fucking do." She drains the beer and opens another one. "I plan to get good and drunk. Sorry. You'll have to call a taxi to take us home."

"I feel like I'm wearing half the dust of the city."

"Same." Jules takes a long draw. "Tomorrow's flight will be a breeze after today."

Despite not being a fan of random physical contact, gratitude has me itching to hug Jules. Without her, I wouldn't have gotten this far. I'd still be stuck at home waiting for a text from Boyoung. Whether Jules is here for the entertainment of seeing me unravel or for the mystery or for some reason only my flatmate knows, she's still here. She could've bailed hours ago. "Thanks for coming."

"Eh. It was better than sitting at home." She's not big on warm moments. I get it. They make me uncomfortable, too. Jules peels off the paper cover of her ramen.

I follow suit, unwrapping the chopsticks, breaking them apart, and then digging in before the noodles become too swollen with water to eat. For a while, there's nothing but the sound of two girls slurping down noodles. When my stomach is full, I push the bowl away and take a sip of my beer. Korean beer tastes about the same as American beer.

"Tell me about him. The ex in the big house." I want to hear this story and I think Jules needs to share it. Plans to storm the Kwon castle can be cooked up later. She's not going anywhere and neither am I.

Jules heaves herself away from the table. "I'm gonna need some ice cream before I talk about this."

"We had it for lunch."

"I didn't realize there was a daily limit."

When she disappears inside the store, I pull out my phone and check my messages. Still nothing from Boyoung, but there are two from Yujun.

> YUJUN: Dinner doesn't taste as good when it's not with you.

> YUJUN: Have a meeting in the morning but plan to take off early. Will meet you at the metro stop since you love it so much.

"Why are you smiling? I haven't even given you your cone."

I look up from my phone to see Jules handing me a paper-wrapped ice cream treat. "Nothing much." It'd be like rubbing salt in her open sore.

"Okay, keep your boyfriend secrets to yourself." She slumps in her plastic chair across from me.

"He says he's working tomorrow morning."

"That's probably accurate. Koreans are workaholics."

"You were going to tell me about the ex," I remind her. The ice cream treat is one of those chocolate-dipped cones with a nut topping. I guess some desserts are universal. I mean, who doesn't love ice cream and chocolate?

"Lee Bowon teaches math at a private boys' school. Teaching is considered a very honorable profession here. It's not like back home where no one gives a shit about a teacher. Here they're like revered. *Seonsaengnim* is one of the most respectful titles you can call a person, and it literally means 'teacher.' So, anyway, he's considered good husband material and his mom was always sending him blind date candidates. This girl is a med student at SNU—that's Seoul National University. This other girl is studying law at Yonsei. This one is getting an engineering degree at Korea University. They call it SKY. He graduated from Seoul, of course." Jules chomps down on her cone and chews the ice cream angrily. "He ignored all of the summons, or so I thought. I mean, we were like you and Choi Yujun. We were together every night. We went to Seokcho and kissed on the beach, held hands by the lake in Ilsan, did other stuff in other places."

She picks up her beer and takes a deep gulp. "And then one day he announces that he can't see me anymore because he is getting engaged."

Geez, he could have stuck a knife in her heart and it would've been kinder. "Was it the Korea Uni girl?"

Jules's brows furrow together. "How'd you know?"

"Math and engineering. Sounded like they went together, unlike this ice cream and beer."

"You just haven't had enough," Jules declares, her mouth full of ice cream again. "What's your boyfriend do anyway?"

I stop denying that Yujun and I are dating because we sort of are, but he's not really my boyfriend. He's a . . . vacation romance. A voyfriend? A vayfriend? Is there a word for this? I toy with the paper wrapping around the base of the cone. "Logistics—although I don't know what all that means. He has meetings. He wears dress pants to work." I recall his evening plans. "He takes employees out to dinner."

"And has a driver and a big-ass black car, so I'd bet my salary he's in one of the *chaebols*."

"*Chaebol* means what again?"

"*Chaebols* are those superconglomerates that basically own everything from the ice cream you're eating to the cooler that it's kept in to the land that the store sits on." Jules drinks more of her beer before returning to the ice cream cone. She screws up her face.

"You're right. This is a foul concoction—beer and ice cream. Maybe you can never drink enough to make this taste good."

"I don't know about that." I'm on my third can and the buzz is feeling good. My feet aren't aching and I no longer smell like dirt and sweat—or maybe I do but the beer buzz is covering it up. I also don't know how rich Yujun is, and does it matter? It's not like I'm going to be affected by his social position. We're enjoying each other's company. A voyfriend's social status is irrelevant because it doesn't affect you in real life. I finish my cone and break open another beer.

"I thought my story was tragic," Jules says, reaching for the last of the beer. "Foreign girl falls in love with local boy only to be replaced by a local, but yours trumps mine. You come here and find out your real old man has kicked the bucket but he's also a turd, spreading his sperm around like he's some kind of farmer during the planting season." She tips her beer can in my direction. "Congrats."

I can't even be angry at this summary. It's only the truth. I clank my beer against Jules's. "Thanks."

"I should've known when he never introduced me to his parents that it was going nowhere. It means something here in Korea."

"Isn't that a big deal in America, too?"

"Not like here. Here it's basically a sign he's going to marry you. I knew one Korean girl who didn't even learn her boyfriend's parents' names until he proposed."

"Well." I drain the rest of my beer.

"I know. This is a sign." She leans forward.

"Of what? That we're out of beer?" I set down my now empty can.

"No. That we should both leave Korea behind. There's got to be better countries with better stories for us. I opt for New Zealand."

"Why there?"

"Because everyone's nice there. Even their birds are flightless."

I am buzzed enough that this makes sense. "Okay. New Zealand it is." I stand up. "But first, let's have another beer."

IT'S DARK WHEN we arrive home. At some point, I remembered that alcohol was a depressant and stopped drinking. Jules, however, declared that coming down off her buzz would be a mistake and moved from beer to soju, downing the potent rice wine like it was water. She totters on her wedges as we climb up the hill. I have one hand attached to Jules's elbow to keep her from falling and the other holding a six-pack I no longer have any interest in drinking. I had second thoughts at the convenience store, but when the irritated clerk snapped something at me in Korean while I counted out coins I found in the bottom of my purse, I decided the beer was a necessity I could not live without. In retrospect, buying something because I was mad at the clerk doesn't make any sense, but I was determined to pay for my beer.

"He doesn't like your coins," Jules informed me in an overly loud voice.

"I figured." He kept pointing at my phone. I ignored him and methodically counted out all the won I had. But now, with the six-pack weighing my arm down and a layer of dust coating every inch of my skin, I think that maybe the coins would've been better spent on a pack of wet wipes.

I swipe the six-pack across my forehead. "Is this hill getting steeper?"

"No. Korea is mountainous. You'll get used to it."

"I'm leaving in seven, no, six days." There's no time to get used to anything. There's no time to learn the language. There's no time to download a payment app. There's no time to fall in love with Yujun.

"Oh." Jules falls silent.

Up ahead a pair of headlights flash. A car door opens and then thuds shut quietly. A tall man emerges from the darkness and strolls toward us, his hands in his pockets. I can't see his face but I'd bet this six-pack and the imaginary wipes I really, really wish I had that he has a smile on his face.

Jules makes a disgusted noise in the back of her throat. "I still can't believe you picked up this guy at the airport. I live at airports and no one there looks like him." She slaps me on the back. "Better spend your last six days here wisely."

"I thought you told me to beware of Korean boys who wanted to take advantage of loose Americans."

"But look at him." Jules points toward the approaching Yujun. "Why go out with him unless you're going to see him with his shirt off?"

I ponder this. It does seem right that after all the crap things I've endured that I get one good thing out of this trip. It would be a crime not to see Yujun shirtless.

"I bet he has abs." Jules nods emphatically and practically falls over.

I grab her arm and haul her upright.

"Did you have a nice night?" Yujun calls out, amusement tinging his voice.

"It looks better than it actually was," I reply. "No offense, Jules."

"None taken, Hara." She waves tipsily. "Choi Yujun-ssi, take care of my friend."

"I think it is you who needs the help." Yujun loops one of Jules's arms around his neck and half walks, half carries her up the rest of the incline.

"How was your dinner tonight?" I ask, hurrying by to open the gate.

"It was not as good as yours." He hauls Jules in and helps her to the front step. Anna opens the door and the light spills out, highlighting his perfect form—the broad shoulders encased in the still-crisp white shirt and his trim waist accented by a pair of dark trousers hemmed right at the ankle bone. He's so tall and so fine, and being near him makes me almost forget every bad thing that happened today.

I dawdle outside while he hands Jules over to our roommates. It's late. He probably wants to go home to bed, and yet . . . he's here. And has been here waiting for me.

He says something to Anna, who giggles in a way that makes my territorial instincts rise, but before I can do anything stupid like rush over and rub lip gloss on his white shirt, the door closes.

Yujun ambles toward me with his sexy long-legged stride eating up the distance between us, stopping when his shiny black shoes are but a few inches from my dusty flats. I curl my toes into the bed of my shoes.

"Are you tired?"

"No." It's not entirely a lie. I'm in this strange suspended state where I'm exhausted but my mind is buzzing. I don't have many coherent thoughts. One question tumbles after another like rocks in a washing machine. Nothing in my head makes sense, but there's a lot of noise. I wish I could shut it out. "If you were tired but couldn't sleep, where would you go?"

"By the river," he answers promptly.

"Take me there. Please."

He doesn't ask any questions. He doesn't talk. He merely leads me to his car, tucks me inside like I'm some precious package, and drives off. There's a deep-voiced rapper going off in the background, a low-grade noise. Some of it's in English and I catch a word here and there like "love" and "hate" and "Seoul," but it's mostly Korean. I lean back against the headrest and allow the synth and thrum of the beat wend their way into my bloodstream.

We drive for about thirty minutes. This late at night, the traffic is sparse. The wide-laned roads that usually have four or six cars abreast have one, maybe two. The occasional blue bus rumbles by. Even the buildings are mostly dark, with pockets glowing amber like small stars in a dark sky. The city is slumbering, resting up for its new day tomorrow. The park is deserted when we arrive, and actually calling it a park is sort of a stretch. There isn't much more here than cement stairs, a bench, and a few metal exercise contraptions.

"The Han." Yujun throws out his arm toward the river. He reaches into the back seat of his car and pulls out a paper bag. Something sweet and fried wafts into the front seat and my mouth begins to water. When we reach the bench, he produces beer and two thick pancake-looking things. "This is *hotteok*, which is basically pan-fried dough with a brown sugar center. Nuts or no nuts?"

I nearly cry with delight. "No nuts, please."

He hands me a beer and a *hotteok*. "It's better when it's hot, but it's still good."

I bite into the crispy dough and let the sugar melt onto my tongue. "It's delicious," I say, my mouth full.

"Masitda," he tells me. "It's Korean for 'delicious.'"

"Mas-i-t-da," I repeat slowly, and then remembering Jules's fingers around my mouth, I say it again, this time faster, pushing the sounds together. *"Masitda."*

"Good." He approves.

I bask in that compliment as if the sun broke out in the dead of night. Everything is good. The food, the weather, the company. My head doesn't hurt so much and neither does my heart.

"What do you like about the river?"

He stretches his legs out and I stare at his ankle bone like I'm a Victorian maiden who gets to see bare skin once every eclipse. Jules said it would be a crime if I didn't get to see Yujun's abs, but what about his calves and his thighs? What about his defined pecs and the hairline that arrows down to his groin?

The last time we were on a bench near the river, I kissed him and then I climbed onto his lap, threaded my fingers through his hair, and tried to tongue his throat. It was the only time I've really touched him. The tips of my fingers tingle at the memory of his bare throat. I want to feel his warm skin under my hand. I want to stick my nose into the hollow of his neck and fill my lungs with his scent.

"You like the *hotteok*?" he asks.

I tear my eyes from his lap and peer up guiltily through my lashes. "Yes."

The corner of his mouth rises. "I'm glad."

Is he smirking? I take another bite of my *hotteok*. I was staring at his lap. Maybe he deserves to be smirking.

"I like it, too," he says, and this time his voice is deeper and throatier. Are we even talking about *hotteok* anymore? He clears his throat and, in a mercy move, turns his gaze to the river. "I like that it's here. The city changes every day, but the Han River was here before the buildings and the cars and the people and it will be here long after all of this is gone."

I wipe the corner of my mouth, checking for drool, and redirect my attention to the river. I asked for him to take me to a place to clear my thoughts, not one where I'd jump his bones. Across the river, the southern part of the city rises high into the air. The distinctive tweezer-shaped Lotte Tower sits to the left, and the faint outlines of the southern mountain ridges loom behind half-constructed high-rises taking their places next to the smaller apartment buildings that were once the height of modernity. The dark river is speckled with the lights from the high-rises.

The city changes every day, he said. This modern, fast-moving, coffee-shop-on-every-corner, face-mask-at-every-counter society is not how it was twenty-five years ago. While the water in the Han is always there, it changes daily. It flows from the mountains and races down to the Yellow Sea, every current bringing something new.

I close my eyes and lean forward to hear the river speaking as it strikes against the base of the bridge columns that rise to my left. Did my mother ever come here to the river? Did she ask the water what to do? Did she think that if she got rid of me like the water, she could start new?

The next bite of *hotteok* lodges itself in my thickening throat. I should go back to imagining Yujun without clothes. Everything was sweeter then. I reach for the beer to wash it down and meet Yujun's concerned gaze. His hand wraps around mine.

"I'm a good listener," he reminds me.

I drop the beer onto the bench and lean my head back. There aren't many visible stars so it's hard to say whether the inky-dark river is reflecting the sky or whether it's the other way around. "I'm adopted, you know."

"Yes, you mentioned it before."

"I came here to look for my birth parents."

"Yes."

I stop and twist around to stare at Yujun. "Yes? What do you mean by yes?"

"Your English is too perfect and you had no family to visit here. The pieces fit together." He interlocks his fingers.

"What do you mean my English is too perfect?"

"Most Koreans who learn English have an accent, and even second-generation Korean Americans speak with a slight one because their parents or grandparents speak it at home. Your English is the kind that is uninfluenced by a non-native speaker. And Westerners generally don't come here if they don't have family. That's changing a lot lately, but I had a feeling." He shrugs, almost apologetic for his accuracy. "One other thing: My *eomma* works with adoptees. Or, not directly; she gives money to a foundation that is working to normalize it here."

Normalize it. "Because it's looked down on, right?"

He hesitates and then gives a terse nod.

"Why didn't you say something?"

"You didn't seem to want to share." He grimaces. "There is a stigma attached to it. Blood is very important to us culturally. We believe that people born in a certain year have certain characteristics. We believe that people with a certain blood type act a certain way. These beliefs are embedded in our culture like the mountains that surround us and, I suppose, an earthquake can make great changes. Until then, we can chip at its base."

The thought that my adoptive status is an impediment the size of a mountain isn't a comfortable one, but hadn't I experienced some of that idiot-ology back home? From kids taunting me that I wasn't wanted to grown adults saying I wasn't a real child of Pat's?

"It's not just here," I admit. "Back home, I once had someone tell me that they would never adopt because you never know what you're going to get."

He slides a hand over mine. "People will always be a surprise to others—no matter the circumstances of their birth."

The river is so still in the early summer night that it looks like black glass. I can almost see my insecurities rippling on the surface next to the reflected neon lights of the buildings looming along the shore. "When I first came here, I would get asked why I wanted to find my biological parents, and I didn't have any answer, but it wasn't because I didn't know. Rather I didn't want to admit the reason. It's dumb."

"I do not believe that."

Of course he doesn't, but the world isn't full of Yujuns, and I don't know if he fully understands, but he wants to hear me. And isn't that all I've ever longed for myself? To be heard and to be understood?

"Being adopted is when everyone is wearing a striped dress but all I own are polka-dotted dresses," I find myself saying. "My mom wore a striped dress and when we went out together people would ask her why she was holding hands with a child in a polka-dotted dress. Shouldn't the polka-dotted dress be with the other polka dots? But there aren't any polka dots around—only stripes. You spend so much time looking at people with stripes that you start thinking you're wearing stripes, too, until you catch a glimpse of your polka-dotted self in a store window and realize that you are not a striped person. Then you learn that there's a place that only wears polka dots. You come to that place and you're very excited because for once you don't stand out. For once, you feel like you belong.

"But then you open your mouth and the polka-dot people know instantly you're a fraud. They know you're a stripe on the inside or, at least, not one of them. And the place where you once thought you belonged, you don't. You're still on the outside." Beside me Yujun takes a breath, but I'm not finished. "Don't tell me that's where you can see the best. No one likes being on the outside. People say that they do because they're trying to convince themselves that their half-full bowl fills them up. Everyone wants to belong—to someone. Somewhere."

Yujun waits for me to finish my outburst and then says, "Do you know the meaning of *han*, Hara?"

"Like the Han River?"

"The word *han* itself has meaning. This small peninsula has been the object of envy for all the neighboring countries and they have fought for it, pushing us out, hurting the people, and yet, we always survive. The cost is high. Our land is divided. Our most precious relics taken from us. Our palaces burned and rebuilt and burned and rebuilt. And that is the meaning of *han*. You may think that you don't belong here because you don't speak the language or you think you do not belong in America because your polka-dotted dress is so different than all the striped dresses, but inside you have the same blood that I have. It's the blood of everyone that came from here. There's *han* in you. No matter where your journey takes you, you are filled with it."

I let his words seep beneath my skin, sink into my blood. I don't know that I've ever thought about what I was made of—what my heritage was—because I was left on the street in some foreign country. My breath slows and deepens.

"*Eomma* gives money to the education and support of adoptees. Helps them find jobs. It's a cause very important to her. She also hires many single mothers. She would want to help you. Will you allow this, Hara?"

It's so gently asked, as if I'm doing him such a great favor. Jules's comment that meeting someone's parents is the same as a marriage proposal gallops through my mind, but I know it's different in this circumstance. This is like if I broke my leg and his mom was a doctor. Would I refuse that? No, it'd be stupid to say no. It still feels off, as if I've moved past a line I shouldn't, and I don't know if I've done right or not, but when I open my mouth to speak, I say, "Yes."

His hand squeezes mine tight. I hadn't realized we were still holding hands, but maybe we've been holding hands since that first encounter at the airport. We don't talk much the rest of the night. We simply sit there, holding hands, listening to the slap of the water against concrete, watching the city in the reflection of the river as the red string of fate binds my heart to his.

CHAPTER TWENTY

A PHONE CALL WAKES ME UP, OR MAYBE IT'S THE UNRELENTING
stream of sun shining in my eyes. I came in at dawn, crashed facedown on the bed, and didn't take the time to close the blinds. My
mistake. I roll over and grab my phone. Through bleary eyes, I make
out a text from my mom.

> **MOM:** I haven't heard from you in days. I miss you. Are you
> okay? Text me back or I'll have to start looking for flights.

The two smiley-face emojis at the end look vaguely threatening. I
try to think back to the last time I texted Mom. Was it two days
ago? Three? I engage in the mental math of time zones, give up, and
use the world clock feature on my phone. It's past midnight back
home, so I default to texting.

> **ME:** I'm good. I walked a hundred miles yesterday but I ate
> two ice cream cones and according to my health app I broke
> even. I love you.

I'm about to put the phone down when I notice there is another text tucked inside my unknown senders folder. Curious, I tap the alert and read the message in growing shock.

KWON HYEUN: It is Kwon Hyeun. I would like to meet with you today. There is a coffee shop off of Gangnam Station exit 10 called Angel's Brew.

My heart leaps. When was the message sent? I scan the time. The display says almost an hour ago. *Please*, I plead internally, *don't back out*. My hands are shaking so badly, I can barely type my reply.

ME: Yes. When.

The three animated dots appear immediately. My fingers fold tight around the phone. "Say yes, say yes, say yes," I chant.

KWON HYEUN: Yes. In an hour?

I confirm and then leap to my feet. I want to look nice but I also have no time. The map app tells me it'll take at least a half hour to get to Gangnam even in a taxi. I briefly contemplate texting Yujun for his black car service but decide that it'll take longer for a car to get here from wherever he is than it will for me to hail a cab. After washing up, I throw on a dress—the black-and-white-*striped* sundress—grab my purse and cardigan, and rush to the door. I don't even own a single polka-dotted thing. I got my metaphors all mixed up last night. I'm shoving my feet into a pair of sandals when I hear, "Hara?"

I jerk upright and see Boyoung sitting at the kitchen table. As she rises from her chair, I check my phone in confusion. Had I missed something?

"I didn't get a message from you."

"Yes, I know. One of your flatmates let me in on their way out of the house. I found something and wanted to bring it to you in person." She pulls a piece of paper out of the pocket of her crisply pleated wide-legged pants. I feel dingy in comparison. One of these days, I'm going to look as good as a regular Seoulite, but that would require me spending less time walking around and more time in underground shopping venues. There are tons of cute things on racks lining the halls of the tunnels. Next week— I cut myself off. I won't be here next week.

"Can you text it to me? Jules found two of the women in a university database and one of them wants to meet in Gangnam."

Her brows shoot up. "I'll come with you. Be your interpreter, yes?" Before I can say no, Boyoung is beside me, toeing on a pair of black sneakers.

I smush my lips together, trying to figure out if this is the best course of action. While I can use the subway and catch a taxi, I have trouble with simple transactions at the store. If this Kwon Hyeun's spoken English isn't as fluent as her written English, we'll have a hard time communicating. On the other hand, if Kwon Hyeun is my mother, it would be nice for me to break down in privacy and not in front of Boyoung. Then again, I could completely misunderstand Kwon and miss something important. I opt to include my friend. "Okay. Let's go."

Boyoung looks relieved. "I'm sorry I did not contact you earlier. I could not find anything at first and did not want to disappoint you."

"It's fine." It's ironic that for a week I was floundering, and now I'm getting aid from all corners—my flatmates, Boyoung, and Yujun's mom. What are the odds? Although I guess the odds were better with Yujun. He'd known I was adopted from almost the beginning. I guess that's why he took an interest in me.

Boyoung trots to keep up. "Well . . . that's good. That's really good. How did you find your information?"

"Jules had a passenger that was a professor at some university who was working on a genealogy project. We went to the university and searched their database. I'm sorry. I should've said something, but I hadn't realized you were still working on it."

"No. No. It's, what do you say, all good?" Boyoung gives me a small smile. "I did find information, though. Maybe it"—she crosses one flat hand over the other—"overlaps?"

I stop walking. "Really? On who?"

Boyoung's face brightens. "One of the names we could not make out, I believe I found her. She does not live in Seoul but is from Gangwon-do. It's to the east of Seoul. She came to the city for work and moved back home when her parents were too elderly to continue working. It is about three hours from here. We can take a train and then a bus or taxi from there. It will take all day, but that's okay, right?"

I hesitate. It's another day out of my fast-dwindling time left, and that means I won't get to spend much more of it with Yujun. Disappointment dims my spirit, but this is why I came to Seoul. Not to hang around the city, drinking beer at isolated parks along the Han River, holding hands with a guy. "Yes," I say finally, moving again. "That sounds good." But I might not need to go because I have this feeling about Kwon. I think she's the one.

"The other women were not— They did not work out?" Boyoung queries.

"No. One didn't know him and the other, well, she denied having any children and I believed her."

"Then who is it today?"

"Kwon Hyeun. I was at her house yesterday but she refused to talk to me. Then today I got a text saying she would meet with me."

"Ah, that's good, then."

"Right. Very good." Excitement surges inside of me and wipes away the irritation I felt toward Boyoung for disappearing for two days. Even if Kwon Hyeun is not my birth mother, she knows something. She must or she'd never have contacted me. I carry this hope in my heart the whole cab ride. My heart beats faster at every stoplight.

The coffee shop is a sleek, modern building with smoky glass windows and black signage with crisp white lettering. "Angel's Brew" is written in English. There is no corresponding *Hangul*. I halt in front of the door, take a deep breath, and nearly tip over from lightheadedness. I haven't eaten anything since the cup of ramen and *hotteok* the night before.

Anxiety is twisting me up inside and I'm not sure what I'm most leery of—not finding out information or discovering something new. Either way, I feel like I could throw up.

"We don't have to go in," Boyoung says quietly at my side.

"No. I do have to go in." I push open the doors and let the air-conditioning blow away my nervous sweat. The first floor has a few tables and they are all full of people far too young to have given birth to me.

"Do you want something to drink?"

"Yeah, but I can order." I've watched Boyoung do this before. I get my card out and ask for an Americano, which is espresso with ice and water, not because I need the caffeine jolt but so I'll have something to hold on to. Boyoung takes the buzzer as I scan the room a second time.

"Maybe she is upstairs?" Boyoung suggests when I come up empty.

"Yeah."

"I can wait here." Boyoung holds up the buzzer. "I'll bring the order up when it's ready."

"Sounds good." I'm not sure why I'm nervous since I've already met Kwon Hyeun before, but my feet feel encased in cement as I climb the wooden stairs to the second floor of the coffee shop. I spot her immediately, sitting at a small table overlooking the street. Her face is pointed out the window; perhaps she is looking for me.

I study her for a moment. Is there something familiar in the slope of the small nose, in the shape of those lips? Is her forehead four fingers or three? It's hard to tell from this angle. When Kwon Hyeun senses me staring and turns toward the stairs, I see nothing but the pretty face of an older Korean woman.

I walk over and bow slightly. *"Annyeonghaseyo."*

I must be getting better at my pronunciation, because approval briefly flits across Kwon Hyeun's face. She rises halfway out of her chair and gestures for me to take a seat. *"Annyeonghaseyo.* Please sit. Did you get something to drink? I can order for you."

"No. I'm fine."

There's a small cup of coffee in front of Kwon Hyeun, but it looks untouched. Now that I'm sitting across from her, I see she has a three-finger forehead—like mine. Her hair is long, parted in the middle, and tied in a bun at the base of her neck. Her face is unlined and she's wearing minimal makeup—light gloss, some eyeshadow at the corners. A beige silk shirt that's almost pink flows around her fine-boned frame. Dangling from her neck is a simple gold necklace with a star pendant that glimmers in the light. On the ring finger of her left hand, there's a solid-gold band. No one element is ostentatious or gaudy but she gives off an aura of wealth.

If Kwon Hyeun did give me up for adoption, I'm going to be mad.

"I am sorry about yesterday. I was not prepared. May I ask how you found my address?" One of her hands is lightly curled around the coffee. She looks relaxed and at ease, which makes me think she isn't my mother, because if we were meeting formally for the first time, shouldn't she be a basket of nerves like me?

I clear my throat a couple of times before explaining, "My friend Jules knew a person who was building a digital genealogy database. They ran a search of names, potential dates, and locations. There weren't that many Kwon Hyeuns around the district where my father lived twenty-five years ago." I'm fortunate, too, that in Korea, women don't change their names upon marriage.

A rueful smile touches her lips. "Our country is too connected. I was at my husband's father's house. They would not have understood."

My mouth grows dry. So she is—

"I am not your mother, but"—she pushes a piece of paper across the table—"I may know who you are looking for. This woman was with Lee Jonghyung for a short while. They were together when he was with me. It was not a happy time for me. My parents did not approve, but I told them he was a good man. Then I found him with this woman. They were at a café, holding hands, in Itaewon. Back then no good Korean girl would go there, so they thought they would not be discovered."

I don't know what to say, my tongue frozen in my mouth. It doesn't matter. Kwon Hyeun isn't interested in hearing from me anyway. She's lost in her own memories.

"Choi Wansu and I went to the same school. She wasn't Choi Wansu then. Her name was Na Wansu. She was a scholarship student with a remarkable aptitude for language. We were the only two that spoke English well. Jonghyung-oppa ran a food stand right outside of the school. He would give you free samples if you were a pretty girl. If you were a pretty girl, he would slip you some soju or a cigarette. Do you understand what I am saying?"

I nod slowly. My father was a predator, then. An older man who hung around high schools to woo young girls. I feel sick.

"I got pregnant, too, you see. But my baby did not survive and I could not have any children after that, so you cannot be my daughter." She recites these details as if she's reading the ingredients list off a bottle of detergent. *Alcohol, sulfate, citric acid, I had a miscarriage, ethanol.* Kwon Hyeun reaches over and taps the paper. "But her. She is your mother."

"H-how can you be sure?"

"Choi Wansu left school and then returned to the city after a year. I've kept track of her." Kwon Hyeun shrugs nonchalantly because low-key stalking a woman for a quarter of a century is no big deal. "She married very well to a widower and then took his company for herself. You can look her up on Naver. There are many articles about her success. She fosters young women, particularly single mothers, and donates many won to adoption charities." Kwon Hyeun arches an eyebrow. "We do not have to wonder why those are things she chooses to champion, do we?"

"No." A coldness is creeping through my veins. I fold my hands on top of each other and try to squeeze some warmth back into the chilled digits.

"She is very wealthy now. I am surprised she hasn't tried to find you, but maybe she does not want to." Kwon Hyeun may not have meant to be hurtful, but it feels like she's taken my fork and stabbed me with it.

Wounded, I struggle for breath before pulling out my phone and swiping to the album I'd made with the scans of the photos. I have to be sure. "Which one of these is Choi Wansu?"

"A test?" Kwon Hyeun takes the phone and flips through the images. She stops at one and lays the screen in front of me. "Her."

It's the photo that's labeled Na Y——, but I realize now that the *Y* was actually a *W* and the coffee Boyoung spilled washed away most of the ink, leaving the last name and a distorted part of the first letter—or *Hangul* character in this case.

My head is reeling with all the information that Kwon Hyeun has shared. The woman was once pregnant with my half sister. My dad was a horrible person. My mother . . . *fuck* . . . my mother's name is Choi Wansu.

"What will you do?" The question is accompanied by a piercing stare. The flat brown eyes bore into mine.

Look her up, storm her castle, tear down her gates, wave my adoption papers in front of her face, scream *why why why* over and over again. "I don't know."

Disappointment flashes through the other woman's eyes, but her tone is calm, friendly even, when she speaks again. "The paper I have given you has her name, her work address, her home address, and KakaoTalk profile. You have everything you need to contact her. Your friend is coming." Kwon Hyeun stands and swings an expensive Chanel bag over her shoulder, but she doesn't leave. She plants a hand on the table and leans down to stare at me, and this time her eyes are swimming in emotion. She's been holding back all this time, trying not to break down in front of me.

Her voice thick, she says, "If you were my daughter and I had the means, I would've spent anything to track you down instead of avoiding you as if you weren't the most important thing to me." She reaches out to press a finger against my face. "I would not have given you up. I would have fought my parents for you. I would have fought King Sejong for you. Remember that when you meet Choi Wansu." Something—

bitterness, regret, pain—twists Kwon Hyeun's mouth. Her finger falls away, leaving a burning sensation where she touched me. Then, as if she can't hold back the flood of tears, she hurries off. I don't try to stop her. I can't even move. Her words have hammered me into my chair.

Boyoung approaches with concern on her face. "Was that . . . Kwon Hyeun?"

I manage a nod but no words. Choi Wansu . . . a poor woman who married money . . . who is into adoption causes. It's a coincidence. It has to be a coincidence. This is a country with fifty million people. Choi isn't an uncommon last name. There have to be hundreds of thousands of Chois here in Seoul. I turn the paper over and over in my hands. A coincidence. I jump to my feet, rush past a bewildered Boyoung, and take the steps two at a time, but Kwon Hyeun is gone when I reach the street.

I grab my neck and squeeze it to prevent the scream of frustration that is building at the base of my throat. I drop my hand to my purse and pluck out my phone. My text to Yujun is half-written when I stop.

What if he knows and this is all a huge setup? What if he knew I was coming? Although how unless Choi Wansu and Lee Jonghyung plotted this together? Except Lee died and Choi decided she didn't want to get to know her daughter after all. That's a ridiculous plot. *Ridiculous!* I shout in my head because why would they want to set me up in the first place? The thing to do would be to ignore me. Maybe Lee Jonghyung wanted to meet me but Choi Wansu did not, and Yujun doesn't want me to find my mother because that would mean some of his inheritance would go to me.

I shake my head again. These are wild imaginings. Soap-operatic imaginings. The next thing someone will tell me is I have a twin sister.

It's a coincidence. It must be. I keep repeating it to myself as I search for a taxi.

"Hara. Hara. Wait." Boyoung is at my heels. "What's going on?"

"I need to get to this address." I shove the piece of paper into Boyoung's hands. "Should I take the subway or a taxi?"

"Yongsan-gu. That's across the river, but—" She stops abruptly, her eyes nearly falling out of her head. "This is IF Group. The woman told you to go to IF Group?"

"Across the river." I latch on to that and ignore the rest. What had Jules said? It's almost faster taking the subway across the river? I pull up the travel app and type in the address. It's four subway stops away. Barely fifteen minutes via the train. I start down the escalator, running past the riders on the right.

Boyoung yells after me, "Wait. Hara, wait."

"I can hear you." I wave for her to catch up.

"Are you going to see her right now?" she asks when she reaches me.

"Yeah."

"Don't you think you should wait a day?"

"I don't have a day to wait. I only have five left."

I hit the tiled subway tunnel floor and start running, weaving through the crowd of people. It's probably considered super rude in this country where politeness is baked into the culture, but I don't care. Not at this moment. I can hear the train coming, the ground rumbling under my feet, and I want to be on this train. I speed up until I'm running so fast the air turns to wind against my cheeks. The train is pulling in when I burst out of the tunnel. Impatiently, I wait until the passengers spill out, hopping from one foot to the other. I want to yell at them to move faster. I have an appointment to make, a person to meet. It's very important. Move. Move. *Move.* The last passenger off is a woman, whom I glare at for taking so *damn* long. I collapse into a seat and try to catch my breath, but my heart can't stop racing. The train begins to move, but inside the subway car, it feels like time has slowed. The train isn't moving fast enough. Each minute ticks by as if the cars are being pulled by actual horses, but old ones whose joints are arthritic and who can't have more than one hoof off the ground at any given time. I drum my fingertips against my thigh. I need to be in Yongsan-gu yesterday.

The train stops and the doors start to part. I dart out, past someone who likely curses at me. The building's address is outside of exit five. I bolt down the long subway tunnel, watching the yellow arrows and signs until I find the stairs to exit five.

The building where IF Group is headquartered is tall, with blue glass windows. The lettering is discreet and in *Hangul*, but my map is telling me it's the right place. Unlike the time that I waited outside for hours looking for Kim Jihye, this time I march through the glass doors and make straight for the elevator bank. Out of the corner of my eye, I see a tall, dark-haired man exiting. I whip around and see a broad suit-covered back duck into a waiting town car. My eyes narrow. Was that Yujun or am I imaging things?

"Hara, I don't think you should do this. Let me help you send an email."

I turn away from the car to find Boyoung has caught up. Did she take a taxi? I didn't see her on the train. The other girl is panting and a light sheen of sweat dots her forehead.

"What's the point of waiting? I've waited twenty-five years. I think that's long enough."

"How will you get past security?"

For the first time I notice that the entrance to the elevators is blocked by a row of clear gates and manned by two security guards. I don't give two flying fingers about security. I'll jump the stiles if I have to.

"Pretend like you're sick and distract them for me," I tell my friend.

"No. I can't do that. Wait, Hara, please."

But I'm determined. I draft behind another employee, and when the woman swipes her badge and the acrylic gates part, I slide in behind her.

I hear the male voices, presumably from the security guards, call out something, but I pretend I don't hear them. It's not like I understand what they are saying anyway. The woman in front of me hesitates and looks over her shoulder. I walk by, pretending like nothing out of the ordinary is occurring, straight to the elevators. I'm going to IF Group and nothing is stopping me. I jab the up button and silently urge the doors to open. Hard footsteps slap against the ground, growing louder as they near. Out of the corner of my eye, I see two uniformed men walking toward me. The two men almost reach me but the doors of the elevator car slide open. My escape! I leap forward and run smack dab into a wall of human chest.

"Hara?"

I look up from the blue cotton shirt and smart blue tie with the tiny polka dots to see Yujun smiling crookedly down at me, his hands on my shoulders so I don't fall.

"Yujun," I croak.

"You're . . . here?" He's surprised.

I am, too, but not in a good way. Not in any good way. My skin feels clammy and that cold wave that washed over me at the café returns. I sway and he tightens his grip. "Are you not feeling well, Hara?"

"Are you . . . Is this . . ." The question sits on my tongue like a rotted piece of fruit that I can't swallow. I have to get it out but it's stuck there. I grab the paper from my pocket and shove it into his chest. "Is this your mother?"

With one hand still on my shoulder, he takes the sheet and scans it. "Where did you get this?"

"Is this your mother? Your *eomma*? The one who taught you not to stutter anymore." *The one you adore, who gave you all this self-confidence, the one you're so proud of because of all the good she's doing in the world. Is this your mother?* I scream silently. I want him to say no. I need him to deny this.

"Yes. Choi Wansu is Eomeo-nim. I was going to text you that I was inviting her to dinner with us tonight so you could talk about your search, but you're here. Would you like to come up and meet her now?"

My eyelids flutter shut and I gulp down a rock that would fill the Grand Canyon before nodding. "Yes. I would."

CHAPTER TWENTY-ONE

I BARELY REGISTER THE OTHER PEOPLE IN THE ELEVATOR.

"Do you know me?" I blurt out.

Yujun smiles down but he looks confused. "Yes. I do."

Maybe I'm reading the confusion into his face and voice. Maybe I'm seeing what I want to see, because if this has all been a setup from the beginning and he's been pretending to like me the whole time . . . well, the mix of anger and humiliation swirling in my gut is an awful concoction. I want to throw up on his shiny shoes and then punch him hard enough that the dimple becomes a permanent dent.

"Did you know me before I came? Did you purposely meet me at the airport?"

"No." He shakes his head. He's still smiling lightly but the questions are growing. "But I am glad that we did meet."

"Why? Why did you drive out of your way for me? I was a stranger. I mistook you for someone else."

"Hara." He reaches up and touches my shoulder again. I didn't realize I was trembling. "Are you okay?"

"Tell me," I demand.

His smile fades away entirely. "I saw you come through the exit. You went and rented an internet modem and struggled a bit until you realized they all spoke English. I had stepped forward to help you but you were able to complete the transaction. When you looked for your driver and didn't find him, I thought I could not allow such a pretty girl to have a bad first day in Seoul."

I want so desperately to believe him. "But the other night, you said you knew I was here to find my birth parents."

"I suspected, yes. When we met at the airport, you said you were not visiting family and that you were adopted."

I rub clammy hands over my face. Was it luck, then? Or coincidence? Seoul is such a big city. There are millions of people here. *It seems big, but it's small. Everyone's connected,* Jules had said that day when we ran into a coworker of hers in the subway.

"I think we should get you something to eat. You're shaking, Hara." He turns to someone in the elevator and says something in Korean. *Bap?* Rice?

I don't know. My head is aching and I can't concentrate. The elevator speeds to the fourteenth floor and then the doors open. No one moves.

"Hara?" Yujun says gently. "This is our floor."

I curl my trembling fingers around the strap of my purse and follow Yujun off the elevator. My sandals slap against the wooden floor and down toward a set of glass doors. Inside, a slickly dressed woman rises and bows. I barely manage a nod in return.

"This way, Hara." Yujun touches my elbow lightly. Behind us I hear the slight inhale of breath as if this casual touch is shocking. I turn down the hallway. On either side are glass walls with a thick band of frosting starting about two feet off the floor and ending right at my shoulder. I can see people's heads above the privacy screens and

I keep peering over them in the misguided belief that I will suddenly recognize my mother. But today is no different than the one where I stood watching all the workers stream out of the building. There are many faces but none are familiar.

The corridors of glass give way to another large reception area dominated by a gigantic marble desk with white and chrome accessories. A very attractive woman sits behind the wall of marble. To the right of the desk are a set of four curved white leather chairs. Behind her is an enormous abstract painting with slashes of red and blue set on a white canvas. Besides the black suit of the receptionist, the painting provides the sole color.

My already chilled hands grow colder.

"Park Seolhyun, is Choi Wansu available? Someone is here to see her." Yujun uses English, presumably for my benefit.

"She is. Does your . . ." The woman is unsure of how to address me and I make no move to clarify because I don't know what my role is here. Daughter? Stranger? Investigator?

"My friend," Yujun answers.

That surprises the woman, but she's too professional to allow more than a slight eyebrow raise that I might have missed had I not been staring intently. The woman presses a button and murmurs something in Korean. Last night's *hotteok* climbs into my throat. I stumble back and Yujun has to reach out to brace me. The shock in the secretary's face is too great to hide this time, but the importance of that doesn't register. I'm thinking about something else. Do I need to meet my mother? What's it going to solve? Will I suddenly feel like I fit in with all the other people wearing stripes? Or is it polka dots? I don't even know anymore. Half of me thinks I should grab Yujun's hand and drag him outside to the river where we can eat *gimbap* and drink beer and kiss and pretend this never happened. The thoughts whip up like a tornado, swirling around with gale-force winds that threaten to flay me open from the inside. I can't even remember the purpose of this whole excursion. Something about polka dots and stripes and my neglectful father and my own inability to come to terms with my identity. None of that is going to be resolved by coming face-to-face with her—

All of my thoughts dissolve when the door opens. Choi Wansu is tall—aided by four-inch heels. Her frame is encased in a smart cream-colored suit with a pale yellow shirt. Needle-thin gold spikes dangle from her ears. Red adorns her lips. She has jet-black hair cut into an angular chin-length bob. Rectangular glasses slide down her nose because, like me, she has almost no bridge. Unconsciously, I reach up and stroke my bridge bone. We barely look alike except for the eyes. Our eyes are exactly the same, and in them I see shock and something that looks like resignation before Wansu blinks and then there's nothing but dark glass, as if I was staring at the Han River on a windless night.

"You have your father's face," Wansu says, breaking the silence.

My hand drops to my throat. I apply some pressure, maybe instinctively, maybe subconsciously, so I don't scream or vomit. It's hard to get the words out past the giant lump, but I manage to say, "I guess so."

Wansu steps aside and pushes the door open. "Come in."

"*Eomma*?" Yujun is confused. His mind is trying to fit all the puzzle pieces together but he doesn't like the picture they're forming so he scatters them and tries again. Or, at least, that's what it looks like is happening as Yujun's gaze ping-pongs from me to his stepmother and back again.

"I'll see you at home tonight, son. Please, come in," she repeats to me.

I grab onto Yujun as if he's a life raft in the middle of a hurricane. *Don't leave me*, I plead silently. *I don't know what I'm doing here.*

Yujun laces his fingers through mine. "It's going to be okay."

"Yujun-ah, when your father brought me home that first time so many years ago, he left us alone so that we could talk. We needed that time together. Do you remember?"

I can feel the pressure lessen on my hand, so I grip him harder. Wansu somehow senses he's wavering, too, that mother's intuition, and presses forward. "I promise to bring your friend for dinner tonight. It will be a celebration."

"No."

Yujun squeezes my hand and then releases me. "*Eomma* is right. You should talk by yourselves. I'll wait here, though." He points to one of the white leather chairs.

I want to haul him back by my side.

"It will be a long time," Wansu interjects. She doesn't want him to stick around, which makes me instantly suspicious. Does Wansu plan to get rid of me somehow? Have the office assistant drive me to Incheon and shove me onto the first flight back to America? Or maybe she will just toss me out the window.

"I'll wait here." He says it with a slight smile and a brief nod, but the tone is firm. He walks over to one of the white leather chairs, flips back his suitcoat, and seats himself. He's not moving and it reassures me in a hundred different ways. I won't be left behind—at least not by Yujun.

The two stare at each other for a long, silent moment. A whole conversation takes place that I don't understand because I don't have the years of familiarity that these two have built. I'm on the outside of their family circle even though Wansu is my blood mother and Yujun's stepmother. The unfairness of it is like a slap across my face, and bitterness fills my mouth.

Wansu's lips tighten almost imperceptibly. She's annoyed, maybe even angered, but other than the slight twitch of her lips, none of it

shows. She turns away dismissively and gestures me inside the office
again.

My limbs are heavy and the drumbeat in my head thuds loud
enough that I'm certain everyone in a twenty-foot radius can hear it,
but I move forward.

Choi Wansu's office is glass and steel and white walls with mono-
chromatic paintings. There's a tiny bit of color in the paintings, but
it's negligible and could be mistaken for shadows cast by the light
overhead. Either Wansu or her decorator hates color, and all of it has
been discarded, much like me. I was like a blot of color in Wansu's
life and so she abandoned me to make way for something sleeker,
smarter—my eyes slide to the door that Wansu is closing—someone
tall, handsome, smart, kind . . . better.

I stiffen my spine and raise my head. I'm not the one at fault here.
Why should I be cowering in the middle of the room like a child
called to the front of the class to explain some infraction? I'm the
one with the questions. I'm the one who didn't screw up here.

I clasp my hands at my back and pretend that it's a privilege for
her to have me standing here. I resume my inspection of Wansu's
surgically precise setup. One side of the room holds floor-to-ceiling
glass panels overlooking downtown Seoul. There's a large painting
on the wall facing the desk that looks like two giant brushes dipped
in black paint where whipped across a canvas. Behind the desk is a
marble-clad wall with illuminated niches holding metal and glass
sculptures. The wall opposite the windows holds the only signs of
personalization. There are framed plaques and a console table with
pictures, but everything is precisely placed.

Most of the photos are of Wansu getting an award. She's depicted
shaking hands with someone while holding a padded portfolio open
displaying something important that I don't understand. One of the
award photos is not with Koreans, and the banner hanging behind

Wansu is in English. I pick it up. *Entrepreneur of the Year, International Association for the Advancement of Women.*

Ellen's home has none of these. Ellen doesn't even have an office. She has a kitchen and a craft room that's messy and maddening because I can't ever find a safety pin when I need one because Ellen doesn't believe in organization. Or white things. I engage in a moment of self-loathing as I think of all the times that I've mentally criticized Ellen for being messy. I send my mom a silent apology.

"Sit," Wansu barks with the demeanor of someone who is used to giving orders and having them followed. "Please," she adds.

I don't do as she's ordered. Wansu doesn't get to tell me what to do. Wansu has no hold over me—not like she has over Yujun. Because Yujun loves her and that love holds him in check. The thought makes my stomach clench. He's had my mother's love all these years.

I once watched the tail end of a show where adoptees were reunited with their birth parents. Usually I avoided those emotional-porn shows like the plague but this one caught my attention. There were three adoptees onstage and one by one, each kid's parents came out. Every time someone appeared from offstage, the crowd would erupt in cheers. The camera panned to the audience wiping away tears. The people on the stage were crying. The host was beaming, likely thinking of the giant ratings. It all made me so uncomfortable. I wondered what I would be doing. Would I cry? Would I break down? I imagined a lot of scenarios but none of them where my birth mother and I would be circling each other like caged tigers or perhaps gladiators waiting for the thumbs-up or thumbs-down from the emperor in order to know whether we should try to kill each other or whether we should retreat to our quarters.

"If you would rather stand, then do so," Wansu concedes as if making a huge and meaningful gesture. She stops at the side of her desk, one hand lightly resting on the shiny wooden surface. "You must have many questions."

"No. Only one."

Wansu's eyebrows go up. "Only one?"

"Why?" I look around the expensive office, at the discreet glass nameplate on Wansu's desk, at the suit that Wansu is wearing that lies perfectly across her shoulders without a crease or a wrinkle. I think of Yujun's expensive car, his US education, his designer clothes. I think of my home back in Iowa, the inheritance my adoptive father decided to leave his *real* son, and the near-empty funeral of my biological father. Yes, I have many questions, but they all start with *why*.

She doesn't pretend she doesn't know what I'm talking about. "My life when I was pregnant was very different than it is now."

"And when it changed? When you had money and opportunity, you did nothing. Why?"

"Did you seek me out?" Wansu parries.

It is like a fight. Wansu wants to be right and I want to be aggrieved.

"No. I was left *on the street*. It wouldn't be rational to think I could find my birth parents. All I have is a sheet of paper that says I eat rice and fish and can handle a spoon well." A picture of myself with a number across my chest. It's a mugshot of an abandoned child. I never look at it because I'm not a poor waif from a foreign country. I *hated* thinking of myself like that. Ellen made a point to tell me that I was wanted. At night when I cried for no reason, she held me and said that I was loved, that she chose me, that she wanted me over everything in the world and didn't the divorce prove that? She chose me over Pat. She has always chosen me, but this woman in front of me with the frozen expression on her face, she threw me away. I clench my teeth to keep all those awful, vulnerable words from spilling out. This woman does not deserve to see my pain.

"Despite all of that, you have found me."

"Not because of anything you did. Because of this." I fumble in my purse and pull out the printed email that I've been carrying since I received it. The creases that I've made and the ones that Ellen made and those of my friends like Boyoung have softened it, and when I shove it in Wansu's face it flops like a wet towel.

Wansu barely scans it. "A DNA test?"

Anger burns through me, rendering the lump in my throat to ash. "Yeah. Sorry, but you can't reconnect with your old boyfriend because he's dead."

Not even a flinch. Had she known already?

"That which is yesterday should stay yesterday," Wansu says.

"What's that supposed to mean?"

"The past is in the past." She shakes her head lightly. "We should look to tomorrow. What is it that you need? Money? A place to live? A car?"

She could've slapped me and it would've hurt less. "Nothing. I don't want anything." This was a mistake. A huge mistake. While I refused to admit it, I thought that I'd find *belonging*, not from being in Korea but from finding my mother. I figured my mother would live in a small, barren room like Lee Jonghyung, not sit in a museum's worth of marble and chrome with a bank account that would likely make millionaires blush.

I don't belong here with the polka dots, particularly ones that are carved out of platinum and sprinkled with diamonds.

"I'm done here." I walk to the door.

Wansu follows immediately. "What do you mean you're done here?"

"I mean, I don't care that you gave birth to me. I don't want to know why any longer. The answers no longer interest me." I stop and hold up a hand. "Don't follow me. I know how to get home." Besides, I have Yujun. I wrench open the door to tell him I'm ready to leave only to find the four chairs completely empty.

"His father needed him," Wansu says quietly, in a tone too soft to be genuine.

I blink rapidly. I haven't cried since I was ten and I'm not starting because some *male* left me.

"Hara, I will drive you home. Wait here."

Not in a million years.

CHAPTER TWENTY-TWO

PERHAPS IT WAS FOOLISH TO RUN OUT OF THE BUILDING, AWAY from my mother, but being left behind once again dredged up so many hurt feelings that I felt like I might drown in them.

It was all too much. I couldn't sit in a car with Wansu, a car that was undoubtedly expensive, a visible sign of her full and happy life here in Seoul with her perfect son. I move toward the stairs because standing and waiting for an elevator would allow Wansu to drag me back into her office, or even worse, she'd get in the car with me and I'd have to stand in her presence, which I can't do—not for another second. I take the stairs, all fourteen flights of them. By the last one, I'm blinded by spots in my eyes, my breath is choppy and short, my skin is clammy, but I know I have to keep moving. I can still hear her tersely telling me to stop and come back to discuss this—whatever "this" is—with her like an adult, so I plan to never stop. If I do, I'll collapse and my body will decay here in the stairwell of a foreign country because I won't get up again. Boyoung is in the lobby, but I pretend I don't see her. It's not hard. I can't really see anything at this point. My anger and hurt and frustration are all I can see and I use all of those emotions to power me forward. If Boyoung and Wansu are behind me, I don't hear them. But I don't look back either. Forward, forward, forward. What had Wansu said? Let's keep yesterday in the past? Good idea. In the subway, I pick the first train that stops and ride it until the third stop, one I don't even know the name of. I keep moving, past the coffee shops, the restaurants, the Olive Youngs, the small shops selling shoes and socks and T-shirts with English sayings that are sometimes vulgar, sometimes funny, sometimes indecipherable.

The cars and buses and occasional motorbikes with their big delivery boxes strapped to the back whiz by. The glass doors and windows of the office buildings reflect a distorted image of me, the street, the people. Ahead, through a break between buildings, I can see the river. I start toward it, walking first and then running, not caring that I might look like I've lost my mind.

I have lost my mind. I left it back in Iowa when I decided to come over here looking for answers that did not exist, answers I didn't need. What was wrong with my life anyway? I had a job. I had friends. Yes, I wasn't close with any of them and sometimes I felt like I was adrift in a sea of humanity without an anchor or a life vest, but that was normal. Who didn't feel disconnected at some point in their lives or even at a lot of points in their lives? Normal people drank or smoke or slept around or took up needlepoint. I should have picked any one of those options instead of flying halfway across the world to find something that didn't exist.

I keep running, ignoring my aching side and sore feet, across the six lanes of traffic, down the spiral stairs, and out onto the river's edge. The railing puts an end to my progress. I grip it, winded, panting. I can barely make out the sounds of the river over the engines of the cars running on the bridge overhead.

In my pocket, the phone rings. I let it go to voicemail but the caller is persistent. It keeps ringing and keeps ringing and it's so irritating I pull the device out and almost toss it in the river. Realizing how dumb that is, I pull back, but my hands are sweaty and I'm weak and dumb and the phone slips out of my hand and sails into the water, landing with an inaudible splash below me.

"Fuck." I stare at the ripples in the dark water in full display. Of course I would drop my phone. I hate life. I *hate* it. I press my thumbs to my temples hard enough that my eyes sting and then I tell myself to stop the pity party and get the stupid thing. I climb over the metal railing and scramble down the steep side, but by the time I reach the edge, the phone is gone. There's no shallow entry here. It's a drop-off and I have no idea how deep it is. The water laps against the rocks like a tease.

I sink to my haunches and cover my face with my hands. A laugh burbles out of me. I swallow back my hysteria and start undressing. I slip my sweater and purse off, shed my shoes and socks, and lower myself into the water.

The water is cool and there's a vague odor that I didn't detect before when I sat along the riverbank with Yujun. The sides of the river here are rocky and slippery. The stones cut into my palms and the soles of my feet. I crane my neck and think I see the vague outline of my phone. I reach for it, but the basin of the river gives way to a well of water. I go under. My arms fly up instinctively looking for something to grasp, but there's only air.

I scream, like a dumbass, and dirty river water floods into my mouth. My elementary school swimming lessons kick in and I surface spitting out water and who knows what else. I scramble toward the slippery rocks and drag myself to safety.

"Hara, you are the dumbest person alive," I mutter as I lie on my stomach like a beached whale and spit out water onto the stones under my cheek. The sun is setting and the heat of the day is being replaced by a cool night breeze. It chills my skin. Goose pimples chase their way from my neck down to the backs of my knees. The river doesn't hold any answers, not that I thought it would. It seemed like a good place to vent my feelings of frustration and anger and hurt. Now I feel foolish on top of all that. I better get home and get dry. I push up to my feet and start squeezing the water out of my dress. It doesn't work very well. I swipe my sweater and purse off the ground and shove my feet into my sandals. The socks go into my purse.

Thankfully, there's a bus stop close by. The people waiting under the shelter eye me suspiciously. They should. Who knows how much further I could unravel.

The bus driver gives me a strange look as I climb aboard. I tap my card against the reader and march defiantly down the aisle toward the back, ignoring the trickle of water dripping down my leg. The bus doesn't take off immediately. The driver is likely debating whether to come to the back and kick me off, but his need to be timely outweighs his distaste at some random passenger getting his bus all wet. I tug the sweater tight across my body.

"It's the Han River," I mutter under my breath. This is Choi Wansu's fault. With each passing block, as I grow colder and more uncomfortable, as the wet clothes stick to my skin like plaster, the anger grows.

If Wansu hadn't abandoned me, I would've grown up here in Korea. I wouldn't feel stupid every time I opened my mouth here and I wouldn't feel like a stranger back in Iowa. I would've never seen Iowa. Yujun, who went to college in the US and who lived with his aunt for three years, only visited Chicago.

But then Ellen would be all alone. She would've married Pat, never had a kid, and ended up by herself after Pat moved on and created a new family—a real one. That alternate reality isn't great either.

I press my head against the bar of the seat in front of me and will my brain to shut down. It doesn't. The hamster wheel is in full spinning motion and the same questions tumble around in my head. The ache in my head spreads all through my frame until even the tips of my fingers feel sore.

It takes me two hours to get home between the buses and the subways and the connections I have to make, and I'm only able to accomplish it because a kind lady in the subway station spoke English and drew a map for me. By the end of the trip, I'm still damp— which is somehow worse than wet—and cold by the time I make it to the bottom of the hill. The number of stairs looms large in front of me and I briefly entertain curling up against the base until morning. Or until it's time for me to go back to America.

Lights flash behind me and then an engine cuts off. I turn to see a shiny black car idling. I know immediately who it is without anyone getting out of the vehicle or rolling down the windows. I should've stopped at the convenience store two blocks back and bought a carton of eggs. In fact, I'm going to do that immediately. I turn on my wet heel and stomp toward the store. I'm going to buy two cartons and I'm going to paint that shiny black vehicle with so much egg that it's going to look like an omelet when I'm done.

"Hara," a brisk voice calls out.

I keep walking. An engine purrs to life and I can practically feel the heat of the vehicle at my heels. I speed up. The car does as well. "Hara. Hara," the voice calls.

I run, only I can't see because it's so damn dark in this alley, and I don't notice the large rock until my toe hits it and I go flying face-first onto the asphalt.

"*Omo!*" Brakes screech. A car door slams. There's a clatter of heels and then a soft hand at my shoulder.

I jerk away. "I don't need your help."

"You are wet and uncomfortable. If you stay out in that condition you are likely to get sick and then you will blame me for that as well."

Wansu isn't wrong, but I'm too mad to acknowledge this. I struggle to my feet and force myself to move. The big black car keeps pace behind me. Wansu clips along, her high heels clicking against the pavement.

"What do you want?" she asks. "I have money and I'm happy to provide for you."

"Money?" I screech to a halt and whirl on my mother. "You think money is what I want from you?"

"Then what is it?" Wansu appears to be legitimately confused, and that is all the more infuriating.

"You're my mother! You gave birth to me! You carried me in your body for nine months and all you want to do is buy me off?"

"That's right, I did," Wansu says, her voice as chilly as the clothes clinging to my body. "I gave birth to you. I nurtured you. I did not *throw you away*. I placed you outside of a police station and waited there until someone found you and took you inside. I gave you up so you could have a better life. And now that you have sought me out, against my wishes, I am willing to provide for you like a mother does. What more do you want?"

I want you to love me, my heart cries out, but there's no point in admitting that. No point in laying my heart out there to be trampled on. I've got some pride left. "Nothing. Literally nothing, which is why I'm walking away. You're the one following me, trying to erase your guilt by throwing money at my face."

"Maybe I am. How much will it take?"

"All of it," I snap. "Give me all of it."

Wansu's face hardens. "Then you wish to ruin me and hurt my son and all the people that work for our company. I can't allow that to happen."

I hate that Wansu can't see through my curtain of hurt—that she's not even attempting to reach me. "Then leave me alone. That's all I want."

ALL THE LIGHTS are on at the house, which makes me even wearier. It would've been nice if I could've crept inside, gone up to my room, climbed into my bed, and covered my head with my blankets.

Instead, I have to face my roommates and Jules will demand to know what is going on. I have no energy for an inquisition. Every last bit of it is in the river.

I push open the gate and trudge reluctantly toward the front door. The illumination should be welcoming but the dark spot in the alley next to the convenience store is looking more appealing by the second. The door opens before I reach it and Yujun's concerned face appears. I hate that my stupid heart leaps at the sight of him, dressed in his work clothes with his white shirtsleeves rolled up to show his fine forearms, the expensive watch, and his capable hands that reach to pull me inside. This is Wansu's son, the child she chose to raise instead of me.

Bitterness floods my mouth. *"You."*

He flinches slightly. "Hara, please."

My credit card isn't maxed out yet. This is a big city. There has to be a hotel that has a room available. I turn around and walk away from the door, from the lights, from him. I should keep going until I reach Incheon, where I can climb aboard a plane, any one of them, and have it take me away.

"I didn't know." His hand reaches out to press against the gate so I can't leave.

"I don't believe you." And I don't want to be convinced otherwise. He's so charming, and if he is given time and an opportunity,

I'm certain that he'll spin a story that will result in me begging forgiveness from Wansu. *I'm sorry I came here. I'm sorry I sought you out. I'm sorry I exist.*

"How could I have known?" The plea in his voice is earnest, so very earnest, but I'm not the same girl that he took to the top of Namsan and looked through the telescope with all the way to Busan. I'm the girl who learned her very rich mother threw her away like garbage and kept a boy instead. A boy I'd kissed, held in my arms. A boy about whom I had fantasies that I would be embarrassed to share with a friend. A boy who makes me want to bury my face in his shoulder and cry the tears I never let fall. I don't, though. I've never let things like feelings drag me down before, and I won't this time either.

I pull on the gate and it falls open so easily that I stumble back into his solid frame. His hand circles my shoulder to steady me and we stand there, breaths held, for a half second, maybe more. At any other time, his hand on my arm, his heart against my ear, his larger body engulfing mine, would be welcome, wanted. From the moment I spotted him in the airport, he's been the safe port in this foreign city, and a part of me wants to cling to him.

"You're the one she kept. Even if you didn't know, you're still the one she kept."

He has no response to this because there isn't one. Facts are facts. I can sense he's searching for words, for a way to convince me to forgive and move on, so when he says, "Where will you go?" I'm caught off guard.

"I— I—" But this time it's me with no response. A hotel, I suppose, but I'd need one where they speak English and that isn't too expensive.

"A hotel?" he guesses like he can read my mind. "Let me take you to one. Let me do this small thing for you. My car is here. I will drive you, check you in, and then leave."

His words have an edge to them, somewhere between a plea and a demand, because the former is unfamiliar and the latter is too harsh. When I don't immediately turn him down, he presses. "I'm not here because *Eomma*—Choi Wansu asked me to be. I came because of you. Because I needed you and I wondered if you needed me."

Again, he surprises me. "Why would you need me?"

A pained expression crosses his face, tightening the skin across his prominent cheekbones, drawing a line in his forehead. "Because, Hara, when I wake up I think of you and when I go to sleep, you're there. Since I saw you in the airport . . ." He shakes his head. "I don't know if it's the same for you and I didn't want to rush things even though in my head I wanted to spend every minute of the day with you. When I had to leave to go see my father, I could feel you slipping away. When you didn't answer your phone, when Choi Wansu-nim didn't answer her phone . . . it was as if you'd already left, and I am not ready for you to leave. Not yet." He pushes my hair away from my face. "Not yet."

I close my eyes and swallow hard. He sounds earnest. He sounds like these are his true feelings, and they are a soft salve on my wounds. I totter on my feet, weakening into that person I just said I'm not.

"Hara, let me take care of you. I am only Yujun from Seoul. Nothing more."

I close my eyes and slot him into a place far away from Choi Wansu. "All right, but we can't go down to your car." I'm afraid she's still there.

"We'll get a cab," he replies immediately. He tucks my hand into the crook of his arm and we walk silently to the top of the hill. There are no cabs around, which is why everyone goes down the hill instead of up, and so we keep walking toward lights and people and traffic. Neither of us speaks, not that I know what to say. I suspect it is the same for him. At a bright intersection, we stop and Yujun from Seoul hails a taxi. He holds the door open for me and I climb inside. After he gives instructions to the driver, we take off. The two engage in some short conversation and I stare out the window as the neon signs, streetlamps, and headlights blur into one giant stream of light. I close my eyes and lean my head against the glass. When the taxi comes to a halt, it's in front of a tall, fancy hotel. A doorman wearing white gloves approaches.

"Stay a moment," Yujun says to me, and then he's gone before I can respond.

The driver and I meet each other's eyes in his rearview mirror and I steel myself for a question in Korean that I will not understand followed by a faint look of disappointment if I'm lucky and disgust if I'm not. But he only gives me a brief nod before fiddling with the GPS screen. The quiet in the car becomes almost oppressive. I wonder if I should pay him. Then I glance at the doorman waiting by the amber-lit entry and wonder if I can afford to pay for even a cup of coffee here. Yujun from Seoul may be able to swing this, but Hara from Iowa only has a little room left on her credit card. I pull up my translation app. If there's one person in this city who knows of a cheap hotel, it has to be a taxi driver. I type in the question and hope that it translates it decently. What was "Excuse me" in Korean? The word pops into my head.

I clear my throat and try it out. *"Jamkkanmanyo."*

I must've pronounced it well enough because the driver turns to me. *"Ne?"*

Yes, I translate in my head. *"Jeolyeomhan hoteli eodi isseoyo."* The words come out halting and, from the confusion on the driver's face, possibly incoherent. I open my mouth to try again when the door flies open. Yujun's face appears.

"Come," he says, and then tacks on a "please."

"I don't think—"

"Everything has been taken care of," he rushes to interrupt me. "But for me you would be home, so please, come." Before I can respond he hands the cabdriver a handful of bills.

The cabdriver takes the money with a smile and says something in rapid Korean and waves his hand, pointing out the window. I look past Yujun to see a couple of women behind him. Their cheeks are flushed from alcohol and one is swaying on her feet.

Yujun gives me wincing smile. "Our driver would like to take these two to their destination. Why don't you look at the room, and if you don't like it, I'll find you another."

In other words, I'm being a hassle. I slide out of the seat and step aside as the two girls push by us to get into the car. The one that wasn't on her way to passing out stops before Yujun and cocks her head. She drags her lower lip down with her thumb and the words that trip off her tongue are Korean, but I know from the sweet, coy tone exactly what they mean. I'm right here, but since I don't know how to say that, I reach into my shallow puddle of a vocabulary and loudly say, *"Jamkkanmanyo."*

The girl starts and swings toward me in surprise, as if she forgot or didn't even realize I was there. Yujun presses his lips together and averts his face to cough into his fist. Is he laughing? Before I can get too outraged, Yujun reaches for my hand and tugs me to his side. "My girlfriend is here with me."

"Yeoja chingu?"

It's the shock that digs under my skin and causes me to lean into Yujun's frame. I bat my eyelashes at the other girl and, while she inspects me, draw my thumb across my lower lip and press bare remnants of my lipstick onto Yujun's crisp white shirt. It leaves a tiny, almost imperceptible stain. Yujun coughs into his fist again and this time I realize he's covering a smirk.

I roll my eyes, but since I brought this on, I guess I should end it. "Let's go." I arrow toward the entrance, but Yujun catches my arm and nudges me down a different path toward a smaller door. A man steps out and holds the door open for us. It reminds me of the time when we were at the club. "Is your friend DJ Song here?" I joke.

A line appears between Yujun's eyes. "Ahn Sangki?"

"Yeah, him." I flutter my hand toward the side entrance. "We went through the side door of the club, remember?"

"I remember. He does make an impression." Yujun sounds slightly peeved. "I asked a friend for a favor, as I didn't think you wanted to go through the lobby."

I glance down at my wrinkled clothes. I'd momentarily forgotten I took a bath in the Han. "Good call," I say and give him a thumbs-up.

The hotel guy leads us down a back hallway. With its plain floor tiles and white walls, it's apparent that we're in some employee area. He leaves us at the service elevator, which takes us to the eleventh floor. At a room near the end of the hall, Yujun stops, produces a key card, and then waves me inside. Unsurprisingly, the room is posh, with dark wood floors and wood paneling on the walls. The curtains are open and even though it is dark, I can make out the outline of a mountain in the background. Yujun flicks on some lights and opens a closet that I missed on the way in. He holds out a robe for me.

"I was worried about you." There's a slight chiding note in his voice. "I texted you as I was leaving but didn't hear back." He grimaces and I realize he's more angry at himself than me. "I promised I'd be there for you and I wasn't. My father's nurse called and asked that I come quickly. He fell ill a few years ago. That's when Choi Wansu was appointed *sajangnim*, the head of IF Group. I would've told you before, but . . . I didn't want you to be concerned."

We hadn't had that kind of relationship—the one that shared

the bad things in our lives. Ours was a vacation fling, no matter how many cameras and Wi-Fi bands connected us. I used him the same way he used me. We allowed ourselves the luxury of joy, but that meant all the dark, dirty spots in our lives were ones we had to clean ourselves. There's a certain freedom in the knowing, a lightness that I hadn't felt before, and because anger is such a tiring, corrosive emotion, I let that slide away, too.

"My phone took a swim in the river and I went in after it." I attempt to explain the sodden, wrinkled mess of clothes I'm currently wearing.

"That is how you got wet."

"Yes, and thank you for not assuming I did it on purpose."

"It doesn't seem like a thing you would do."

For some reason, the story of the young couple that killed themselves by jumping into the river flashes into my mind, and I wonder if we're talking about the same thing.

"I was mad that it kept ringing and I pretended to throw the thing into the water, but it slipped from my hand."

"So you decided that you would dive in after it?"

"Yes." I cross my arms.

"I don't think all the rice in Korea would've saved it. Sometimes it is best to let lost things go." Is he giving me advice about his mother? Before I can ask, he moves on. "How are you feeling?"

"Not great," I admit.

"*Eomma* can be difficult at times. She doesn't like surprises."

"Did you know?" I don't think he did but I have to be sure.

"No, and even when I saw her name on your paper today, I didn't immediately put it together." His fingers curl around the edge of the robe he's still holding.

"Does it surprise you at all that we met? It seems almost too coincidental."

"Not at all. It is fate. Your red string of destiny and mine must be tied together so we will always meet, no matter what life we are in."

He says it so simply, so matter-of-factly, as if our coupling was as certain as the tides rising with the moon. And I need to hear it, even if it's not sincere. My heart takes those words and wraps them around the fragile, sore edges like a Band-Aid.

"I don't look like her."

"Oh, I wouldn't say that. You have the same eyes. Do you look like your father?"

"I don't think so." I reach for my purse and pull out the photos.

Yujun tucks the robe under his arm and flips through the images, his eyebrows arching up like Wansu's do when he reaches her picture. Na Wansu doesn't look much like Choi Wansu. The eighteen-year-old has long hair with bangs that are curled under. She's wearing tight jeans with a wide brown belt and a plain blue blouse with a wide collar. If she has earrings on, I can't make them out, but there's a leather necklace dangling around her neck. The most shocking part of the photo is that Wansu is smiling. It's not a big smile. There aren't any teeth showing, but there's a distinct upward curve of the corners of her lips. She looks happy.

"You recognize her," I say.

"Yes. I do."

"And if I'd shown these to you earlier, you would have told me?"

He nods. "I would have. I know that this is hard—for all of us—but once we get over the shock, it will all work out. You'll see."

He sounds certain and confident as he always does, and because I'm tired and it's been a very long day, I decide not to argue with him. He lives with a certain optimism that I'm reluctant to chip away at. Why should everyone be miserable?

"Take a shower. I'm going down to the gift store to get you some clothes so you don't have to sleep in that."

I rub an awkward hand down my front. How terrible do I look? "I don't need anything fancy," I tell him.

He allows himself a small sigh of relief, one that I might have missed if I wasn't standing so close, if I wasn't paying such careful attention. His broad chest expands and the urge to press my ear against his heart, allow his strong hands to clasp me close, descends. Before I can make a bad decision, I step back toward the bathroom. "And nothing too expensive because I'm paying you back."

He gives me one of those tiny head bows and leaves. I sag against the closed door. As much as I want to think of him solely as Yujun from Seoul, the reality is that he is Choi Yujun, the stepson of my biological mother. I should be creeped out by my feelings for him. But I am not, and in the shower, with the hot water sluicing over my frame, my mind wanders. It's the exhaustion and the loneliness. It's the fineness of the hotel room and the scent of him lingering in the air.

I take the shower head off the wall and press it between my legs. Better to do this and get it out of my system than be a weak kitten when he returns. The water jets against me in hard pulses. My knees give out and I press my hand against the wet tile to keep me upright. The orgasm tingles along my spine only to sputter out like a fire with too little kindling. I laugh at myself and replace the shower head. God, I'm pathetic. I might as well admit that I want to screw Yujun's brains out even though he is the kid Choi Wansu chose and even though he is only a vacation romance and even though I know everything now is so complicated. None of that really matters to my vagina.

I scowl at my crotch. "Get your act together," I scold and start to dry off.

There are times I regret not allowing people to get closer, times when I wished I'd spent more time with Kelly instead of at home with my television so I would have someone to whom I could pour out my untimely lusts. I pause mid-toweling off, recalling some of the dumb things that came out of Jeff's mouth, like asking if Boyoung and I were sisters and coming to me every time he had a question about Asia. No, I don't think I could've spent more time with Kelly because that would've meant enduring Jeff. The irony is that the person I should text is Jules. That acerbic, slightly mean girl helped me find Wansu, and maybe if I had my phone, I would've shared this debacle with her, but I already know what her response would be. *Girl, how dumb are you? There are dildos here in Korea, too.*

I squeeze the water out of my hair and finger comb it. The nice thing about having Asian hair is its relatively low maintenance, although I've noticed a lot of hair products in the beauty shops. I'm probably missing out on some key ingredient for keeping my black hair shiny like Boyoung's. I need a whole lesson in Korean stuff, from food to makeup to hair care. It's something I should've gotten from my mother. Wansu's face appears next to mine in the mirror. I run my finger along my eyebrow and down the slope of my nose that looks just like hers. A chill runs up my spine as I remember the cold way she looked at me. My stomach tightens and my hand trembles. I clasp my fingers tight against each other and order myself to breathe. Vaguely, as if I'm deep in the back of a cave, I hear the door open. Footsteps brush against the wooden floor and then louder on the tile as Yujun approaches. I feel his solid mass displace the empty air beside me, and warmth spreads from his palm, which he presses against my back. "You okay?"

Wansu had been so cold, so hurtful, and here is Yujun from Seoul with his broad shoulders and his warm touch. *I needed you and I wondered if you needed me.* I'm that moth in the night seeking out the slightest bit of light, not caring that the fancy golden god has killed so many of my companions. All I know in this moment is that no one here in Seoul wants me more than Yujun, which is why when my mouth opens, the words "kiss me" fall out.

Yujun has never been slow. He was probably born premature, eager to get out into the world and show everyone how great he is. He doesn't pause, doesn't allow me to take another breath, think another thought. His mouth seals itself across mine. His hands come up to cup my face. Something falls to the ground. My scruples, definitely my inhibitions. Maybe the bag of things from the gift shop. He kisses with the same surety that he does everything in life—full of confidence and knowing. It's sexy as hell. I pluck at the buttons of his shirtfront. He parts the lapels of my robe. The chill of the room pebbles the surface of my skin but I'm only exposed for a moment. He lifts me in his arms, drawing my legs around his waist and carrying me effortlessly out of the bathroom to the giant bed with its snowy down comforter. The bed cradles me in its softness while Yujun's steel frame pins me down. His hands are everywhere, stroking down my arms, the sides of my torso, the expanse of my legs. We push his shirt off, unzip his pants. I cup his hard length and swallow the groan that comes from deep in his chest. His mouth moves away from mine to map its way down my throat, along my collarbone, making a long, thorough stop at my breasts before he moves even lower.

I knew the shower head was a pitiful replacement for him, but I didn't realize how much of a difference it would be until his mouth found my sensitive flesh. He pushes my thighs apart rather roughly and I nearly expire then and there. He licks me, feasting on me like I'm some kind of delicious dessert he is only allowed to eat once in his lifetime. If I ever felt this good during sex, I don't remember it. My toes curl and my limbs tense as the first orgasm rushes through me.

When he returns to me, he is fully nude—his shirt and pants abandoned somewhere. His condom-covered shaft hangs heavy between his legs and I can't stop my tongue from creeping out to wet my lips. A look of hunger flashes across his face and then he's on me again, his tongue so thoroughly exploring my mouth that he must know me better than my own dentist. My own busy fingers scrape across his back and dip into the hollow of his spine where two indentations rest right above his tight, gorgeous ass.

A whoosh of air escapes when his thick head penetrates my sex for the first time. He pauses immediately. *"Gwaenchana?"*

"Yes, I'm okay." I dig my fingers into his shoulders and urge him on. "I'm good. Very good."

He grins wickedly and slides home. I close my eyes and ride the sensations—his shaft rubbing along all those nerves, his chest making contact with my nipples, his mouth devouring mine. He's furnace hot, and that heat sweeps through me, burning away the hurt and replacing it with bliss. I let the waves pull me under into a cocoon of euphoria. His own body heaves and shudders before he drops to my side. The moment that he leaves me, though, I can feel dark thoughts encroach.

"Don't think anymore, Hara. Not tonight." He presses my head against his chest. His heart is still thundering. "There will be time for that tomorrow. "

My mind doesn't work like that. My brain refuses to rest though my body is deliciously relaxed, and Yujun seems to sense my inner turmoil. His chest rumbles as he speaks again. "We can have a Korean lesson. Will that help you fall asleep?"

"Maybe."

"Okay. New word. Repeat after me: *choahaeyo*."

"Chohay-o."

"More like *choaiyo*. Swallow the *h*."

"Choaiyo."

"Good. I like you, too."

"What?" I bolt up.

He drags me back down to his side. "I like you. *Choahaeyo.* Lie down next to me. I need to rest before I take a taxi back to your place to fetch my car." I'm torn between wanting him to leave and appreciating that he's giving me space. "It's too bad you lost your phone."

"Beyond the obvious reasons, why?"

"I was going to enter this date so that in a month you could buy me a gift. It's the twenty-first century. Women should be buying men gifts."

He says this so cheekily that I can't help but smile. It might be the first one I've worn all day. I feel out of practice. "Is that right?"

I can feel Yujun smiling. "Yes. In Korea, Valentine's Day is where you must give me a present. I will expect flowers and chocolate. I like the chocolates with raspberries inside."

I burst out laughing. "Are you kidding? Valentine's Day is for women to buy men gifts?"

"Yes. Don't forget."

My laughter dies off when I think of how far away that made-up holiday is. "Valentine's Day is months away. I may not even be here."

"Of course you will," he says, as if there isn't even a question of me staying here for months at a time. "Christmas is sooner, I suppose. You can give me a gift at that time, too, although it's not common. We're Buddhists, you know." I did not know. "Usually couples do things together. We can ice-skate or go to a ski resort. Do you ski?"

"No. I'm not very good at anything physical. I excel at all indoor activities such as drinking coffee, reading, napping. Those sorts of things."

"Sounds perfect. It's why lodges exist at all ski resorts."

"You make it sound like I'll be here for a while. It's June and Christmas is six months away."

"Finding Wansu was not the hard part, was it? It is figuring out how to go on from here that is the challenge, but we will wrestle the pig together." I think that's a general saying and that he's not calling Wansu an animal. He likes her too much, more's the pity. "You will learn about Chuseok," he is saying, "which is our Thanksgiving, and the Lunar New Year and White Day, and we will get you a stamp so you can sign all your documents and—" He stops and his body tenses.

"And," I prompt.

He gives himself a tiny shake. "And we will enter you into the registry, move you into a nicer place, find you a job, introduce you to all my relatives, which are not many, but still they will love you."

"What about . . . her . . . relatives?"

"Both her parents died shortly after she married my father. They were in a car accident on the Mapo Bridge."

"Oh."

"Yes. This life . . . it has not always been easy for—" He cuts himself off. "It doesn't matter. Let's rest. Don't move," he says when I attempt to lie on my back.

"This can't be comfortable for you. I'm lying on your arm. It's going to fall asleep."

"As if that wasn't the reason I have arms," he teases, folding his long limb around me. "We will untangle all of this," he whispers.

I let him believe that. Maybe he can believe it enough for both of us.

"It could be worse," he says.

"How?"

"We could actually be related."

CHAPTER TWENTY-THREE

THE BED IS TOASTY WHEN I LEAVE IT. I SLIDE OUT OF BED AND hobble to the bathroom. On the floor is the bag of clothes that Yujun got me from the gift shop. I shake out the contents and rummage through until I find a fresh pair of underwear. I clean up with a washcloth and dress myself. As I button the wide-legged trousers and tuck in the striped knit long-sleeve shirt, I wonder whether Yujun picked this outfit out or the salesperson did. Either way, it's stylish and comfortable, which I appreciate. The hotel bathroom comes equipped with a toothbrush, toothpaste, and even a small disposable hairbrush. Just luxury-hotel things. If I had an active Instagram account, this would be perfect fodder for it, but my social media presence, much like my current life, is empty.

There's something about me having sex with my somewhat, not exactly, but in some fashion, stepbrother, in a random hotel in Seoul that is fitting—an inappropriate person in a soulless place. The marble counter is empty but for the hotel-size soap and the plastic-wrapped toothbrush ready for the next traveler. My life is like that. Other than my mom, Ellen, I don't have people to share things with. I've let my high school and college friendships lapse. I have no deep connection with the people I work with. The last time I had sex was with the minor league baseball player that last summer of college.

Hooking up with a vacation fling is perfect for me. No commitment means no emotional investment. I've never allowed anyone to get too comfortable with me. I've held myself aloof from people, never letting anyone create too much permanency in my heart, never letting anyone come too close, always leaving the door half-open. It's why it was so easy to come to Korea. I hadn't anything back home that I wanted to cling to, and it's not because people back home aren't special or that there aren't things to become attached to, but because I want to be the one to do the leaving. I was abandoned by Wansu and then Pat. By age eleven, I was done with that nonsense.

At least, that was the lie I told myself. But, of course, I wanted a connection. I'm human, so when Lee Jonghyung sent me the email, I thought that this was my opportunity to forge something meaningful, something lasting. It was the idea of that connection that lured me here, because if I had put any thought into it, I would've recognized that I was only running halfway across the world because I was ashamed or afraid to admit the problem was me.

It was easier for me that Lee Jonghyung was dead. If he was alive, I would've had to open myself up to be hurt again, which is why I lashed out at Wansu. When she asked me what I wanted, I made sure to be as cruel as possible. Better that I say those disappointing words than wait for her to say them. But I'm here now and I'm no longer a child. I'm a woman, fully grown, and so I should face what I started and then cope with the fallout, no matter what it is. I have only four days left here in Seoul, and I will not spend them hiding. I pull on the socks and set the shoes by the door.

Saying that is fine, but executing my new resolutions are another thing. I don't have a phone. I don't know where Choi Wansu lives, but Yujun would know. He's still lying in bed, one strong arm across his eyes. The sheets are pulled down far enough that I allow myself a three-second leer before reaching for the phone he casually tossed on the table last night before I attacked him. I turn it on and stare at the lock screen. I don't know enough about Yujun to make any kind of guess at his password.

"I can feel you frown from here." His sleep-rough voice scares the shit out of me. I fumble with the phone and nearly drop it. "Bring it over."

Guiltily, I cross to the bed. He sits up and the sheets fall even farther. God really took his time with Yujun. It's unfair, really. He wiggles his fingers until I hand over the phone. He presses his thumb against the keyboard and waits expectantly. "What do you need? Hungry?"

"I want to talk to Wansu and my phone is in the river."

"That's right." His finger hovers over the screen and then the phone is back in my hands. "She's probably home. Give this to the taxi driver and he'll take you there. Use this button to pay for it."

INSTEAD OF TOWARD the high-rises that line the land in front of the river, the taxi moves north along a busy highway. The Namsan Tower gets smaller in the distance. The high-rises give way to tree-lined streets, stone walls, and detached homes. The horizon is no longer buildings and the river, but mountain peaks. Rooflines peek over the top of concrete and stone walls, some with decorative brick on top. Greenery is in profusion, spilling over the walls in some places like a floral necklace. There's an aging, quiet wealth here. If someone were to ask what money smelled like, I would tell them it was old and green.

After I've paid, the taxi deposits me in front of a garage door set into a stone wall. To the right is a door and one of those outdoor intercoms that Kwon Hyeon had next to her entrance. A light turns on above my head as I approach, and before I can engage the comm system, a small buzzing sound is made and the door latch disengages. My shoes make almost no noise as I climb the stone stairs behind the gate. When I turn the corner at the top of the stairs, Wansu waits. Her body is stiff and stick straight. It's hard to say whether she's uncomfortable or angry. The urge to turn tail and flee is strong. There's something imposing about mothers, a sort of ingrained obedience that's hammered into your bones, and my first instinct is to cower. I take a deep breath and let it out slowly as I approach.

"Good morning." Little fingerlings of light are breaking through the night's sky but not enough for me to make out her expression.

"Good morning, Hara. Come inside."

The entrance is lined with marble and so are the walls. I shed my shoes and then awkwardly hand them to a staff person dressed in all black who gives me a pair of gray felt slippers that match the ones that Wansu is wearing. Silently, I follow my birth mother down the hall. We end up in a living room overlooking a terraced garden. The furniture is tufted white leather with gold accents. Whoever decorated Choi Wansu's office made their cold, colorless way here. Yujun had this place coded as home in his phone, and he once said his place was white but for the yellow pillows Wansu forced on him, but I can't envision him here. He's too warm for this place.

"Does Yujun live here?" I blurt out.

Wansu's shoulders tighten as she places a tray on top of a concrete coffee table. "No. He lives in Yongsan-gu with a view of his favorite place."

"The river?"

"IF Group." His work is his favorite place? "He can see the river if he positions himself in the right place in his bathroom," Wansu continues, and I don't know if she's telling me these things to be informative or to drive home her superior relationship with Yujun.

It strikes me how little I know about Wansu that I can't confidently arrive at any conclusion. Sadly, the same thing can be said about Yujun. I might know that his neck is sensitive or that he has a mole on the inside of his right thigh, but I don't know how he likes his coffee, what his favorite color is, or even the last book he read. If Wansu means to make a point of my ignorance, she's doing a great job. I feel outmatched in this stark opulence and my borrowed clothes. This is a house full of polka-dot couture and I'm made up of ten-dollar stripes from the underground mall stall.

Wansu pours me a cup of dark coffee. "Milk or sugar?" she asks, her hand poised over a small china bowl.

"I'll take it black." I need the punch in the face that the caffeine will provide. The house is so quiet that I can hear the puff of air from the purifying machine in the corner. That sound is joined by the clink of porcelain on porcelain as Wansu places the cup onto a saucer.

"Does Mr. Choi live here? Yujun said he was ill."

Wansu nods. "Yes. We care for him here. He suffered a stroke five years ago and has not fully recovered."

"I'm sorry." Five years ago, I was twenty and dicking around in college while Yujun and Wansu were grappling with this trauma. I had no idea. That said, she doesn't know about my life either.

"Can I ask how you met my—Yujun?"

She was going to say her son. I hate that he's connected to her. On the other hand, this confirms what he told me—that he had no idea who I was when we met in the airport.

"I met him in the airport. I thought he was the driver my friend had sent me to take me to my Airbnb."

Wansu's eyebrows twitch in surprise. "That is a coincidence."

"I don't even know what to call you. In my head, I keep switching back and forth between Choi Wansu and Wansu. I know that if you were a regular person, it would be Choi Wansu, right? But you aren't a regular person. You're my mother but only because you gave birth to me. You didn't raise me. That was Ellen."

"You can call me whatever you like."

When Yujun said that to me, I melted. It doesn't have the same charm coming out of Choi Wansu's mouth.

"In Korea, because we believe in honoring our elders, most people refer to others by titles, not names," she continues after a sip of coffee. "Teachers and doctors are not Mrs. Lee or Mr. Choi but *seonsaengnim*. The older woman that works with you is *sunbaenim*. But among friends, it is fine to call us by our first name."

"And if we aren't friends?"

"*Samonim* or *seonsaengnim* if you want to be very formal."

"Yujun calls you *Eomma*." It's starting to make sense. To Yujun, Wansu is the mother figure that he lost when he was very young. So what is Wansu to me? She is not my mother exactly.

"How about *imo*? It is what a young person would call the mother of a close friend. It's a type of aunt in Korean." Then she smiles, an almost imperceptible curve of the corners of her mouth upward. "Or *michinyeon*. It means crazy bitch."

An involuntary laugh escapes me at this unexpected level of perception from Wansu. "I'm okay with Wansu."

Her response is to drink her coffee. I notice that her knuckles are white. She's not as cool and unaffected by our interaction as she makes herself out to be. Oddly that puts me at ease. I sag against the cushions and drink. For a heartbeat, a breath, there's only the sound of our china in the still room.

"Hara-ya. Look at me."

I raise my eyes to Wansu's. Her emotionless gaze steadies me in a way that I find surprising.

"I will tell you this not because I want your sympathy or your forgiveness, but because you do deserve to know. When I was in high school, I met your father. He was very kind to me." *He was a predatory jerk who took advantage of you*, I think. "I was lonely. My parents worked very hard, very long hours, and I did not see much of them. I became enamored of Lee Jonghyung and we made you. When I told my parents . . . my father . . . he did not understand."

The pause said a lot. He beat her. I know this without her saying it. There's a shadow of pain in her eyes that I recognize. I see it sometimes when I look in the mirror. There's a stain that the betrayal of your parent leaves on your heart. Pat never raised a hand against me, but he hurt me nonetheless. Sympathy stirs and I try to quash it. Sympathy leads to forgiveness and I'm not there yet. I don't want to be there yet. Still, I want to know more. I'm so thirsty for every morsel of information that I'd do anything to keep Wansu talking. "Your mother? Did she understand?"

That ghost smile appears again. "She understood even less. I told them that I would raise you myself but I did not know what that meant. There are not many jobs for girls who have no education and no skills. I tried for twelve weeks but I could not feed you enough. You were sick and tiny. A church family I cleaned for had fostered a baby that was adopted by a foreign family. The foreign family was very well off. The foster mother would show the infant pictures of the foreign family's large home and many cars. I thought, if I cannot have that life, my daughter can, so one night I went to the police, and when no one was looking, I set you at the gate. I watched for forty-two minutes until a police officer came out for a smoke break and found you."

Forty-two minutes. She remembers the exact amount of time.

My eyes grow tight and hot. "Then you were married and gained Yu-jun." *And no longer missed me.*

Wansu sets her cup down and clasps her hands together. One finger rubs along a thin silver band. "What good would it have done if I searched for you and found you? Would you have me take you from your mother? Would you have me disrupt your life? Would anything have changed for you?"

I rub one hand down the side of my face. "I think so." But I don't know if I'm right.

"I cannot change the past, but I would like it if we can have a new future. In whatever way you want to go forward, I will follow."

That's a strange way of putting it. My brow furrows. "What do you mean by that?"

Her eyes flick to the phone on the table. Yujun's phone. It's not in a case but somehow she recognizes that it is his. "It has not escaped my attention that you and Yujun share . . . soft feelings for one another."

I lift my chin. "So what if we do?"

"Do you remember the young couple who were being mourned the same day your father was?"

"Yes, but . . ." The image of the tall, elegant woman sweeping by in the big hat flashes in front of my eyes. "That was you at the funeral home, wasn't it?"

She nods tersely. How funny. I'd been upset that I hadn't experienced an inkling of recognition with any of the women I'd met these past ten days, but there was a spark and I'd missed it. I had known something was different about the woman in black. At the time, I had believed it was because she was a striking figure, but . . . something in her must have spoken to something in me. An unfamiliar, but not unwelcome, feeling spreads through me.

"That couple died because the public disapproval of their union was so strong, they could not bear it. If I acknowledge you, then you will become my daughter and the *sister* of Choi Yujun."

My heart bumps against my chest as understanding sets in. In order to be a Choi, I have to give up Yujun. I can keep him as Yujun from Seoul forever, but if I do, I can't be a part of the family I was born into.

I leave Wansu's place without any clarity of purpose. I've found everything I came to find—Lee Jonghyung, Wansu, why I was abandoned, why she never searched for me—but I don't feel better. My heart still aches. I don't suddenly feel like I belong. My stripes and polka dots are all mixed up.

Lee Jonghyung, my birth father, turned out to be a predatory asshole who deserved to die, yet I never got to confront him. Wansu today isn't the poor mouse she was when she had me. Choi Yujun is the sibling I didn't know I wanted but the man I've always dreamed of. My motherland is beautiful and warm but still so foreign, and my time here is slipping away.

But to dwell on those things seems pointless. I should be like Wansu and take what I can from life. I'll suck all the heat and charm from Yujun and store it in my body like squirrels store nuts in their cheeks. When I return to Iowa, I'll pull out my memories when I'm lonely, one morsel at a time during the long, cold winters. If I only have these four days, then I'm going to spend each minute enjoying myself. Yujun once proposed a dinner with Ahn Sangki and Boyoung, and the idea of matching those two is appealing. It'll be fun, something ordinary Koreans would do.

I let Wansu's driver take me home. I left Yujun's phone with Wansu and I'm going to try to make it through the next few days without a phone. When I get home, I'll buy a new one. *Home.* My mind thinks it's Iowa, which tells me that I'm making the right decision. Once I'm back in Des Moines, these two weeks will be a memory and I can tuck it away and forget it about it. My head pounds and my hands are shaky as I reach for the front door, but that's because I'm hungry, not because I'm upset.

The app everyone in Korea uses on their phones has a PC version, so I download that to my laptop and text Yujun.

ME: Dinner tonight?

YUJUN: Yes

I love that I don't have to wait for a response from him.

ME: Let's invite Ahn Sangki

He sends me a frowny-face emoji.

YUJUN: Let's not

ME: I thought I could invite Boyoung and we could introduce them

YUJUN: Let's invite Ahn Sangki

ME: Brilliant idea

YUJUN: Let's eat here

He sends me an address. From the photos, the food looks amazing, so of course I say yes.

ME: Yes

YUJUN: Are you doing well?

I sort of want to know whether he's talked to Wansu, but I sort of don't. If I'm to keep him in my head as Yujun from Seoul, I need that separation.

ME: Yup gotta run my roommate is here

I move on to Boyoung before I am tempted to ask Yujun any more questions.

ME: Dinner tonight?

BOYOUNG: Oh my god yes of course how did it go with your mother?

I like Boyoung. I consider her a friend. She helped me search for my birth mother and maybe is owed some kind of explanation, but I do not want to get into this with her either.

ME: As good as can be expected gotta run my roommate is here

I snap the laptop shut and go find Jules. She's out on the patio smoking.

"I'm using you as an excuse to avoid questions I don't want to answer."

"Glad to be of service." She holds out the cigarette to me.

"No, thanks. Want to spend the very last of my money with me?"

"Sure. What are we doing?"

"I need to buy some gifts. I'm having dinner tonight with Yujun and a couple of friends."

"Nice." She stubs the smoke out in a dish set on the railing. "So you and Yujun are a real thing? You think it's going to last?"

I think of our trip to the top of Namsan Tower and how he had me look through the viewfinder at the people in Busan. I'd spun up dreams that maybe we could write and he would visit me and I would visit him and perhaps something lasting might form. That night seems another lifetime ago.

"No."

"How was he?"

I arch an eyebrow.

"I can tell you slept with him. You have that look. That and you have a small bruise on your neck."

I clap a hand around my throat. "You're kidding." I sat in front of Wansu with a hickey? Is that why she said we had soft feelings for each other?

"Nah." Jules smirks. "But your response tells me everything I need to know."

"You're evil." I drop my hand away.

"I have a shitty job and a nonexistent love life. I have to get my thrills in where I can. So how was he?"

"If he was a tourist attraction, the national debt would be retired," I admit.

"That good? I'm going to have to shoot my shot after you leave."

"The hell you will. Try it and I'll murder you."

Jules's eyes drop to my hands, which I realize I've fisted at my sides.

"Not going to try to make it last but you're ready to go to prison at the thought of him being with another woman. Make it make sense." Jules makes a tsking sound.

"Maybe I'll just murder you for being annoying."

"They hated her for she spoke the truth," Jules says, her chin in the air. She pushes away from the deck and heads toward the house. I make a booing sound as I follow her inside. My plans to make my trip to Seoul into a beautiful memory are going to take a lot of work.

CHAPTER TWENTY-FOUR

"THERE YOU ARE," SANGKI CRIES WHEN I CLIMB OUT OF THE
subway. He rips the bouquet out of Yujun's hands and runs forward
to embrace me. "Are you taking a picture of us?" he calls over his
shoulder to Yujun, who is standing a few feet away with an endearing smile playing around his lips.

Yujun, who always looks delicious, is wearing a fairly form-fitting
white T-shirt with interlocking *C*s across his chest tucked into a pair
of flat-front black slacks. His brown eyes are covered in big tinted
shades and I'd like to go over and lick the column of his neck where
his vein sits prominently. Will I ever be able to forget him? I avert
my gaze in an effort to hide my reaction, but when Sangki starts
laughing, I know I've been caught.

"Are you happy to see me?" he says between bursts.

"Of course." I try to keep my eyes on the man in front of me and
not the one waiting patiently ten feet away. I'm so glad I bought a
new outfit. Down in the underground shopping centers, clothes are
cheap and plentiful. It was easy to find a short black miniskirt and

an oversize off-white cotton top with black trim. The wide neck shows off my collarbones, and despite the volume, the cut makes me look slender. I even have a pair of new flats I purchased for the criminally low price of twenty thousand won. They might fall apart tomorrow, but they're perfect for now. I guess that's my new life motto. Tomorrow may be miserable, but this moment is great.

"These are for you. Yujun will say he bought them but it was my idea." Sangki tucks the flowers in my hand and takes the bag I am holding. "What's this?"

"A gift." I mentally pat myself on the back. "For my friends."

While he digs into the bag, I bring the flowers to my nose. Out-of-season tulips are a quiet extravagance. How Yujun-like. I clutch them tightly, pleased that I finally remembered to bring gifts of my own. "It's nothing extravagant," I call out to Sangki, who pulls out the first gift. In fact, now that I look at the flowers, I wish I'd spent a little more.

"Oh, there are three gifts here," the DJ notes. "This one is yours, Yujun-ah. I know this because it has your name on it written in *Hangul*." They both turn to me with impressed faces.

I feel especially proud of my effort.

"The third is for Boyoung," Sangki reads out loud. "Is that one of your roommates or do you have friends here we don't know about?"

"I have friends here you don't know about," I tease.

"Impossible." He pretends to be outraged.

Yujun watches us banter with an extremely fond expression. He likes that we get along so well. I like it, too. *Choahaeyo.* I lock eyes with him and his smile grows. His dimples appear, exclamations of his happiness. This dinner, this meeting, was exactly the right thing to do tonight. So enraptured am I with Yujun, I don't notice Boyoung climbing out of the taxi or the horrified shock that causes her mouth to fall open. I hear her cry out, though.

"Boyoung. You're here."

"No. No." She stutters out an apology and stumbles backward. "I thought we were meeting for dinner. Just you and I, Hara."

"Kim Bomi-ssi?" Yujun says. "How do you two know each other?"

Bomi-ssi? That's what I want to know. "I came over with her. She's my friend from America but I know her as Boyoung, not Bomi-ssi. How do you know each other?"

Confusion flickers over Yujun's face and then settles into suspicion. His narrow-eyed, almost flinty expression is what puts all the puzzle pieces together for me. It wasn't all a coincidence—not the meeting at the coffee shop that I went to regularly, not the friendship, not the long delay in hunting down the women in the photographs, not the intentional misdirection. Bile creeps up my throat, and a hot, sickly feeling washes over me. Boyoung—no, Bomi—brings a hand up, as either a shield or a mask, and then spins on her heel, but I'm too fast for her. I catch her by the elbow.

"No. You don't get to leave. Not until you explain everything."

"I don't know what you mean." Bomi tries to wrench free but I'm not having it. My hand is glued to her arm.

"Let's go," I tell Yujun.

"Where?" he asks, not even questioning my order.

"The restaurant, where else?"

"Are you sure?"

"Absolutely. Yes." For once, being a foreign speaker in this country is going to play in my favor. All four of us speak English and I'm going to squeeze every last detail from Bomi tonight. If I let her go, I bet I won't ever see her again. We can have this talk—oh, and we are going to talk—because no one else at the restaurant will understand us.

"Let me go," Bomi cries.

"Nope. You're coming with us." I march her down the street to the *hanwoo* restaurant. Yujun says something to the host, and in short order, we're shown to a table tucked around a corner.

"There are no private rooms here," Yujun murmurs. "There are other restaurants—"

"This is fine." I push Bomi into the chair in the very corner and sit down next to her, blocking her exit. I do not want to waste the time finding another restaurant, making another reservation, when I have Bomi right here.

"How long were you going to carry this on?" I confront her.

"You would not understand."

"Explain it to me. I have all night." I am so enraged that my vision blurs and Bomi becomes a hazy blob. I don't believe in violence, but I could punch her in the face and not feel bad about it.

"Is it too much for me to ask what's going on here?" Ahn Sangki inquires. "I want to know because it will impact how much soju I order. Is this a four-bottle or fourteen-bottle night?"

"I wish to know as well, Kim Bomi-ssi," Yujun demands in a hard voice I've never heard him use. "I thought you were in America for the last six months doing outreach on behalf of IF Group. That is what it states in your personnel file."

Boyoung or Bomi or whatever her name's mouth is glued shut.

"I'm thinking fourteen. I'll be right back." Ahn Sangki excuses himself from the table. None of us pays any attention.

"She was in America," I answer. "She was in Iowa, studying at my local college, in a new cultural studies program. Is there even a cultural studies program?" I never checked. Why would I?

Bomi looks away. I clench my fingers into fists. "Your name is Bomi and not Boyoung? Is there anything you didn't lie about?"

Before she can answer, Ahn Sangki appears with the soju. Bomi leaps forward, grabs a bottle and, ignoring all the rules, pours her own drink. She tosses it back and pours another. And then another.

"Should I stop her?" he asks, looking to Yujun and then me.

"Nope." Maybe the booze will loosen Bomi's tongue.

Yujun orders food. The waiter brings out bowls of *banchan*, which everyone but Ahn Sangki ignores, but after a while even he grows disinterested in the food. Bomi opens the second bottle.

Ahn Sangki, tired of waiting, reaches out and swipes the liquor away. "Speak," he orders.

Bomi hangs her head, the black silk curtain of her hair hiding her face. "I went to America because Choi Wansu was not receiving her reports about you."

"Not receiving her reports . . ." I stop and horror almost floors me. The only person who would be in a position to send her reports is Ellen.

"Yes, that's right." Bomi's face pops up and her chin comes out. "Your American mother is to send Choi Wansu a report on your activities every month, but for six months there was nothing, so *Sajangnim* sent me." She taps her chest. "She trusted me with this important task. I, who am nothing, was someone Choi Wansu believed in. I'm sorry, Hara, that I lied to you. I do like you. I am your friend." She grabs my cold hand. "Please, I told Choi Wansu nothing that you would be ashamed of."

I snatch my hand back. "Ashamed? Why would I be ashamed? I'm not the one who abandoned their kid. I'm the one who grew up—"

"In a nice home that Choi Wansu paid for," Bomi interrupts. "She did not abandon you all your life. She has provided for you. She paid for your home, your schooling. You have had everything because of her. Choi Wansu is a good woman. Very good." She leans across the table to Yujun. "Tell Hara how good a woman your *eomeonim* is."

"Don't fucking say a word." I glare at him.

Yujun appears too stunned to speak anyway. How could Wansu have sat in front of me this morning and divulged none of this? She is *michinyeon*, a crazy bitch. I want to go up to the mountains, invade that sanctuary of hers, and throw paint on her white marble, slap her face, scream at her, shake her until she breaks down and admits that she's a horrible, horrible liar. And Ellen. How could she? How could she let me come all the way here, run around this city, and tell me nothing? How could she text me and ask me if I was getting along okay? Of course I wasn't getting along okay! I shove a fist in my mouth and bite down with shaking teeth to keep the anger inside.

"I need to leave. I can't breathe in here." I feel so small right now. If I could, I would pull my shirt over my head and hide. I don't know how my life came to this—how the people I loved and trusted have all betrayed me in big and small ways.

"Okay." Yujun's chair scrapes against the tile as he stands. He fishes his wallet out and lays some bills on the table. "Take care of this, will you?"

"Yes," Ahn Sangki answers. "Go. I will see her home, too."

"Wait." Bomi grabs the bottom of my shirt. "Promise that you won't say anything to anyone. If you tell someone, your roommates, anyone, it could get to the internet and it would ruin IF Group."

"No, it won't," Yujun cuts in tersely.

"Yes, it will," Bomi insists. "*Sajangnim* has been a recognizable champion of adoption rights and single motherhood. She has made a practice, a loud one, of hiring women who don't have education or experience, who a major corporation would turn away. That she abandoned her own child, married a rich man, became famously wealthy herself, and did not seek out her own child? She would be ruined. The company would be ruined. The board will take the company away from her. They've hated her ever since—"

"Enough." Yujun slaps his hand on the table. Heads turn and hands fly up to cover whispered observations.

Ahn Sangki tries to melt into his seat.

"Enough," Yujun repeats, this time in a more moderate tone. He tries to smile at me, but it's a grim stretch of his lips. "The only people who are responsible for the success of the IF Group are the people who work there, and at this table it is Choi Yujun and Kim Bomi. No one else."

Bomi glares at Yujun before turning to the other man. "What do you say, Ahn Sangki-nim?"

I'm interested as well. My eyes cut toward Sangki, who finds his empty plate very interesting.

"Ah, I, well," he stammers, and then clamps his mouth shut when Yujun sends him a piercing look. He quickly fills everyone's glass including his own and drinks his glass down.

His nonanswer is answer enough.

I sink back into the chair. "If you don't start talking, then perhaps I will go to the press and tell them my story. As you say, someone will be very interested."

Across from me Yujun stiffens, but he remains silent. There's a tension in the air that's different from before, flavored by the worry from both Yujun and Bomi.

The girl licks her lips. "What do you want to know?"

"Everything." I place my hand over her soju glass. "And no more of this until you are done."

She begins to talk. "I started working for IF Group when I was nineteen. I did not have a college education but I got hired after I interviewed at a job fair. Even then I had good English and I was hired because of it. I worked my way up and took distance learning courses to obtain a college degree. *Sajang*—"

"It means CEO and she's not to use those titles at IF Group. We're a family," Yujun interjects.

"That's right." Bomi nods fiercely. "A family. Choi Wansu-nim took care of me. She has paid for my education. She is helping me support my family, as she does all of her employees. She does not take a salary. She is *good*." Bomi says this as if by repeating it enough, she will compel me to eventually repeat it, but my heart's a rock at the moment and no amount of sad stories or heroic deeds is going to penetrate.

The other girl sighs. "Because of my English skills, I have been promoted and have worked closely with Choi Wansu-nim on several projects. Last year, she asked me to do a very great favor for her. She asked me to leave my family for a short time and go abroad. There was someone she knew who lived overseas that she had not heard from in a long time, and would I be so kind as to check in on that person. I was—and am—so grateful that she asked this of me."

Choi Wansu had collected all of these children in place of me. I should be impressed, but it only makes me sick.

I hold up a hand. "Please. I don't need any more editorial comments about how great and wonderful Choi Wansu is. I want to know about these reports. How long have they been going on? How long has Wansu been paying for 'everything,' as you say."

"I do not know how long. I know that they existed and stopped."

"And they were provided by Ellen Wilson?" I want to be wrong.

Bomi nods. "Yes. I saw the last report. It was on Choi Wansu-nim's desk when she gave me the tickets to America. I did not see the entire thing. It was a printout of an email. The subject line said 'Monthly Report.'"

"And what did you tell Wansu about me?"

"That you were doing well. That you watched a drama with me. That . . . your father died. That you had contact with Lee Jong-hyung."

That bitch hadn't mentioned a word of any of it to me. "How do you know that Choi Wansu paid for everything?"

"She told me. She told me because after I met you, Hara-ya, and we became friends, it was very hard to do this thing." She leans close and her eyes plead for my understanding, my forgiveness. I stare stonily back at her. "She told me that she had provided for you all her life and this is the payment she wanted in return—to know that you were well and healthy."

"That is enough for tonight, I think," Yujun says softly. "Let's eat."

"I can't." I shake my head. The thought of putting any food down my throat sickens me.

"I'm sorry." Bomi takes my hand again. "Please, Hara, I did not mean for any of this to hurt you. My family is—they need me. I did this for them, and you lived so well, it seemed like a small harm, but now I see that it is very large and I am sorry."

I wish I had more compassion in me. I wish I was a better person and could tell Bomi that it doesn't matter, but it does. It fucking hurts. I can't even say anything because the words I have are angry ones and I'm afraid if I open my mouth a torrent of hateful things will fall out. I gently remove my hand from hers and get to my feet.

"I'm going now."

"I'll come with." Yujun starts to rise.

I look at him, the son my mother loved and cherished, and shake my head. "No."

CHAPTER TWENTY-FIVE

THERE ARE PEOPLE AT THE RIVER. I HAD THOUGHT IT WOULD BE empty like before but, no, tonight, of all nights, it's crowded. Rationally, I know that in a city with ten million inhabitants, it's going to be more rare to find places that are empty, but right now seeing people in my spot is maddening. Also maddening is that Yujun has followed me.

"Are you worried I'm going to jump in?" I say without turning around. I saw him climb out of the taxi two cars behind mine. He didn't come and join me right away, opting to hang out at street level while I staked out a space below at the railing and stared moodily into the river.

I guess he got tired of watching me because he finally descended the stairs.

"It's been known to happen."

"Well, I'm not jumping, so you can go."

He doesn't leave, but neither does he say anything, and I don't know if that makes me happy or madder. "Don't you have any advice?" I say sarcastically and regret it immediately. He's not at fault, but he's here and I'm hurting.

"I don't know that I'm the right person to give you anything—even comfort. But I'm here if you need me."

I drop my head to press against the backs of my hands. His response is so classic Yujun—kind and understanding. I wish he was anyone's son but hers.

"My *eo*—someone told me that my worst trait is talking too much."

He was going to say his mother—*our mother*, I mentally correct. Head still down, I say, "I thought listening was your best skill."

"That was a learned trait. I wasn't always good at it. I guess once I stopped stuttering I wanted to prove how good a talker I was."

He'd stopped stuttering because of Wansu. He never refers to his father. It's always his mother. She was the one who told him listening was his best trait. She helped him to stop stuttering. She's why he left a job in the US to return to Seoul.

"You love Wansu, don't you?"

"Yes." His response is a bare whisper, as if he's concerned I'll run off if he says it too loud.

"I don't understand how she can be so good to you and have never once tried to find me. She's out here mothering you and Boyou—Bomi. Her countless other rescues, but why not me?" I sound pitiful and I hate it.

Yujun practices not talking, and during his silence I try to gather my composure. I'm not mad at him. I'm mad at the world.

"A Korean's life is centered around food. We don't all believe in the same god or the same economic policies or the same dreams of the future, but we all believe that food can heal." There's a crinkling sound and then a small fish-shaped pastry appears in front of me. "It's *bungeo samanco*. There's cream inside the wafer. Someday, you'll have to have *bungeo ppang*. That's kind of like a pancake with ice cream inside, but for now, this will do."

Someday? He still talks like there's a future between us. My stomach squeezes, reminding me that I haven't eaten much other than some fish cakes that Jules and I bought from a street vendor when we were shopping for my gifts.

"When I planned this dinner, I thought it would be the four of us getting drunk together and maybe ending the night singing karaoke. I wanted to have an ordinary night of fun. Not this." I crunch down into the wafer. It's delicious, as is everything I've eaten here. Why Korean food is so good, I will never know.

"The notecards are very nice." He pulls a box out of his pants pocket. "They're very pretty. *Yeppuh*."

I cock my head to see my gift in Yujun's palm. Jules took me to a small but elegant craft store filled with delicately carved wood sculptures that had shockingly high prices but also a collection of smaller goods like the hand-painted notecards I bought for Yujun. Each card features a different part of Seoul. I recognized the river and Namsan Mountain but not the others. For Boyoung, I bought a key chain with an enameled cherry blossom and her initials KBY, which is useless now because that's not even her name.

"Sangki-ah laughed very loudly when he opened his gift and then refused to tell me why." Yujun sounds peeved.

"He was the hardest to buy for," I admit. "I don't know him very well, but Jules said it's well-known he likes butter bread, so when I saw the small stuffed bread toy, it seemed fitting."

"You'll have to give me a plushie as well to be fair," Yujun declares, tucking the box away.

I'm not sure if it's a joke. His face gives nothing away. "I promise to buy you—"

"Wait. If you're going to make promises, let's negotiate. First, not only do you have to buy me a plushie, but Ahn Sangki can never receive more presents than me." He holds up his pinky. "Second, for every note I send to you, you need to send me one in return. Third, you give us a chance."

I stare at that pinky. It doesn't seem wise given Wansu, the distance, the time. The path forward has more obstacles than a military training course.

"It's just a chance. Nothing more."

The pinky looks lonely and brave . . . I'm the first part, but I'd like to be the second part, too. I hook my own small finger with his. "A chance, then."

He covers my hand and brings it to rest on the metal railing. While he eats the wafer, I stare at the water thinking of Wansu's story of being poor and frightened and pregnant. *I waited forty-two minutes. She received monthly reports.*

All this time I thought I'd been abandoned, but she'd been secretly checking up on me. When her monthly reports stopped, she sent an employee all the way from South Korea with a fake identity and a fake story to find out how I was doing. She provided for me and I sat in her house and basically told her she was a terrible person. Then there's Ellen. She raised me, loved me, cared for me, but she also harbored a huge lie. A cocktail of shame and anger swirls inside me, a cyclone of jumbled emotions. I hang on to the rail and the sensation of Yujun's hand on mine like a life raft. I sift through the tangled web and find the one strand I need to unravel the most—the one where I admit my own complicity.

"Remember how I told you that I wanted to look in the mirror and know who I was? I came to the sad realization that the reason I hated seeing my reflection was because I didn't like my Koreanness. I didn't like the way my eyes were shaped or that my profile was so, well, nonexistent. I didn't like the color of my skin and the way I could never find one shade of foundation that matched. I hated my jet-black hair and my dull brown eyes. I didn't like to be around other Koreans or other Asians because it reinforced all the things I never liked. When I came here and everyone around me had the same things—the same hair color, the same eyes, the same delicate profile, the eye smiles, all of it, it reminded me of how I'd shunned my own culture. If I don't belong, is that really anyone's fault but my own?"

It's easier to blame this all on Wansu or Ellen or Bomi, but none of them made me separate people into stripes and dots. I did that all on my own. I othered myself.

He threads his fingers through mine and squeezes, not judging, just accepting. Saying the words felt like a confession and I feel better. Good enough to go on, at least.

"After my dad died, after hearing that he didn't feel like I was his real kid, I jumped on a plane and came running over here, thinking that I was going to find all the parental approval I didn't get as a kid from the two people who abandoned me in the first place."

"A Korean person would be the last one to scoff at you for that. We are always seeking our parents' approval. It's literally the gas in our engines. At the age of fifty, my father would still bow to his mother, still take direct orders from her. One Chuseok, she said she didn't like his tie—it was one that had pumpkins on it. I'd picked it out with *Eomma*. He took it off and I never saw it again."

"Well."

"Well," he agrees, a small sympathetic smile dotting the corners of his mouth. The barest hint of his dimple peeks through.

I've never felt this comfortable with anyone before. It's as if there is no flaw, no admission that I can make that will turn him from me.

"If I confessed that I'd killed someone, what would you do?" I ask suddenly.

"I'd likely ask where the body was. If there is no body, it's hard to convict someone."

My throat gets tight. "I haven't had that hard a time here. I met Yujun from Seoul after all."

He smiles wider; the dimple grows deeper.

"Will you come to visit me in America?" The thought of never seeing him again slices through me.

"Of course. Will you return?"

"Yes." The sooner the better.

"Even though your experiences here haven't been the best?"

"What are you saying? I love it here."

We both laugh. His hand comes up to cup my face. "Hara-ya, I believe in fate. Our red strings are tied together somehow. It's not a coincidence that we met at the airport. It was meant to be. We Koreans are a romantic people. We like couple clothes and one true pairings. First loves. Destiny. First snowfalls where you meet your love. Come back in the fall and see the winter with me, Hara-ya."

I lean forward and kiss him. And the feeling of his lips on mine explodes in my chest. Unfurls like one of those midnight blooms that open under the moonlight. It's Paris in the rain, the desert under the moonlight. It's Iowa in the fall when the leaves turn golden red and the air is crisp. It's Seoul with its gray skies, tall buildings, constant rumble of car engines on the pavement, the lapping of the river against the shore. It's the rolled *r*'s and the guttural emphasis, the smell of fish cakes deep-fried and salty. It's his taste, his warmth, his long fingers spread across my cheek, angling my head so he can drive the kiss deeper. I could heal under this. Under him. Under the hot Seoul sun. The same place that wounded me so long ago could cover the sore I tried to pretend for so long never existed.

The tears come, hot and furious and so out of place I don't realize I'm crying until I taste the salt on my lips. I pull back and try to wipe the wetness away, but the tears are like a flood bursting through a dam, and a little finger or two isn't going to stem the deluge.

"I don't cry," I say, weeping.

"Of course not." His smile is tender and it makes me weep even harder. I don't even know what I'm crying about. Is it Pat's death? Is it Lee Jonghyung's death? Is it Ellen's betrayal? Is it Wansu? Is it me feeling like I don't belong in the one place I thought I could call home? Is it that I found Yujun, who has suddenly become so precious and vital to me, but that I'm about to leave him to go back to my boring existence where I fill my cup with books and television shows? I feel like I'm crying for everything at the same time. My nose starts to run and my chest and throat ache. My knees begin to buckle. Yujun catches me and pulls me against his chest, pressing my face against his shirt. He tries to dry my face with his own hands, but he doesn't have enough fingers, so he pulls a tie out of his pocket and presses the expensive silk against my eyes.

"I've never kissed a girl until she's cried before. Not even as a kid."

"I'm going to pretend that you've never kissed anyone until me because I feel fragile right now and the thought of you with other girls is a little too much." I snivel into the silk.

"It would be the truth." He places an arm on either side of me, a protective shield against the outside. "Plus, you are the only woman I've allowed to use my Hermès tie as a handkerchief."

I laugh but a sob catches in my throat, choking off the sound. Yujun pats my back until I stop coughing.

Someone comes over and says something to Yujun. He answers in English, probably for me. "She dropped her phone in the river."

"You should buy her a new one," admonishes the woman.

"I will," Yujun promises while I hide my face in embarrassment. This is only slightly less humiliating than walking out of the bathroom with your skirt tucked into your tights, but not by much. A public breakdown so loud and obvious that strangers are coming up to Yujun to see if I need help? Dig a hole in the concrete and cover me with the leftovers.

"I'm not much of a crier," I say when the tears subside to a small trickle. "I didn't even cry at my dad's funeral. Either of them. Pat, my adoptive dad, didn't like it when I cried. It made him uncomfortable." I draw the damp silk across my swollen eyes. "What about you?"

"I've been known to shed a tear or two." He bends down to gauge the tear status.

I wave him off. "I'm so confused right now."

"I wish I could say I understand what you're going through but I can't. But I do know one thing. You're Korean, Hara. Even though you grew up in America. Even though you speak English and not Korean. Even though you feel like you're different when you open your mouth. You are Korean where it counts. Here." He draws a finger across the blue veins in my wrist. "The same blood that flows in me flows in you. My ancestors are your ancestors. Where you were raised and who you were raised by doesn't change that. If anything, your experience makes you all the more Korean because what is a Korean but someone who has experienced loss and still survived?"

I have only four nights left with Yujun. When the taxi transports me from the river to the bottom of the mountain of stairs, I tug him out with me. I pull him through the gate, up the stairs, and into my bedroom. He leans against the door and takes me into his arms. His kisses are slow and lazy, as if to say without any words that time has no meaning. Blood pumps through my veins, hot and heavy.

My limbs feel curiously weighted as I lift my arms to unbutton his wrinkled soggy shirt that is still damp from my tears. His hand comes up to cradle my head as if he doesn't want us to break contact for even a second.

I push his shirt off his broad shoulders, warm my palms against his heated skin, breathe in the scent of the river, soap, and mint from a candy he popped into his mouth on the ride here.

My hands find his waistband and then his zipper. I pause, not sure if I should go on, but his fingers fold around mine and together we tug the fastener down. His slacks fall to the floor as he dances me backward to the bed. Goose bumps pebble my flesh as the cool air hits my lower back where his free hand has pushed up my shirt.

"Cold?" he murmurs against my lips.

"No." And that statement is made true when his body covers what he bared.

He's all long limbs, capable hands, confident mouth. I give myself over to him, let him console me with his strength. Of all the memories I want to take back home from Seoul, Yujun features in all of them. The river is more seductive, the sun is brighter, the food is tastier, when I'm with him. There are no parents here in this bed. No responsibilities between the sheets. There is only his body worshipping my body. His lips on my breast, his hot breath on my stomach, his mouth lower still. I twine my fingers through his hair, part my legs, and allow myself to crest one wave of pleasure after another.

And when he takes me, when his mouth returns to mine and he whispers broken things to me in a language that sounds like music, he is not anyone but my Yujun from Seoul.

CHAPTER TWENTY-SIX

I WAKE UP WITH A POUNDING HEADACHE AND AN EMPTY BED. Beside my pillow is a phone box with a note that reads, "As promised, here is your new phone. You can't return it because it's already activated. I put my phone number as your first contact."

As promised? I can't remember when— Oh. Last night he had that conversation with the stranger.

She threw her phone in the river.

You should buy her a new one.

I will.

Yujun from Seoul.

I curl my fingers around the edge and smile rucfully. I do need a phone.

I push myself out of bed and get ready. First order is to text Ellen.

ME: Am coming home soon. Give me a call. I don't care what time it is here

That sounds inviting rather than threatening. Actually, if I really want a response, I should send some vague panicky text like omg pls call right now, but I don't know what to say to her yet. I'm hurt and mad and maybe this conversation would be better in person, but I can't swallow this down like I've done everything in the past. It's too big to put in its own box and be forgotten.

I don't really want to talk to Wansu until I talk to Mom, and I'm not sure what I should do about Bomi. Yujun is working, so that leaves Jules. I go downstairs to find her.

Except it's not her at the kitchen table. It's a good thing the phone is in my pocket and not in my hand or I would've dropped it.

"Mom."

Ellen rises, an uncertain smile quavering across her mouth, before she pastes on a bright expression and rushes over to hug me.

I step to the side and her arms fall to her sides.

"One of your roommates let me in before they left. I decided to come over and surprise you."

"I know."

I can tell she's about to say something else, some excuse, so I shake my head. I don't want to hear the lies anymore.

"Are you going tell me about it or try to pretend like nothing is wrong?"

"There are options?" she tries to joke. Her voice wobbles as tears threaten to spill. I look away because crying makes me uncomfortable. Plus, I might be tempted to rashly move on.

"No. No options." I jerk my head to the chair. "Let's talk."

Ellen slumps into the chair and it reminds me of the times when I got in trouble as a kid and she would tick off all my wrongs on her fingers, including the ones I'd committed years before. Ellen had the memory of an elephant.

"I'll start. I met Choi Wansu."

Ellen flinches as if I struck her. I fold my arms across my chest and wait as Ellen looks at the ceiling, rubs her lips together, and basically does anything but answer my question. When I was eight or nine or maybe ten—it was before Pat left us—I'd snuck into Ellen's bathroom and tried on her Yves Saint Laurent lipstick. It was a gorgeous red color and I'd always wanted to use it. She told me no because I was too young and because it was expensive at thirty bucks a tube. Not having much of any experience with makeup, I wound the whole stub up and applied it one day while she was running an errand. The lipstick broke off and dropped on the counter. I cleaned up the red stain, placed the broken makeup back into the tube, and shoved the container back into Ellen's purse. Three days later, she dragged me into the kitchen, sat me in a chair, and waggled the tube in front of me. I remained silent, thinking stupidly that if I never spoke, the problem would go away. I guess I learned that tactic from her.

"You sent her reports about me every month until six months ago. Why'd you stop?"

"You turned twenty-five."

I blink in surprise. I hadn't made the connection to my birthday and the stoppage. The reasoning still escapes me. "Why twenty-five? Why not eighteen or twenty or sixteen? Why send them at all? Why not tell me? Why hide it? Why?" I demand.

"Because you're mine!" Ellen cries out. She pounds her chest. "Mine. I raised you. It was me. Not her. She gave you up and I chose you. I sent her thirteen years of reports and I was done. Done, do you hear me?"

My ears ring with her words as I grab the roll of paper towels off the counter and hold it in front of her. She tears off a sheet and presses it to her face.

"I know you hate it when I cry," she sobs. I pat her shoulder awkwardly. Yes, I do. I'm Pat's child, too, after all. Curse him anyway. "I knew this would happen. I should've ripped up your ticket the minute I saw it."

And I should've known then.

"Making me out to be some kind of secretary. Demanding to see you."

My hand flies to my throat. "What did you say?"

"She wanted to meet you. Said that it was her right. She had no rights to you. Just because she gave me some money to help through the lean times doesn't mean that she had rights to you."

I draw back the paper towels to my chest. The things I'd said to Choi Wansu, how I accused her of trying to buy me off, settle inside me like a rotten fruit. No wonder her first instinct was to ask how much. Mom had been taking her money all these years, and then, when Wansu wanted something more than impersonal monthly reports, she'd been shut out. I feel like a piece of shit. I swallow around the hard rock in my throat.

"What exactly was the deal?"

Ellen sniffles, wipes her eyes, and then reaches for another towel, but I keep the roll pressed to my chest. "What was the deal? When did it happen? What did you tell her? How much did she pay you?" I want to know it all.

The corners of Mom's mouth tighten. The tears are still falling, but maybe she reads the resoluteness in my expression because she begins talking. "Choi Wansu reached out to me many years ago and told me she was your birth mother. She had hired a private investigator and said she'd been looking for you for a long time. You have to understand, I was just divorced and struggling to make ends meet. I had a small inheritance from your grandmother, but that was running out. I'd spent all those years as a homemaker and had no marketable skills. She proposed that she send money every month—like a child support payment—and all she wanted in return was regular reports on what you were up to. What grades you were getting. How tall you were. What foods you liked. The books you read. The friends you made. Photos. All of that."

I rip off a paper towel and hand it over like a reward. "Why'd you hide it from me?"

"Hara, you have never properly grieved for your father." Ellen tsks, avoiding my question. "I know that you were angry with him and you had every right to be, but he's gone now. You hating him doesn't bring him back to life. It doesn't rewind the clock. It doesn't make him feel regret. He's not here anymore but you are. He wasn't the father that you needed, but he was still the man who worked hard to put food on your table, who taught you how to throw a punch"—*Tuck that thumb in, girl.* "Running away to another country doesn't make him any less of your father. Finding the man who donated the sperm to make you doesn't erase all that Pat did for you."

"Are we talking about Dad or you now?"

Ellen's jaw tightens, but she continues as if I never said a thing. "You never wanted for anything because of the decisions I made for you."

And the money that Choi Wansu sent. These excuses make me angry, though, hitting me right in that cross section of guilt and unjustness. Yes, I've had it good, but the two people who are supposed to love and cherish me most—the woman who gave birth to me and the woman who raised me—have lied to me all my life.

There's a spot in my chest where the wound of my abandonment has festered ever since I knew what adoption was, and Ellen knows that. She held me when I cried. She told me I was precious when I wondered why my birth mother had given me up. She had raised me, had loved me, and yet, when she had answers that might've healed me, she hid those. I know she reads the resentment glowing in my eyes.

"You were fine, Hara," she cries. "Before you knew anything about this—about Choi Wansu, about Korea, about anything. You didn't want to know. I tried to take you to cultural events, food fairs, language lessons. Wansu would send me extra money for those things, but you hated being Korean."

"I know!" The shame makes me angrier—at myself, at Wansu, at Ellen. "I know. I know I was embarrassed of it. I was embarrassed of being different, of looking different and smelling different, and lots of times I had convinced myself that I wasn't different at all until I looked in the mirror and saw I looked nothing like you. And then one day I wanted to feel what it was like not to be the different one, and I came here and there was . . ." I close my eyes and drag in a shuddering breath. "There was no peace here either."

There's endless confusion and noise, and the only time it's quiet in my head is when Yujun is holding my hand. But Wansu is telling me that even that small refuge has to be given up if I want to find a place in her family.

"Oh, baby, I'm sorry. I really am sorry." Ellen jumps up and tries to force me into a hug. I freeze, wanting to wrestle away, but her mom strength keeps me tight against her. "Because I was afraid," she rasps in my ear. "I don't want to be replaced, and because when you were younger, you used to cry yourself to sleep some nights wondering why your mother had abandoned you. I thought I was protecting you."

And yourself.

"Eventually you stopped asking those questions, so when Wansu contacted me the first time, it had been years since you'd asked that question and I didn't want to bring that pain up again." Ellen pulls back and grabs my cold hand between hers. "You're my daughter. You've been the light of my life since I took you off that plane twenty-four years ago. To me, those people who created you, the woman who gave birth to you, they didn't exist anymore. It has always been you and me against the world. We have never needed anyone else."

I remember the stories that I'd comforted myself with—that even though I'd been abandoned, I'd also been chosen. And it was Ellen who had chosen me. Who had bought me those books, who had taken those pictures, who had made cookies for those friends, who had measured how tall I was and recorded it in a book, who'd praised my good grades and scolded me for bad ones. She had made my lunches, gone to my recitals, sat through the endless hours of softball I struggled through to please my father even though I know that Ellen hated those games.

"I know that one day you'll marry and have a family of your own, but it's one thing for you to fall in love with a man, and it's an entirely other thing for you to love another woman as your mother."

My gaze falls to our clasped hands. Mine are short and small. Ellen's are long and elegant. There are few similarities between us. Ellen's skin is reddish with freckles dotting the surface—some of that is her German heritage and some is due to the sun exposure from outdoor work. Mine is pale and warm, a product of an office environment, not enough sunlight, and my Korean genes. Ellen has green eyes mixed with blue. Mine are brown, bordering on black. We look nothing alike, and maybe that made Ellen hold on to me a little tighter.

"I did what I thought was right at the time. You're my daughter, Hara. Pat had left me with no money. Choi Wansu offered me a lifeline and I took it. Please don't hate me. I love you so much." She brings my hand up to her mouth and presses a kiss to it. Water from her tears dampens my fingertips.

I need time to think, away from her, away from everyone. "Do you have a hotel room?"

She nods. "Yes, why?"

"You should go to it."

"Hara—"

"No. Please. No more. I've heard enough." I wanted all the answers, and now that I have them, I'm more confused than ever.

After Mom leaves, I take a bottle of soju and go out to the tiny deck. The little pottery dish that Jules uses to stub out her cigarettes rests by my hand. The smell of the burned ashes and smoke infects this corner space. I take a deep breath and wish I had a smoke of my own. Maybe the nicotine would calm my racing mind. Time passes; the sun lowers its head, and the summer day grows chilly. I don't move, not even when Jules comes out to set a dish of fruit by my hand.

My new phone vibrates—once and then twice. I drop my head against the back of my hand and wish I could shut the world out. I remember that moment when I slipped into the river. Under the water, there's no sound. It's complete silence. I can see why people seek it. I don't wish for that, but I understand. The one side of me argues that Ellen did raise me, her fears are valid, she was abandoned, too. The other side is ashamed of how I acted in front of Wansu. She's suffered a lot and I added a bunch of shit on top of her pain, thinking mine was the only valid hurt out there. She deserves something from me, but what she asks for is so much.

The phone beeps again. I take a swig of the soju for courage and turn my device over.

BOMI: I'm sorry for everything. I hope you can forgive me. I do regard you as a friend although I understand if you do not believe this. Yujun said it would be okay for me to reach out. Don't be mad at him, though. You know how he is.

Yeah, I do. He wants the people he cares about to be happy. I don't reply because I don't know what I want to say. I feel like I'm being forced to forgive everyone. Can't a girl be mad for even a day? Damn. Yujun's message is next.

YUJUN: I can't believe I'm eating dinner without you.

He sends me a picture of a box of takeout. My stomach growls at the sight of food. I haven't eaten all day.

YUJUN: I wanted to come by but thought I should wait for an invitation. Please send me one.

A laugh bursts through. He's so endearing and the only one who deserves a response.

ME: My American mom showed up. I'm not in a good place right now.

YUJUN: Ah. Then you are busy. Call me when you are not. I would like to see you. I went to the river tonight and it said it missed you. Or maybe that was me.

My eyesight blurs while reading his text and I blink back tears. Can I really give him up?

My life is full of questions and there are no answers. For now, the only thing I am certain of is this—

ME: I miss you too

CHAPTER TWENTY-SEVEN

MOM ARRIVES FROM THE HOTEL FIRST THING IN THE MORNING. I go out to the gate to let her in. She holds up a prettily wrapped box with strawberries on the paper cover. "These were sitting outside. The box has your name on it but I also brought breakfast."

There's a forlorn note in her voice as if she is anticipating my rejection of her gift. "Come in. I think the strawberry pastries are from Yujun."

"Yujun? Who is she?"

Oh God, I didn't even think about explaining Yujun to my mom. *Hey, so I hooked up with a guy from Seoul and he happens to be Wansu's sort of adopted son. Crazy how that works? Keeping it all in the family! Yes, I'm super dysfunctional!*

Mom would haul me to the airport before I could take another breath.

We barely clear the threshold when Ellen hits me with a curveball. "I think we should both meet Wansu together." I stumble on the shoes and Ellen has to catch me by the elbow. "It's the right thing to do. Let's face her together."

"Face her? What did she do wrong?"

Ellen's face grows tight. "So you've decided I'm the villain."

"No. That's not what I meant. I'm not trying to leave you, Mom. I'm trying to figure out my place in this world. I'm trying to come to terms with all of it. I said some bad things to Wansu the other day and I need to apologize for that."

A deep, shuddery sigh of relief rushes through Mom's body.

"Oh, Hara, I couldn't sleep last night." The tears are coming again. I brace myself. "I thought you would hate me." She dashes the back of her hand against her cheek. "I'm sorry for crying."

"It's okay."

"Let me get it all out here so I don't look foolish in front of Wansu. I bet she doesn't cry."

"No. I don't think so."

"Just like you."

I stand frozen as Ellen makes her way into the house. *Just like me.* I'd thought I wasn't a crier because Pat had trained it out of me, but maybe it's part of my genes.

"Come in and show me how to make coffee with this machine. Is this a coffee maker?"

I get a grip and hurry inside. "No. Koreans drink instant coffee a lot. It's just a hot-water dispenser. You can get real coffee from a coffee shop."

"I noticed so many of them on the way here! By the way, my calves are killing me. You should have rented someplace that didn't have so many stairs." She sits at the table while I make her a cup.

"I'm sure that's why the cost was low."

"I suppose so."

I hand her the coffee and take a seat. The *ttalgi* café box is full of small cakes and pastries. I take one and push the box in front of Ellen.

"When do you want to see Wansu?"

"Soon. I might lose my courage if we wait much longer."

"Let me change, then." I go upstairs and trade my sweats for the last of my new clothes, a pumpkin-colored oversize apron dress tied at the back with a thin string that dangles down to my waist. When I look presentable, I shoot off a text to Yujun.

ME: My mom would like to meet Wansu. I'd text Wansu but I don't have her number.

Yujun replies instantly.

YUJUN: I'll come and get you.

ME: No please. We'll take a taxi

Dots appear and then disappear and then appear again, only for me to suffer what feels like a long period of silence, but it is only a couple of minutes. Finally a response comes through.

YUJUN: Ok will see you soon. Choi Wansu will want to eat with you. What kind of food does your mother like?

I hesitate because my first instinct was to say we'd eat Korean but Mom has had a long flight and this meal might be challenging to get through. It's better she have something familiar.

ME: Italian

YUJUN: We will eat at Rubrica at the Westin Hotel. Very good. Your mother will like. Is it okay if we meet at the office and go together to the hotel?

ME: Sounds perfect

Downstairs, I tell her the plan. "Sorry, we have to walk to catch the cab."

"It's fine, Hara. I need the exercise." She pats her stomach. "What's Wansu like?"

"Imposing."

"Really?" Ellen's eyebrows shoot upward. "I wouldn't have assumed that, although her emails were always very short. I assumed she didn't know much English, though."

"She speaks it perfectly." I stop at the gate. "Wait, do you not know what she does?"

Ellen's brow furrows. "She said she worked for her husband's company doing administrative work."

"She's the CEO."

Mom's jaw drops. "The CEO?"

"Yes."

"Isn't it a workday? We should call her? Or maybe wait?" Ellen's flustered state rouses my protective instincts.

"No. She'll see us." I tuck Mom's hand into the crook of my elbow. Not for the first time, I note how fragile it feels. She's getting older. Is this how I want to spend my time? Being angry with the woman who loved and raised me all of my years. It's a question I asked myself all night. I'm still mad but I resolve to be less of a bitch. We settle into a taxi, and after I show the driver a photo of the IF Group address, he takes off.

"Where are your pictures?" Mom makes a *give me* gesture with her fingers pointed up and it catches me off guard because for nearly two weeks all I've seen is people making the same motion with the same meaning but with their fingers pointed down.

"I lost my phone. Didn't I text you that? I haven't downloaded the old ones onto my new phone yet."

"Oh, that's right. I hope it wasn't too expensive. Did you have phone insurance? They say that's a scam, you know, but it sounds like you could've used it."

I glance at the device in my hand. Yujun said he bought this but I wonder if it was Wansu's doing. "I had phone insurance." I mean, Wansu had paid for it as she'd paid for so many things in the past that I didn't know about. Before Ellen can ask any more unintentionally discomfiting questions, I tell her about Namsan and the Seoul Tower, eating *soondubu jjigae*, shopping in the underground. I make it sound like my days were busy doing touristy things and not traipsing all over Seoul looking for my birth mother.

The trip to Yongsan-gu is quick, which is good because my list of sightseeing in Seoul is pitifully short for a nearly two-week stay and I was running out of commentary. Oddly, there's a crowd in front of the building and many of them are holding signs.

"What does it say?" Ellen asks.

"No clue." I squint as if that will help my brain decipher the *Hangul* better, but while I recognize the characters, I don't have the vocabulary to figure out the meaning.

In front of what looks like a group of protestors are people with cameras and handheld microphones. What had Bomi told me that one day in the café? *Protesting is a Korean hobby. We will protest anything from our favorite yogurt drink being discontinued to ousting a corrupt president. It works and so we keep doing it.*

"Protesting is part of a Korean's DNA."

"It's not a bad thing," Ellen replies, stepping lightly out of the cab.

"That's what I said!" I exclaim as I climb out behind her.

Mom pats my face. "Because you're my child."

At my mother's praise, a reflexive smile appears before I remember to squash it, but when I wipe the appreciation off my face, Mom appears crestfallen. Going forward is not going to be easy.

There's a hush in the crowd noise, and suddenly the cameras are pointing in our direction. I look over my shoulder but there's no one there. The doors to IF Group slam open and Bomi comes rushing out. There's an urgency in her face that I can read even from here. Something isn't right here.

"Let's go, Mom," I urge. We need to get inside.

Ellen's confusion causes her to fight me for a second. The crowd of cameras swings around to close in on Bomi. "We need to go now."

I grab Mom's hand, cover my eyes, and pull her toward the front door. Bomi emerges from the pack and waves her fingers—pointed down—for me to hurry. *"Ppalli ppalli,"* I can hear her saying. *Hurry.*

"Is there something wrong?"

"I think so but I don't know what."

The reporters shout at Bomi, who ignores them. "Please come inside." Her fingers close around my wrist at about the same time I see something white and small hurtle toward us.

"Bomi," I shout, but it's too late. The thing strikes the girl on the side of the head. Yellow slimy egg yolk explodes across her shiny black hair. She raises a hand and it comes away sticky and gross.

Mom stops and tries to find the perpetrator. "Who did that?" she shouts. "That's entirely not okay."

"No. No. It's fine. Come inside," Bomi begs. Another projectile flies through the air, but now an army of black-suited men appears and drags us inside before any of us can get pelted again. The reporters press against the glass front windows like zombie ghouls trying to claw inside to eat the undead. A handful of gawking office workers mill around, trying not to stare but not fully succeeding.

"Are you okay?" I reach up and try to flick some of the gooey mess onto the ground. Better that it's on the tile floor than dripping onto Bomi's black suit.

Bomi ducks away from my hand. "Yes. I'm fine. Are you okay? You didn't get hit by anything, did you?" She tries to inspect me.

"I'm not the one that was egged. Holy crap, Bomi, what is happening? Did someone from the IF Group kill a person?"

She stops moving. "Not exactly."

Her words make me freeze, too. Something *did* happen to the IF Group. Bomi says something to the man next to her, who whips out a handkerchief, but instead of using it on herself she grabs my hand and tries to wipe the egg off my fingers. I shake her off. "I'm okay, Bomi. Please tell me what's going on."

"Upstairs. Choi Yujun-nim is going to be so mad when he sees this. I am going to go wash my hair out. Take her to *Sajangnim's* office," she orders one of the security officers.

I turn to Mom. "Are you okay?"

"Yes, but this is very confusing. They must be protesting something serious." She casts a worried glance over her shoulder.

"Yeah. I don't know what, though."

We follow one of the security officers to the elevator bank.

"Could you understand any of the questions the reporters were asking?" Ellen whispers loudly.

"No, Mom."

"Me either. I listened to a beginner's audio lesson on the plane, but I don't remember anything beyond 'hello.' I regret taking that sleeping pill now." She squeezes her hands together in distress, as if one more hour on the plane would've allowed her to magically understand the language.

My chest is tight. Something is wrong with Yujun's company—enough so that there is a gaggle of reporters standing outside the building and a smattering of protestors. When the elevator opens on the fourteenth floor, Yujun is waiting. The smile on his face is thin and tired and he looks unusually disheveled.

"I'm sorry I didn't come down. I was on the phone. Where's Kim Bomi?" He cranes his neck to peer into the elevator as if she was hiding in there behind the security guard.

"She had to go to the restroom."

He frowns. "She shouldn't have left you."

"We're good." I'm not so sure about the other woman. "What's going on?"

He jerks his head in the direction of Wansu's office. "I'll tell you in *Eomma's* office." He bows deeply to Ellen. "I'm sorry we are meeting under these conditions."

"This is Yujun. Choi Yujun. He's Wansu's son. Stepson," I correct myself.

Ellen's eyebrows shoot up. Evidently, she hadn't known that Wansu had a son. I guess the two mothers never really talked. Ellen wrote out the reports and Wansu wrote out the checks. That was the sum of their exchanges—because Ellen was afraid of losing me and Wansu was afraid of wanting more.

The office is eerily quiet. Everyone's heads are down and tension hangs in the air like a dense fog. We trudge through it but it sticks to the back of my neck like the egg yolk in Bomi's hair.

The double doors to Wansu's office are ajar. Through the opening, I can see her standing behind her desk, her hands fisted on top of the wooden surface. Her complexion is as pale as her cream suit. Her normally sleek and polished exterior looks frayed, as if someone took a big wet brush and dragged it over her image. Her red lipstick is feathering at the corners of her lips. There's eyeliner smudged under her eyes, as if she's rubbed them too hard. A coffee stain decorates the front of her blouse. Yujun has his jacket off and his sleeves rolled up. His vest is unbuttoned and his hair is mussed, probably from him shoving his hand through it. He looks like he's worked a hundred hours and it's barely ten a.m.

The minute we are inside the office and the doors are closed, Yujun speaks.

"Someone reported on you."

"What do you mean? Reported on me?" I point to my chest.

"Someone overheard us in the restaurant, I think. We were speaking English but other Koreans speak English and must've put it all together. That you were *Eomma's* daughter who she gave up many years ago. The gossip columns say that you did not know of this and were angry when you made the discovery."

"Oh my God." I rock back on my heels, stunned. I'd been so brash the other night, dragging everyone inside, not waiting for a private room. Not brash, but arrogant. I thought only of myself, and this is what happened. But why would anyone care enough to go to the press? I know the IF Group is big news, but this seems more of a personal attack on Choi Wansu . . . Sick, I clamp a hand to my stomach as a niggling thought crosses my mind and then refuses to be banished.

Maybe it was a person at the restaurant, but other than the people in the dining room sitting near enough to overhear, there was only one other person in full possession of the entire drama, and that was Kwon Hyeun. She also had a reason to go to the press. Kwon Hyeun and Wansu had been rivals for the same man. They both got pregnant by the same man around the same time but Wansu delivered and gave her baby away while Kwon Hyeun miscarried and then could no longer conceive. Choi Wansu had everything that Kwon Hyeun wanted, especially the daughter that Kwon Hyeun lost and Wansu had given away.

I gulp. "Yujun, what if it was Kwon Hyeun?"

"Kwon Hyeun?" Wansu cuts in before Yujun can respond.

"Yes, she is the one who gave me your information. She and my dad—at the same time—well, you know." I don't feel like piling shit on Wansu's already horrible day by bringing up bad memories.

"It could be her. She knows the whole story, yes?" Yujun asks.

"Yeah. Should I call her?"

"What's going on?" Ellen asks. "Are you Choi Wansu? I'm Ellen

Wilson, and oh my God, you're so pretty, which of course you are because Hara is beautiful, so her mother—I mean, I'm her mother but you are, too." Ellen bursts into tears.

Wansu looks mildly horrified and physically leans away as if the tears are some contagious disease. I put my arm around Mom and lead her over to the sofa. Wansu watches us carefully the whole way, with an odd expression of longing on her face. Does she want me to take her by the arm and help her sit down, too? The moment is fleeting, though, for in the next instant, Wansu's face is perfectly smooth. She lifts the phone and barks out an order, and a second later, an assistant appears at the doorway bearing a tray with four cups.

"Mom got in yesterday. She's jet-lagged," I try to explain.

"Don't apologize. It's a challenging day." Yujun presses tissues into my hand, which I pass on to Ellen.

"I'm a crier," Ellen says as she dabs her eyes. "I cry over everything. Tell them, Hara."

"It's true. She cries during commercials, and not just because there is one every five minutes."

No one even cracks a smile at my bad joke. Yujun takes a seat on the other side of my mom and pours out a cup of coffee. "It's brewed, not instant," he informs us as he hands the beverage to Mom. "I know Americans love their coffee." Then he bows his head. "Please accept our apologies for what happened outside."

"What is going on?"

The two Chois exchange looks that I can't decipher. Mom is just as confused. The coffee rests in her hand untouched.

"Yujun?"

He won't meet my eyes. "Let me call you a car. Mr. Park will drive you back to your house or to your mother's hotel."

"What hotel are you staying at?" Wansu breaks in.

"Oh, me?" Ellen points at her chest. "The Best Western in Gangnam." She gives us a watery smile. "Like the song."

Wansu wrinkles her nose ever so slightly. "Yujun-ah, call the Four Seasons and get our Ellen a suite. It would not be good for the Chois to have the mother of Hara not be in our best hotel."

CHAPTER TWENTY-EIGHT

BOMI ACCOMPANIES US FIRST TO THE BEST WESTERN, WHERE she handles the checkout, and then to the Four Seasons, where she handles the check-in. The check-in does not take place at the front desk. Oh no. We are shown to a private lounge, handed champagne glasses and hot towels, and invited to feast on the cheese and olives and fruit and jellies and tiny cups of pudding.

"This is nice," Ellen whispers as she smooths a hand over the creamy leather sofa.

"Everything the Chois have is nice." I stare at the back of Bomi's head, which is bent over a hotel document. She knows everything. All the answers I need are sitting a few feet away from me.

"I'm not sure I should accept this room. I bet it's superexpensive."

"There's no point in arguing with the Chois." Yujun might be tight-lipped, but I'm going to drag the facts out of Bomi.

She ends her conversation with the staff person at the front and comes over to hand Mom a key card. "The room isn't ready yet but it will be soon. You're welcome to help yourself to anything here including the wine or beer. If there's something that you want, tell me and the staff here will get it for you."

"I could really use the restroom," Mom says. "Hara? Would you like to come with?"

"No." I don't take my eyes off Bomi.

"Oh, all right. I'll only be a moment."

The minute she's out of earshot, I grab Bomi's hand. "Tell me everything."

The girl twists away. "I don't know what you're talking about."

"Bull. Shit. Your hair is still wet from the egg wash, by the way." I glare at her. "You owe this to me, so start speaking."

Bomi presses her lips together but I know I'm going to win this skirmish because *she* wants to spill. She's dying to tell me something or she wouldn't be sitting across from me wringing her hands. She'd be back at the IF Group next to her favorite person in the world—Choi Wansu. That she's still sitting here with me tells me she's got something to confess and is trying to find the courage to do so. I cross my arms across my chest and wait.

It doesn't take long for Bomi to start talking. "Choi Wansu took charge of this company about five years ago. Choi Yujun came home from Harvard with many radical ideas, but they were the same ones that *Sajangnim* has always had. IF Group would hire based solely on merit, without regard to anyone's religion, educational background, gender, or connections. They would open an on-site day care so that mothers, particularly single mothers, could find employment with them. This was a huge change and it's rumored that Choi Yusuk—that is Choi Yujun's father—argued for days, weeks, about it."

Choi Yusuk. I realize this is the first time I've heard his name.

"In America, maybe this is not heard of, but here, we are taught to honor our elders, give deference to their knowledge and experience. In return, they foster and guide us, provide for us."

A Korean person would be the last one to scoff at you for that, Yujun had said. *We are always seeking our parents' approval. It's literally the gas in our engines. At the age of fifty, my father would still bow to his mother, still take direct orders from her. One Chuseok, she said she didn't like his tie—it was one that had pumpkins on it. I'd picked it out with* Eomma. *He took it off and I never saw it again.*

To stand up against his father must have taken a lot of effort for Yujun.

"There is another rumor that Choi Yujun's fights with his father caused his stroke, but even as Choi Yusuk lay in the hospital, his son worked with his stepmother to make sure she took power, and with the shares he owns along with his father's proxy, he supports her at every board meeting. This unwavering support from the heir brought the board to heel, and Choi Wansu has been able to run IF Group without challenge."

"But?" There's a catch.

"But the board is always waiting for her to make a mistake so that they can nod and say that they were right about her all along. A woman doesn't have the balls to run a business like the IF Group, they say. They don't like her policies because they are perceived as weak. They don't want people like me"—Bomi taps her chest—"people who went to small rural schools or who don't have a college degree. They want to brag that they have the most Seoul National University graduates or even the most Western-educated employees, but *Sajang-nim* says that as long as our balance sheet shows a profit, they cannot touch her."

This is the Bomi I know, the one who spoke passionately about women's rights. I didn't realize at the time that it was because it was an issue that hit so close to her, had so much of a real-life impact on her.

"And if it is widely known that this champion of women who

gives money to adoptee programs abandoned her own child, it will be used as a weapon against her," I conclude.

Bomi nods vigorously. "Yes. Much of *Sajangnim's* power here rests in the belief that what she is doing is right. Her—our—reputation is built on it. That she gave up a child and that child was never aware of it will not be welcomed by the board. They will say that Choi Wansu speaks with two tongues when she leaves you behind but advocates for other adoptees and therefore is not fit to run this company."

"Oh my gosh, we should do something. Hara, what should we do?"

Bomi and I both jump at the sound of my mom's voice. I'd forgotten about her and so had Bomi. I look around to see if anyone else has overheard, but the lounge is empty but for the two staff members at the front desk, who are too far away from us to have heard anything.

"There's nothing we can do." But even as I say that I realize how wrong I am. I can fix this for Wansu, for Yujun, for Bomi, for the hundreds of women that Wansu employs. I just have to give up one thing. There's sympathy in Bomi's eyes when she sees I've come to the conclusion she's led me to—sympathy and hope. My heart clenches and cries, but I know the right, the honorable, course of action.

Hot tears prick my eyes and I blink them back furiously.

When I was a child, I spoke as a child, I understood as a child, I thought as a child: but when I became an adult, I put away childish things.

What right do I have to Yujun if so many others suffer? What happiness could he have with me if his company would be taken from him and Wansu? How could I live with the fallout? A result that I had a direct hand in, accidentally or not, whether it stemmed from being overheard at the restaurant or Kwon Hyeun letting her festering bitterness have free rein.

Simply put, I could not.

CHAPTER TWENTY-NINE

WHEN I STEP OUT OF THE SHOWER OF THE FOUR SEASONS HO-
tel suite, I discover an unfamiliar black garment bag lying across my
bed. The *Hangul* characters are the same as the ones that were on
the bag that Bomi had brought me two weeks ago on just my second
day in Seoul. I had suspected that Wansu had bought my funeral
dress, and this confirms it. I know enough now to make out the
name—Hwaiteu Ip. I'm not sure what the second characters mean,
but I think the first one is "white." "White-eu."

"It's White Leaf," Wansu informs me. "It's a very nice shop." She
walks over to the bed and draws down the zipper. "It's owned by sisters and they employ women who can't find employment because of
their past. The white leaf represents a new start."

The dress isn't white, but the palest pink—the color of the inside
of a flower that's too shy to show itself to the sun. It's simple and
lovely and will make me look like I'm the sacrificial virgin to the god
of business.

"I have my outfit," I say. I pull out the pinstripe gray pants suit Bomi bought with the very last available credit on my card. The straight-legged pants have cuffs that break right at the top of my black two-inch pumps. I pair it with a beautiful light blue blouse embroidered with white and pink cherry blossoms on the collar and down the front.

If Wansu is disappointed that I've opted for a different outfit, she doesn't show it. Without a word, she returns the dress to the garment bag and zips it up. I step back inside the en suite bathroom and change. Wansu and Ellen don't speak, so it's eerily quiet. The only sounds are the ones made by fabric sliding over skin, the metallic slide of the zipper, and the breaths I take as I button, fasten, and smooth everything into place.

"Leave your jacket off. I have a makeup artist and a stylist," Wansu says when I open the bathroom door. Since I already won the clothing battle, I meekly follow her out into the living room, which has been transformed into a salon. An army of staff appears to be milling about with brushes and curling wands and hair dryers.

I'm stunned at how quickly this has all been put together. One minute, I'm listening to Bomi's story about Wansu's rise to power, and two hours later, I'm preparing for an emergency board meeting. I have no idea where Yujun is. While Bomi called Wansu to tell her my decision, I called Yujun, but he never answered. Wansu informed me that she passed on the plan to Yujun and he was in agreement that this was the best course of action.

That really hurt, even though it was my damn decision. I guess a tiny part of me wanted him to protest or, rather, a big part of me wanted him to swarm in here on a white horse and save me, save all of us. How humiliating. I shove the misery I have no right to feel aside and give myself over to Wansu's miracle squad.

Ellen is already in a chair. "Come here, darling, and get your battle gear put on." She pats the arm of the seat next to her. "Do you like my dress? Wansu brought it."

"It's very pretty." What I can see of it looks nice. There's a cloth draped around Ellen's shoulders, but it is a lovely color of tulip yellow. Wansu is dressing us to all look soft, like flowers, and I've ruined it. "Thank you."

"*Eomoni.*"

"What?"

"You will need to call me *Eomoni* in front of the board. It is a more formal version of 'Mother,'" she explains for Ellen.

"Right. I forgot," I reply stiffly. Not the same as what Yujun calls her, but close enough. *It could be worse,* I can hear him saying, *we could actually be related*. He was right. Things could be worse than they were the other night, and this is living proof.

"Come sit down," Ellen says, this time tugging on my pants. "Let's get this over with."

I do as I'm told. My hair is tucked back into an elegant bun at the base of my neck and the hairdresser gives way to the makeup artist, who smooths on one cream and then another before she even starts with foundation. Light eye makeup is stroked across my lids. Blush is dabbed on my cheekbones. Highlighter is added to my nose and forehead. The stylist shakes a tube of liquid eyeliner and starts to apply it. I feel the wet liner drawn across my lid, hear a mutter, and then a cotton pad swipes across my eye. This process happens twice more. I tell myself that this isn't a bad omen, that not even a Korean can apply eyeliner correctly to my eyes.

Wansu—I can't quite bring myself to call her *Eomoni* yet—says something sharply in Korean. When I pop open my eyes, I see the makeup artist bowing and stepping backward. Wansu picks up the tube and shakes it again.

"Your eyes are uneven and that's why the eyeliner is hard to apply. They turn down at the ends and you need to—" Wansu flicks the applicator across my lid. "Close," she orders. I obey. Two more swipes and Wansu is done.

I check the mirror. The black lines are perfectly done, highlighting the shape of my eyes, evening them out and making them look larger. Our eyes are the same. I don't have my father's eyes. They are Wansu's. I touch the corner of my eye and feel a spot of wetness.

Wansu is busy capping the tube, so she doesn't see the tears slip down my cheek. I didn't even realize that tears were threatening to fall. If I'd had warning, maybe I could've stopped them. But they climbed my throat and spilled out my eyes before I could even blink. The makeup artist makes a sound in the back of her throat and comes over with a puff to dab away the evidence of my emotional fallout. But the discovery that the only way I was ever going to learn to put on eye makeup correctly was to find my birth mother who had the same eye shape as mine is too much for me, and like the night at the river, I can't quell the torrent.

"Are you crying, Hara?" Sounding horrified, Ellen comes over and crouches down next to the chair.

"No," I weep into my hands.

"You never cry." She looks over at Wansu. "She didn't even cry at her father's funeral."

"Tears will smudge her makeup," Wansu replies, as if I merely got a speck of dust stuck under an eyelid. The answer is so matter-of-fact, so cold, so typical of Wansu, that it wrenches a laugh from me. I laugh and laugh and cry until the two are so mixed up that I don't know what's coming out of my mouth and no one knows how to deal with me. They all just wait until I can get hold of myself.

"We don't have to do this today. We can wait until you're comfortable. Isn't that right, Wansu?" Ellen turns to the other woman for confirmation, but Wansu's face is granite hard. She does not want a delay and neither do I. Waiting only makes things harder. Under Wansu's unflinching gaze, I pull myself together, sucking in deep breaths until the flood of tears is quelled and the hysteria-induced laughter is tamped down. There's something so reassuring about Wansu's steadiness. It's easy to understand how Yujun overcame his stuttering. Wansu simply wouldn't allow it to exist, and as the force of her personality has carried her through all the past hardships, it will carry all of us through this one.

The makeup artist fixes my makeup, and at the end, I pat my perfectly lined eyes dry and rise. "I'm ready."

THE PHONE IN my hand vibrates gently. I know it's Yujun but I refuse to look at it. What if he asks me not to speak? What if he tells me he has a different solution? I'll cave, so I take the coward's way out and refuse to even tempt myself.

When we arrive at the IF Group building, there is a wall of photographers standing in the underground parking garage.

Ellen squeaks out her surprise. "Isn't this private property?"

"It is," Wansu replies grimly. She snaps a command out to the driver in Korean and then turns to Ellen and me. "Park Minho will clear a path, but we can't wait until everyone leaves or we will be late. When I open the door, follow me. Do not answer any questions."

"We can't speak Korean anyway." Ellen smooths her hair back.

"There will be questions in English," Wansu warns.

"We'll be fine, won't we, Hara?" Ellen replies.

I make some noise, which Ellen takes as agreement, but in truth I don't feel fine at all. I bend over slightly and start breathing through my mouth. There's a hurricane stirring up in my stomach and I'm afraid that I'll lose the strawberry cake that I managed to choke down earlier this morning before my personal snow globe got up-ended and shaken to pieces.

In my head, I recite the small speech that I'm to give in front of the board of directors. In high school, I was only able to give half of my prepared paper in speech and debate before I got so tongue-tied that I could not squeeze another word out of my mouth. My teacher, a large, balding man by the name of Johannessen, took pity on me and sent me back to my seat. I remember his name because it took me half of the term to remember how many *n*'s and *s*'s there were. Yes, *Hangul* was a lot easier language to learn.

If I have a repeat of speech class, Wansu will pitch me out the boardroom window. I'm certain of it.

Park Minho holds open the door. Wansu steps out with her head up, and I wonder if she's ever had a moment of uncertainty in her entire life and why she didn't hand down an ounce of that nerve to me. Selfish woman. She strides toward the glass doors of the basement entrance. Ellen follows, a little less confident but with bright, curious eyes. A few questions are shouted out in English. "Are you the English mother?" "When did you find out Choi Wansu-nim was the biological mother?" "Are you giving up your parental rights?"

Ellen stops at that question and opens her mouth. Before she can say a word, I grab her arm and push her forward.

"Really, Hara, that question should've been answered. Of course I'm not going to give up my parental rights," Ellen huffs once inside the double glass doors. Wansu pushes the up button.

"Wansu told us not to answer any questions."

"*Eomoni*," Wansu corrects.

"I didn't expect there to be those types of questions," Ellen protests. She looks like she wants to go out and fight. Fortunately, the elevator doors slide open. I nudge my mother inside.

"Wansu says—"

"Oh, for God's sake, I know what Wansu said, but she's not your mother!" Ellen throws her hands up. "I'm the one that's the mother. I raised you. I was there for you when you skinned your knees, when you ran home crying because that boy in fourth grade asked you if your face was flat because you fell off the monkey bars or when that wretched girl in the sixth grade said you smelled weird. I was the one who dried your face, fed you ice cream, and tucked you into bed. I paid for your—" She cuts herself off suddenly. Her eyes dart to Wansu's face. Her breath comes out in short pants. Wansu's already porcelain complexion grows even more pale.

"I know." I place a hand over Ellen's. "You're not losing me because I'm going to call Wansu *Eomoni*. I'm still your daughter. I will always be your daughter."

Ellen sniffles, but she manages to gather her composure. This time when the doors open, I'm the first one out, walking forward with my head high and my eyes focused. We can't all lose our shit at the same time.

The boardroom is already full, but not everyone has taken their seats. The members range in age, although none look as young as Wansu. No one except Yujun. I avoid his eyes, afraid that I'll lose my resolve. He looks edible in his three-piece suit and with his dark hair swept off his forehead. His face is set in hard lines and I wish I could be a fraction as comforting to him as he has been to me these past two weeks.

But there are no good options here. We had two weeks together and that's not enough to form a lifelong love. That's not reason enough to upend the lives of potentially thousands of people who wouldn't otherwise have a way to put a roof over their heads or food on their tables. If we gave in to our own selfish feelings, it wouldn't be Bomi who would suffer but Bomi's family. It would be the brothers and sisters and sons and daughters of all the families under the IF

Group umbrella. It would be one more sacrifice Wansu had to make, and she's made enough of them in this lifetime.

I have to stop feeling sorry for myself and grow up. Maybe if Yujun and I had known each other longer, maybe if it wasn't some vacation romance, we could have convinced ourselves that our feelings mattered more than anyone else's lives. But that isn't the case and so here I am, facing down the den of hungry, greedy wolves that want to devour Yujun's future. I can't be with him, but I can give him this. I force my gaze away from Yujun and survey the room.

It's surprisingly diverse in terms of sex, with roughly half women and half men. Yujun did say that Wansu had made sweeping changes to the company when she took charge, and I guess that included the board. Too bad it wasn't enough to weather this scandal.

I bow, a full ninety degrees, and wait for Wansu to introduce me.

"This is Hara Wilson. As you know from the news reports and my internal communications, Ms. Wilson is my biological daughter. Because her adoptive mother and she do not speak Korean, I am requesting that you all speak English for their sake." Wansu pauses, but when no one objects, she powers on. "Today, this emergency board meeting has been called because some of you are concerned that my role as the head of this company is jeopardizing its future. I know that there are many changes—"

"I am sorry to interrupt, *Sajang*, but the very mission of this company has been to provide opportunities for girls and women who do not have the good fortune to attend a good university. The mission is in jeopardy due to your actions," interjects a female board member. Older, with a head of black-and-white hair, she speaks with authority. Others are listening to her.

"I realize that and I will humbly step aside should the board consider that the best course of action. However, I think it is obvious why I have been devoted to single mothers, the issues of adoption, and the promotion of women's rights. I have been supporting Hara financially for some time. While I may not have been physically present, from the moment I've been able to I have done my duty toward my daughter."

"And what does Hara Wilson say?" questions the older woman. All eyes swing toward me like a bright spotlight. The desire to shrink back behind my mother—either one of them—is strong.

After two deep gulps that do nothing to settle my nerves, I step forward.

"Hello. Thank you for having me." My voice is quaking. I'm not a good public speaker. What was the joke the famous comedian once made? That you'd rather be in the coffin than giving the eulogy? I've never felt so seen by a joke. I would give anything right now to be in a pine box in the center of the room rather than standing here in front of a bunch of strangers who are twice my age and are looking at me as if I stole money from their pockets.

"I am Choi Hara, daughter of Choi Wansu, and sister to Choi Yujun." I don't look in Yujun's direction as I recite this little speech. "I am grateful for the choices *Eomoni* has made for me. I have lived a very good life in America with my adoptive mother, Ellen. *Eomoni* sent us money and paid for my college education and my apartment. I am grateful for all the opportunities she gave to me. She should be praised"—I blow out a deep breath—"and not vilified." I'm not sure if there's a direct translation, but everyone seems to understand. "If I were able to vote, I would keep Choi Wansu as *sajang.*"

"What about the rumors about your relationship with Choi Yujun-ssi?" This comes from a male wearing a suit that looks to be one size too tight.

Yujun opens his mouth but stops when I hold up my hand. "I love him like the brother I don't have."

The man grows disappointed. It wasn't the answer he wanted.

Before he can ask another question, Wansu jumps in and says something in Korean. It must be directed toward Yujun, because he stands and bows. "I am in agreement with Hara-ssi."

Wansu wants him to say something more, but he's done. I finally meet his gaze and I'm surprised to see determination rather than anger. A spark kindles inside me. This is not the look of someone who's giving something up, but of someone who is fighting for something. What does it mean? I curse myself for not talking to him before. Have I made the wrong decision? Bomi and Wansu and Ellen all think this is the right course, but is there a way out I haven't considered?

"What position will you be giving your daughter?" the man asks.

Wansu is startled—so startled she replies in Korean. *"Museun marieyo?"*

"What do I mean? Your daughter should be given a position here so others can see she is a valued member of our family. That is what our company stands for. We are a family. We cannot ignore our family."

"Yes, I agree. She should be given a job," Yujun speaks up. This wasn't part of the plan. My eyes fly to meet his again. He stares boldly back. *Trust me*, he seems to be saying.

"I do not speak Korean," I interject. Work here? In Korea? Next to Yujun? This is not a good idea.

"She can help with the English translations. Hara works at the American magazine *Perfect Home* as a copy editor. She can do the same for us as we move forward in our globalization endeavors," Yujun suggests.

I need him to stop being so helpful. I can't stay here in Korea, be in the same city as Yujun and not want to be *with* him. I need an ocean and a continent or three between us. I need to return to the cows and the cornfields, the endless discussion of insurance premiums, pizza, and pancakes, and forget that this country, this man, exists. I try to telegraph this to him, but he is pretending not to notice.

A murmur spreads among the board members. They like this scheme. Not only do they like it, but they are seriously considering it. I turn to Wansu. Surely she will put a stop to this, but the woman is avidly watching the other members, gauging their reaction, calculating a hundred different scenarios, and when a small smile crosses her lips, I know I've lost.

The conversation is over. After a short discussion a vote is held and Wansu's position is retained. There is more business that is discussed but I've stopped listening. Earlier, I thought the worst thing I'd face was not ever seeing Yujun again. I hadn't even contemplated that the worst thing would be to see him every day and not be able to have him. *That* scenario hadn't occurred to me.

Finally, the meeting concludes and everyone files out, leaving Ellen, Wansu, Yujun, and me—the Choi family.

"You did well," Wansu says. There's a smugness in her voice that grates on me. Everything has worked out for her. She gets to keep her position and her company. Ellen and I are properly grateful for all that she's done. She's a heroine in her son's eyes once again. I have been forced to forgive everyone—Ellen, Wansu, Bomi.

"Yes. You did a marvelous job, Hara. I was so proud of you. I know you hated it. She hates speaking in front of others," Ellen explains.

I'm angry. I feel like a pawn in my own life. Wansu has moved me adroitly around the chessboard. Yes, she was wronged in her life, but everything has worked out for her. She gave up one child but gained a perfect son. She was born poor but now she lives in a house that is not only nicer than the one in *Parasite* but I'm sure has only expensive cars in the basement. I felt sorry for her and she used that against me. Now they want me to live here in South Korea, the land of polka dots, when I'm so clearly a stripe?

"Stop talking about me as if I'm not here," I fume. "Stop treating me as if I'm a toy. I agreed to come here to save this company, not for you, Choi Wansu, but for Yujun and Bomi and all the other people that would suffer. I did it for them. I didn't do it for you. I wouldn't do anything for you."

Ellen gasps. "No. No. She doesn't mean those things. She's in shock right now. Hara, apologize to Wansu right now."

"Why? Because she paid for a few things. Have you seen the house she lives in or the car she drives? Actually, she doesn't even drive. She sits in the back seat because she has a driver! Everything in her life is perfect. This is but a tiny blip in her well-planned life. And now she's moving me to Korea to live and you're okay with it?"

"Well, actually, Wansu has offered a place for me . . ." Ellen trails off at the sudden look of fury on my face.

"Did you all plot this out beforehand without telling me?"

"No." This rejection comes from Yujun. "I hadn't thought of it until Kim Jungkwon brought it up just now. But it's a perfect solution. It'll buy us time."

"Time for what? For everyone around you to know us as brother and sister?" I speak bitterly.

"I raised her better. I swear I did." Ellen wipes the tears away from her face. "She's grateful. We all are. You've done so much for her."

"No." Wansu's voice comes out harsh and brittle. "I can never make up for what I did. Hara's rejection is appropriate. You reap what you sow. I made the decision to give you up, Hara, and I am not sorry. I would do it again. I would do it again." Her voice breaks then and she begins to bend. Her knees fold, her head dips. The motions are all smooth and meaningful, but it doesn't make sense to me. To see this very proud, very elegant woman in her tailored ivory suit go down to the floor seems like a scene from a movie and not real life. It's not a ninety-degree bow of respect. It's a full bow, on her knees, arms stretched forward, back bent. I shut my eyes because I do not want to see this.

Ellen collapses to the floor. "No. No. What are you doing?"

"Thank you. Thank you." The perfect English that Wansu normally speaks is gone. She struggles for the words. "For caring for my child. For protecting her all these years. For raising her right."

A rock lodges in my throat. I struggle to keep a grip on my bitterness. I don't want to feel compassion or empathy. I want to be mad. I should be mad. Mad at Ellen for keeping secrets. Mad at Wansu for abandoning me. Mad at Yujun for being so damned understanding.

"This is your daughter, Hara," Ellen begins to say, as if she's introducing me for the first time. "She was an early reader. She spoke early, too. Her first word was 'milk.' I thought it was 'mom' but Pat said it was 'milk' and he was right. She was hungry. She can be clumsy and impatient. Stoic. So stoic. I think she got that from you."

"I told you not to cry," Wansu says rather unexpectedly. "When I left you on the street, I told you not to cry. Adults don't like criers and I worried if you cried that they wouldn't take you, they wouldn't love you. I laid my hand on your tiny chest and prayed that you wouldn't be a crier. And I vowed I wouldn't cry either." Wansu's tongue is so thick and the words are heavy like lead, and it's hard for me to make out what my mother is saying.

A keening noise escapes Wansu, and suddenly it's too much. I fling out an arm, searching for the door. I find it and push it open. Someone yelps and jumps out of the way. I make it to the hallway before collapsing. My heart is broken and full at the same time.

"Everyone out. Park Minho, get everyone out."

Two strong, warm arms close around my shoulders. A large hand comes up to cup the back of my head and press it against a solid chest covered in crisp white cotton. Yujun doesn't tell me it will be all right. He doesn't say that my mothers' reconciliation should make me happy. He doesn't tell me to stop crying. He just holds me.

He's always been so good, so perfect, so present whenever I've needed him, from the time that I showed up at the airport to the night we sat in front of the Han River for hours and he held my hand in silence to this moment right now.

"Why is doing the right thing so hard?" I blubber.

"It's like asking why everything that tastes good is fattening," he replies.

I choke out a laugh. "This is going to be terrible."

"No. We'll figure something out." Yujun tips my head up and kisses my swollen eyelids. "Our fates are tied together." Kiss. "There will be a solution." Kiss. Kiss. Kiss.

My hands find his shirt buttons. His fingers tug at my blouse. I don't know exactly where we are, but I don't care. An earthquake could take place, an air raid siren could go off, and I still wouldn't relinquish my hold on Yujun. My fingers scrape across the base of his spine. He shudders and clutches me closer. His tongue sweeps inside my mouth, rousing every nerve ending inside me and awakening some I didn't know existed. I slide my palms under his shirt and up his bare back. His muscles clench and flow under my grip. He lifts me suddenly and swings me around until my butt lands on a solid surface. I regret wearing pants today. His fingers dig into my thighs as he pulls me close.

"Yujun-ah, please come out. The press is downstairs. They are waiting for a statement." Wansu's voice breaks through the fog of arousal.

Yujun stops moving for a second. Just for one second, but it's long enough for me to come to my senses. I push him off me and slide off the counter. He brought me into a bathroom. How convenient that the bathrooms at IF Group are unisex, I think mundanely as I button my shirt up.

"Your hair is a mess," I tell Yujun, gazing at the back of his head reflected in the mirror. He's turned into a statue—*Coitus Interrup-*

tus would be the title of his sculpture. His head is bent and his shoulders are slumped forward. He still looks delicious—more so because his shirt is hanging out and I can see a tiny sliver of flesh around his waistband. His body is so fine that it's criminal. A shiver courses down my spine.

He shoves a frustrated hand through his hair, lets out a low curse before straightening. He avoids eye contact with me as he goes about repairing the damage I made. He wets his hands and pats down his hair, buttons his shirt, tucks everything away. I lean against the counter and watch the show. It might be the last one I'll ever see. There is something wildly erotic about seeing Yujun put himself back together. When he's done, he wipes his hands dry and then reaches for the door.

"Meet me at the river. Nine p.m." And then he leaves.

CHAPTER THIRTY

YUJUN IS STANDING BY THE BENCH WHEN I ARRIVE. THERE'S A bag at his feet. My heart sinks. A gift? I should've known. Koreans give gifts all the time. Why wouldn't a breakup include one, too?

"I didn't bring anything," I say when I reach him. I'm always empty-handed.

He smiles, that devastating half smile with the tiny divot punctuating his expression. "Perhaps it's not for you."

I let out a reluctant chuckle. He can always make me smile. "How bold of me."

He grins, but he can't hold it for long. The strain pulls the corners of his lips down. His two dimples wink out and when they're gone it's as if all the light in the night sky has been snuffed. I hate it.

"It's for you," he says quietly. "Please sit."

I don't want to sit. I can't look at Yujun as well when we're sitting side by side and I'm afraid that after tonight, I won't have another chance to stare at him. Everyone will be watching how we look at each other, how close we stand, how we address each other. There will be no more Yujun for me. I will have to call him *oppa* but not with any kind of flirtation or affection. If I'm to stay here, my tone with Yujun must be tempered with the right amount of respect and the right amount of deference and, most important, the right amount of distance.

"I can't." Not tonight. Tonight, he is still my Yujun from Seoul. Tonight, I will stare at him for as long as I can, memorizing the way his eyes crease when he smiles, the placement of each tiny mole, the roundness of his cheeks, the slope of his nose, the long fingers, the prominent veins, the breadth of his shoulders that he thinks can shoulder every burden in the world.

"Okay." He accepts my strangeness without question. The summer breeze blows across the river. It's warm and heavy but I still shiver. Yujun reaches out instinctively to warm me, but I step away. Hurt flickers across his face and it's like a paper cut against my thumb—small but a wound that I'll recall every day because small wounds can be sharper than the big ones.

"I'm sorry," I say as the silence turns uncomfortable. "I didn't want to make that choice, but—"

He holds up his hand. "I know. I *know*," he repeats, biting his bottom lip slightly. He breaks his gaze away from mine to stare out across the river. In the dark, even with Seoul's bright lights bouncing off its surface, the Han looks menacing.

What is he seeing there? The drowning of our hopes? The tears I've shed? The ones that swim in his eyes.

Last night, I made a family tree. I put Ellen and Patrick on one side and Wansu and Jonghyung on the other. I held the images up and realized the pictures were the same: two parents and one child. But even if the end point—me—was the same, the start was different, and so while I looked like Wansu and Jonghyung, and Yujun may say pretty words about me being Korean where it counts, I grew up in Iowa. I ate birthday cake instead of seaweed soup. My comfort food was peanut butter and jelly sandwiches and not kimchi and rice. Football meant helmets and pads and touchdowns, not pitches and goals.

Last night, I made up my mind to leave. I didn't come here to hurt anyone. I came here to heal. I suffered all these tiny cuts back home. Small ones from when I was old enough to hear how different I was. How I must smell strange. How my house smelled fishy or my face was flat. How I didn't belong to my mother. How I wasn't my dad's real child. How I knew nothing about my past so how could I have a future? How I wasn't good enough, pretty enough, smart enough, to have been kept. How leaving me, abandoning me, was the very best option. That last wasn't a small cut. That was a big one. It was one that hadn't healed. Perhaps if I returned home to my birthday cake and peanut butter and jelly sandwiches, then I could go back to living my normal, ordinary life and I would be okay. Then my aching heart would return to normal, but now I'm here in this city that is both familiar and strange next to a man who fills me with so much happiness that I could burst.

Only I don't get to keep that happiness. I have to shove it into a box and set it aside.

Yujun reaches for the big bag, and a small square box with a red bow fills the palm of his hand. "It's nothing very big, but I wanted you to have this."

My hands tremble and I nearly drop it as he sets it in my hands. The red bow goes into my pocket. It's a keepsake now. I have a moment of worry that I'll end up being one of those old ladies who has nothing but a houseful of cats and a room filled with mementos—bows, boxes, napkins. If I'm desperate and start to steal used tissues, I'll know I've gone too far.

Yujun waits in silence as I peel back the lid. A gasp escapes me when the jade first comes into view. Intricately carved out of the precious stone, a tiny duck rests on a deep green lotus leaf.

"Ducks mate for life. When one dies, the other pines until its heart stops. A mated pair can't live apart. They must always swim in the same pond, fly the same path, rest in the same haven." Yujun lifts the red silk cord out of the box. I lower my head so that Yujun can drape the cord into place. The jade duck drops between my breasts, heavy and comforting.

He steps back. Through a hazy veil of tears, I see him unbutton the top two buttons of his shirt. He tugs the loosened fabric to the side and the edge of the same red cord that dangles around my neck slides into view.

"They say that the gods tie red threads around our ankles and pull on them when they need help, but these same red threads can bind two people as well. We are meant to be and so we will work through this for however many weeks or months or years it will take. Our threads became entangled before we even met, and once tied together, the bond can never break. It can stretch and get knotted but nothing can sever it."

My hand rises to grip the cord. I want to believe. We are two smart people. Surely there's a solution that we simply haven't yet thought of. "You taught me how to say 'I like you' in Korean. How do I say 'I love you'?"

He sucks in a breath. *"Saranghaeyo."*

I repeat it to myself. I can't say it out loud, but I memorize the sound of his voice as he says it again, quietly, almost under his breath. I want to stay in this moment, simply standing next to Yujun, breathing the same air as him, repeating our love, in English and Korean as many times as possible until it takes shape and is too big for anyone or anything to undo. I love you. *Saranghaeyo.* I love you. *Saranghaeyo.*

"You have a beautiful eye smile," I tell him.

A muscle in his jaw jumps. "You're a true Korean now. The bitter and the sweet flowing through your blood," he says, his tone dark. Yujun, who never gets angry at anything or anyone, is finally mad. Somehow it makes it all a tiny bit better. "I've had a lot of good fortune in my life. Too much, I guess."

Yujun stretches out his hand to cup my face but, perhaps realizing the fragility of my emotions, lets his arm fall to his side.

"I . . . I'll go first, then." He knows, as always, that I need time alone. And I know he'll sit in his car parked along the street and wait for me. This is how it will be for us. We will go to the same place of work—him on the fourteenth floor and me on the ninth where the marketing team is lodged. We will sit across the table from each other, within arm's reach. We will be together, but not in the way that either of us wants.

I came to Seoul to find myself, and instead I found everything I could ever want—a family, a love, a life. Yet it's not what I envisioned—that perfect life just out of my reach.

Not wanting Yujun to stay out too late or too long, I force myself to leave. There's a car waiting for me at the top of the stairs. Yujun must've called for it the moment he got in his car. I keep my eyes straight in front of me, not allowing myself to look in Yujun's direction for fear I'll lose control of myself and dash to his car, demanding that we run away together. Each foot moves forward until I reach the taxi.

"Address?" the taxi driver asks when I climb into the back.

I mumble the Four Seasons Hotel low because my voice is hoarse from unshed tears, the syllables slurring together, and for once, I sound like a proper Korean. The man nods and pulls away.

None of the pretty skyline registers. There is only Yujun. And then he is joined by Wansu and Lee Jonghyung and Ellen and Pat and Kwon Hyeun and Ahn Sangki and Jules and Bomi. Korea is all of these people just as I am not one thing or the other. I am complicated and contradictory and I don't know how all of it can coexist, but it has to because these versions are all me.

I lean my head against the window and let the tears fall, reciting the refrain of my heart over and over and over again. I love you. *Saranghaeyo.* I love you. *Saranghaeyo. Saranghaeyo. Saranghaeyo.*

ACKNOWLEDGMENTS

When I first started writing, I never imagined that there would be a market for books like this, but the world changes and so do opportunities. These past few years have been a challenge from a writing standpoint and there were so many times during the course of this story that I looked at my keyboard and wondered what I was trying to attempt here. My fingers were forming words on my screen but I'd lost my ability to judge whether those words were good, whether they made sense. I'd really lost myself.

I don't know who said this but you can never make anything great from a place of fear. It's not a universal truth but it was a truth for me. I had been holding myself back. When you write about a culture not entirely your own, you stand the chance of misrepresenting that culture. The Korea that I've written about is one tiny viewpoint, as is the story of this one adoptee. This book is not intended to portray all adoptees or all Koreans. If I write another adoptee story, it will not have the same storyline or the same characters because no one story can portray all people. While there still exists a fear that I will make a mistake and offend someone through my portrayal, I did my best. I took creative license at some points to tell the story that made sense. I appreciate the reader's understanding in those parts.

I'm so grateful for my friends who told me to keep going: Jeanette Mancine, Melissa K., Meljean Brook, Jessica Clare, Robin Harders, Syreeta Jennings, Lea Robinson.

Extra special thanks go to Christina Hobbs, who would send me a photo of my favorite band member as a reward and incentive. I can't wait to go to concerts again and hold your hand during our favorite parts. May we always get sound check! Or at least once a tour.

Elyssa Patrick read this story in parts and gave me immeasurably good feedback. I'll always treasure your friendship.

Nicole, author assistant extraordinaire, I often wonder if I would still be writing if not for you. Thank you for all the work you do.

Diane Park, my dear Korean friend, thank you for reading this, helping with romanization of our beautiful language, and assisting in details about the beautiful city of Seoul. Thank you for all the other things you do. You're a precious human. All errors are mine.

My endless thanks go out to Cindy Hwang, my editor, who took a chance on this story and me. Thank you to Steve Axelrod for guiding this project into Cindy's hands.

No book makes it to the market without the enormous help of a publishing team. Thank you to Angela Kim, Fareeda Bullert, Jessica Brock, and everyone else at Berkley/Penguin Random House.

To all the readers, bookstagrammers, Facebook groups, You-Tubers; people who interact with me on Twitter, who send me messages on Instagram, who follow me on Facebook; people who leave reviews on B&N, Amazon, Goodreads: Thank you for the time and effort you put into the reading community.

Finally, to my mother who chose me, I love you. To the mother who gave me up, I love you, too. To my brothers and sister, thank you for being part of my life. To my husband and my daughter, you are the most important beings in my life. Thank you for loving and supporting me.

To you who reads this book and finds comfort, I love you and I'm rooting for you.

Heart and Seoul

Jen Frederick

QUESTIONS FOR DISCUSSION

1. Is Hara's othering of herself the result of her wanting to fit in or the result of her trying to avoid more exposure to the racism in the world where she lived?

2. Which character did you relate to the most?

3. Who changes the most over the course of the story?

4. Did you empathize more with one mother than the other?

5. Did you have a new perspective on adoptees from this book?

6. Did you learn things about Korea that you hadn't known before?

JEN FREDERICK is a Korean adoptee living in the Midwest with her husband, daughter, and rambunctious dog. Under the psuedonym Erin Watt, Frederick has cowritten two #1 *New York Times* bestselling novels.

Ready to find
your next great read?

Let us help.

Visit prh.com/nextread